FINBLOOD

To Joan,

Thankyou for the
Support

Best Wishes,

Luio xxx

FINBLOOD

Lucie Howorth

Edited by: Pete Howorth

Howorth Publishing

Cover designed by Howorth Publishing

This book is a work of fiction. Names, characters, places, and incidents
either are products of the author's imagination or are used fictitiously. Any
resemblance to actual persons, living or dead, events, or locales is entirely
coincidental.

Lucie Howorth

Printed in the United Kingdom
First Printing: January 2020
Kindle Direct Publishing
ISBN- 979-8-60-137466-8

PART 1

DAUGHTER OF THE SEA

Prologue

here was and is a house which stands alone within the waters of Orkney. Upon Eynhallow. The winters were always long and bleak, with no sunshine or hope. The summers seemed to laugh at us in those dark months, mocking us with memories of stolen days in the warmth. If there was such a thing as summer. The Hylands seemed to exist in a world forgotten and us, in turn, forgotten too. As the cold began to creep closer, it was as if the rest of the world was saying Goodbye. Nobody came to us and we came to nobody.

Mammy was a god-fearing woman. She told us always, that the water would never claim us. That God would save us because we had earnt our place in Heaven.

I knew as much about Heaven as I did about life and desired it less than I should have. I wondered if the Sinners had disregarded it too and damned their souls regardless?

I was a good girl who said her prayers. But I was never certain who I was saying them to.

Daddy was like the house itself. He would never let the elements take him without a fight. The Hylands was his castle, and the lonely rocks were his land. I think, perhaps, he saw something else when he looked around us. Never did I see the desperation in his eyes that I saw when I looked at myself.

Even during that winter my brother came in the middle of the night, not even then did he wish to be anywhere else. As storms raged, bringing the ghosts which lived in the wind whistling through the walls, he held Mammy's hand and allowed me to stand at the foot of the bed. I was so young, so uninitiated in pain. I thought she was going to die. Though I hated the little pink thing in her arms for hurting her, I grew to love him in the winters which passed. A sorry substitute for the friends which we had lost, eventually we became grateful for the company in each other. Whether through choice or necessity, we came to love each other beyond all others.

The winter of my fifteenth year was one of intolerable desolation. The Hylands, my family home, was cut off from the mainland by waters so treacherous not even the fishermen dared set sail. We lived on an Island of our own. A craggy rock of land that seemed to have broken off from the world thousands of years ago in search of absolute solitude. The Hylands wasn't meant to exist here. Sometimes it was as if the earth beneath our feet tried to tell us to go, that this place wasn't meant for us. But we remained. Every winter like the last, we remained in our stone-built house by the water. Even as the water licked the bay with a savage tongue, threatening to move closer we would stand and watch the foam whipped into a frenzy.

We stood together by the stone wall which ran around The Hylands, by the gate we watched as heavy clouds danced above the water and shrouded the mainland in an impenetrable mist. It was my fifteenth winter, but never did I cease to feel that clench in my throat as I watched the rain descend.

On that day, Mammy walked down the garden to watch with us, a solid hand on each of our shoulders. There was a sense of foreboding. I was never certain if they shared it, or if they simply stood to watch at the sorrowful beauty of the savage weather.

My face was flushed red, my lips quivering against the biting wind. But still, I stood and wrapped my shawl tighter around me.

"Ah, not today… not today." Mammy said, her voice almost lost in the wind.

I closed my eyes and imagined the boat coming through the mist. But there was nothing but the shadow of Rousay.

"Why Mammy? Why not today?" My brother asked, his stubborn reluctance as strong as mine.

Mammy tucked him under her shawl, though he was already at her height and pulled him away from the oncoming storm.

"Ah Rohan, the waters are too rough for sailing. You'll watch tomorrow, when they'll be calmer."

But his eyes turned away and I knew he would watch until nightfall.

"Finola? Will you not come back into the house?"

I turned and went with them. I could not withstand another day waiting for salvation that would not come.

I had long since grown sick of the smell which came from the fire in the kitchen. Of vegetables boiling in the same water as the night before. In the larder was the remnants of the bannock bread which had gone hard and stale, which we sopped in the soup to make it soft again. The frost had killed the best of what little crops we'd grown, the wild foxes which were not native to Eynhallow had been circling the chicken coop for weeks. Hunger was setting in and we were no exception.

It seemed to cry out from the very stones. The Typhoid had finished off the other Eynhallow families. Perhaps hunger would be the end of us?

A year had passed since the others had died or fled to the mainland. I often wondered if Daddy had descended into madness by keeping us here. I thought Mammy would protest but instead, she went to the kirk on the other side of the Island and prayed for us to survive.

That old church and its roofless byre was Mammy's place of pilgrimage. It gave her comfort to go there when it seemed all other hope was lost. There was no comfort for me here. The old stones of the ancient church were like false idols. Whoever had built it was no longer there. Even God had fled this once Holy Isle.

"Finola, will you go out and fetch your Daddy from the garden?" Mammy asked, before I had chance to remove my broken shoes. "I'll be serving your suppers."

He was standing behind the house, bringing the pail up from the well. The rain had reached us and was lashing at his shirt.

"Ah, Daddy! Will you put your coat on!" I said through the howling of the wind, taking his coat off the wall before it blew away.

He let me slip it around his shoulders. "Get you back in the house girl, it's raining tears from God himself out here!"

Daddy was a strong man. But the fierce wind was against him.

"I'll have to tie it off, get you back into the house Finola Gray!" But his orders went unheard.

The winter chill had already set in my bones. I heard the chickens clucking at the end of the lawn where our plot of land met the wilderness. I saw a flurry of feathers and knew they were frightened. I fought against the wind until I was standing above them, their wings trying to take flight. I gathered the eggs which had been abandoned on the ground and my eyes met with the creature of their fear. Facing me was one of the wild foxes which had been left to roam by one of the families who went to the mainland. His eyes were burning into me, that hunger which was so familiar. For a moment, the wind seemed too calm and I could sense his desperation. I never knew what made me do it, or why it meant so much to me. As I opened the coop I watched as one of the chickens broke free and into the path of the waiting fox. I thought I saw him bow gracefully as he took the chicken in his mouth and retreated across the barren fields. He would eat a fine meal that night. I could not regret what I had done if the creature filled their belly.

But I would pay for it. For what I had done for that Fox. For in the night when the skies cleared and the moon shone its full light on our tiny Island, the Fox returned for more.

In the calm morning there was a frost like no other, ice that had kept the blood fresh. The corpses were laid out above the white grass, their heads taken, and their bodies savaged. Not one chicken had survived the massacre.

"What in God's name has occurred here!" Mammy screamed, her footsteps crisp on the ground as she hurried back into the house.

Daddy rose from his breakfast, the last of the bannock bread and some salted fish, his eyes casting a glance at me.

"Finola, how were them chickens when last you saw them?" He asked, his voice low and authoritative.

They feared for their lives, but they were as fine as any well-kept creature. But I could not say the words. I chose their fate the moment I allowed one of them to slip free. I cursed the day the McDonnal's returned from the mainland one summer, their youngest son Angus clutching a tiny bundle in his lap.

He'd found them in the hedgerows in the village of Evie, their mother had abandoned them, and they would have starved. But they weren't like the domesticated animals we kept in house. They were meant for the wild, when the day came that the tiny foxes grew to maturity there was nothing could be done to stop them roaming the shores… too afraid to head into the water.

So, they remained. As did we. Even when the McDonnal's had gone. Perhaps that's why I had fed them. They didn't ask to be here anymore than I had.

"Finola, I ask you again. How were them chickens when last you saw them?" Daddy said, breaking into my thoughts.

I stared at him gravely. "They were just fine."

He flexed his bearded jaw and I wondered if Mammy's God would strike me dead for the lie. She was pale as a ghost on the church steps and fell into one of the chairs in a faint.

"God save us." She whispered. "Those waters have calmed when we have need of safe passage most."

I went to the window and peered down to the water. The frost had brought a cloudless sky, blue and eternal. The tidal water swelled and receded like it was licking the wounds of the previous day.

"Rohan, be a good boy and fetch my gun from underneath the bed." Daddy ordered.

My brother was quick to do his bidding, none of us wished to anger him on a day as grave as this. Those chickens had been a source of food when all others had run out.

Mammy sighed in relief. "Of all God's creatures! Will you have them on this table by supper."

By the calm of the frozen shores, it seemed to me that lying hadn't hurt much. I was not struck down dead. I did not see there had been much difference, save for my Mammy and Daddy's disapproval.

Which I had avoided with the lie. Already my resentment was finding its own way into other aspects of my character.

I had begun to hate these rocks under feet. I watched the birds flying overhead and found an aching in my heart to join them.

There was a quietness here which seemed to scream into my very veins. The sound of the water hitting the shore, always moving, never relenting in its quest to raid the sand and then retreating to where it came.

The wind through the grass, sending it into disarray. Even the most content people would be haunted by it. Or perhaps it was only me.

Picking up one of the stones by the water's edge, I returned it to the tide. I threw it as far as I could and watched it hit the water.

But all too soon it was too cold to stand more. The bite of the cold had reached my exposed hands and was sending a chill through me. I knew if I returned to The Hylands there would be the reminder of my grievous deed. I knew that if I stayed in the path of the wind, I would give myself the fever. The shelter of the ruined kirk was my only respite and I did not want to go there.

Churches mocked me, even when ruined. Instead I went to the ashes which once were home to the other Eynhallow families.

The McDonnal's were the first to succumb to the typhoid. All of them died within fourteen days of each other. I recalled Angus. His flame red hair standing by the wall around The Hylands, waiting for me to come and greet him. He was a wee boy of seven. The first on the island to die.

Their house was burned and the family within it. The parish thought it would rid us of the disease. But when the Munro's were struck down, fear began to spread.

But they did not die, not all of them. Only Aaron Munro. He was eighteen the week of his death and had a sweetheart waiting for him in the village of Evie. The other Munro's could not stay. They were the first to flee in the cold morning light, taking Aaron's body with them. We burned their house regardless.

The McAvoy's came to pray with Mammy and Daddy in those last days. But their prayers went unanswered, so began the plague of my doubt. Jenny McAvoy had been to me what I was now in most need of. A friend I had grown with since birth until the last day of her life. I had cried for Jenny when there had been no tears in me left to shed. Her brother Benjamin soon followed into that realm where the living cannot follow. So, the others left, as the Munro's had done before them, taking the bodies of their children in the prow of their boat towards the mainland. Forever gone from me and when it seemed as if there could be no more sorrow bestowed on our houses, The Guthrie's died in their beds.

The old couple had not been parted and in that we took solace as we watched their home taken by flames. What remained, along with the charred stones and grey dust was a memory I could not shake. We were all that was left. The Gray's and their Hylands home. We waited for our deaths, wondering when it would come to claim us. But death smiled on The Hylands.

We did not greet the typhoid at our doorstep. We did not see the sickness which took the others, either into death or the mainland. Perhaps it was waiting for us now. So that the winter could claim us instead.

As I lamented my friend, taking a moment to miss her and think of her, I knew that if I did not turn my back I would descend into madness. I walked away from what was no longer there and shrouded myself within my shawl as the first flurry of snow fell silently onto Eynhallow.

With the snow came the darkness and with the darkness, Daddy and Rohan called off the search and returned home. I watched them from the brow of the hill above, carrying the corpse of something I could not determine in the paling light. They hurried inside, eager to be out of the freezing air. But I lingered. Perhaps tempting the fever to claim my body and rid me of this melancholy.

We ate the meat of the wild Fox that night. It was not the succulent meat of the chicken or the duck, but it satisfied the hunger.

"We'll be having the other one on the morrow." Daddy said, picking bones from his teeth. "Snow or no."

Rohan was finishing his meal, chewing the fat enthusiastically. His thirteen-year-old bones had not yet caught up to the strength of his mind. Hunting kept him content with his lot. He seemed content here and in that, I knew we were worlds apart.

"Before winter's done, we'll have meat in our bellies again." He continued, eyeing his empty plate proudly.

Mammy stirred the pot above the fire and stared intently into the flames.

"God grant it." She sighed.

I moved my plate away from me, unable to touch the food. Daddy looked at me almost with contempt. Forever we turned away the food he provided; it was a grave insult in these hard times.

"I cannot stomach it. I feel a little unwell." I said and it was not a lie.

Daddy's face softened a little, his eyes moving towards where Mammy stood over the hearth. She stooped now. Her body rounded with age and time; the fair hair of her youth was starting to turn to silver.

"Finola, have you the fever?" She asked, hurrying to place her hot hands upon my brow.

But perhaps there had been some harm in lying. There it was in the beating of my heart as I looked down at the food on my plate and could not bear the thought of it.

What was this ache which riddled my soul? The regret that I had done what I had done. The guilt that I had lied about what I had done. The sense that this one act would shape the rest of our lives. Or at the very least, my life.

"I think I'll go to bed." I said, taking my leave of the table.

The winter of 1852 was unrelenting. It drove us to the edges of tolerance.

For Daddy, who's very soul was etched in the land it tested every bone in his body to stay. For Mammy, the God she loved so appeared to have gone from us in the days when we thought we would starve. For Rohan, whose life had yet to take on any meaning, the weather only dampened his soul when it prevented him from going outside.

For me, there was a longing which would not be slaked. There was no release from it. No time where I did not curse my birth upon this lonely place. Then, like a beacon of light to slay the hellish night, standing by the wall I watched.

As the red sun moved across the water, I saw the tiny form moving between the waves. At first, I could have sworn my eyes deceived me. That it was but a dream that I saw the boat heading towards us. Was it truly the end of winter? Had we truly survived?

I felt the shackles of all which had passed ease a little, enough for me to rush down to the water to greet our first visitors in three months.

I stood and waved erratically and did not come to my senses until the boat reached the shore. I was utterly consumed by relief. Like I had recovered from a madness I had no recollection of. Winter was gone. I could forget, for a moment, that I was unhappy.

Lucie Howorth

Chapter One

THE VISITOR

In the hours before sunrise, on the first day of spring, I awoke early and regarded myself in the mirror by candlelight. Today I would not bind my shawl about me or wear my warmest petticoat. Today I put my bonnet aside and braided my hair high on each side of my head, allowing whispers of hair to fall around my neck.

I noted the bones protruding from my shoulders and my dress was loose around my burgeoning hips. I had not survived without sacrifice. But I would amend that in the coming months. With ripened fruit and fresh fish.

My eyes were still the same colour blue and my hair that same shade of raven black. If I had lost anything, it could be restored.

Everything else was as it had ever been. Except older. I felt older. I saw it in myself even in the flickering candlelight. Last spring, I had been a child. But as I ran my hands down the contours of my body, I knew the sacrifice had been too great. My childhood was gone.

It was a thought I could not give much mind to. The sun was rising over Eynhallow sound, the red turning the sky into almighty blue and the tide was turning.

The water was trying to retreat from us, but the waves pushed it forward creating white peaks that crashed into one another thoughtlessly.

It was always at this time I liked to stand and watch the Arctic birds circle above us and wonder where they had been what they had seen.

But today we had a guest and as I turned away from the window, I went to fetch water from the well. There was dew on the ground, sending broken rainbows across the grass and the sun shone down. A truly marvellous spectacle.

I let the pail down and stared at the broken colours on the ground. Daddy had always called me a creature of thought. Unable to keep my mind to the task at hand without breaking free into thoughts of other things.

Even now as the pail hit the water, I stood for a moment, hypnotized, before I remembered why I was there. All morning I had been distracted. Like there was something more important just waiting to grasp my attention, but I could not fathom what it might be. I found myself drifting from one task to another, floating above the conversation. God, King or beast could have spoken with me this day and I would have still looked out over the sound in silence.

"Come with me, Finola..." I heard a voice say, penetrating my reverie at the sound of my name being called.

I was standing by the front door, a cloth in my hand and an unwashed floor behind me. I turned to find our guest lacing his boots at the kitchen table.

"Mammy wants me to clean this floor." I protested, but I knew I would adhere to his request.

"There's none here to stop us. If the floor does not get cleaned today, I shall scrub it myself."

I smiled at Nathan Munro and was glad he had come. He had come back to set his affairs in order before his wedding.

He wanted to sell the land where his house once stood but came to give Daddy first refusal.

I had never given much thought to Nathan Munro. I had never noticed the sweetness in his voice when he spoke or the kindness in each request. Truly I had lost my childhood.

But if I should no longer be a girl, I would be glad of these stirrings within which I had never known before. It was not that I wanted Nathan for a sweetheart. He was too old and already engaged to be married. I reasoned with myself that it was because I had seen no other face in so long. Perhaps

I was simply flattered by his request for my company. Regardless, I joined him as he ventured down to the rocks near the water.

"I had thought returning here would somehow mark the end of my mourning, but I find myself more melancholy than ever." He said to me, as we sat by the rushing water.

"It's only the memory." I said, glancing in the direction of where the old houses once stood. "I went myself only the other day to see where once we were all together. But there is nothing there now, except for what I remember."

Nathan was much like his brother. Tall and fair haired. In the year which had passed since last I had seen, him he had grown a moustache and taken to wearing it into a beard. He was twenty-three and had met the woman he wanted to marry. If I had not had such a liking for him, I would have screamed until my lungs bled of the jealousy I felt towards his life after leaving Eynhallow. But I could not. He had lost something in return.

"They were fine days indeed. But Eynhallow slips further and further away, it seems. As I crossed the sound, it was as if it slipped entirely from view and I could not find my way. If I were any less of a reasonable man, I would fair say there was no way back at all."

I believed him. When the mist shrouded us, it was as if we had completely vanished and were not hidden, but it was as if we had never been there at all.

"I think, sometimes, Eynhallow is not a place but a living being. It speaks to us if we listen hard enough." I said, and the water rushed towards me as if it had heard me.

Nathan gestured for me to move back; his hand stretched out to me to aid me across the rocks. He had learned something of being a gentleman in the past year, I noticed. In a world of gentlemen, I wondered, would I ever find one of my own?

"What does it say?" He asked, as we moved towards the higher rocks.

"It does not want us here. It wants to be alone with the tide and the mist and old ruined kirk..." I ventured to say, but as I said the words out loud, I knew it wasn't true.

Eynhallow had always been the same. It would not change to suit our needs. It was not that it did not want us, simply that it did not know how to be anywhere else. Or perhaps I was wrong, and once it had been a prosperous place of warmth and good nature. It had turned barren because we invaded it.

Nathan put his coat down so that I might sit. "If I might be so bold, but is it not you that does not want to be here?"

I thought I would cry at his assumption. There was a seal somewhere out in the water which shrieked above the sound of the crashing tide and I felt my own voice within it.

The strangled sound carried far and as I looked out, I could not see the creature but only listen to its low rumble. Had I become so ingrained in this place that the creatures were now speaking for me? I shuddered. I put the thought away, like all my other thoughts, so that I may not forget myself.

"There is no hope that I should ever leave here. I wonder, sometimes, even when I come of age if I could truly leave Rohan here. I do not like to think of Mammy and Daddy without us either, so I am utterly lost."

"You cannot live for them. There is much in the world to touch, to see. They would not begrudge you your dearest wish."

My dearest wish. I had not considered it that way. What had become an impossibility now seemed possible. To leave with their blessing was something I had not considered. But it would be a blessing indeed.

"I am afraid to leave here. As much as I have wanted it." I confessed.

Nathan stared at the bird's overhead, his eyes watching where they swooped from the sky down onto the land.

"How strange that I should miss this place, even now when I am more content than I have ever been. Do not be afraid of what lies beyond the water. There is nothing to fear except for the unknown. You will soon come to know it."

I wondered what he had seen on the morning they took Aaron's body. Had he closed his eyes and waited for absolution? There was no fear in the unknown when it was shared. I would be alone on that day.

"I fear not the unknown. I fear that I shall flounder without this place, or it shall crumble away without me. If it should, it will take my family into the mists and I shall never see them again."

The clouds seem to turn and cast shadows across the land. It changed the colour of the ground completely and for a moment we were shrouded in relative darkness.

But the wind swept across us and the clouds moved, allowing the sun to triumph and once again shine upon us. Nathan pulled a flask from his pocket and took a quick swig. He winced before swallowing, but after he seemed to be refreshed and gestured for us to continue walking.

"Shall we continue? I would like to see more before I leave. I have forgotten the landscape. I dare say there will ever come a time where I shall return again."

I was dismayed, but I knew there was nothing here for him now. So I followed him across the shore, never certain of where we were heading. I found him good enough company not to care. As we headed away from the sea and onto the dirt path leading through the rough terrain he stopped and stood and looked back to where we had come from.

"This is it..." He said quietly, running a thoughtful hand through his beard. "This is the path we took… that day."

We were standing in the middle of a wild field. The path was hidden unless you knew where to find it. It leads from over the brow of the hill before us right down to the water below.

"Finola, would you indulge me a moment?" He asked, putting his coat down once again so that I could sit comfortably on the ground.

He seemed to change immediately. As he sat beside me, he took another swig from his flask and then offered me a taste. I declined, so he took another sip.

His eyes glazed over. It seemed as if he was far away, remembering something he did not want to remember. I began to regret that we had come this far.

It had been only a year since he had lost his brother. There was a raw memory here that had not been grieved for. I sat with him until he was ready to speak, unable to say anything in the meantime.

When finally, he spoke, I was surprised to hear the steady tone in his lovely voice. He did not crack; he did not stutter. I had thought there would be tears to shed. But when I looked, they were gone, and his eyes were only red rimmed.

"Did your Daddy ever tell you about the Goodman of Thorodale?" He asked me, quite soberly.

The name evaded me; I did not recall. "No, I have not heard of him."

"It might be that an imaginative soul like you did not need to hear such stories." Nathan presumed, his brow raising a little with the thought.

"If there were stories to be told, they were told from the Bible." I told him; he did not seem surprised. "Mammy insisted on it."

"My father told it to me when I was a child. I had thought it but a story, but now I find myself believing it could well be true. There's a feeling to this place unfelt by those who dwell here. But I come here now as an outsider, and I tell you, I feel it."

A cold spill went down my spine. I shuddered, but I was not particularly cold in myself. It went as suddenly as it came.

"They say he came from Evie, and his wife bore him three sons. But she died in childbed with the third and Thorodale was left to raise the boys alone."

He had my complete attention. There was no other thought to contend with, nothing to distract me from the sound of Nathan Munro's voice. It was a welcome relief.

"Many years later he married the bonniest lass in Evie. She was younger than his sons, who had now grown to manhood. He loved her like he had loved no other. But because of her youth and beauty, he guarded her closely. He did not anticipate that it would be a day like any other that she would be taken from him."

Enchanted, I was, hanging on every word. Wishing he would not pause for breath.

"One morning he took his wife down to the shores and as he stumbled upon a rock, he stopped to tie his shoestring. He took his eyes from her but for a brief moment, but it was enough for him to turn upon hearing her begin to scream. He saw his bride being taken from the shore by a man he had never seen before. He held her tightly and dragged her into a waiting boat.

Thorodale followed them into the water, but the strange man had already begun to row where Thorodale could not follow. He knew, with the intuition of a man who had lived long by the sea, that she had been taken by one of the Finmen who lived beneath the waves. Because as he watched them go, knowing he could not get to his own boat in time, they simply vanished into nothing but air."

My breath stuck in my throat, I swallowed hard only to find my mouth was dry.

"It is known that Finfolk can do magic. Making their vessels unseen and swifter than a bird in flight. But despite their sorcery, Thorodale was not a man who could take such a blow without seeking revenge. There, on the same shore where his beloved wife had been taken, he knelt into the sand and swore that living or dead, he would have his revenge. Every waking moment afterwards he thought long on it. But he could not see how it could be done against their magic.

Until one day he was fishing in the sound between Evie and Rousay and there, during the slack tide, he heard a woman's voice singing. He knew the voice and listened closely and though he could not see her, he knew it was his wife.

Goodman grieve no more for me. For me again you'll never see. If you would have of Vengeance joy. Go ask the wise spae-wife of Hoy.

So Thorodale returned to the shore with his staff in hand and silver in his pocket and set out for the holy isle of Hoy."

I could barely speak, but in a whisper, I asked, "What then? Did Thorodale find his wife?"

"It is not written that which the wise woman told him. But it is fair to say that she gave him the knowledge he would need to seek the Hildaland. The home of the Finfolk."

Nathan turned to me with a knowing look. "Know you not that once this placed was called that? Here is the Hildaland of the Finfolk. When Thorodale came to it, he knew that taking any part of it was the greatest punishment of all. For nine moons he had waited, on the full moon he went to the Odin Stone of Stenness and on his knees he looked through the hole in the stone and asked to see the hidden ways to the Hildaland. He did this for nine moons, finally when the answer he sought came to him he filled a meal chest with salt and set three large straw baskets beside it.

He sent word to his grown sons to come and help him and told them the tale of his sorrow. He told them what they should do on the morrow, when finally, it came he looked out onto Eynhallow sound and saw the island there which had never been before. Calling to his sons to fill the baskets with the salt and bring them to the boat, the four men began to row out into the sea.

The sons were not fools, but they were perplexed because only Thorodale himself could see the mystical island towards which they rowed. But before they could question, they found themselves surrounded by a pod of whales. The sons insisted on driving them away, but Thorodale knew better. He called to his sons to pull for their lives. *The devil catch the delayer...* It was then that the greatest of the whales came within their path and reared its head before the boat.

Its mouth was open as if to swallow them whole, but Thorodale bade his sons to bend their oars and as they did so he stood and threw a handful of salt into the waiting mouth. The whale vanished. It was but an image of the Finman's magic, which the consecrated salt had destroyed. But they were not done with sorcery.

As they neared the island two mermaids stood in the water awaiting them. Their beautiful faces and haunting voices enchanted the sons and they put down their oars. But Thorodale did not take his eyes away from the Isle and kicked his sons into picking up their oars once more. He called to the mermaids and warned them *be gone! Ye unholy limmers!*

He threw crosses made of tangled weed at them and they sank into the waters shrieking pitifully. The boat reached the enchanted shore. But their troubles did not end there, for on the shore awaiting them there was a terrible monster. With great striking tusks and feet as broad as quern stones. With blazing eyes, it spat fire from its mouth. But Thorodale was not afraid and as he leapt onto the sand; he threw more salt between the beast's eyes. It let out a terrible growl, then vanished just as the whale had. But this time, in its place stood a dark man who was tall and angry. He had a sword in his hand and was ready for Thorodale and his sons.

Go Back said the man. *Go back you human thief, you who come to rob the Finfolk's land! Or by my father's head I shall defile the Hildaland with your nasty blood!*

The sons turned in fear and begged their father to return. But Thorodale ignored his sons' pleas and instead met the finman in combat. But Thorodale knew the finman's weakness and stepped aside as he thrust his sword and instead with a flick of his wrist threw a cross into the strange finman's face. He turned and fled, his anguished screams of pain and fury sounding across the whole land.

Thorodale ordered his sons to bring the salt ashore and instructed them to walk the length and breadth of the island, sowing the salt into the ground as they went. There arose a great outcry from the Finfolk and their beasts, they ran into the water screaming their doleful cries of agony. In the end, there was no beast or man living of the Finfolk left. All had fled into the water. Their homes went into ruin, their crops failed. When Thorodale was satisfied he cut nine crosses in the turf and sowed nine rings of salt in all.

So the finfolk's Hildaland was laid bare for all to see. No longer enchanted. Empty and clean to human eyes, so that none of the Finfolk could ever reclaim it. Thorodale had his revenge. We had Eynhallow, the holy isle."

I watched Nathan sigh and take out his flask again. I did not decline this time and sipped gratefully on the hot whisky that burned as it went down. I was lost in dreams that I could not wake from.

"Where did they go?" I asked in that far away voice that was not entirely my own.

"My father said only that there is a place we cannot go to, under the sea. Finfolkaheem. The kingdom of the Finfolk. Where they came from. Before they stepped onto the land."

I looked onto the sound and tried to fathom a kingdom beneath it. "Do you think one day they shall return?" I asked, unable to take my eyes away from the water.

Nathan shook his head, his face taking on a playful look. "It's just a story Finola. There's no truth in it. While I'm certain there's something here which does not belong in the world beyond, I dare say it's nothing to do with mystical beings from the water." He had changed his tune.

But I was utterly spellbound. It was as if I had been sleeping and had awoken for the first time. As we made our way back down towards The Hylands I could not speak of it. Nathan was quiet too, although I was never sure if his reasons mirrored my own.

That night as he sat at the table with Daddy, discussing things I had no mind to pay attention to, I sat by the fire and began to wonder if I should tell Rohan. He was the most logical of boys. The tale I had heard that day defied all logic.

He would ask too many questions. He would not believe in the possibility of it. So, I decided not to tell him. But my distance did not go unnoticed. As ever, I was lost in thought and he demanded to know why. I did not have the strength to lie to him.

"I am weary of this place." I sighed, taking one of the pokers to slake the fire.

Confusion wracked his face. He could not fathom it. Here was his world and there was nothing beyond it. I envied his simple mind. For it kept him content, and I could not share it.

I thought of him watching for the boats even when we knew none would come and wondered if it was my desire to leave which he had shared, or if he simply wanted us to stay disconnected from the rest of the world and feared the boats would bring an end to our solitary confinement?

"Daddy said this Sunday is the first of the month and we shall go to church in Evie for the morning service. So, you need no longer feel weary."

But he did not understand. Once a month, when the weather permitted, we would get in our boat and attend the morning services in the church in the village of Evie.

Mammy reserved it for time to reflect and prayed fastidiously, for all our souls before taking in the polite conversation of the local parishioners. Daddy would speak with other crofters and farmers about their crops and cattle and they seemed to be fascinated with the family who remained on that strange island. I knew they did, because Rohan and I were subject to whispers amongst the Evie children.

They pointed and spoke in hushed tones about us. But would never engage us. It was as if we didn't really exist. I could not help but share their sentiment.

"I do not think going to church will satisfy my weariness." I confessed.

But, like any thirteen-year-old boy who had no patience for the deepest feelings of a young girl, he shrugged and went over to where Daddy was shaking Nathan Munro's hand. They had reached a deal. Soon it would be time for Nathan to leave forever.

I could not sleep. The sound of the sea seemed to encroach on my dreams and kept me awake. It seemed that I was climbing trees to try and reach the sky, but they continued to grow beyond my reach. So, I looked out across the land instead and watched the water swallow Eynhallow.

But I was not asleep. My eyes were open and fixed on the pale moon shining through the window. There was something sinister and beautiful about the moonlight. How it shifted and changed, becoming full and dazzling and then hiding its light under the crescent bow.

Tonight, it was full and round, looking down at me as if it offered its light to no one else. It roused me. I could not lie still a moment longer. I pulled my shawl over my nightgown and on light feet I went down to where the fire had died into embers. Every soul under The Hylands roof slept soundly. I envied their content slumber.

Quietly I managed to build up the fire and gather some warmth about me. But I could not shake the cold in my heart. It would remain winter for me no matter if the sun bore down on us. *Time to die...* I thought.

Then the thought was gone from me almost as swiftly as it came. Perhaps it was this that kept me from noticing the figure sat at the table. So silent and observant as he was, he only made his presence known once the firelight filled the room and there was no darkness left to hide in.

"Forgive me. I did not mean to startle you." He whispered, leaning forward into the flickering light.

He was cloaked with the blanket we had given him to sleep with. But underneath he was dressed for the day. He rested his chin into his hands and would not look directly at me.

"Nathan..." I breathed, afraid even a whisper would break the silence. "What do you down here?"

He was again that other man. That man who lamented his woes and could not rest his soul.

"I could not sleep. I did not mean to wake you. I thought I might sit here a while. I shall return to my chamber if it would suit you..."

When he stood the blanket slipped from his shoulders. I knew it was bold of me to protest, but I could not face the night alone.

"No. You can stay. It makes little difference to me that you are here." I said, catching his eyes as he pulled the blanket back over himself.

His face was clean shaven, I noticed, though he did not look at me. His skin seemed to glow under the dim light and though I wondered why it was so, I did not ask. His eyes averted to the ground, and his sadness was resonating against the very foundations of the house.

"I suppose, although I have no right to presume otherwise, that it would make little difference to you if I were here or not." He said, his voice altering from a whisper to a low hum.

His words struck me like walking through a garden of thorns. Perhaps I misunderstood, or was the misunderstanding his? Were I more equipped with the right words, I could have set his mind at ease? But I was just a girl and he, was a man.

"I only meant that it would not displease me if you stayed, but I shall not put upon you if you wish to return to your chamber." I simply said.

Had I trusted my first initial feeling, I would have turned around and returned to my moon filled fantasies of trees and water. But there was something about his sadness I could not turn away from. I did not want to go back to those idiotic, futile thoughts.

He shifted in his chair and pulled open the one next to him so that I might sit beside him. I pulled the pot from above the fire and poured some of the weak tea out, avoiding the chair he had intended me to sit in.

There was something about the night which changed everything. In the day he was my old neighbour and family friend. But in the dark of night he was simply a man and I was afraid of him. I slipped into the seat opposite him and hoped he would not speak of it.

"So, you have done what you came here to do?" I innocently inquired, taking the cup of tea to my lips to steady my nerves.

There was something about the way he did not look at me which unnerved me. He would not meet my gaze.

"I have done the business I came to do. I did not want to sell to anyone but William Gray."

I shuddered at the sound of him using Daddy's Christian name. I so seldom heard it that sometimes I forgot he possessed one. Mammy referred to him as we did, calling him Daddy in our presence most of the time. I did not know what she called him when they were alone. It was much the same for him, referring only to Mammy by her Christian name on those days when we attended church.

When there were others, he could refer her to. He called her Mary, and I always thought of the virgin mother when I heard him call her so. I thought it was the most perfect name for Mammy, because she loved the Mary who we heard so much about from the Bible.

I put my cup down and saw that he was looking at me. I had allowed my thoughts to take me away again, and I cursed myself for it. I felt my heartbeat pulse through my veins faster. His eyes were fixed on me, but he did not smile. He did not move to alter his stare on me. All sense of propriety was gone, and although I was afraid, I could not deny that if he had looked away, I would have fallen apart.

"And now you can go back with everything in order." I sighed.

Those eyes were burning me now. Blue and yet red in the firelight.

"It will be as if we were never here, someday. When I am gone will you not..." He swallowed hard and his jaw flexed. "Will you not mourn that I have gone as I shall mourn that you remain here?"

His eyes became desperate then. I could not move. His face took on all the intensity of someone fighting to stay alive. I wanted to run from him and yet I could not leave him. His fists were curled into balls which shook the table. If it was fear which gripped me then it did well to release me, but it was not fear which made me stay. It was the ache I knew that would come if I did run, and inevitably I knew I would mourn him once he was gone.

"I shall be sorry to see you go." I said, and I knew it was true.

Nathan pushed his chair back sending an almighty screech resounding through the room. I held my breath, waited for someone to hear us and rush into our presence. Nathan was standing now, his great height shadowing me. Nobody stirred, and I wondered if he had pushed the chair back at all or if I had just imagined it?

"Well..." He said, uncurling his fists and letting his shoulders sink back down from the tension. "I find myself in a most peculiar position then."

He walked around the table and came to where I sat. I felt something peculiar myself as I watched him drop to his knees beside me. All the desperation was gone and in its place was a sorrow I could not fathom. His face had softened, and I could see a handsomeness I had not noticed before. It was I who had to look away. I was afraid of his warm breath on my neck, the way he leaned closer to me without permission.

"Would that I could somehow honourably rid myself of this engagement I have found myself in..." He said, and the words were hot on my skin. "But what honour do I own when I trespass upon you like this..."

I could not find it within me to utter a word in response. I was frozen to my seat like the ice which had clung to the window shutters in darkest winter.

"You are of such beauty; I cannot be reasonable in your presence. It is a great mystery to me that I did not notice before... How I could have ever lived beside you and not been driven completely mad by the sight of you. Forgive me... I do not know myself."

He stood and inched back, as if surrendering to some unknown foe. I could not comfort him, there was much confusion.

How could he have taken notice of me before? I was a feckless child. So I still was, as I tried to bring the conflicts within me together. His advance had both flattered and scared me. I did not know how to resolve it.

"Worry not, Nathan..." I whispered, "On the morrow you shall be reunited with your bride and you shall forget me."

But he shook his head as if in pain. "She is the daughter of my father's new friend on the mainland. He is a rich man. A finely orchestrated engagement to suit my father's financial gains. While I thought myself content, I find myself unable to think of her now... Today I have not thought of her once. Only that when I walked with you there was no wish to be anywhere else. There was something in your face, I could not deny to myself that you are beautiful. But enchanting... Have you enchanted me, Finola?"

I knew very little of enchantments. As I knew very little of men. If I had truly enchanted him, it had been without my knowledge.

"I do not know." I swallowed. "It was not my intention to enchant you, but if I have then I am sorry."

In the firelight which was dying once again I saw his face break into a strange smile. He almost laughed, but only gasped and tried to fight against it.

"Of course. How infantile of me to suggest such a thing." He said, coming to his senses. "Have I scared you, Finola?"

It would have been foolish for me to admit that he had, and so I shook my head and hoped that it would satisfy his question.

"Good. For that would have grieved me so, if I had scared you. I do not know what came over me. Except that it has troubled me, that I should harbour such feelings towards one as young as you are."

Like any child who was on the brink of adulthood I took great offence to this. I could only respond in the way any child would have, defending their right to be addressed as the adult they pretended to be.

"I am almost sixteen." I protested. "I am hardly as young as that."

"I recall when you were born. But perhaps that is more a testament to my own age." He said, once again lamenting that which had already passed.

"Ah, you are not old yet Nathan. You will know that you are old when your grandchildren sit at your feet and you have not the sight to see them with. Or so Daddy says..."

"So, you do know something of wisdom?" He asked then.

But I could not say it was wisdom I had learned of myself, only that which had been passed down to me. I wondered why it should matter. But then perhaps that is what made the difference between a childhood and what came after.

"I know that which I am taught. If there is wisdom to be learnt elsewhere then I have not been given the chance to learn it. Nor shall I ever be given that chance. If you pine for this place, perhaps that makes you the bigger fool than I. But certainly, only in that respect. You are an educated man. Because you were given the chance to be educated. I can read and write and know something of mathematics, but I shall never know what you know."

"Such eloquent words for one so uneducated." Nathan said, his voice sincere and yet somehow, I knew he was mocking me. "Proof indeed that you are more woman than you consider yourself."

He dared to take a step forward. But I had found my voice, I reasoned that nothing untoward could happen under my own roof and so I went to slake the fire and moved from the path of his advance. He watched me closely and I was not entirely dissatisfied to think that his eyes could not move away from me.

There was a great pleasure in knowing he wanted me. But even that, in the cold light of day, would most probably disturb me.

"You are too bold Nathan." I told him, trying to assert my newfound power. But still it felt like wearing new shoes. I was never certain if I sounded like the master or an imposter. "You talk to me of enchantments and wisdom. But what for? I dare say your intended would be grieved to hear you talk to me so."

For a moment I thought he would agree with me and put aside his nonsense for reason. But there was that flash in his eyes again. Something of madness and desire.

"Do not pretend to me, Finola. I have told you that I do not love her. You know very well what I am saying to you. Bold or no, you have already shown me that you are no fool. Do not pretend that you do not know why I speak so to you."

Without hesitation he moved towards me. I had thought I would move once again, but I found myself unable to refrain from allowing him to take whatever liberty he would.

There had been some truth in what he said. I could no longer deny that I knew very well what his intentions were. Only now I was afraid.

His large hands crushed against my sparrow like arms. What sort of man was he to lay hands so rough on his host's daughter? What sort of girl was I to allow it without murmuring a sound? There was something in the urgency of his touch that told me he did not mean to hurt me, only that he could no longer withstand to be in my company without holding me.

All too soon I felt the cool stone of the wall behind me and I realised he had inched me between that and himself. There was no escape. I was more afraid now, not of him, but of myself and the realisation that I did not wish to escape. The room was dark behind him. Nothing but shadow. There was only his huge body before me and the sharp line of his jaw that I could make out.

"Tell me to stop, and I shall stop. I shall leave here and never return. You will never have to look upon me again, but if you do not, I shall take you with me now and I shall make an enemy of this place, and your Daddy with it."

He was deadly serious. The whites of his eyes barely visible but boring into me like ice.

I was quietly hysterical. "You do not know what you are saying..."

His grasp on me tightened. "Do you protest, then? Do you send me to exile with a woman I do not love and a father I now resent? In a house I cannot abide, surrounded by the memory of this one sweet moment with you?"

Content... He had said he was content. Had he forgotten himself? Had I enchanted him with sorcery I never knew I possessed?

"Truly Nathan... you are mad." I said, shaking now under the iron grip.

I looked up into his eyes and there our souls met. For a moment, The Hylands slipped away and it was as if I stood atop that tallest tree and could taste the sky around me. But Nathan was beside me, every sin and every thought laid bare. Those blue eyes seemed to become one with the sky and I saw that he was still that boy I paid no mind to. Whose face was familiar, whose greetings were polite and formal. Just a life being lived in the same part of the world as my own, with no more connection than that. Yet he was connected, somehow, he had come to me and looked upon me with new eyes. I had enslaved him to me, without knowing I had the power to do it.

And then he gasped, fell away from me. The bruises of his hands still burning on my skin.

"What are you doing?!" He demanded.

I could barely keep myself from screaming. He had held me so much tighter than I'd thought, with an ache inside me that was neither pleasure nor pain. The echo of his grip remained. For a moment, I could not comprehend what he had done to me. Yet he had the audacity to ask what I was doing?

"You..." He said, in a voice which was not entirely his own. "You will not have me!"

In two great strides he backed away from me as if repelled by something unholy.

"I do not want you Nathan Munro!" I spat. "You are a dog more foul than any dirty stray!"

And yet I was compelled to feel some sorrow that he was turning against me. Such sweet words as he had spoken to me were seldom heard in any girl's lifetime.

Certainly, words I had never expected to be spoken to me. But they were tainted now, and I was angry that I had allowed this mad man to speak to me at all.

"You call me dog, but I have seen... your eyes... I know what you are!" He shook his head against his own words. "I have seen!"

I closed my eyes. They were but only eyes. Tools for vision and enlightenment. Nothing more, nothing less.

"I tell you Nathan I do not know what you have seen. Will you end this madness and return to your chamber with some sanity intact?"

I was weary and wished for our encounter to be over.

"I shall not sleep another night under this roof. For now, I know why it remains here, and your family with it. I dare not speak of it, that which lingers here. But you will know one thing from me. Though you might not know it yourself, even your very name speaks that which must not be told."

If I had been flattered by his attention, It had given way to a very real fear.

"You speak in riddles. I will not listen to you a moment longer!" I flared, stepping back into the doorway.

But he would not rest. Pointing an ominous finger at me he spoke to curse me, "Cast no more spells upon me. I am but a man without wit nor power against them."

Fear gave way to despair and broken and confused, I felt the salty tears of sorrow fall. But he only laughed at me then, a low rumble to mock me. I thought I would kill him in that moment, if he had not quieted.

There was a rage building within me that my body could not withstand. White heat rose from my chest and stabbed my throat as I tried to swallow.

"Why do you laugh at me, Nathan Munro? How do you dare! You who are mad man! I have cast nothing upon you!"

His laughter was thin and shaky, his nerves laying waste to each bone and sinew in his body. He looked pale and sick as he eyed me suspiciously.

"Aye. I can well believe that. You have been well sheltered. Even here on this Isle. But I dare say the truth will come to you... in time."

I could not stop the flow of tears. I felt them roll down my cheeks and into my mouth. Bittersweet they were and hard to swallow. Of all the things I had tolerated I had not cried a single tear. For me to shed them now seemed almost a waste.

"Enough!" Said a voice, hushed but enraged.

I had not heard Daddy come into the room. Nor had I known he had been there, listening. He strode towards Nathan, standing below him but with the strength of a man twice his age. If there was relief to be had, I could not feel it. Only dread clung to me as I watched Daddy approach Nathan with fists clenched.

"I know what you harbour here." Nathan said, with the arrogant assuredness of someone unaware of their foe. "You think I do not see her..."

Daddy said something under his breath and then opened the front door slowly. Moonlight flooded the room, and I was able to see his true rage. His eyes were wide and incensed.

"Aye, Nathan, and I see you Boy. What madness breeds within you is of no concern of mine. Whatever you saw, I tell you boy it is not real. I will not have you puttin' fear in my daughter. You are no longer welcome in my house."

He gestured the way out and Nathan hesitated. "What is real here? I was asleep my whole life and only awoke the day we left. Forgive me, William, I did not mean to cause distress. But *she...*" And he pointed again that finger at me. "I never looked a day upon her with desire. Not in all the years I have known her. Today it seemed... something within me stirred and it was not of my own doing. It has driven me insane, for certain I could not look upon her without being so. Perhaps it is but illusion. But there's a truth in this... Those bible stories will not slake her thirst. You can hide the truth, but to what end? She's bound for that fate you keep from her. There will be no way to stop it. There's a power there unutilised, and she too will be driven mad if she does not learn of it. I know what she is... I have seen in her eyes. So the stories are true, then?"

Daddy lowered his head so that none could see his face. I thought he would admit defeat, but three things seemed to happen at once.

The first, which struck me the hardest, was the way he turned to me for the briefest moment with a look of twisted despair. The second, and I was never certain what force drove him, but he seemed to act with the strength of ten men behind him as he struck Nathan around the mouth sending blood across the doorstep. Then the third, I could only watch as Daddy shoved him out of the house and down the garden to the gate.

There was no mercy in him, none of the gentle man I knew. Though Nathan was bigger and younger, he could not come against Daddy's rage.

I watched them in the moonlight as Daddy kicked him down, almost taking the gate off with him. He took something out of his pocket and threw it at Nathan as he scrambled to compose himself.

"I shall take no land from you...you foul scoundrel of the devil!" Daddy raged, "Be gone from here and take your evil tongue with you or I shall not hesitate to strike you again!"

Blood came from the corner of Nathan's swollen jaw and he spat out a broken tooth. I winced. I had not wanted this.

"William Gray." Nathan said, almost inaudibly, through broken teeth and swollen jaw, "I have known you all my life. My family have worked alongside yours since time forgotten. I said that I recalled the day Finola was born. But I say to you now, I do not know of what, or who she was born. For certainly she is not of you. I implore you, William, to deliver yourselves from this secret and of this desolate place."

He did not wait for Daddy to say another word but turned and went down to his boat. In the blackest of night, he set sail for the mainland with only the moon to guide him. Daddy would not speak of it. Or if he did, then he did not speak of it to me.

I had not wished to see Nathan go under such hostile circumstances, but I could not think of that. If I did, then surely, I would have driven myself to the brink of despair, longing for the answers to my questions.

Chapter Two

THE FIRST SUNDAY

For endless nights I had tangled myself in confusion and resentment. Perhaps it had only been two nights, or three but the long hours seemed to go on and on until I slept fitfully and deep. Without dreams. There was nothing.

The days were equally numbing. Strange, because a silence hung above us that was so loud it deafened me.

Daddy, in his usual manner, would go across the fields to check on the cattle. But he did not linger over breakfast. Mammy was not entirely with us. Her attention turned towards the sea and she could not take her eyes from it. I wondered what Rohan had heard, if he had been told to keep his thoughts to himself.

He would sit to the table and read from books and learn the words the way I had done before him but the way his eyes looked up from the pages betrayed his concentration. A hundred years could have passed in those days until Sunday morning arrived like a beacon of hope. I was solely frustrated. I could feel my whole body tense up into stone as we loaded the sailboat we used to travel to the mainland.

The sun was coming up over the horizon, spilling its light over the rippled water. I turned my face away and put the food basket underneath my seat.

Rohan was throwing skimming stones as we waited for Mammy and Daddy to finish preparing for when we returned at supper time. It always seemed to me that these journeys to the mainland were becoming more difficult. Or perhaps that's how I perceived it, because it seemed so seldom that we went.

"Rohan, get you in the boat before Mammy and Daddy come down!" I called to my restless brother.

He threw his stones down like the petulant child he still was and came to the boat. These journeys were a nuisance to him. The church service was a nuisance to him. I pitied that he could not drift away as I did.

"Shall we go to Aunt Hannah's house today?" He asked, climbing aboard with long legs that could not carry his new height. "Do you think they have missed us?"

There was a twinkle in his eye at the thought of going to see our cousins. They at least did not stare at us like we were cattle with two heads or spectres in the mist.

Aunt Hannah was our Mammy's younger sister who had once lived on Eynhallow as we did now. But she had married a boy from Evie and not once returned since her babies had been born. First came Ewan in the same year Rohan came, and then came Bethan.

She was a nuisance child who insisted on following my every move on our infrequent visits. Ewan was too quiet for my liking, always too afraid to play with Rohan the way he would have had them play.

But it was not in Rohan's nature to give up and I recalled one Sunday afternoon after dinner when he managed to coax the shy boy into the fields behind their home to play on The Knowe O'Aikerness. A soggy mound of earth that overlooked the water, there was not much to do but roll down it and ruin their Sunday best.

After that they had managed to find some pleasure in each other's company. Rohan was wild and Ewan was tame, but they had some common ground. I wished that I had known at the time that it would be as fleeting as the turn of spring.

Bethan was still a nuisance to me though, but as I had grown, I had found some patience for her. I found myself quite looking forward to seeing them.

"If they have not then I shall say that I have missed them." I said, glad for a moment that we were leaving.

Rohan smiled at the moment of optimism within me. "You'll be singin' a merry tune next." He teased.

I felt like lifting my voice to sing as The Hylands became nothing but a shape in the distance. The curve of the island came into sight and Daddy raised the small white sail above our heads. It was like being reborn, being on the water. I turned my back on Eynhallow and watched as the mainland came closer.

The water was clear and calm, the tide ready to move back out towards the open sea. Daddy knew the tides like he knew the beat of his own heart. He would never sail on low tide, always we would have to wait for the water to rise before we embarked upon it. He always said it made for a swifter journey, but sometimes it seemed that no matter what the tide it would take forever.

When finally, we reached the shore, I busied myself with carrying the food basket up towards the village. Rohan kept looking back but soon his fickle nature would steal his concentration elsewhere.

I felt somewhat nervous as the houses seemed to loom above us, rows of them side by side. Daddy lead us through the streets until we came to the house of our Aunt and Uncle. Since last we had been there the ivy had grown higher on the front of the house. I looked up at the smoking chimney and the way it seemed to stand so firm. It made The Hylands look like piles of stones which had been thrown on top of one another under the guise of a home. But this place was solid and new, the windows clear and free of smudge marks. The front lawn was immaculately cut, and I could not help but feel envious of how their hanging baskets were starting to bloom. Nothing bloomed on Eynhallow. Not even people. If there was some beauty to be found here, it did not extend inside the house.

Aunt Hannah came to the door, her face pale and sallow. She was not the bonny woman I remembered from last summer. Her very life seemed to have evaporated. She smiled in warm relief to see us and embraced us one by one.

"Ah, God save us Mary! Thanks be to Him that you're here!" She cried, holding Mammy close to her.

Her bony hands clamped around Mammy and it didn't seem natural. There was a darkness in the house where once there had been light.

Bethan did not run to me, instead staying by her brother's side as they stood in the parlour waiting for us. Ewan, quiet as ever, had grown a good head above me now. There was something sad about the way he stooped, his arm wrapped protectively around his sister's shoulder.

"In God's name, what has befallen here?" Mammy gasped, pulling Hannah away from her so that she could look into her eyes.

Always God. They were as pious as each other. They both worshipped and blamed Him in their own way. But God hadn't done this. God hadn't kept the curtains closed, keeping out the morning light. God hadn't forgotten to sweep the floor and beat the rugs. God had not put that sour look on Ewan's face or taken Bethan's excitable nature. Something else had occurred here.

Aunt Hannah broke into tears as she told us that her husband had died during the winter. Her heart broke on every word and she could not speak afterwards.

"Ah poor wretches." Daddy said, extending a hand to Ewan's shoulder. "What shall you do now?"

Aunt Hannah managed to compose herself and went over to a chest in the corner of the room. The dust flew into the air as she opened it and I had to look away.

"Seamus never told me about it when he was alive, I only discovered it once he had gone. The damned fool must have known he wasn't for this world. There's enough money in that account to keep us in good health until Ewan is old enough to find work."

Her hands were trembling as she passed Daddy a slip of paper. His eyes widened as he inspected it.

"Seamus!" He exclaimed. "Well, he might be gone but at least you have *this*."

"Aye, but it cannot make my children smile. But that will come in time." She said sentimentally, sending Ewan to put the water on to boil and Bethan to draw the curtains open.

The light burst into the room like a hungry animal. The dust was revealed, swirling in the air and I held my breath until it settled. We sat and drank tea in the parlour and ate a little bread and cheese. But still they did not smile, and I wondered if this was what I inflicted on others? This melancholy, this sadness. But no, theirs was momentary. There would come a time where they would smile again, and happiness would return.

Daddy spoke of the garden and how it had been well kept and Aunt Hannah told us about a boy from across the way who had insisted on tending it for him after Seamus died.

Mammy implored her to keep the house in good shape, but Aunt Hannah tactfully dismissed it. Ewan spoke little, but Bethan seemed to return to some semblance of her old self after a while.

Her little eyes were red rimmed and tired, but Mammy coaxed out of her a little of the excitement I knew must still be there. She inquired about school and Bethan told us everything she had learnt. There was that bitter twist of resentment again, that I had never been to school. Never known a day in a classroom and had learnt everything in our parlour from books and Daddy. It was the only time I really listened, when Bethan told us about her teacher and Benjamin McDonald, the annoying boy she sat behind. Then I would leave again, my mind elsewhere as my body sat stationary.

And then Aunt Hannah said something I could not ignore.

"How seemed Nathan Munro when last you saw him?" She asked innocently.

The room seemed to shift into a reluctant silence. I saw the look Mammy gave Daddy but could not hope they would speak of it.

My heart began to burn as it beat more swiftly.

Daddy coughed nervously. "He was in good health."

Mammy clasped her hands together and, in a voice, which was unnaturally high, she suggested Ewan and Bethan go to play in the garden with Rohan, who was already outside inspecting the flowers. He never could tolerate the indoors, especially when they were not his own.

"Finola, dear, would you like to join them?" She asked, her eyes pleading.

But she knew I would not. I was too old for such games.

"No thank you Mammy." I said politely, for Aunt Hannah. "I am weary from our journey."

Aunt Hannah shook her head. "Ah yes, I have forgotten that journey. Treacherous as it is in winter, it must still be so in spring. I spoke with Nathan's mother at the market and she informed me that he was to return to Eynhallow before his wedding to settle the sale of their land. Did you buy their land William?"

Daddy took the stance of a great bull protecting his field. "Well, you see. I have no use for that land. I was tempted, for certain. But I have all the land I have need of."

Aunt Hannah looked perplexed. "I see. So he left you in good spirits, then?"

Mammy sipped the last of her tea and placed it back on the saucer a little more abruptly than was seemly.

"Hannah, what is this about Nathan Munro? Why do you ask?"

Aunt Hannah's face fell. She swallowed hard and shook her head. "I had forgotten news from the land does not reach you. Why, it has been a full ten days since last anybody saw him. So, he left you and did not return. His poor mother has lost one son, and so it seems she has lost another."

There was an audible gasp. I was never sure if it was my own, but I couldn't hide my astonishment. Daddy went pale and put down his drink, the cup almost shaking in his hands. He patted down his Sunday shirt and waistcoat, searching the pockets for his pipe and tobacco.

"Has there been no sight of him?" Mammy asked nervously.

If their guilty consciences were written on their faces, Aunt Hannah could not read them.

"They waited on the shore for him, and when he did not come, they sent for his mother and father. Old Mabel wept and said she knew he was gone from us and instead of waiting for his return, she waited for his body to wash up. Hamish Munro set out onto the water to find his son, or the wreckage. But there has been nothing."

I felt a shudder of cold run down my spine. That we had caused this was too much to bear. I wished I could have gone to him on that night and tried to prevent him taking his boat out in the blackest night. But there was much against me, the way he had looked at me I knew he would not have listened.

I could not make sense of that night. Now he had paid the dearest price. I wanted to find Mabel Munro and convey my sincerest condolences. But I would have broken at the sight of her, the intolerable cruelty of not knowing etched on her face.

I would have told her all which had come to pass that night and she would have looked at me with hate and malice. It occurred to me, in that moment, that indeed I had harboured feelings towards him. It pained me that some misfortune had found him.

And it hurt, like hands twisting my stomach from the inside, that I did not help him. I had somehow orchestrated his fate, and I was chained to him now. I felt my knees tremble and ache to stand and run to the water's edge and search for him. But I was rooted to the spot and could not move. Mammy's eyes were boring into me, the words unspoken screaming at me to sit and keep quiet.

"How sad." Mammy said calmly. "I shall pray for him today."

But when it came the time for us to go to Church and take our places amongst the other parishioners, I looked around me and wondered how many of them were truly without sin.

Even Mammy, who was pious beyond all reason, had lied today.

The doleful sound of the church bells sounded as we made our way down the cold stone aisle and to our seats. I heard the whispers before I had even removed my bonnet.

There be William Gray... Hamish be wanting a word with him... Do yer think he knows? Ah... there's not a soul knows what happened to him here.

I did not dare to lift my head and see where the whispers came from. In the house of God, I wondered if all my sins would lay themselves bare with one look. I sensed their wonderment and wished to be out in the fresh air where the wind could cast my sins free. Or was it the sins of others I was so burdened with?

I looked at Mammy and her eyes were pressed firmly into her hymn book. Daddy too, but he was not reading it. Only looking absently through the pages as if it were a tool to keep the devil away. Their secrets were buried so deep not even God could penetrate on this holiest of days. They were as dear to me as my own heart. But today, they were strangers.

The sermon was long and monotonous, as it always seemed to me. The words echoed down the aisle and made no sense. Rohan shuffled in his seat, his eyes wandering to the colours of the window and the image of Jesus Christ made from glass. The sun sent the colours dancing onto the cold floor. I found myself lending my attention to this, rather than the meandering heads of the crowd before me and the alter before them.

"I cannot contend with this every Sunday." Rohan whispered almost silently as he inclined his head towards mine. "Even if it should take us from the Island."

I smiled in agreement and kept my voice low. "For that at least, I am thankful for where we live."

Mammy moved in her seat next to me, her hand clamping around my wrist tightly. "Do you wish to draw attention to us?" She whispered venomously.

I pulled away seeing the dark bruise where her hand had been upon my skin and almost broke the silence with rage. I bit my lip and resolved to bide my time. This was not my God and not my worship and I did not care if they stared. Let them! Their judgement did not make my soul bleed. I would look past their faces untouched.

And so, I did as the sermon ended and the masses began to make their way out into the churchyard. The accusers and sympathisers met my eyes with sadness and hate. But they could not hold my attention. Out in the sunshine, no longer stifled by the darkness of the church, I sighed in relief and closed my eyes against the blinding rays and then Mammy's hand was upon me again and I remembered my previous anger.

"Finola, go and wait by the gate with your brother and your cousins." She instructed. "I must speak with Hamish Munro."

I hadn't noticed the fair-haired man until I saw him standing behind the gravestone of his youngest son, underneath the shade of the blossom tree. The Munro's never came to church, except for weddings and burials. Now, as the old man stood almost weeping, his eyes searching us out, I knew it was a great wrench to his heart to come today.

He had waited for us; had known we would be here. He seemed so much older now. His fair hair grey and his eyes lined with the loss of two sons. I wanted to comfort him if only I knew how. I watched as Daddy went to him, his hand extended for Hamish to shake. I winced. I could not forget that that same hand had thrown Nathan Munro out of our house that fateful night.

I would have gone to wait by the gate, but Hamish sought me out from the crowd. His eyes resting on me like a hunter to its prey. I was compelled to greet him.

"Finola..." He said, his voice low and aggrieved. "How you have grown." And he took me in a brief embrace.

I recoiled but allowed him to plant a customary kiss on my hand. Could I lie to this man as I had lied before? Somehow the sin seemed so much greater now. Even if I did not believe in God, I did not wish to hurt this man who had already suffered enough.

"Thank you." I replied softly.

Daddy was shaking his head as if in great thought, his hand rested against his jaw as it flexed. *Speak ill of him... I shall dare you to speak ill of him...* I thought.

"I wish I could tell you something of comfort Hamish." Daddy said, "But when last I saw Nathan he was as alive as you or I standing here now."

Hamish winced. "I would have come to Eynhallow myself, but Mabel would not have it that any of us set a foot back on that island. I have waited the longest of days to speak with you. Will you not give me better news, William?"

But there was no comfort. Not here. There were secrets so deeply buried not even the dead could raise them. Not even the burning face of a man tortured with the unknowing nightmares of where his lost son could be could make my Daddy tell. I felt like standing beside Hamish, to force them for the answers I still had not received.

"Would that I could Hamish. I did not know he had not returned until this morn. Had I known; my search would have been as fervent as your own."

I wanted to laugh. If sincerity had another face, this was it. A cold and calculating face which did not smile.

"Mabel will not give up her weeping for him. I have wept enough for many lost sons. I will weep no more. God be with you William, and you Mary..." And then he turned to me with desperate eyes. "And you Finola. May you remain in the bosom of your family."

And then he turned and walked into the church. I did not venture to wonder why. When all comfort is lost, perhaps all that there is left is futile prayer. Mammy crossed herself again as she watched him enter.

"There goes a broken man." She said, almost unrepentant that they had sinned on hallowed ground.

"Aye, and there'll be no use for any of us to prolong his pain. There's an end to it." Daddy said, speaking directly to me.

Was I to forget then? Console myself with nothing but darkness and wondering? If I had been angry before, now there was a rage there which would not be slaked. I had waited, I had been patient and questioned not when they would have had me remain silent.

"An end for who?" I inquired, as they began to lead me away from the church.

Mammy looked at me peculiarly. "For all of us."

All but one.

We returned to Aunt Hannah's house for afternoon tea and the realisation that the day was not going to improve. Rain began to fall in earnest, preventing Rohan from escaping outside and making the house, however large it had seemed that morning, close in on us like a proverbial tomb.

We spoke of Uncle Seamus and the fond memories we had in his company. But I could not mourn him. He had little time for me in life, besides the obvious courtesy extended to a niece of his wife's side of the family.

Daddy stayed by the window, smoking his pipe absently as he inspected the conditions over the horizon. As time wore on, I slowly began to realise that we would not return that night and instead would stay in our tomb until the rain cleared.

Rohan was sent to sleep with Ewan, and Mammy with Aunt Hannah. I was to share a bed with Bethan and Daddy slept between the two armchairs in the parlour. The rain was still beating down as I put the candle out and slipped into the bed beside my cousin.

But the moon was full and fought for dominance of the sky between the dark clouds that seemed to fight back. I saw it as a good omen. That light would prevail and with it, the truth...

"Cousin?" Bethan whispered; her white skin visible to me in the pale moonlight. "May I ask something of you?"

She had been quiet for most of the day. Keeping her voice for responses rather than offering conversation of her own. Here in the darkness where four walls kept all others out, I was touched that now she spoke and only to me.

"Of course you may." I whispered back.

She sighed heavily and moved her head towards the small opening in the curtains, where the shaft of moonlight slipped into the room.

"When you return to Eynhallow, will you take me with you?"

It suddenly struck me that here was her prison. As Eynhallow was mine. I could not take her from one and put her in another.

"You do not want to come to Eynhallow, as much as you think you might." I told her quietly. "There is nothing for you there."

But she seemed not to care. "Mammy does not smile anymore. She is only ever sad here. I do not want to be here anymore, and neither does Ewan."

But still I could not take that sadness to Eynhallow. Where sadness seemed to flourish. My own sadness, if nobody else's.

"I tell you Cousin, someday you will all smile again. You will have no wish to leave here. For me it is different. There is no respite like church and school and the faces of others when I am sick of the faces before me. There is nothing but wreck and ruin and memories that do not sleep."

Her childish face turned to me in wonder. "Perhaps we could take each other's place?"

I smiled at the thought of it but knew it could not be. "That would be nice. But Ewan would miss you and Rohan would miss me. As we all know, boys are silly and need their sisters to ensure they remain with all their wit intact!"

I heard the muffled laughed under the blanket and turned to sleep, satisfied I had slaked her whim. But in moments I could feel her small body shifting towards me.

"At school, they say Benjamin McDonald likes me. That's why he throws paper at my head and teases me about my hair." She said, and I could feel her warm breath on the back of my neck. I did not turn. "But how can that be so when he does nothing but irritate me?"

"You are asking the wrong person." I yawned. "I know little of matters of the heart."

I didn't want to know. What little I did know gave me such grief that I intended to push it away from me for all my life. Whatever I did not know, I did not wish to know. If all men were like Nathan Munro, then all men were mad. If I should feel something for a mad man, then I too in turn must be mad.

"Have you kissed a boy?" Bethan asked then, her whispers turning into excited giggles.

I would tell her this and no more. If I had wanted her to smile, I had succeeded.

"No." I simply said. "Now we must try to sleep. I must rise early."

"I don't suppose you have." She surmised, dismissing my request for sleep entirely. "Would you like to kiss a boy?"

I sighed heavily. "I shall not know until I do. This talk is folly, you are a child of eleven. You must think only of school and church and childish games with your dolls."

She gasped at my reprimand and shifted back onto her side of the bed. If I had wanted silence, I had achieved it. But now there was a sense of that sadness I had wanted to remove. So, I turned to her and tried to soothe her with the story of the Goodman of Thorodale.

But I could not tell it like Nathan. My words in comparison to his did no justice to the tale which had enchanted me. When I was done, I was almost sorry I had told it, and there was no way to tell if it had enchanted Bethan as it had with me.

She slept soundly by my side, her low breath somehow a warm comfort to me as I slipped into dreams of terrible whales trying to capture my soul as I tried to return to Eynhallow.

Their great bodies leapt from the water and tried to take me back down with them. Part of me longed for them to drag me under.

And then I remembered I could not breathe under water and awoke with a panic, struggling for breath.

The sky was red. Like blood streaked across the clouds. Soon it would be light, and I could forget my hellish dreams. But then would come the night again. It seemed futile that I would ever rest.

I slipped away, leaving Bethan to her peaceful slumber and went out to sit and watch the tide.

Chapter Three
THE WATER

I t was too still. The birds did not take to the sky. The wind was low and silent. Something in the way the water moved told me not to encroach upon it.

The grass was still covered in morning dew as I overlooked the sound and my broken shoe began to let the moisture in.

With wet feet and a heavy heart, I went down to the boat and waited. There was a fresh breeze which came after the rain and I closed my eyes against the coolness of it on my skin.

I did not know where to look. I did not belong here in this village; I did not belong out there on that Island I had spent my entire life. So, I kept my eyes closed and imagined myself remaining in this boat out on the water, hanging between the two places forever more.

Darkness moved overhead, the clouds gathering in stormy clusters above. The wind picked up, and I felt the chill of it down my spine. A bad omen. But there was no way to foretell its meaning.

I watched as my brother came down to greet me, the empty food basket now full as he placed it back into the boat. Mammy and Daddy followed, their solemn faces saying silent goodbye as we pushed out and away from the shore.

It seemed as though the rain had waited for us to begin our journey and began lashing down on us as we took to the waves. It was no longer still. Like it, too, had been waiting to unleash some misfortune upon us. I pulled my shawl above my head and waited for it to be over. But time stood still, when it seemed we had been sailing aimlessly I peered out and saw that Eynhallow was nowhere to be found.

"In God's name!" Mammy cried out, her arms reaching upward as if to take God's hand.

I looked at Daddy, but his face did not change. Those determined eyes seemed focused on the mist which had descended, and he would not look away.

"William, turn back! What folly is this? Ah, we have roamed into hell!" She bellowed.

And for all the bravery he had shown before, Rohan crumbled into her arms and allowed her to hold him close like a babe. She urged me to come forward and lean against her, but panic had already set in. I would not be soothed.

My heart racing, I looked to the empty space across the water and felt my body turn to stone as I wondered if my eyes deceived me. But, how could they? The fear was real.

"Mammy, where have we gone?!" Rohan screamed, his youthful voice turning into the high-pitched sound of a wailing banshee.

She placed a hand across his face and tried to make him look away, but he broke free and stared unrelenting at the lashing water and the empty space before us.

"Rohan, will you not look son… We have found ourselves in bad weather. We shall come across it soon." She soothed, trying to placate his fear.

But mine had taken flight. My body of stone began to move and sway with the rocking of the boat.

"Sit you down, Finola!" I heard someone cry.

But I could see it now, the shadow lying beyond the mist and rain. It was there, but it was hidden. It didn't want to be found. For all I had ever felt, I knew now it was trying to abort us. *Leave me be, I am barren. I want to be alone…* but we hadn't listened. We had remained and now the Island was punishing us.

"I see it! Beyond… I see it, there!" I screamed, my voice somehow floating above the roar of the waves and wind.

But Daddy did not hear me. It was as if he had always kept his eye upon it. He had not flinched. His determination was both arrogant and frightening. If the waves truly wished to claim him, they would whip him into their clutches and not let go.

"But I see it, I do..." But nobody listened. They heard me; I knew they heard me. But I could only see their waving arms, their demands for me to sit. I would not loosen my grip on it, nor give it chance to disappear again.

I stood in the prow as the storm raged on and watched as we broke through the mist and near the shores of Eynhallow again.

There was a strange feeling within me. Like something unholy had occurred. Rohan did not dare look, in case it were not real. He stayed in Mammy's arms, shaking and crying in a low, dull tone into her skirts. I was not afraid anymore. I wondered if Daddy had ever been afraid to begin with. He broke his solid stance and looked at me, his mouth moving into the smallest of smiles.

"You knew we would come to it, didn't you?" I asked, but he would only smile. "You know much and will not tell me."

He sighed heavily and tied off the sail as the wind dropped. "Aye. Because you do not need to know all which I know."

"What occurred here, just now?" I whispered, and I knew somehow, he could hear me.

"Nothing but wind and rain." He whispered back, his eyes narrow and distant. "Do not seek to find anything untoward here. Your brother is scared, and there's no need to scare him more. Here, we are almost home. Do not worry about things which require no explanation. Now, sit you down Finola."

Sit me down? I bit down on my tongue, but it was not enough to quiet it. I recalled the linger of Daddy's eyes which would not move away from that distant shadow. Nathan's voice filtered down from my mind and into my consciousness. *But Thorodale did not take his eyes away from the Isle...*

"These mysteries are but hidden truths. I say you reveal them to me, or I shall cast myself forth into the water. You shall not see me more."

There was an unspoken look between us. He would not have me thrust myself into the waves, but he would not reveal that which I desired to know either.

"You are a fantasist, child. Whatever dreams you have, keep them for your sleep. Because there is no place for them here." He said, shaking his head and pausing on the clear sky ahead.

How strange it had been. So momentarily stuck in a nightmare only to wake and find the sun shining through. But it did not fool me. I knew what dreams were, and what existed in reality. Nathan had been more real to me in those days than anyone had ever been to me in the years before.

But I could not say it, could not confess that I had somehow loved him.

"Nathan said he knew what I was. But how can that be, when I do not myself? Do you know, then? Daddy?"

He closed his eyes for the first time, and I thought he would speak. Instead, what happened would remain with me for the rest of my life.

For a moment, it seemed like the storm had not done with us yet. The wind picked up, and the sail moved to accommodate.

Daddy did not open his eyes in time to stop as I lost my grip and plunged into the icy sea.

I heard them scream my name through muffled water, but I did not fight to respond. The surface was already beyond my reach, the light fading with the sound of their voices. The cold soon numbed me, and I waited for the pain of it to subside.

Why do I not fight? Why do I not search for the boat which I know is above me? It was as if there was no need. That allowing myself to sink further was more natural than breathing.

And soon it became so. I forgot that I was drowning, and I lost sight of which direction I was going.

If I am dying, then it is pleasant enough… I will not fight it.

But it was not death which greeted me. Within the darkness of the water I began to feel that I was not alone. Though I could not see my hands resisting before me, I knew I was not alone. Perhaps it was euphoria which gripped me. The unrelenting knowledge that I had come to meet my death and I greeted it with surprising joy.

But it was not that, it was not within me. It was beyond me. I could have sworn I had been submerged for hours; my breath still stuck within my lungs with no wish to expire. But surely it had been but a moment. Was it not the surface I saw before me? Its light beating like a beacon on the horizon.

No, there was no light such as this that I had ever seen above the waves of Eynhallow sound. Its golden glow radiated towards me like arms trying to embrace me. Its warmth was almost more than I could bear.

It took away the piercing cold and reminded me that I was alive. The glow illuminated the blood running through my veins. I could not even gasp for the fear of water engulfing me. Whatever this spectre was, I was not afraid. It was not afraid of me. It pulled me towards its inferno and soon I knew that I had come to die. For no living creature could withstand a dream so vivid.

Through light greater than the great fire ball in the sky, I moved down and recalled the sense that I had stepped onto firm ground. But there was nothing beneath me. Only above were ornate gardens of flowing weeds of colours I could not describe.

Their texture gleamed against the blinding light. I felt my heartbreak at the sight of them. Where crystals seemed to hang from ceilings which were not there, I had somehow earned my place in Heaven. I felt the tears of relief come, but they did not flow. The water took them, and I was left only with a sense that I had been crying.

But I was no longer sad. This was something else entirely. Never would I have been able to find the words. As I moved between the crystal gardens, I felt the water shift behind me. I turned to see a pair of curtains close, their movements slow and deliberate. Enclosing me within a room littered with pearls and coral. Within their smooth surface I saw faces reflected at me, but as I turned, they disappeared into the phosphorus glow.

Only their voices remained, calling my name. In a tongue I did not recognise, they spoke to me. Whoever they were, those around me. They would not show themselves to me.

"Finola... Where have you been?" They chorused, the water altering their voices. *"Finola... Stay here with us..."*

For a moment I recalled another place I had once known. Almost as quickly as it had come, the memory faded, and I could only recall this magnificent place before me. Drifting through curtains of fabric I had no name for, there seemed to be no end to these halls of decadence.

Until finally I came to a room of gold and there upon a wall which seemed to shimmer in the dim light of the surface there was a grand mirror. Or was it a window? For as I peered into it there was no reflection of my own. Only a view of a grand and opulent gate which seemed to sit comfortably on the seabed.

And then I saw, through whatever this was, a face which looked back but would not come close enough to touch. Saddened by something I could not grasp, he came to me and stood in reproach.

"Finola Gray..." He said solemnly. *"Tell them I did not come of my free will. Tell them I shall return some day. You must. For I shall dwell here until the world changes and none shall remember my name.*

What did this place have to do with free will? If I had known of its existence before I would have flung myself into the waves and allowed myself to drown sooner.

"You may return, But I shall not go there more. Here I shall stay." I replied, hearing those voices once again requesting that I remain.

Nathan stared blankly into the beautiful abyss. *"I am not one of them... I wish to see my father's face again. Tell my mother I am well. Only you must do that for me... but you must go now!!!"*

I watched him turn and disappear into the weeds. As if there had been rope around him and pulled from sight.

I wondered why it should not seem strange to me to see him here. But I had already accepted the possibility that I was dead and so was he and somehow, we dwelt in the same heaven.

Perhaps it was Angels which called to me to stay. Their velvet voices carrying like air through the water.

But they still would not show themselves to me. Instead, remaining just beyond my sight. Making their presence known without revealing their faces.

I called Nathan's name once, but there was only myself to hear. I was alone, as much as anyone could be alone when no other could be seen.

But as I touched one of the brightly coloured weeds which weaved its way into the golden room I shuddered. It was not of any weed I had ever felt before, its texture was warm and pulsating.

As if it were a living creature born of this place and not planted in the earth. I shuddered again. For the first time I came to my senses.

The tightening in my chest bore down on me and I began to swim. Searching for Nathan, searching for a way to the surface. I did not want to leave him, But I could not breathe. The more I recalled that loss of breath the more I began to see that golden surface fade away.

"The spell is broken..." I heard them say. *"Finola Gray... The spell is broken! When you shall weep the land shall weep. When you shall hunger so the creature's hunger. When you love so it shall be as it has always been..."*

Was it hands or weeds which clutched my body so? In the darkness I was bound to them but still they would not reveal their faces.

"You do not enslave them as they enslave themselves..." And then I heard them no more.

It was a gentle breeze which roused me. The cool touch of the wind forced me to acknowledge the ground beneath me.

For a moment it seemed I remembered a fox calling to me to be fed. Birds crying as they flew overhead, because they had shared my tears. A man declaring his maddening love, because I had looked upon him with desire... Then it was gone.

And all that remained was the taste of the ocean on my tongue and a body which would not move enough for me to purge.

They found me on the rocks by the shore. Their screams were fevered with anguish and relief. I did not protest when Daddy picked me up and carried me back to The Hylands. I could not even speak. But I could hear their rage and despair. Mammy prayed over me as sickness ravaged my body. Her doleful hymns hanging over me like an ominous shadow.

Daddy would come and sit by my bed and read to me when he thought I was asleep. Always the same book, always in that slow drone that he insisted reading aloud in. Rohan would then come and speak to me, to tell me of his day and what he wished for when I was better.

In those weeks where I was never sure what was real or fantasy I began to speak in my sleep. I discovered, quite by accident, that I recalled much more than I had dared to.

The dreams were vivid and came to me in succession each time I closed my eyes. When fever clutched me, I heard my own screams as if I were standing from another room. The hallucinations were terrifying, and yet when I saw Nathan Munro's face, I knew there was something I must say. He haunted me then. I was sorry I could not fulfil his ghostly requests.

But when the sickness faded, so did his face. I did not see him again. Nor did any other. Wherever he was, and part of me knew he was in that place I had seen in some half-forgotten memory, he would remain there until the world had changed and none remembered his name.

But when I thought of it, always I recalled the words in his voice and not my own. As if he had said it to me somewhere, sometime. But I could not place it.

Time seemed to shift. In the dark of night, I would forget myself and reach out for the golden walls of that land beneath the waves. Then I would awake at the break of dawn and wonder why I should weep for a place I dared not think of.

And then, on one of those peaceful nights where dreams evaded me and I could sleep without fear, Daddy came to my room and sat with me until dawn. When the sun broke over the horizon and I heard the cockerels sound, I opened my eyes and found him waiting at the foot of my bed.

"Are you well enough to rise?" He asked dolefully.

"I shall not know until I try." I replied, my fragile body resisting the pull as Daddy helped me to sit.

I had not seen the view from my window in weeks. The barren landscape was washed in red light. Like it was bleeding.

"I would have stayed away. Let you get your strength back. But there's not much good can come from it. Not now."

He lit his pipe and fell into the chair by the door, his weary face pale and covered in sweat. There was a broken man in his place.

"Your Mammy, she prayed for you. She believes her God saved you, and that's as well enough for her. But I think we both know, and you'll not deny it to me lass, that God had no part in this."

The sweat was beading around his forehead now. I saw it glimmer in the morning light. He had been sitting too close to the fire, too lost in thought to move away.

"Why do you say that?" I asked in a voice much weaker than it had once been.

He was not forthcoming. The dawn had begun to give way to the morning and already there were birds stirring in the trees outside. Their song was familiar and haunting, and reminded me there would be no other joy for the day.

"I'll not speak ill of her God while she's present. But I dare say you've known for some time I am no God-fearing man. I'll say the same for your brother as it is with your Mammy. But not you. There'll be no more talk of God between you and I."

It was strange that he should speak so. There was an edge of desperation in his voice that worried me. Where the morning light met the horizon, a great shaft stole its way into the room and into my eyes. I closed them and turned my head away and was suddenly reminded of that gold.

"As you wish." I whispered. "Then what shall we talk of?"

His reluctance was burdened with a need I could not fathom. Something haunted him which would not rest. These mysteries held the answers I longed for.

"I had hoped that this day would not come. But there's ghosts that need to rest. I'll put them to rest. It has plagued my soul, and I'll not let it fester more."

He spoke as if it would be the last time. That it would be easier and kinder to bury himself underneath the rocks than speak now. I was still too weak to burden him with questions. But perhaps this was why he came to me now. Before I was recovered enough to respond.

He came to the bed and sat beside my feet. Despite the glowing sunlight he turned to look outside the window and did not blink. The light did nothing to dispel his fears. They seemed to age him with each passing moment.

"A man has many sides to him." He began, finally looking away. But he would not look at me. "When I was young, I did not thank my father for bringing us here. The winters of my childhood will always remain bleaker than any I have endured since. But when my father died, I was of an age where I could become a man. So, when I longed to return to the mainland, I remained. My mother would not leave, nor would my brothers leave her. I was certain they would perish without me. A man does not own his own destiny. My father knew that, and he taught us well. I could not weep as my mother died. I could not feel envy as my brothers left for the mainland and as the eldest, I had paved that pathway for them. But not for myself. I'd ingrained myself so deeply in this place I could not leave it, not even when I was the only one left."

He hung his head in sorrow. As if remembering these things were like ripping open scars which had long healed. I had never heard him speak of the life he had before I had come into the world. What child can really know the person that their mother and father used to be? We can only know them as protectors and providers. But not as those people who loved and hurt, lived and lost.

It pained me to see him so distressed. I almost wanted to protest that he speak further. But he would have motioned me to silence. His hand was already poised to gesture that I let him speak.

"I was little older than you are now. Eighteen. My brothers had chosen to go and live with our mother's sister on the mainland after she passed. But they could not make me go. I had a reason to stay. It will be with me always. That reason. It keeps me here, even now. When the winters get bleaker still, and disease takes our neighbours." His voice shook. Through tears he could not shed, he looked at me then.

"It was before your Mammy came. I had been fishing on the rocks and I saw her standing there. She was looking out to sea wearing nothing, but a dress made of rags. Her hair was wet, and it clung to her skin in the wind. I'll never forget the way she moved towards me. Like waves. I knew she did not mean me any harm but still I feared her. She was beautiful and I had not seen a beautiful girl in many a year. She would not speak to me though, only stood with me until I could take it no more. I begged her to tell me her name, but she would only smile at me as if I should already know it. I knew then I must be content to have her by my side and nothing more. She had cast some spell upon me, that much I knew. But I could not protest. I would have ripped my own beating heart out for her if she had requested it. I was consumed by her. I have not shed tears since that night I lay with her on the rocks and awoke to find her gone. I did not sleep for searching. The other families would watch me and whisper that I had gone mad with grief after losing my mother and father so young. But they had died, there was no madness in knowing that truth.

The only ones who did not mock was the Munro family. They invited me to supper one night, they took pity on me. The house still belonged to Hamish Munro's father and Hamish was still young enough to obey him. But still he was older than I, and it was a bitter reminder that I was too young to be alone in this world. They told me the stories. Aye, those stories I know you have heard. Then I knew why they did not mock me.

These were not mere stories. They had seen me with her. They knew for whom I searched. But I did not see her again, not until I had made a good marriage with the daughter of a new family who had come to Eynhallow after their crops had failed on the mainland. We had married before Winter set in, and she had gotten with child. But the wee boy was strangled before he could be born, by his own belly chord. She mourned him and cursed her God to that hell she fears so much.

When the spring came, still she mourned. She would not let me touch her. So, I went from her, always back to those rocks. Always searching without knowing what it was that I looked for. It had been almost a year when I saw her again, by the shore. She was waiting for me. I have never felt such blind relief as when I once again took her into my arms, and I knew nothing more. She came to me three more times before she could come no more. On that last time, I knew I would not see her again. She handed me the child of her belly. The seed, which was mine, and finally she spoke to me. *Finola*... She said in a tongue I had not heard before. It was a strange dialect not of anywhere around here. I never knew if she was telling me her name... Or yours."

The wind stopped. Like it had been commanded to die. My breath caught in my chest and I could not breathe.

"Your Mammy made her peace with God that day. When I brought you to her she took you from me and said that it did not matter where you had come from. You were a daughter of mine and a gift to take away the loss of our wee boy. She had it put about that she was with child again and had been so consumed with grief she had not known. Hamish Munro's mother had given birth to him in such circumstances, and it was a well-known story that Fanny Munro had gone to bed one night only wake with Hamish between her thighs. So, it was with you. But I'll not survive another winter without you knowing. There's no hope for it now. Not now you have seen... Aye, and I know you have seen for such dreams as those you have spoken of could not be mere coincidence. But you must tell me and there'll be no more secrets between us. Did you see her?"

His face was riddled with that madness he had spoken of. I had only seen it once before, in the face of Nathan Munro.

"I did not see anyone." I said quietly. "And even if I had, how could I have known who it was?"

His face fell. "Aye. I would never have known. She would have kept you, no doubt."

I began to feel rage in my weak body. This broken man told me these things for the answer to his own question. So that he might rest his own soul. There was no peace for my own. These discoveries did nothing to quieten my sobbing. But I did not show my tears. I cried inwardly.

"Do you dare?" I spat. "Do you truly dare to tell me these things and think that I shall not hate you for them? I shall not look to my Mammy again as her who gave birth to me. I shall not think of those stories in wonder and amazement but only disdain and regret. That madness which consumed you, was it the same madness which consumed Nathan? Is that my curse? Was that my true mother's curse?!"

He shook his head, as if he would not change things even if he could. "You have heard the stories. She could have dragged me into the water and taken me forever. But not her. She came to me. She would not have you do the same. But there's things that can't be changed. That is desire. It can reduce the most reasonable man into nothing more than a lonely shadow. But it is not a curse. It is the way it has always been between the Finfolk and man."

I know what you are... I gasped. Nathan's voice echoed through the water and I heard him say it again. Suddenly everything made sense.

"You sent Nathan to his fate because he knew what I was. You would not have him reveal it, now you come to me when I am too weak to comprehend it! This is the greatest evil you could do to me..."

I pushed the bed sheets from me and tried to retreat. But my legs had not walked for weeks and had forgotten how to move. I could do nothing but fall to the ground and allow myself to be held up in Daddy's arms.

"Do not say so, the greatest evil was concealing it from you. I should have known you would not find contentment here. That you would soon find that part of yourself. Of all my regrets as a man I shall not regret you. But for all my regrets as a father I shall always lament that I did not do better by you. But this is my torture. That you look like her. You can enslave the way she could. Without even knowing it."

Somewhere I heard a gull cry. With it my own tears came. I clung to Daddy's shirt and let him hold me to him. If nothing else, he had kept me. When *she* had not.

"Hush now, Finola." He soothed. "There'll be an end to it now. But do not forget there's magic in your blood. It is why the birds cry when you do. Why those wild foxes came to you for a feed? Aye, I know it was you who sent those chickens to their death. Why men will follow you until they know not where their own feet carry them. Shall you not forgive me?"

For all the anger and bitterness there was no desire to resent him for what he had done. Through the haze of confusion there was relief. But I could not rejoice in it. Whatever truth I had once known had now become a lie, and so I would not punish myself for lying again. Nor fear God. Or say my prayers. I would try to make sense of it. If there was any to be found.

Chapter Four

THE BODY

I imagined myself standing on a high plane above the entire world. Above me was nothing but sky, but below me was the flesh of man struggling to reach me.

They wanted only to be where I was. I, with my feet hanging over the edge of the grey clouds, wanted only to sink into the murky waters below.

I found myself no longer aching to attain my place in Heaven. Instead there was a morbid curiosity of that place I scarcely remembered save for in sour dreams that came to me seldom now.

I had recovered well enough to resume my daily duties and my bible studies. But what did it matter now? I looked at Mammy as she read the Psalms to us and her face took on that of a stranger. How dear she was to me, and how I longed for her to be that one to give me birth. Now it was tainted by the image of another. One I had no recollection of.

In a strange way I loved her more. I gave thanks that she had taken me into her heart and raised me as her own. But I would always return to those wandering thoughts about the strange woman on the rocks.

Legend had always said the Finfolk had dragged their chosen ones down into the waters against their own will. But not her. She had come to Daddy of her own free will and allowed him to remain on the land.

These fantastic tales of shape shifting creatures who could make themselves in the image of whales and great beasts was surely the imaginings of one driven mad. I looked at my own skin. My own bones. They grew only in my own image and would surely break should they shift into that of a creature greater than myself.

I could not dwell under the water either, for certain my breath would cease, and I would drown. Perhaps these were the parts of me which were human, and perhaps this was why she brought me to the surface. That woman, I could not think of her as my mother, but still it broke my heart to think she had given me away against her wishes. I would then cry and taste the salt of my tears and wondered if she had cried too.

I had not even begun to understand the magnitude of these discoveries when something else came along to distract me.

It was the eve of my Sixteenth birthday. Mammy had given me leave of my chores and Rohan asked me to accompany him fishing. It was a welcome request to me.

There had been evenings of temptation as we had sat by the fire where I had almost spoken those words, I know would change everything. I wondered what she might say if I told her that I knew their secret. But I could never bring myself to say the words out loud. Not as I watched her content face watching the flames lick the brick of the fireplace. She was happy enough and one day when her flesh was gone from this world I would whisper on the wind and hope that she heard me.

The wind was low as we made our way down to the shore. Rohan was overjoyed to be able to pursue his greatest pleasure at leisure.

In the weeks of my incapacity he had grown above me and his shoulders had broadened. Soon after my sixteenth birthday he would have his fourteenth. As I watched him cast his line, I tenderly recalled the night of his birth once again with a bitter renewal of old memories. I wished that I could tell him all that was in my heart. But he was Mammy's boy, and I could no more tell him than I could tell her.

"Shall you be glad to be sixteen?" He asked me as we sat waiting patiently for something to bite.

The sun was trying to shine through the passing clouds. In one moment, we were basked in its light, and in the next it was overcast once more.

"I couldn't say. I've never been sixteen before." I surmised.

He thought about this for a moment, his brow furrowing. Then his mind cleared, and he returned his gaze to the fishing line. How I had always envied this carefree side of him. To be able to put away my thoughts. Now there was some true magic.

"I shall be glad to be fourteen. Daddy says I can have my own rifle." He said triumphantly, his eyebrow raising.

"Perhaps I'll be given the use of a rifle."

"A wee girl like you?!" He teased. "You'll blow your eye out."

He was in a playful mood. As ever when he was relieved from his schooling and bible studies. It was hard to feel melancholy when around a spirit such as his. I dearly loved him and feared for the day we would be parted. However, it would come about, I knew now that one day we would be irrevocably parted.

If I had hated Eynhallow, then surely, I was cursed. To hate that which I am now tied to more than ever. I sighed and tried to rid my mind of the thoughts, but they remained. On the edges of my mind. Threatening to spill into my consciousness. Always there. Perhaps I should try to love this place?

"Don't be so quick to judge." I retorted. "I'll be sixteen tomorrow and I'll brandish a rifle if I choose to. Wee one..."

And he smiled ruefully, his eyes rolling.

"I think I prefer you like this. When you're not being miserable or drowning."

I knew he was jesting, but I knew he meant it. "Aye, I dare say you do."

"You miss Mr. Munro? I heard Mammy talking. I hear them talk all the time when they think I can't hear. You say his name when you're asleep."

There was no explanation worthy of him. Despite his broadening shoulders and burgeoning manhood, he was still my little brother. I would always protect him.

"He was a good man. I pray they find him soon." I simply said, turning away.

Rohan shrugged and return to his line which had caught a bite. He reeled it in quickly and inspected his catch.

"Ah, I've got to set it back there. Here look." He caught my hand up and ran it across the fish's underside. "See here, she's ready for spawning."

I wondered why it meant so much to him that he returns the spawning fish. But I did not trouble myself to ask. He was a kind soul, or perhaps it was simply because we could not eat them when they were that way.

I was happy to sit and listen to him. There was no other way to forget. But I was being haunted, I knew I was as I watched the birds begin to circle above us. Their laboured cries reaching out to me from up above. I watched them for a moment as they gathered in numbers. Then as if lured by something down below they swooped, something caught my eye.

"Rohan, you see those birds?" I asked, pointing to the shoreline where they had gathered.

He looked away from his fishing line for a moment and shrugged. "Of course, I do. There's nothing unholy about them."

I might not have known much about the fish, but I knew the birds. They were not squawking for their own merriment. I could almost hear them call my name.

"No, there's something..." My voice trailed off as I stood to get a closer look.

I fought against the wind. The coolness of it making my eyes water. Underneath the swooping and scurrying around I could make out the dark form beneath. The birds flew into disarray, their wings flapping urgently. As they flew off, screaming like little children I wiped the dew from my eyes and blinked.

"Stay here if you wish." I said absently as I made my way down to the water.

Slowly at first, moving across the rocks with my skirt hitched up. Then, as I reached the sand, I allowed my skirt to fall and my pace quickened. I will never know what drove me to run. But I did, I ran towards the heap which lie covered in the sea foam.

The waves still lapping, I disregarded my broken shoes so that I could run faster. The water in my eyes grew salty. I was crying before I reached him.

The helpless form which haunted me. That face I had seen in both life and death. Why had he come to me like this? Lips which once spoke to me of both love and hate were now the deep colour of blue.

They would not move to speak again. His eyes looked beyond, glazed and terrified. Time had not changed him. He wore the same clothes, the same enigmatic stare. As the water pooled around him only then could I truly see his stillness. I could not move, could not scream that painful cry I felt surging through my veins.

Somehow his eyes seemed to look at something I could not see. I wondered how he had managed to find himself on this shore.

"I remember you..." I sobbed quietly, leaning over his body. "I know you..."

I recalled his face in a mirror, or was it a window? *He knows me as I know him.*

"You should have stayed where you were..." I whispered. "I would have come for you..."

I heard Rohan shift behind me. "Jesus, Mary!"

"Go and fetch Daddy. He will know what to do."

The body of Nathan Munro washed up onto the shores of Eynhallow and I could not run anymore.

Yes, I had loved him. For only a moment. It was that which had driven him insane. I wondered if I could ever reconcile that within myself. I felt a twinge of guilt and desolation, and somehow, I knew it was that part of me which I shared with those people under the sea.

I could never love a human man without binding him to me against his own will. It was that magic which haunted me. But how could I have known before? I was just a child. Love and desire were not toying or games. They held no interest for me. Not until Nathan Munro had brought the sunshine after that longest of winters.

To see him now, my heart broke. He was meant to be married and having children on his land in Evie. Not lying here like this, with no life within his bones. I felt the salt of tears on my lips and realised I had begun to cry harder.

"I'll never let this happen again, I swear..." I sobbed into his wet chest, which was still and quiet.

I stayed there until I felt the pull of hands take me away.

Daddy shrouded his body and placed him in the boat ready to return to his family at the break of dawn. I did not speak, nor eat that night. I went to bed knowing his body was waiting for absolution.

It seemed that he was calling my name, but I was too afraid to respond. When I finally slipped into a fitful sleep I could not rest for dreams. It seemed that I closed my eyes for just a moment and when I opened them again the sun was creeping over the horizon. It was time.

I had not been back to the mainland since that fateful day I fell from the boat. I was afraid to make that journey again, but I could not protest. I sat in the back, as far from Nathan as I could.

Somehow it felt like if I touched him one more time I would die too.

Rohan would not look at him. But it was nothing more than innocent revulsion. He came and sat beside me, facing away from Nathan's shrouded form.

"He looks strange." Rohan sighed, recalling the sight of him over and over again. As I had. "Like he'd been in the water only for a moment. But he's been gone for such a long time..."

I flinched at the thought. Wherever he had been, he had not been dead for long. Horror rushed through me as I began to imagine him trying to escape that beautiful place. He must have tried to reach the surface, and not made it.

"I do not know. Whatever his fate, his family can rest now." I said quietly as Mammy handed me the food basket and we prepared to set sail.

My heart began to beat so fast I could feel myself become faint. I rested my head against Rohan's shoulder and fought against the onslaught of more tears.

All was silent save for the sound of the waves. The motion turned my stomach, or was it the fear? There was a sense of sadness hanging above us that none of us could speak of. Daddy had not come to me, to speak of what had befallen him. Perhaps he would in time, as everything did with Daddy.

"I'll go to see Hamish, get you to Hannah's house and wait for me there." Daddy said, breaking the silence as we approached that other shoreline.

"No William, you can't bring that burden alone. I'll come with you." Mammy protested.

He looked at her with grave concern but did not give his final word on it. He did not want to bring the news alone, but he would have to spare us the grief in doing so.

Despite his failings, he had only ever wished to shelter us. I could never hate him again.

"Finola?" He said, and I moved my head from Rohan's shoulder. "Can you take yourself and Rohan to your Aunt Hannah's house?"

I nodded obediently. Forcing a smile upon his lips, he nodded in thanks. "Then we shall try to celebrate. You shall only be sixteen once."

I had forgotten. Today I was sixteen years old. I checked myself, my body and my face. Neither felt any different. There was nothing fundamental about it.

"Of course." I mumbled softly.

I wondered what they would say to Hamish and Mabel Munro. They decided to leave Nathan's body in the boat and bring them to him rather than parade him through the village. I ambled slowly towards Aunt Hannah's house and could not deny there was a part of me that wished to go in that other direction.

Rohan was quiet and subdued, for once refraining from asking questions. The dawn was breaking way to the morning and as we made our way up Aunt Hannah's garden path, I thought I heard a scream in the distance. I closed my eyes and knocked on the door.

Bethan answered with her hair still looped in the rags which would secure her curls. She squinted into the early morning light and her tired face broke into a smile.

"Oh, I am so glad to see you!" She beamed, wrapping her arms around my waist.

She ushered us inside. The smell of freshly baked bread filled the air, but I was too preoccupied to be hungry. Aunt Hannah was pleased to see us and remembered that it was my birthday.

"I was going to save this, for the first Sunday of the month. But being as you are here today..." She passed me a parcel wrapped in brown paper.

I opened it gingerly as I felt the round hardness of a shoe within the folds of the paper. I was elated and felt guilty for managing to raise a smile.

"Thank you, Aunt Hannah." I said, rising to place a kiss on her cheek.

She offered me a kiss in return, and I stared at the black shoes, feeling the cold buckle between my fingers. I had never had shoes with a buckle before.

"Ah, I'm sorry I couldn't buy you a new pair. These came from Jenny Kennedy; she lives in the house by the Church. She had them for her daughter but no sooner had she worn them a day and she had grown too wide for them. But they'll do you better than those broken things."

I stared out of the window where the curtains weren't drawn, waiting for Mammy and Daddy to appear. Time had begun to shift slowly. Perhaps time had stopped entirely.

"I don't know why your Mammy kept you in them so long. Will you try them on?"

I wanted to run outside. To run all the way to Hamish Munro's farm on the outskirts of the village. I wanted to tell them everything and throw myself at their mercy. I wanted to be anywhere but here, in this dark room with the curtains still drawn halfway.

I heard them talking about shoes, but their voices were muffled below the inner sounds of my own silent screams. I ached to run. I could no longer sit there and speak of such trivial things. I went to the window and opened the curtains so that I might see down the garden path.

"Something distracts you, Finola." Aunt Hannah finally said, coming to me by the window. "What could distract you so on your birthday?"

I sighed gravely. "They will be here in a moment."

I felt Aunt Hannah's hand stroke my back comfortingly, but the touch burned me. I did not deserve it. I had brought this fate; I had cursed him. I looked down towards the water where I knew the boat was waiting. I began to wonder if she knew. Did she know there was no blood between us? Or was she outside the secret circle?

"Where did they go?" She asked, her voice low and soft as if she sensed my unease.

"To Hamish and Mabel Munro's place. To tell them their son is dead."

I could have folded myself in the silence. Aunt Hannah stared at me, her face a mixture of horror and disbelief.

"Say it is not so." She whispered. "No… There's not more heartache!"

I edged towards the door, laying waste to any sense of politeness.

"I must go to him!" I cried, before heading down the garden path and back towards the boat.

There, in the prow of the boat lay the shrouded form of Nathan Munro. I could no longer distract myself. There was no help for one as cursed as I. I stepped into the boat and held my breath. The salt of tears pooled in my eyes and dropped onto my lips.

With shaking hands, I pulled back the white sheet and gasped at the sight of him. Not one part of him had altered. Yes, he truly was dead. They would find me here with him, crying over his body as if we had been lovers. They would see the blood on my hands. But not so much as a kiss had passed between us. Never would there be.

"Nathan..." I whispered through anguished sobs. "If you shall wake now, I shall return to Finfolkaheem and never bewitch another man as long as I live. I swear it, open your eyes and I shall go into the water this very moment..."

I knew it was the ramblings of despair. But still I waited for a sign of life. His eyes remained still. His chest did not move to breathe. I was consumed by guilt I did not fully understand. I could have done something. But when enchantments behold you, what help is there for those who are enchanted? It was too late. There was no magic here.

"Finola, what do you do here?" Said a voice that sounded over the wind.

I turned and saw Aunt Hannah move towards the boat; her face lined with concern.

"I know not." I replied, returning the shroud to Nathan's lifeless face.

"Come back to the house and there we will wait for your Mammy and Daddy. Will you come with me?" And she extended her hand to me.

I looked my last and closed my eyes. Silently I took Aunt Hannah's hand and found myself lost in thought which could not be penetrated.

I heard the clatter of teacups and the sound of tea being poured. The quiet conversation between my cousins and my brother. It seemed to rattle on forever until the sound of footsteps broke the monotony.

Looking up towards the door before they opened it, I felt my heart choke me within my throat. Mammy's eyes mirrored my own. Raw from tears that would not cease and an age of sadness within them.

She looked at me once before greeting Aunt Hannah and my cousins. Daddy seemed untouched, as ever. A little tired perhaps, but relieved to have delivered his terrible news. Always I would remember his indifference towards Nathan Munro's death, and with great sadness I wondered if he did not feel a little pleased that his secret would go to Nathan's grave.

"They have taken his body and shall bury him on the morrow. There'll be no speak of their loss now. It is done. Today is a day of celebration!"

Daddy said, his voice low and authoritative. "Tomorrow we shall join the Munro's in their sorrow."

But there was a shadow hanging above us. We drank tea and ate cake. I wore my new shoes and Bethan sang for us. Still I could not shake the dread of watching them bury him in the ground. If it were not for me, he would still be alive. I could not celebrate as long as that haunted me.

"Finola, will you not smile for your old Daddy?" He asked me, as I stood in the garden watching Ewan and Rohan play with an old leather ball.

"I don't feel much like smiling today."

His strong hands circled my shoulders as if to protect me.

"Ah, you'll someday know what it is to love, and it will be more real than any of this."

His words drove a knife through me and left the bitterest taste in my mouth.

"I do not mourn him in that way. He was nothing to me in that way you speak of. But..." And the words caught in my mouth. "I could have saved him. I did not. I sent him to his death twice."

Daddy shook his head and closed his eyes. "Do not blame yourself. He did not have to go out onto the waters, he chose to go of his own free will."

"I'm not entirely certain that he did go of his own free will." And I closed my eyes against the memory of the blood on the doorstep.

But Daddy was unrepentant. "I throw a man out of my house. It does not make me responsible for his fate. I'll not have you blame yourself Finola. It was not your desire that sent him to his madness, or his death. If that were so then I would not be standing here now almost an old man."

And there it was again. That vision of that woman I had never seen.

"I'll not know myself anymore." I sighed, pushing his hand away from me. "You think you have ended the torture of your secret but for me, it has only begun. I am bound to a place I loathe and despise. Abandoned by the Finfolk. Segregated from mankind. Shall I ever know what is real?"

Daddy looked at me as if I had ripped his heart from within his body. Crestfallen, he stepped away from me. For a moment, I thought he would cry.

"Abandoned?!" He gasped. "No, never that. I see I have done you a great injustice. My only daughter. Will you hate me now?"

"No." I replied, turning my gaze towards the brother I loved dearly. "No, not hate. Never hate."

But it was more than I could hope for that I would not resent him. I think he knew it. He walked solemnly away from me and allowed me to be a child for one more day.

I chalked a hopscotch on the garden path and there I played with Bethan while the boys watched. But my heart could not rest. It was false joy. But it was better than complete oblivion.

Chapter Five

THE FINHAG

amish Munro stood by his youngest son's grave and wept. The mourners began to dissipate, standing close by as they exchanged their condolences. I could feel their eyes on me. *She found him, that strange Finola Gray...* Their whispers were curious and accusatory.

I looked down at the new shoes underneath my black dress. I did not look up until the funeral service was over. Mabel Munro was notably absent. So, their whispers soon turned from me to her. I was grateful I could not cry.

Why would Finola Gray weep for Nathan Munro? They would ask me, and I would not say.

A few of them asked how I was feeling since our absence from church had been noticed. Aunt Hannah had put it about that I had been ill. For once I was grateful for her desire to gossip. A few of them approached Hamish, but he did not speak. His shoulders carried the burden of grief and none could take it from him. Perhaps Mabel could not bring herself to see Nathan buried. No mother should bury any child. I could only begin to imagine the pain of burying two. I decided to wait by the churchyard gate, as I always did, whilst Mammy and Daddy spoke to the other parishioners.

"Nobody will go to Hamish." Rohan said, staring towards the lonely man.

I could only shrug. "Perhaps he does not want them to."

"Where is Mabel and the other Munro's?" He inquired, scanning the small groups of people who had stayed behind.

"Perhaps they are too grieved to come." I surmised.

I peeked from underneath by bonnet and watched as Hamish dropped to his knees. But still none went to him. He had rebuffed their comfort. I could not watch and turned away, grasping the hard wood of the churchyard gate in fear of sobbing.

"Finola..." Rohan said quietly, pulling me back. "He's looking at you."

His body was on the ground, knees in the mud. But his eyes had moved from the mound towards where I stood. Slowly raising his hand, Hamish beckoned me to him.

"What is he doing that for?" Rohan asked, an edge of worry in his voice.

But I could not reply.

He rose from his knees as I approached him. His face was racked with tears and desolation. A man pushed too far. He had aged ten years in one night. He extended his hands to me and I was compelled to take them in my own. Those who had offered their comfort only to be turned away looked on in distaste. I shared their sentiment. I had done nothing to deserve this man's attention, nor had I wanted it.

"Finola." He whispered through gritted teeth. "I shall thank you for finding my boy."

Do not thank me. Anything but that.

"I am sorry." Was all I could manage to say as the edge of hysteria threatened to break over the barriers.

"There's no need for that. The boy knew those waters like the back of his hand. Even in darkness. Whatever befell him, there's none here need be sorry for it."

He seemed to sober a little and draw himself out of the melancholy. He recognised the churchyard and the people around him as if for the first time.

"I was hoping to come back to Eynhallow and sell my land to your father myself. I shall always regret that I sent Nathan. I was to give him the money from the sale for his wedding and to start his life with his new wife. Will he not reconsider our offer?"

He knew that I could not give him an answer. His eyes lingered on mine for a moment before shaking his head wildly.

"Of course not. My apologies Finola. A wee girl like you knows nothing about the affairs of their fathers."

I almost allowed laughter to escape my lips. I would repent of my father's affairs until my dying breath.

"I remember the fishing boats off Rousay. I had an Uncle who worked on them. There was an accident and he was found in the water weeks after he went under. They said his body was bloated and tarnished by the creatures that had tried to devour him. Weeks he'd been floating on the waves. I do wonder why Nathan..." His voice broke at the sound of his son's name. "Why he seemed so untouched. If he had been in the water all this time..."

He closed his eyes tight and dropped my hands. There was no comfort, no solace. None that I could give. I should have run from him in floods of shame. But I could not make my feet move. I was beholden to him.

"I wish I could tell you." Was all I could mutter. It was not a lie, but a simple fact.

Hamish nodded in agreement. His shoulders slumping under the strain.

"He was a good boy. A good son and a good brother. Aaron will have kept him a good place. I will try to remember them as boys. By the hearth fire at the house on Eynhallow, listening to stories and eating their supper like starved pups!"

"He told me those stories." I said, hoping this at least would be something of value to him. "Of the Finfolk."

And the word stuck in my throat like hard bread that could not be swallowed.

Hamish smiled fondly as if I had struck a chord with him. *Do not smile, or if you do then do not smile because of me.*

"Did your father not tell them to you? I had thought all the children of Eynhallow were told."

"No, my mammy liked us to read the bible."

Hamish sniffed. Perhaps we shared a distaste for religion.

"Well, you had you a good storyteller. Nathan..." He hesitated again. "He was always good at telling it in a way I never could. I dare say he believed they could have been real."

"Would that I could hear them again." I lamented.

But I had lost Hamish. His eyes had grown vacant again. The light in them had gone out. He whispered something to himself, something I could not hear.

"Do you think..." He said quietly, leaning closer towards me so that I visibly stepped back. "He believed in them. He may have said they were only stories, but I saw him looking for them. Do you think they had him? In their land under the sea?"

There was a maddening edge to his voice. In that moment it was a bitter reminder of his son's face as he stared at me expectantly.

"The stories tell of the Finwife. She will remain beautiful only if she takes a human husband. Or if she does not, she will become the Finhag. Have you heard of that, Finola?"

His mouth curled around my name and he seemed to taste treachery. "Hmmm..." He said thoughtfully. "I had never thought of your name. *Finola...*"

"No." I said calmly. "I have not heard that one."

He nodded ruefully and turned away as if invisible pain. "Forgive me, I am not myself."

"Do not ask for my forgiveness!" I said, my voice breaking into sobs.

Perhaps it was the sight of this sorry man. Or his assumptions that were sliding on a double-edged sword. But I could no longer contain the tears which had been threatening to spill for days.

"Ah, wee lassie. I didn't mean to upset you. I'm just an old man who has lost too much. I have always valued your father as a friend, and you as his daughter. Aye, I'll go now. I'll go..."

I was just a girl. That I knew, as I stood there watching the old man go. For truly he was old now, with too many scars to bear. I felt pain in my heart for him, or was it for Nathan?

I turned his words over and over in my mind. As we ate our supper in Aunt Hannah's parlour, I could not taste the fish and bread. I listened to them talk of the old days and of people I had never met. Ewan and Rohan sat with a game of dominoes on the floor while Bethan watched, waiting for her turn to play.

But inside my mind I began to imagine a beautiful woman emerging from the water only to turn into an ugly old hag as she reached the shore. That mother I had no face for, had she grown ugly and old? Had she turned into the Finhag of legend? The blood in me ran cold. Was that my fate? Did I have enough Finfolk blood in me to share that terrible end?

Daddy had not been taken for a human husband. I could have cried for joy at that sacrifice. For if it were true, then truly it was a sacrifice. But he would have willingly followed her. That much I knew.

"Finola, what distracts you?" Mammy asked, her voice breaking my reverie.

"It has been a long day." I sighed.

Her face was sympathetic. I felt the pulse of her love for me in her hand as she brushed it against my cheek in that way only a mother can. I closed my eyes and felt it bite within. *But you are not my mother.*

"Aye, that it has. Get you to bed, if you like." She said, gesturing towards the door.

I would not sleep regardless. Bethan would keep me awake with her childish chatter, and Aunt Hannah would never allow me to share the bed with Rohan. For that matter, even Ewan would be a more appealing bed partner for a night such as this. His reluctance to speak at any time of the day would be a welcome relief when nightmares waited on the periphery of my mind.

"I am not weary for sleep." I explained, pushing my plate to one side and finishing my meal.

Mammy took my plate, her smile fading into something a little more concerned.

"I saw you speaking with Hamish today. I certainly hope he hasn't put on you too much. A wee girl like you."

A wee girl like me? I looked down at my body. Certainly, I no longer looked like a wee girl. I fought against the resentment of being called one.

"He only spoke of his memories." And I shuddered, picturing Hamish as a young man, telling his children the stories of the Finhag.

Mammy nodded. "Did he not say why Mabel could not attend?"

"No." I whispered, acutely aware that she was no longer concerned but simply fishing for gossip.

My Mammy, for such a God-fearing creature, she often committed the smallest of sins. I raised a smile for her, and she ran a loving hand through my hair.

"Ah Finola..." She crooned. "What sweet sadness haunts you?"

I caught my Daddy's eyes resting on me from the corner of the room. His stare was authoritative and apologetic, and it broke my heart. Smouldering from the darkness he sat in an old wooden chair smoking from his pipe. His left arm was draped over the back of the chair, the smoke from his pipe filling the air.

"Leave her be, Mammy." He grumbled.

Her eyes shot up to meet his. Without question she nodded and stalked away. It was a moment that no other bore witness to, and if they had they would not have heard the unspoken words between them. He was warning her, and she was afraid to anger him.

He put the pipe aside and leaned forward. "Finola, come sit by me."

I heard Bethan's cries of joy as she took her turn to play dominoes. The sloshing of water as Mammy filled the sink to clean the supper plates. The distinct sound of Aunt Hannah's knitting needles clashing together. Each of us were lost in our individual pursuits. Confidently, Daddy put a hand upon my shoulder and whispered to me.

"She does not know what you have discovered. I would like it to remain that way. I dare say there'll come a day when all will come to light. But until then, I'll not have her heart broken. She'll be praying to her God ever more. I've had my fill of Him today."

I shuddered at the thought. "Shall I never know, then? Shall I take this knowledge to my grave and never speak of it?"

His face was filled with reproach in the firelight. "You may speak of it with me, if you wish."

"And what shall you tell me? All that I have already heard. Know you anything more of value to me?"

He raised an eyebrow and resumed his smoking, filling his pipe with more tobacco.

"This is not the time or the place. We shall speak more when we are back on Eynhallow."

I felt bile rise in my stomach. How would I endure that journey now that Nathan's body had been buried? I had been consumed with the news of our bearings but now there was nothing to prevent me from being afraid. If I ever went back into those waters, I would surely never return. The biggest fear of all, it would be my own choice. I glanced at Rohan and banished the thought.

"When do we return?" I asked, swallowing hard.

Daddy took a long hard drag on his pipe. "At first light."

There was a sense of relief as Bethan blew out her candle and climbed into the bed beside me. I turned away from her and tried to steady my breathing to sound as if I were asleep.

She felt warm and solid behind me, her little body wriggling around to find comfort. When finally, she stilled I waited for her to speak. But she never did. For whatever reason she let me lie at her side in silence until the moon dipped below the horizon and that murderous red of morning light began to blaze.

I had not slept one wink. Thoughts of the day were ripe and invasive. I could not shake the vision of that beautiful woman standing on the rocks.

When she turned, her face was ravaged with age and ugliness. Her hands reached out to me in rotten claws, her eyes sunken and screaming that once she had been beautiful and never would she be again.

Was it my mother I envisioned, or was it myself?

My heart raced in panic, but I could not move. Who would be there to comfort me in the dark? Nobody here knew what my fate held. There it was the root of my fear. *They won't be there when the time comes. When I am turned into one of those hags of the sea.*

As the world slept and I remained awake, there was a lonely void that could not be filled. I envied their sleep and longed for some of my own, but it would not come.

I remembered that I had turned sixteen, and for the first time I had a moment to piece together what that might mean.

I was no longer a girl. But now I was afraid to be a woman. I had to know, or I would linger in this purgatory. I had to know how much of me was a part of *her*. But it would be a futile search. I did not know where to start.

Bethan stirred beside me, her tightly bound hair beginning to uncurl from the rags. Turning to face me, suddenly I felt an overwhelming need to sleep.

"Good morning." She said, yawning.

I could not deny she had given me respite, if only I could have found some peace. So, I could not be irritated now that she wished to speak with me.

"Morning." I replied softly.

"Are you worried about going home today?" She asked innocently, as if she were asking if I'd like some butter with my bread.

"Why should I be worried?" I inquired.

She shrugged in that way only a child can. "You fell into the sea last time."

"I managed to remain in the boat on our outward journey, I am sure I can manage it on our way back."

What a wretched girl I was. I wanted to scream at her to be quiet and still her foolish tongue.

"I still wish you would take me with you." She sighed, pulling at the rags and revealing a head full of envious curls. "It's still not as it was."

"Believe me, you do not want to come to Eynhallow. I have told you before, there's nothing for you there. There is only me and Rohan. Aunt Mary and Uncle William. The rest is just nothing."

An ancient waste land that was taken from my true mother's people by a man who sought too much of a revenge. A place where nothing will flourish. We only remain there through folly and foolishness.

"But the stories you told me. I have watched for them, the Finfolk. I would so love to see them."

Her eyes were wide with wonder, framed by those magnificent curls. Once again, I envied her. The possibilities of her life, how beautiful it would be. I knew this was the real reason I disliked her. I wanted her life. This feckless child. I wanted to have the certainty she had. She knew she would grow old as nature decreed.

"Be careful what you wish for." I whispered, pulling a hand through my own hair that was matted and flat.

She looked at me speculatively. "I don't believe they are bad. How could anything so magical be bad? Perhaps the Goodman's wife fell in love with the Finman? No one has ever thought of that. But I have. I think she fell in love with him and that's why he took her to that place under the sea."

Her thoughts touched me. "You think that the Finfolk took their human husbands and wives willingly?"

She nodded, becoming excitable that I was entertaining her conversation.

"Oh yes. I believe it would be quite easy to fall in love with a Finman. I think they have enchanting qualities that I would certainly love. When I fall in love." And her words were full of possibility.

"Such a romantic thing, aren't you?" And I patted her curls, traces of my envy dissipating once again into genuine care. "In such a rush to love and be loved."

"I can't wait." She sighed, as if the years were against her. "To be married and have children."

But you are a child yourself. You do not know what you will want when the time comes... And I wasn't sure if I was thinking of Bethan, or myself.

"All in good time." I said, rising from the bed that I wished I could remain in. I was tired.

"When you fall in love, you must have me as bridesmaid at your wedding Finola... I would be such a good bridesmaid!" She suddenly said, her eyes widening in excitement.

"I have no plans to marry." I replied, "There is little opportunity on Eynhallow. One of the many reasons why you would not find happiness there."

But her childlike eyes burned, and something in her face changed. As if all the excitement was gone and in its place was a real sadness she could not shake.

"I think you shall find love before I do. Despite Eynhallow."

And it sent a coldness up my bones, and I shuddered. "Come. Less talk of foolish things. Get you to breakfast."

It was a calm morning. The water swelled and receded as if it was caressing the shore. Blue sky panned above us but exhaustion consumed me. My eyes threatened to close and as I sat in the prow of the boat the slow lull of the waves beneath tried to force me into dreams.

I heard my aunt and cousins cry their goodbyes as we made our way out onto the sound, but I could not turn to respond. Daddy raised the sail but there was little wind.

"Rohan, we'll have to row. Grab an oar." Daddy instructed.

I heard them move the oars into the water and pull. But I could feel myself falling into sleep. *Strange that I can sleep here, but when I am wrapped within blankets on a comfortable bed I cannot...*

"Where is the wind? There's something unholy about it..." Mammy said, her voice drifting into my half-awake consciousness.

"Tis just a clear day." Daddy said, his voice betraying him. He did not believe that.

No, they are calling to me. They want me to sleep, so that I might slip once again underneath that surface....

"How strange..." I heard Mammy remark. "The waves... they break on something."

I opened my eyes slowly and stared into the distance. At first, I could not see it. But then it moved, and I saw the dark form move underneath to where we could not see.

"It's a whale." Daddy snorted, keeping his eyes firmly on Eynhallow.

It seemed to satisfy Mammy, but still she craned to see the gigantic creature as it peaked once again and blew water vapour into the air.

"Rohan, will you concentrate boy!" Daddy roared and fixed a sharp gaze at my brother.

Gracefully, it submerged once again and did not return for air. It moved underneath us like a great black shadow, and it was the first time I ever felt as if they pursued me. Perhaps it was just a lonely whale, lost or searching for something. But this creature did not speak to me as the others had. No, this was not a creature with a soul of this world. I found myself sobbing quietly underneath my shawl, perhaps through tiredness and all that had befallen me. Or perhaps it was that I knew my fate was tied to Eynhallow now. That I should despise this place truly was irrelevant. It had made me despise it. The land had tried to reject me once it knew what I truly was. It spat me into the sea and told me to remain there.

Only in the dead of night did my demons smile. When darkness enveloped the sky and the low wind howled over the land, only then did I allow myself to drift into that dark place where an old woman laughed at me mockingly.

Where Nathan Munro called to me, and those whales tried to capture me for their own. The days were long and barren. When spring gave way to summer and the bleak flowers bloomed still, I could not see their savage beauty.

Often, I would dare myself to go into the water, but I could not leave the shoreline. The Hylands stood lonely behind me, and those who I loved within it. It was as if nothing had changed. The melancholy lingered. Knowing why had not eased it. But something else lingered too. It wasn't entirely unwelcome.

Whether it had been dormant within me or was something I had acquired since coming of age, I was never sure which. But it was there, nonetheless.

That magical element within that now flourished. From bird to beast and fish to flame, there was a deeper understanding of each. My nightmarish nights were only made bearable by the curious days.

It was a revelation to me that I should hear their beating hearts, their anguished cries. A bird can only think in pictures of blinding colour, and I heard them. The Seals that dared to breach their watery home and come onto the shore called my name in their pitched tongue. I heard them. Their hunger, their love. Their every memory was offered to me and I heard them.

Like opening a third eye, I knew the hellish nights were the price I had to pay for the moments of awe in discovering this new magic. So, I tolerated the sadness. Always I knew they were waiting, those creatures which spoke to me. To take my true form, to bend this magic within my own means. *But I am human...* I was conscious not to forget it.

It was a night like any other when I awoke to the sound of the crackling fire calling me.

Coiled within my blankets I heard myself gasp at the sound of the red-hot wood snapping and burning. I had not been asleep long. The arduous task of repeating painful memories had been long and exhausting. The red hue sent shadows into my open door and I held my breath.

Almost silently came the voices above the snapping and crackling. But they were there, hushed and frantic.

From the kitchen, I could smell the scent of broth being boiled. It was not yet sunrise, and my head was heavy from unwanted dreams. My hair fell about my shoulders as I rose from bed. I was dishevelled and did not want to be seen like this. But still I could not ignore my peaked curiosity.

Pulling my blanket about me, I silently went out of my room on the tips of my toes. The cold floor sent chills up my spine, and I shuddered. Without a candle to guide me I lingered in the darkness, the firelight that resonated from behind the kitchen door catching my eye as it flickered.

The kitchen door was old. Older than Daddy, who had witnessed his father fashioning it from a piece of driftwood many years ago. Within its smooth finish were small holes that had been created by the rocks which it had fought against before coming to rest on the shore.

It was an ugly door but held much sentiment. It belonged here so much more than I did. Pressing my face against the cool wood, I could not refrain from watching with eyes that had no right to see. Listen with ears that had no right to hear.

Daddy stood over the fire; his arm placed above him over the hearth. Mammy sat at the table; her hands wrung with worry. She seemed to be praying, but she did not say it out loud. Both of them were as dishevelled as I. Tired and weary I saw Daddy's face in the pale light of the fire. It seemed he had been crying, but there were no tears.

"I tell you William, I have seen it. There'll be no help for her. As God as my witness, the time is upon us."

He raised a hand in disagreement, shaking his head against her words.

"Say it not. I will not hear it." He said vehemently. "She is aware of her birth. I did as you wished. Let this be an end to it."

Mammy almost laughed as she clasped her hands together as if in prayer.

"Do not be a fool William Gray! You know as well as I... Sixteen years have passed. There was never much hope that we could have more than that."

He shook his head, pulling a thoughtful hand through his beard. "There is always hope."

"And would you have it so? Would you have her remain here when her fate lies elsewhere? I tell you I have seen it, as did Nathan Munro. Soon others will see it. There will be no help for it."

For a moment it seemed as if time crept very slowly. The wind ceased. I was forced to hold my breath against the silence.

"Have you not loved her? Have you not any wish for her to remain as she has always been?" Daddy asked, his voice shaken with desperation and vulnerability.

I looked at Mammy. She sighed heavily, her whole-body stiffening at his words. I found myself aching to make my presence known. But my cold feet were locked to the ground. This was not my place, to be here listening. But still I could not make myself move.

Mammy's tears were falling unashamedly. That was the privilege a woman owned. The right to cry without fear of reproach.

"I have loved her. As I love her even now. Perhaps more dearly than if I had carried her myself. These ungodly things do not sit well with me. Still I love her. But I do not deny them. Soon even the blind will see what she is. I knew it on that day I found the slaughtered chickens. She speaks to those beasts, and I dare say they speak back. What other powers does she possess? They will come to her unbidden and she'll not thank you for it!"

"Aye, but I was given the task of raising her. Have I not been a good father? A good husband? Have I not given everything to you all?"

There was a short pause. He hesitated, knowing he spoke out of turn.

"I asked you once, when the other families went to the mainland, should we leave this place and make our lives elsewhere? You said to me that we could not. That we must remain here. You did not tell me why. I did not dare to ask. Have I not been a good mother? A good wife? Even when I knew in my heart, it was for *her* that you would stay?"

His face was drawn. Like a sickness took hold, and he could not hold his anger more. His curled fist came crashing down against the fireplace. It rattled the pan below, and for a moment I thought they might come to see if they had woken us and discover me.

But neither of them moved. Mammy sat motionless and staring into space. She would not look at him. Daddy stood in defiance, breathing heavily against the desire to do more damage.

"I'll not have you speak so, Mary." He said breathlessly. "It is too late for any of that. You gave me a son, and I have loved you long."

"Evil Witchcraft…" She whispered, crossing herself. "Why pretend that you would not have her, if she returned once again to you?"

Daddy shook his head, wearied of opening old wounds. "Mary, my love. I'll repent of that sin until my dying day. For what I've bestowed upon Finola, for what I have bestowed upon you. She cannot come back to me."

Mammy frowned in distaste. "So, she has become Finhag?"

"I know not. If she took another human lover, then there is every hope she did not become Finhag. Or if she did not, then Finhag she will be."

Mammy cocked her head to one side, regarding Daddy as he stared into the dwindling fire. "I wonder why she did not take you."

He seemed to wonder the same thing. "She never told me. But I dare say it was so that I may raise Finola on the land."

Mammy took a handkerchief from her pocket and dabbed at the corners of her eyes. I had barely noticed her tears as the room grew darker.

"And so, you have. Soon it will be time for her to return…" She sobbed quietly.

But Daddy was resolute. "Nay, she has seen that place I am sure of it. Yet she returned."

"She has a hatred for this place that troubles me so." Mammy replied, composing herself. "We cannot hide here forever more. Eynhallow's days are gone. I will not damn Rohan's fate to this forsaken island."

I must not stay here. My love for them will bind them here, and here they will die. If I love them, I must leave them…

"None of us know what fate one man has to another!" Daddy snapped, slaking the fire with an iron poker. He thrust it into the ashes with a hard stab and watched the embers return to life. "I'll no more damn my son than I'll watch my daughter leave! We will await the future and say no more."

But Mammy pointed an ominous finger at him. "I tell you William Gray, she is bound for that fate you will not have for her!"

He pushed her hand away slowly, stepping towards her menacingly. "She is human. A creature of your God. She was raised upon the land, as was the wish of her mother. Whatever part of her she may share with those... *Water folk*... she is still of my blood."

"Blood or no, she is who she is. I will wait, if you wish, to see that part of her come to fruition. But I will not make her stay."

Daddy raised his hand, he was shaking. I thought he would strike her, but he only placed a hand against her cheek softly. This was more than I could bear. I had truly no right to witness this. As he took Mammy into his arms, I forced my cold feet to step back.

"Keep your secrets." I heard her whisper. "They will reveal themselves somehow."

Chapter Six

THE WHITE-HAIRED MAN

I no longer dared myself to go into the water. I knew that if I should, then never again would I see sunlight. The birds had told me to wait, their doleful cries were forever constant. I liked to listen to their inner dialogue of all that they had seen. They were thoughtful creatures who remembered every corner of every land they had been to. It struck me, as it often did now, that many creatures were often not as they were perceived.

The cows were not stupid or docile. They were sentient and spent many hours considering their own spirituality while chewing the grass.

The wild foxes were not sly. They had senses which paralleled no other, and they cursed themselves for it.

The seals that lurked beneath the waves had long been a source of curiosity to mankind. But truly they were selfish creatures, in search only of fish and that most comfortable of bays to lie down and rest in the sand.

And then there were the Orca whales. They had come to us in the night, their souls sang to me and I heard them in my dreams. I had thought it a trick. A shadow, of the same form which had pursued me. But they opened their hearts to me, and I believed them. The whales were protective creatures, with a desire to be playful and joyous. They saw the best in the world, and I envied them. They did not speak to me as the others did, in pictures and emotions. But in their own way. From one mind to another in telepathic form. Always, I would later discover, in riddles that sometimes enraged me to despair.

The first time I heard them I could not stop myself from crying. As the red sun hit the water, I went out into the garden to listen to their mournful songs. Their high-pitched wailing began to shift into words I could decipher, and it was then that I knew I had begun to know my true self.

I was not afraid of it. Animals were easier to understand than mankind. With man I could not see their souls, their intentions.

They were as closed as an old book, forgotten on a dark shelf of the darkest corner. I had decided not tell Mammy or Daddy. Nor did I wish them to know. Their fears for me clouded their judgement. So, I was alone, it would seem.

But I was not afraid of that either. I had lived and breathed loneliness. If I were the only one of my kind, if I were doomed to this life forever, I would have to endure it alone. Perhaps this was why I was gifted with the power to converse with the creatures of the land. Perhaps I would not be entirely alone.

My mind would often drift back to that midnight I had stood behind the kitchen door and I wondered if Mammy was right.

Would our secrets reveal themselves? Each of us had our own to bear.

I knew there was much Daddy had not told me and would never tell me. There was an unspoken sadness now between Mammy and I that I knew would never heal. My dearest Rohan. Whatever secrets there were for him, they were the ones which are kept from the person they would hurt the most.

As spring gave way to summer, I saw him grow from boy to the fringes of manhood. Father allowed him to go hunting alone, as was the privilege of a boy his age. I could not deny the changes in me ran deeper than the eye could see, or the mind could hide.

The raven black hair began to thicken, and I could no longer braid it above my head. I began to let it flow loosely below my shoulders, something which Mammy disapproved of. But as was the new custom between us, she did not protest unless we attended church on the third Sunday.

I grew taller and needed to take down the hems on all my skirts and dresses. The new shoes I had received for my birthday began to pinch.

Even those parts of me that I had taken little notice of before began to bloom. Amidst this barren landscape, I seemed to flourish. But it was an illusion. Everything, as ever, remained uncertain.

From the stable I could hear the sea. It had been many years since this place had seen a horse, instead it had become the place I went to milk the cows.

The beast above me grumbled to herself as I pulled, and the milk spurted forth. Her annoyance resonated with each pull and I was grateful that she did not kick my pail over.

I was distracted, the sound of the waves taking my attention away from the task I had been given to do. I stroked the beast's leg in apology, and she found a little more patience for me. Cows did not like to be milked. It interrupted the flow of their day. But as was their peaceful nature, they would not deny us that which we sought from them and so they stood quietly and did not protest.

"I am sorry." I sighed, more to myself. "I am not in the mood for milking today."

She made a sound of agreement, her hope that I might finish tingling at my fingertips. I regarded the full pail beside me and the half full one beneath me.

"Go…" I said, leading her out of the stables and into the hazy August breeze. "I am done with you. Back to the fields…"

It was a blue and cloudless sky above us. As I untied her and watched her return to graze I wondered if I should return to my chores or allow my distractions to take hold. Of course, I had no choice.

The pod of whales which had come in the night were singing once again and I found myself listening to them from the safety of the shore. The wind was low and cool, brushing the free hair from my face. I was careful not to be seen and hid myself behind the brow of the hill where The Hylands stood.

I had already procrastinated too much. But I could not bring myself to look away. Their shiny black and white heads rose above the water, the spray from their backs sending rainbows into the air. Some of them leapt into the air, their great bodies moving between the waves and crashing back down with such power and grace. There were five of them, the smallest one still a suckling babe. The largest was the one who spoke to me the most. He was a graceful bull, the head of his pod. Always he would call to me.

"What are you doing out here on your own?" Daddy inquired, his gun in one hand and a dead bird in the other.

I winced at the sight of it. "I finished milking, I thought I might sit a while."

He stared at me, floundering in his estimation of me. "You look like you're hiding."

And if I was, then it is no business of yours. "Why would I have need to hide?"

He shrugged. "Get you back to the house, your Mammy will find something for you to better spend your time doing. Come winter these whales will be gone."

It was as if he was trying to diminish my pleasure. He had succeeded.

"I am aware of that." I replied, my tone harsh and clipped.

He did not seem to notice.

"Finola, I'll not have you pondering. The devil makes work for idle hands." He quoted.

"If your disbelief in God is true, then there is little to worry about any truth in the Devil." I replied, using his own words against him.

Once I had troubled myself about lying to my parents. Strange now, it came to me so easy and in such an insolent way. His face was unreadable. He could only stare at me, as I stared back. We had reached an impasse.

"I suppose there is little else to do. The day is waning. Stay here, if you wish. But do not be late for supper." And he walked away, tucking the dead bird underneath his arm.

He said something underneath his breath as he went, but I could not hear him. How could I make him understand that which he did not wish to understand? His reluctance alienated me and so it became between us that we could no longer speak without angering the other.

He would have it that I remain a child. I could not halt my own fate any more than I could halt the rain from falling. He was waiting for something. But for what, he would not say. But it mattered little to me. There was little I could do to placate him. What little I could do, it seemed in vain.

At supper it was the same. We ate the bird he had carried with him earlier, but I could not savour the meat. Eager not to displease him once more I forced it down and felt it stick within my throat.

Rohan was animated, having managed to snare his first kill without any help from Daddy. It was the last of the wild foxes. I could not share his elation. I had come to know these beasts as equals.

"Those damn foxes. I say, I shall not be sad to see them gone." Daddy said, sopping the meat juice with his bannock bread.

Mammy liked it best when he was like this. The head of the household, speaking with pride of his boy.

"It was a fine kill, son. A fine kill." And he placed a firm hand on Rohan's broad shoulders.

His eyes rested upon me for a moment and then shifted away. Could he no longer bear to look at me?

There was a trinity of affection between them that carried no part for me. I sat in silence and drank my water, hoping it would fill me so that I would no longer have to eat that poor bird. As we sat and drank, and chewed until it stuck within our teeth I wondered if it were my own doing or if they were truly excluding me? Had I laid myself victim to paranoia? I had found some joy in this meaningless mire. But I could not share it. That was all.

"We shall take the furs with us to the mainland. Keep something of your first kill, that you might always remember it." He continued, looking up at Mammy expectantly.

"Yes, of course." She said, following his lead. "I shall make something of it for you, Rohan."

So, my brother had become a killer of those creatures I had come to know. It was hard to look at him, and I would not praise him. I had loved him with every fibre of my being. It pained me now to feel such callousness towards him. We must survive, we must eat and harvest and be glad of it. But I could not quieten my soul against the life he had taken.

Chickens were feckless creatures. Their thoughts made little sense and did not extend further than the ends of their beaks. To kill one creature to feed another, I had done it myself and was no better. But not like this. I would not celebrate it.

"I will show Ewan, and may I take my gun to show him too Daddy?" Rohan asked, his excitement unslaked.

Daddy shook his head. "That won't do. On the Lord's day, we will attend Church and have supper with your aunt and cousins. There'll be no guns."

His face fell, as if it had had the shine taken off. He picked at the tiny little bird bones on his plate and I pitied him. For whatever it was he had done, he had only ever wanted to make his father proud. I could not share his need. Pride? What was it to me? Sometimes I wondered if he only loved me because I looked like *her*. So, what would it matter if I made him proud or not? But to Rohan it was all consuming.

"Perhaps one day Ewan will come here, and you can take him hunting with you?" Mammy suggested.

Daddy laughed between clenched teeth, his pipe sitting on his bottom lip as he sucked intermittently.

"Has your sister so much as looked at this Island since the day she left? You'd more likely have Angels fall onto your roof from the heavens than see her step back onto Eynhallow soil."

Mammy had taken offence. She turned away from him and began to stir the pot furiously above the fire. I had no memory of him ever offending her before.

"That does not mean there may not come a day where she might. Now poor Seamus has gone, God rest his soul." She said quietly, eager not to fuel this pompous mood he was in.

"Eynhallow's day is done."

Their eyes moved towards me. I had barely known I had spoken until the words had come out.

"What might you mean by that, Finola?" Daddy asked, removing his pipe so that he might smile sarcastically.

Soon there will be nothing here but the land itself. When they drove the Finfolk back into sea they sealed their own fate.

"Nothing." I lied. "Only that… we are the only ones left. None of us can live forever."

But deep in the back of my mind, a voice spoke to me. It was not the voice of anyone in the room. Certainly not any voice that human ears could hear. That soulful pitch, the faraway sound of it. Yet it was as clear and crisp as if it had been spoken by any sat near to me. I risked a glance towards the window, and I knew it had come from the water.

"How do you know that we will be the last ones? Many may come after our time is done." Rohan said thoughtfully, still burning from his scalding about the gun.

"Perhaps." I replied absently.

I could not stand the way Daddy was looking at me. As if love and hate were battling for supremacy. My face haunted him, now more than ever. Age had made me resemble her more, that much I knew.

He could not bear to see me but could not bear to see me go. It was a double-edged sword. I could not remove his fear entirely.

As silence descended upon us, I could hear the waves more clearly and there was no doubt that I was curious to know what might befall me if I stepped off the shoreline. But the birds had told me to wait.

"You cannot know what will happen when we are gone." Rohan reasoned. "You will be in heaven. It will not matter."

I took another sip of water. "Nor does it matter now."

"I will stay." He said sternly, in an attempt to curry Daddy's favour once more. "Even if you do not. I'll bring a wife here and have our children here."

I did not doubt his sincerity. It would be a suiting fate for him. But I could not imagine why any woman would want to renounce the mainland for *this*. She would have to love him beyond all rational measure.

Daddy clasped him on the shoulder. "Aye lad and let us hope they will be as happy here as we have been."

Rohan's face took on that shine again, and all seemed well. Mammy seemed to forget any insult and returned to the table with a second helping of broth for Daddy. I returned to being insignificant once again. But there was little to dispel that look in Daddy's eyes. He did love me. He could not live with the fear that I might leave. It made him spiteful and belligerent. Perhaps it would be easier this way.

The summer nights gave light enough to illuminate our way until late. After supper it had not begun to grow dark. In summer darkness was never truly found. Only a strange dusk which remained throughout.

The tide had turned and was coming in fast. I slipped away from the house quietly and made my way across the fields towards the ruined kirk, certain that I would not be found there.

Misery craves company. But I only wanted to be alone. I wondered what sort of misery this was, that I could find such joy in the one thing which scared me the most.

And yet what I had always known now seemed so strange. What was happening to me? I pulled out my old copy of The Canterbury Tales and began reading in the fading light.

For a moment I would not think of it and try to dispel the nervous feeling I had whenever I went near the water's edge. Here the water could not touch me, and I could not taunt myself to go near.

I sat until dusk began to darken enough to sweep over the horizon. There was enough light to guide my way home, but I could no longer make out the words upon the pages. My heart sank with the sun as I made my way back towards The Hylands. The familiar glow of the fire burned through the window as I approached the garden path. But inside there were raised voices. I found myself lingering behind another door.

"Certainly, Mr. Gray. As is your prerogative. But I assure you, my plans shall be going ahead." Said a low and stern voice I had never heard before.

It was a dialect I had seldom heard. He was not from Evie, nor was he from anywhere else I recognised.

Slowly I raised my head towards the little parlour window beside the front door. The dying light would hide me.

Through the glass I saw my Mammy standing by the table, her face drawn and unreadable. Daddy was stood beside her, our guest sat with his back to me. He was dressed finely, with a jacket of the finest material and tailored to fit him perfectly. The side of this jacket pocket hung a pocket watch that he played with loosely in his hand. Perhaps most strikingly was his hair, the whitest of white.

He was not a young man. But he had come here alone, at a time where others were retiring for bed. He could not be an old man.

Rohan was nowhere to be found.

"Aye, I don't doubt they will Mr. Bishop. But I can't have it affecting my land. You understand?" Daddy said, quite reasonably.

The man nodded and sipped on a cup of something Mammy had given him to drink.

"Hamish Munro was quite adamant that it should not, when I bought it from him. I hear you did not want the land for yourself?"

Daddy's jaw flexed. "It is no secret that he gave me first refusal. But what need have I for more land? My family here have all we need."

"Indeed, indeed…" Said the white-haired man, nodding. "So, you understand why I might be looking for a similar life for my own?"

He thought about it for a moment, and then sat back down at the table. Mammy followed. She poured more tea for them, her hand visibly shaking.

"You understand there was a great outbreak of the Typhoid here? And that is why the old houses were burned down?" Daddy asked, clearly trying to scare the white-haired man.

"I understand. Hamish Munro made everything clear to me. But it has been more than a year since that time. I am confident that new houses can be built safely."

Mammy dropped the teapot, the sound of it resonating around the room.

"Do you intend to build more than one house, Mr. Bishop?!" She asked incredulously.

The white-haired man turned. But still I could not see his face.

"Two homes. One for myself and my wife and our youngest children. You see, she is the wife of my Autumn years. I have sons from the marriage of my youth. The eldest has just married himself and his wife has expressed a desire to live closely to us. She is with child."

Mammy smiled; her nerves settled. She could not hide her joy that others would return to the Island. But for Daddy it was not so.

"My sons and my boys from the factory will commence work after this winter has passed. But I thought it my duty to come in person and speak with you first. I had hoped to come earlier in the day, but as you can see, I was delayed by the inconceivable difficulty it is to reach this land."

Daddy nodded, taking his pipe out of his pocket. Taking his own, the white-haired man accepted a match from Daddy's pack.

"You will wish you had not come here during your first winter." Daddy said ominously.

But the man did not seem to mind. "In England, we have had winters where the deepest lakes have frozen deep to the core. I have known many a harsh winter and I consider myself hardened to them. Perhaps my youngest children will then become hardened too."

The white-haired man was from England. The flow of his voice made sense. I had heard it once before at church, an English priest had come to do a service at Christmas time. It was a most beautiful way to speak and made our Orcadian way of speaking sound harsh.

"And what of your eldest boys?" Mammy asked, basking in the civilised conversation.

"I have two sons of my first marriage. My eldest, Victor, is recently married as I said before. His wife Jennifer is due at Christmas. My other son, Caleb, has been living with my brother in Lancashire, helping him to build a watermill there. But he will have finished by September."

This seemed to amuse Daddy. He sneered sarcastically and took a long drag on his pipe.

"I wonder, Mr. Bishop, why a man such as yourself would want to waste his time on a near abandoned Island on the edge of nowhere. You said you owned a factory? Is business not going well?"

"On the contrary, Mr. Gray. But I am not getting any younger. I wish for my youngest children to grow up with wide open spaces to fill their lungs with fresh air instead of the smog of the city. Also, my wife has particularly fond memories of this place. She grew up on the Isle of Rousay and moved to England for her schooling."

Mammy raised an eyebrow, seemingly unaware of Daddy's hostility. "Is that so? Well then she will feel as if she is coming home."

The white-haired man said something I could not hear and held his glass up in a gesture of a toast and then downed it whole. He rose from the table and bowed graciously.

"Mr. Gray…" He said, extending his hand to Daddy. "Mrs. Gray. It has been a pleasure. But I must return to the mainland before it is too late. I had hoped my visit would be longer, but the lateness of my arrival prevents it."

Before he could shake their hands, Mammy was already shaking her head. "Mr. Bishop. These waters are… quite strange… at nightfall. It would be in your best interest that I suggest you stay here the night and return at first light."

He turned and peered out of the window. I caught sight of his face before I moved out of view. He had a serious face, long and straight. With a jawline so sharp it belied his years. Only the hair betrayed his true age, and I could well imagine him capturing a younger woman's heart. He was dressed smartly, and I wondered what he made of our humble Hylands. He was like polished crystal in a byre.

"I have left my wife and children at a guest house in Evie. It would not do for me not to return, but I thank you for the offer."

He would have got into his boat and tried to navigate the waters alone. He would have been at the mercy of the waves. But there were some things I would never live with twice.

I opened the door slowly, moonlight flooding the room behind me. My windswept hair was in disarray. I peered out from the curtain before my eyes and knew how I must have looked to them.

The white-haired man regarded me closely. For a moment he did not speak, forgetting himself. Daddy was a man torn apart with rage. A stranger had not looked upon me for many years.

"Mr. Bishop, this is my daughter Finola." He said, through gritted teeth.

Mr. Bishop swallowed hard and bowed his head towards me. Mammy gestured for me to remove my hair from my face and stand up straight. It was already too late for the formalities.

"Please." I said calmly. "You'll not be wanting to go out onto those waters now."

There was a stony silence as I closed the door behind me and prevented the flood of moonlight. In the dim firelight I must have looked bedraggled and weather worn. What well to-do businessman would listen to the ramblings of a wild girl?

Certainly, he was still regarding me as I stood in the doorway and regarded him back. Perhaps he was reconsidering what the fresh air might do to his children. Perhaps they would end up like me? *Ah, but there is no other like me. I am cursed and blessed equally for it...*

"I see." He said finally, with a short intake of breath. "And there is no way to prevent my wife from worrying."

Daddy was stoic and firm. "What woman alive does not worry at the slightest of things?"

Mr. Bishop smiled and nodded in agreement. "Indeed Mr. Gray. In that case I must impose upon your hospitality a while longer."

Of course, Mammy was insistent that he take Rohan's bed. A man so enchanting and upstanding, it was as if Royalty had descended upon us. Daddy chose to ignore the fanfare and his agreement to let Mr. Bishop stay lay only in the need to prevent further tragedy.

I would not let another living soul fall foul to those waters. At night it seemed everything was much more sinister. Perhaps it was the tone of the night that made me grateful not to spend it alone. I found Rohan sitting on my bed, having made his own on the floor.

"I don't like him." He said petulantly.

I closed the door and lit the candle by my bedside. "Why ever would you not like him?"

"He will bring others back to Eynhallow. They don't belong here."

I instructed him to close his eyes and turn away as I undressed for bed.

"Do not be under any illusion that we belong here. I had thought it your wish that others come and that we are not the last?"

"English people! They do not know the land; they are city folk! They will not last long."

I slipped my nightgown over my head and pulled my hair away. "Do not be such a fool. Who are we to decide who comes and goes from here simply because we are the only ones to dwell here? Get you to bed and stop this folly! It will be a great deal better for you when there is company to be had."

I was never certain if I was speaking of his benefit, or mine. He was the only one with any real binding to me. It was with a heavy heart that I spoke.

As the house descended into that otherworldly silence, and Rohan fell into the deep and serene sleep of a boy who gave little consideration to his grievances, I listened to the whales as they serenaded the night. Their sweet songs aided my own sleep and I was glad to sleep without dreams.

Before dawn I opened my eyes to find Rohan sleeping beside me. His place on the floor had been abandoned and he had silently crept in beside me. His body was warm and stifling beside me, and as I slipped out from beside him, he shifted over and stretched.

But he did not wake. It was cool in the darkness and it hit my skin like the first snow. I slipped on the new shoes that were now too small and pulled my shawl over my nightgown. Embers were still glowing in the kitchen fireplace. Empty cups littered the table. The bread knife had been left on the chopping board and crumbs left on the plates, but I disregarded them as I made my way out into the morning darkness.

Dawn was imminent, the red of the sun threatening to spill over the water at any moment. I could make out the boat sitting by the shoreline. It was a grand thing, superior to many boats I had ever seen.

For a moment I was inclined to agree with Rohan. What business did this man have here? There was nothing here for any of us, save anyone trying to make a new life for themselves.

The Hylands would be gone one day, it seemed futile to build anything around it. I imagined a world where only the old ruined kirk remained.

Dawn began to break. The red hue painted the sky and I watched as the world awoke.

Finola... Why do you weep child?

Underneath the black water I saw the shape and form of a whale come to the surface, his great fin breaking the waves. I touched my moist cheek and had not noticed the tears there.

"I do not know." I confessed.

Have no fear, Finola Gray.

The voice was as familiar to me now as if I had heard it all of my life. Even in dreams I would know that ethereal voice and know it spoke only to me.

"I am not afraid." I said, but perhaps I was lying.

Do not deny yourself. Deny to others, but not to yourself.

I edged towards the water. His great body was pacing the shoreline. He could not come any closer.

"If I knew what I were, then perhaps there would be no need for denial."

You are what you are.

"But what is it that I am?"

In the morning light the spray from his back sent rainbows into the air. I liked the sound of it, his great heaving breaths as he sunk beneath the surface and returned once more.

Halfling. Neither this, nor that. The greatest of each. Mated from human blood, and Fin heart. You are what you are…

"And I suppose I shall never know which part of me is this, and which part of me is that."

The whale went below where I could not see. His voice becoming blurred and distant.

If you know what it is to be human, then you will know which parts of you that are not.

"Do they speak to you, then? The… Finfolk? Can they speak to you in this way?"

He broke the surface, his whole body reaching into the air and crashing back down in a sleek fight against the water that was his home and the land that he could not breach.

A thousand years ago, the Orca's leant their form to the Finfolk so that they may resemble us. In return they allowed us to dwell at the gateway to their world and carry their messages.

"Is this why you speak to me? Do you carry their messages now?" I asked.

Footsteps on the sand. I was no longer alone. The whale went down to where I could not follow, and the sun spilled over the horizon. I stared at it bleeding out into the sky. I could not recall the last time I had witnessed the sunrise so beautiful.

"An early riser, I see." Said Mr. Bishop, his jacket draped across his arm and his shirt untucked.

I smiled and nodded, too enchanted to speak. He stood with me a moment to take in the view before recalling his manners.

"I wanted to thank your mother and father for their hospitality, but I had not the heart to wake them. Would you pass on my sincerest thanks to them?"

The whale and his pod had moved out into the middle of the sound. The tide was retreating. Mr. Bishop sighed uneasily.

"You do not like the whales?" I asked.

"I have recently finished reading a newly published book, from America. Moby Dick, by a fellow called Herman Melville. It is the tale of a great whale that destroys a hunting boat and takes off the Captain's leg in one great bite."

I wondered further how an educated man would ever wish to come here and concluded that he must be insane. For only insanity would bring anyone here to remain.

"Such things have no place here." I sighed, keeping my eyes on the water.

Mr. Bishop's eyes were on me. I could feel them penetrate me. In the way one's eyes would regard a spectre in the night.

"Literature has a place in every corner of the world." He reasoned.

"I have The Canterbury Tales. My brother likes to read Gulliver's Travels. They were bought for us by our Aunt from the mainland. We have the Bible. But we have little use for books. Soon you will know."

He scanned the shoreline. Sighed deeply and placed the jacket around his shoulders. The wind had picked up.

"I shall always find a place for literature in my own home."

He was going to bring England to Eynhallow. Plant his own patch of his own world within one that would not allow it to grow. He would come here for beautiful sunrises and expanding vistas. The open spaces and quiet wind. He did not see what I saw.

"You will bring your household here. But your house will not hold." I said quietly, a solemn warning.

Mr. Bishop, the white-haired man, pulled his jacket around him tighter. The wind had died, but something chilled him.

"Is this opinion or prophecy?" He asked, quite seriously.

"I am not a prophet, Mr. Bishop." I replied.

But how could I tell him they were not my words? Once again that soulful pitch spoke to me, and I found myself speaking the inner words aloud. I watched for the water to break, for his shining body to return to the surface. But there was only his voice.

This barren land has given all it can yield.

"We shall see what the spring brings. I shall be sending my lads over in April. Until then I shall be drawing up plans for the houses and barnyard. There is even enough land for stables, my youngest son likes to keep horses. He is much like his mother."

"You will bring horses to Eynhallow?"

"Yes, I doubt that my little Nathan would allow it otherwise! Nor would my wife for that matter." He said jovially.

There was once another little Nathan that lived here. I sent him to his death. Nothing good could come of this. Not even the prospect of horses, and company and books.

Finally, I turned away from the water and looked into the placid eyes of the white-haired man.

"I hope you find whatever it is you are looking for."

He stared back at me. The placid eyes searching for something they would not find.

"Strange child…" He muttered, all trace of manners and propriety gone.

Do not fear, Finola Gray. Said the voice of the whale as I turned to go back into the house. *This one shall not perish…*

And all the while the birds told me to wait.

Lucie Howorth

Chapter Seven

THE REVELATION

I could not mourn Summer's passing. When the sunshine and warmth died, I knew that Winter had come to kill us again.

The whales did not stay to witness the frost. But still I could not regret that I was glad the darkness encroached. There were many memories to bury, and although Nathan Munro was gone, he haunted me. I could not love. For my love would drive the object of my affections to distraction.

To the sea where they would perish, or to the edges of insanity on a barren island always waiting. I would not send any man to either fate. I would never court desire or allow desire to tempt me. Perhaps this was why I'd been kept here. So that I might never set eyes on one I might love and compel him to love me in return.

As the darkness drew in early, I would retreat to my bed and wonder what it might be to be beloved. To be held in arms that desired me. To know that most passionate of kisses on my own lips. *To capture, to enslave, to take!*

In fits of rage I would wake at the memory of those words and recall that my true mother had not captured or taken. But perhaps enslaved. If I could achieve what she could not I would live with Nathan Munro's death avenged.

With each joy there was a curse. With each curse there was a sacrifice I could scarcely conceal. The raven hair grew wild and free. The blue eyes began to change into a deeper shade of green. I grew in height, a full head above Mammy and I knew I had grown into the image of *her*.

Daddy could not bear it. To look at my face and see another there. When we could no longer make the journey to the mainland, he would avoid my presence by making himself busy in the out-house and old stables.

The cold was always unrelenting out there, biting and fierce. For hours he would remain, tending the animals and tinkering with his guns. Any task that would keep him from looking upon me. It would be his undoing.

That Winter he courted death, and he succumbed to the fever. He could no longer avoid me, and I could no longer afford myself those romantic fantasies that would never come.

And so, winter descended into constant darkness. Mammy battled to keep him alive, with no medicine at her disposal she turned to the formidable prayer that Daddy would have protested had he any strength to protest.

Rohan became the man he had always wished to be. Keeping what little meat, he could hunt on our table and tending to the land with the fervor and stamina of a man twice his fourteen years of age.

I could do little more than keep the house and cook the meat while Mammy kept her bedside vigil. There was no time for foolish things, and I could not go to the water to lament the changes within me.

I did not notice when the shoes I had received for my birthday no longer fit me entirely. I could not recall the passing of days, or when Spring might be upon us. If I had been glad to bury memories of the previous year, I found myself wondering what else we might bury. Perhaps it would have been the better for him, to die and end his suffering than live on in constant torture. But there was one that would never forgive him if he left us here alone.

"He is dreaming again. Speaking your name, Finola. Always *your* name. Do you think he knows himself?" Rohan asked, a dry bed pan in his hand and a soaked cloth in the other.

I placed it into the sink and began scrubbing. He fell into one of the chairs, exhausted. I could feel the ache of the day in my own body. But I could not rest.

"I cannot say. But it must mean the fever is breaking, and he will be well soon."

Rohan's face was grave. "I had not realised the extent of his work here. I think if he died, I would not be far behind, worked into the ground."

"You have done well not to catch the fever yourself." And I had thought it a near miracle that he hadn't.

"Perhaps I have, and we haven't noticed." He said, coughing into his hand with a wry smile.

Despite the hardship, there he was. My little Rohan whose spirit could not be dampened.

"Eat something before you truly become ill and I shall have to tend the land myself." I urged, handing him some bread.

He ate heartily and we sat by the fire, silent and tired. Outside the wind howled hungrily for us to let it in. But the Hylands would not succumb. As I watched my Daddy rise from the edges of death, I was grateful to the stones for keeping us protected.

Soon he fell asleep in the chair, his face soft and serene in the firelight. Yes, he was still my precious brother. He would remain in my heart as the baby who had come on that stormy night.

I barely noticed as Mammy came into the room, weary and tired. My eyes remained on Rohan, envious of his serenity.

"Is there much tea left?" Mammy inquired, making her presence known.

I gave her my place by the fire and put the teapot on to boil. She slumped into the chair and rested her head against a sweaty palm.

"He is restless tonight but finally he is asleep. What day is it today? Is Winter almost over?" She inquired.

But I could not tell her. "The moon is full. It must be nearing mid-winter."

She lifted her head. "Have we missed Christmas?"

But I could not tell her that either. If Christmas had been and gone, then there was little could be done. Christmas had never been the jovial affair that I had heard about from my cousins. They spoke of a great feast where they sat around the table together and exchanged gifts. Church was a heartwarming place, where speak of the dead Christ turned to talk of his birth.

Christmas on Eynhallow had been as fruitless as the barren trees.

"Perhaps. But it does not matter. It would be another inconvenience." I surmised, pouring hot tea into a cup and handing to Mammy's trembling hand.

"The real inconvenience is here. I have thought much about it and I think we must now go to the mainland. I will not lose him to these winters."

Rohan raised his sleepy head. "He will not go. Nor will I."

Mammy looked at me, certain I would agree. "Finola. Have you not wished to leave here? Would it not make you happy to go?"

I wanted to say that it would. There was still a part of me that longed for it. But I was bound here now, and I was never certain if it was against my will, or if I had accepted my fate. I could not give her the answer she wished for.

"Oh, I see. Have the tables turned so?" She said, nodding at me knowingly. "Aye, you'll go. But not to the mainland."

"You cannot know that." I whispered in return.

She had never spoken of that secret we shared. That which we had both known, but never shared. Her eyes burned into me now, as if she knew she should not speak of it but would not be silenced. She was exhausted.

"Can I not? I know what I see when I look at you. There is less of *my* daughter and more of *hers*."

Would she reproach me now? When it seemed all else was lost? She was surely delirious. Perhaps she had caught the fever too? She sweated and shivered, her face accusatory and sad. I wanted to give her some comfort, but she would have pushed me away.

"Who do you speak of, Mammy? What is this?" Rohan asked, panic rising in his voice.

Mammy could not hide her triumphant smile. She had come to hate me; I was certain of it.

"He could not bear to see it. He will die when you leave us, whether you know it not yourself, there will come a day you can no longer tolerate the land. He knows it well. If he will not look at you it is because you share *her* face. He will not look upon it without heartbreak. Shall we remain like mutes or shall we speak of it? That he is dying because you are who you are…"

Rohan stepped towards me protectively. But Mammy's face remained resolute. She would have her secrets revealed, and it did not matter that Rohan would get caught in the crossfire. I felt it should have been me to stand protectively before him.

"It seems that you have concluded of your own accord what will be. I have avoided the water and will not go near it. You are certain I will go?"

"Aye. I am certain. You have been human for too long."

Rohan stepped back, pressing me into the corner of the room. He turned to face me slowly, his confusion turning to tears. At the sight of them I could not stop my own.

"Finola? What is this madness?" He asked, on the verge of hysteria. "What does she speak of? Where are you going?"

"I go nowhere." I told him. "Unless you banish me."

The thought seemed to cross her mind, and then like a rogue breeze it was gone. "Banish you? I would not banish you. You do not see it. But you will go of your own free will."

"What does free will have to do with it? I am bound to whatever fate awaits me whether I wish for it or not. Through birthright, or whatever magic this is. Am I no longer your daughter, then?"

She smiled and it was warm and genuine. "God knows I have loved you. Every day I have loved you, but I cannot watch you become… Whatever it is you are destined to become. No more than I could watch you burn. It is destroying your father. Soon it will destroy me. If you will not come to the mainland, best that you return to that other land and soon."

Rohan was trembling with rage. His fists curled into balls that made his knuckles white. He stared at Mammy and demanded through silence to understand what we spoke of. Her face softened towards him, finally she was sorry she had begun this.

"Ah, Rohan. My boy…" She crooned. "The sins of the father shall ruin the son. But it is no sin we can be sorry for. We have had our beautiful Finola with us for sixteen years. I cannot regret that. But times of change are upon us. Sit with me and I shall tell you all."

From the folklore to the moment we sat together by the fire, contemplating whether we would stay or go, Mammy unleashed the truth upon my unwilling brother.

At times her eyes rested upon me, at others she simply stared into space. Her voice was low and weak. But when it seemed she could speak no more she would sigh thoughtfully and continue. She was emotionless as she relayed the tales that had passed down from generation to generation. The ones we had never been told. The ones that had gone into myth and legend.

But they were not the enchanting stories I had heard from Nathan Munro, but bitter tales of blasphemy against God. Unnatural creatures taking forms of great beasts and using magic to enslave humans to a fate of untold misery. The consequence of not taking a human consort.

She took some pleasure in telling of the Finhag. Her jealousy did not go unseen. Her bitterness only subsided as she spoke of the baby she lost and the child of her husband's affair with one of those *creatures* that gave her a reason to end her grief.

She had not asked, nor wanted to know how it came to be that I was given to them. But in time she had learned and loved me regardless. But now it was too late for love. Love could not save me, or Daddy, or any of us. I could not stop my heart from breaking.

Rohan looked at me with sadness. That sadness would never leave. If ever he smiled at me again, I could never replace that look of redemption. My brother. My little boy, the one I had cared for as a babe and held in my arms during the winter storms. He looked to me now and I could not comfort him. Neither could Mammy, her embrace rebuffed as he rose and went to the fireplace, standing above it, watching the flames lick and spit.

"If you do hate me, then hate me for keeping it from you all these years. But do not hate me for what it is." She pleaded.

Rohan shook his head. "Hate? What is hate to me? I do not know what it is to hate."

She did not see the tears I shed. The utter contempt for myself at the way she had spoken. She no longer saw me.

"Then tell me. Tell me what it is that you feel." She asked, her hands still reaching out to him.

But he no longer saw her. He saw my tears, the contempt.

"I feel nothing." He said, as he came towards me with more sorrow than I could take from him. "Tell me, Finola, what should I feel?"

"Do not be sad." I said quietly, wiping away the tears. "Feel whatever you may. But do not be sad."

I stepped into his place, putting myself between him and Mammy.

"If I am my father's murderer then you must shackle me and imprison me. But if he dies of his own stupid heart's wish then I am not to blame. Have pity on me! I grieve that you are not my mother! I know not what will become of me. Even when you claim to know my fate, and I fear your predictions may come true, still I wish to remain here with you. Will you reproach me?"

The words cut like a knife. Her face contorted in pain, the years of anguish rising to the surface.

"Ah, Finola! I do not reproach you. Your beauty and power betray that you are no more my daughter than the rock is like the water. There's no need for reproach. Perhaps regret. But not reproach."

But what was beauty and power to me? I had little need of either.

"Then what reason have you to break my brother's heart? I will not go into the water. The birds…"

She raised an accusatory eyebrow. "Ah yes, the birds. What of the birds?"

They told me to wait. For what, they will not say. But I trust their word.

"Do not think that it goes unnoticed. I am a god-fearing woman, and it puts the fear within me to see you converse with those creatures."

Rohan stepped forward, his hands that were now bigger than mine, resting on my arm.

"Mammy, you must leave it be." He said, quite rationally. "It matters not. Finola is the sister I have always known, and the daughter you have raised as your own. Let magic not be part of it. If these Finfolk were not creatures of God, why would he place them here? It matters not that she is part of us and part of them. She is Finola and that is that."

He moved his hand from my shoulder and placed it firmly down onto the table, nodded once and went towards the fire. He would not speak of it again, for whatever reasons that were his own he had chosen to accept whatever he'd been told with the same acceptance he gave most things.

"It would be unfair of me, would it not? If I did not let it be?" Mammy said, nodding in peace. "And I shall let it be. But not before I have heard what I desire to hear."

She looked at me then, and we exchanged an uneasy glance. I could feel my stomach wretch and I felt a real sickness though I could not feel anything within me to purge. She would ask me what it was to be who I was. She would ask me the things I had seen. I could not deny her the truth.

"Tell me." She sighed, resigned to the fact there was little else she could do to change things. "You have seen the land under the sea, have you not?

I heard your dreams as you spoke of them in sleep. But now I will hear of it as you wake."

My eyes pricked with a sadness I had thought long buried as I recalled those golden rooms. The texture of the weeds, glowing ceilings of water that were not really there.

The voices that would not show themselves, and the face of Nathan Munro at the window... or was it a mirror? There was no way to do it justice. No way to truly convey the happiness or euphoria. The fear that I did not want to return to the land.

"If you were so happy, why did you return?" Rohan asked belligerently.

I smiled at the memory. "For you, brother. Down there it is not as it is up here. I was given a task, and I failed to recall what it was until it was too late. But I never forgot that I had a reason to return, and that was you."

He raised an intrigued eyebrow. "And what task were you given?"

But for that I could raise no smile. "Nathan Munro was taken, I believe. He asked me to tell his father he would return. That he would one day see his mother's face again. But I could not remember. I think he tried to escape. Perhaps they set him free. We all know the fate he met."

"It is truly a terrible deed. To take without consent." Mammy lamented; her eyes glazed as if in deep thought.

Consent? A fire blazed within. What did consent have to do with it? What choice was there to be had? Without a human consort there was little to stop the magic of the Finhag taking hold.

"You dare!" I spat. "You dare to judge even now! You think I do not know the madness that is to love a finwoman? You think I wish for that power? To enslave? If I could know the sort of love that is of free will then I would gladly hand over any birth right I have to any other power. But I shall never know it. I shall enchant the object of my desires, even when I would throw myself onto the rocks to find a violent end. There is no more help for it than there is to prevent the birds from flying or the fish from swimming!"

She was visibly shaken. Her bony hands wrought with the wrath of my words. If I had wanted to silence her, I had succeeded.

But it would not be the end of it. There was a morbid curiosity unslaked, and she would always wonder what I had seen at the bottom of the sea. The powers I shared with those who dwelled down there.

I had no doubt that she loved her daughter. The child I had been, and no longer was. If she loved me now, I would never know.

And she would never say.

Rohan sighed heavily. "Mammy, let there be an end to it."

He came to me and embraced me. His body was hardened against the work he had done, and he had grown a full head above me. I was lost in his embrace. Just a tiny thing, with wild hair that he tamed with one hand as he laid a solitary kiss upon my forehead.

"Dear sister." He said quietly. "We will speak of this another time."

And he strode out of the room leaving Mammy and I to silently make our peace.

How strange it felt, as I slipped into bed, without my secrets burdening me. I fell into a deep sleep almost instantly and was greeted with nothing but silence.

It was well past sunrise when I woke. The red sky had turned blue without me and already the clouds were beginning to darken with the onslaught of the snow.

I could feel the cold of the snow already, it was painful to the tips of my fingers as I pulled my blanket away. There had been no fire lit in the kitchen. All was silent. It was as if the world had turned and my sleep had brought me to a place where no other dwelled.

I wrapped my blanket around me and crept into the hall. Rohan was absent, and Mammy was bringing in water from the well before it froze. In the corner of their chamber, where the only fire had been lit, lay my Daddy.

His chest heaved in great breaths. It was as if each time he could not take in enough air. He shivered beneath the warmth of the thickest blankets we had, and yet the fever in him brought nothing but sweat.

It had been weeks. Had it been a month? I was certain he would die. His body was racked with fever, all the life taken from him.

He would not eat the meagre broth Mammy had brewed for him. He would not drink. But sometimes his eyes would move towards the window, and I knew he was waiting for death. Perhaps he had courted it. Perhaps it was not his avoidance of me that had kept him outdoors in the biting cold. He seemed to be done with this life and had chosen to leave it.

He turned his face away as I came into the room, the bitterness still etched in his sunken eyes. Even now he would not look upon me. But I would make him. I would not let him depart without setting his eyes upon me one last time. He would regret it in death, I was certain of it.

"Daddy…" I whispered, conscious of Mammy lingering at the well outside. "Will you not look at me?"

He resisted still.

"Ah, you're stubborn. But I know you're just pretending. I know it's because you love me."

His eyes stared at me pleadingly. Yes, he looked at me then. I almost wished he hadn't. His hand reached for me, and I took it in my own.

"Finola…" He said, his voice barely there.

"Yes…" I said, bending to his ear. "I am here."

With his other hand, shaking, he pointed to the shelf above the fire. There was a wooden crucifix hanging there.

"No Daddy. There is no need for it. You do not believe in God." I told him, holding his gaze.

But he would not relent. He was staunch as he pointed, telling me silently to bring it to him.

I regarded the shabby craftwork as I brought it down from the shelf. It had been made for some purpose, perhaps other than prayer.

As I handed it to him, he felt the weight in his bony hands that were skin and sinew. For a moment he paused. Eyes closed and brow furrowed he placed it upon his lap and began to move it apart.

To eyes that did not know where to look, it could have been placed anywhere and be seen as nothing more than a wooden crucifix.

But as Daddy's hands moved deftly over the wood, he took the front apart and inside it was hollow. From it he took a piece of paper that had been rolled to fit inside. He did not look at it but handed it to me before turning his face away.

"What is this?" I asked, feeling the paper tremble in my hands.

It was old and worn, edges faded. His closed eyes tightened at my question, but he did not speak to respond.

With silent blessing I opened it to reveal the face I wore as my own. The hand that had drawn this had taken every detail, every laughter line and every eyelash and transformed the white paper into a living memory. Those eyes, much like my own, were wide and sad. The lips full and round, that pouted even when she was smiling. She was framed by raven black hair, so wild it could not be tamed. She was beautiful in a strange and melancholy way. I knew that she was not human.

The things which set us apart were subtle, but still they had been captured. Her face was a different shape, and the wild raven hair was tucked behind ears that could never exist within human flesh. Long and almost pointed like a leaf, I began to notice the wide and side eyes were too large for a human too. She was far more striking than I could ever hope to be.

Looking into her pencil drawn eyes I felt a sadness so real it was as if she came to life. If she could have spoken, what would she have said? I knew her. If I had been blind, I would have known her.

"You drew this?" I whispered, revealing sobs I had not known would come.

But I had taken my eyes from him too long. I had not seen the light go out. I had not heard the rattle, or the shallow breaths cease. I had not held his hand or given him peace. There had been no rest for him in life.

As I searched for his eyes to see me, they looked beyond. He had looked his last upon me. There was a hint of a smile upon his lips. I could not regret that it had been this way.

Slowly I placed the picture of my true mother back into the crucifix and placed it back upon the shelf.

"Do not look more for her." I said, placing the dead eyes shut. "She was with you all along."

I kissed the shrunken cheeks and wept into the folds of my blanket until I fell into a sleep of my own.

Lucie Howorth

Chapter Eight

THE ISLANDERS

With no passage and no priest to guide us, there we laid William Gray to rest within the ruined kirk on Eynhallow. Winter had finally claimed him. It had snared its fated prize and rewarded us with an early spring. How strange it was at first to see his empty place at the table and his shoes by the door. His pipe was left by the fireside to gather dust.

These were things we would not relinquish. These were the things which kept him alive.

And so, the Hylands became a shrine. I could see no sense in it. He was not here. I could not feel his presence in these things.

But they gave comfort to those around me. So I did not protest. Instead I went out into the fields and made my home there.

The birds with their ever-constant stories were of more comfort than the nights I spent holding my bereft brother and when the whales returned, I knew I could endure this heartache that threatened to end me. For it was a heartache like no other. There were no words to convey the depth of it.

Rohan was broken for many weeks. The senselessness of it resculptured his carefree nature. There was an edge to him now, where once there had been a boy with red cheeks and soulful grin there was now a man who had known a grief so cutting, he dared not speak of it.

He came out of the darkness wounded. But he had fought hard. Sometimes, when he thought I could not see, I saw the boy.

Mammy prayed for us. She took her faith and used it to rebuff the grief. But at night it touched her, and I heard the ravaged sobs as she lay beside the empty space where once he had been.

I wondered if she blamed me. If she wished that I had died in his place. But we carved ourselves a life without him, and she never spoke again of the truth. As if it had been removed from memory. Perhaps in her grief she *had* forgotten. Perhaps she chose to forget. Or perhaps she was honouring Rohan's wishes. She was leaving it be.

But I could not. The animals began to seek me out, waiting by the door at first light.

The birds perched on the wall of the well, and the cows would descend from their grazing to appear by the wall at the top of the garden. At night I heard the whales sing. They called to me and requested I join them in the sea. But I would not.

Instead I stood on the shoreline watching their majestic bodies rise and fall from the surface. I could not reproach them that they had left when I had need of them most. They gave me joy and knowledge I could not find anywhere else even if sometimes it made little sense.

For a time, I was content to have it so. That I could milk the cows and have their blessing. That the birds entertained me with their dream like words in pictures, of places I had never seen before. But as with any contentment I had ever known, it would not last.

The life we had carved began to dissipate. Rohan abandoned his schooling in favour of working the land and hunting. Mammy did not protest.

Instead she invited her sister to come and live with us.

Aunt Hannah's avoidance of Eynhallow had stood long. But the money Uncle Seamus had left her began to diminish. So, Bethan had her wish and my quiet contentment was ruined.

The day before my Seventeenth birthday I watched the boat cross the sound carrying the meagre belongings of my Aunt and cousins as they came to make their lives with us. Ewan eyed the land as if it was excrement. His pale face was afraid of the unfamiliar terrain.

But Bethan could not hide her excitement. For many nights she kept me awake with her joy at leaving her friends and Sunday school hopscotch opponents behind. Surely, she was mad? I would have given anything for friends or hopscotch. But I could not lament, I had been given a greater gift for my lonely childhood.

And so, my world was invaded. Aunt Hannah and Mammy shared the room she had once shared with Daddy. Two beds lining the wall instead of one. Ewan was to share a room with Rohan, and Bethan shared mine. But what did I have in common with a squawking twelve-year-old?

Our secrets became secrets again and it was harder to hide them when they screamed in the faces of those who were on the outside.

Aunt Hannah would shoo the birds away from her freshly washed linen that she hung out to dry. She would question my insistence on standing by the shoreline, watching the whales circle the island. If I could have hidden it where would I have gone? There was only one place and the birds had told me to wait.

"She is a strange one, always standing by the water. She should be putting her time to better use, Mary. Should she not be finding a husband? She is seventeen, and beautiful. With a little guidance, she could be a good wife. Time now to stop the folly and distraction, don't you think?" Aunt Hannah said to Mammy when she thought I could not hear.

I was standing by the stable door, leading a cow into milk. They could not see me, and I had been so silent in my approach they had not heard me.

"Perhaps." Mammy replied. "But she is not interested in boys or any of that. I cannot force her."

When I thought of strange it reminded me of the pale boy who would not go outside, who had been so afraid to leave his mother's side he had spent the first night sleeping by her bed on the cold floor. Strange to me was the way he did not speak even when he was spoken to, and seldom offered conversation of his own. Sickly and weak, he spent his days in the parlour schooling himself with books. He did not want to be here; he was afraid of this place. But I did wonder if there was anything in the world that did not scare Ewan.

Every day Rohan grew more tired of him. As his shoulders broadened and his voice became lower, the hair around his chin became coarser so did Ewan's body wither and the age which they shared became less apparent. As their fifteenth birthday approached Rohan had grown into a beast of a man who could easily pass for twenty. But Ewan resembled that child I recalled standing by his mother's side in the house in Evie and yet I was the strange one?

"If she is not interested it is simply because she has had little chance. Now that Bethan is here, she must be feeling stifled."

Stifled? It would have been blessed to be stifled. No, I was trapped. Alienated. Lost. But no longer. Now it was acceptance. Tolerance.

"She'll adapt. It is a hard time for us all. But we'll all adapt. In time." Mammy said thoughtfully.

But Aunt Hannah would not have it. "Would it not be more fitting if she went to the mainland? I was her age when I left. Although it pains me to return, I have done the best for my children. Perhaps she might return with her own children. But if she remains here, I dare say she'll never find a man to have any!"

"We shall see what becomes of her. Mr. Bishop will return soon and build more houses. It may be as it was when we were young with families here and neighbours to call upon. It was not always like this. We were not always the only ones."

But I could only recall the words the whales had told me. *Your house will not hold… Eynhallow's day is done.*

"God bless that day! I have been too long on the mainland. I crave the company of others." Aunt Hannah sighed.

But now that Daddy was gone, Mammy dreaded the day they would come.

But they did come.

As dawn spilled over the horizon I watched as their boats brought rock and stone, chisels and hammers, spades and men.

Two boats headed towards us, the larger one with sails so wide I could not keep my eyes from them. I had never seen anything on the water like it. The other was a barge that carried wooden boxes and stone. I watched them curiously as they navigated the tide and wondered if they would get lost upon the way.

The wind was low, but it pushed them forward. It was an ominous feeling. Not completely without pleasure. I could not deny the excitement.

But it was tinged with fear that these people would take their place in Eynhallow and soon realise it had been a barren investment. There was nothing for them here. They came with hopes and expectations that would never be fulfilled.

But there was no way to tell, no way to warn them save for watching and waiting.

Perhaps Hamish had given tales of the glory days when we had lived together in relative peace and harmony as part of his sales pitch. Perhaps it had been hopes of recreating such an idyll that had brought the white-haired man here.

As they neared the shoreline, I heard the whales speculate about the vessels above. They wondered who would come to a land that was ready to die. They wanted to know what madness drove them. I could not save myself from smiling in agreement. I watched them land and dismount.

The white-haired man stood in the prow of the barge and as he came onto the shore, he held his arms out as if he had stepped into paradise. Two men brought down the wide sail and emerged from the boat carrying wooden chests. They were followed by another two men, who seemed to survey their surroundings before disembarking. The five men stood for a moment, bewildered, their faces in awe and wonderment. But one of them did not. He seemed to look away and turned his back on us.

"They have arrived then?" Rohan asked, as he approached from behind carrying his gun.

"So it would seem."

He eyed them suspiciously and spit upon the ground. "Aye, and now they'll rape the land. With their brick and mortar."

"You think The Hylands appeared from the ground like potatoes? The land has been raped once before, as you so delightfully put it."

He laughed under his breath and nodded. "It seems futile now, though. Doesn't it?"

"Aye, but do not make it known. They will discover it in time and if not, they'll perish here."

We watched them for a while, until we could watch no more. I pitied them. As we walked away, I felt a sadness for them I could not explain.

"I fear no good can come of this." I confessed, as we walked through the grass towards the brow of the hill which hid The Hylands.

Rohan had become my confessor. I could speak freely with him without fear of reproach. No longer the child I had to protect, the baby I had cared for and the boy I had comforted in those first bleak days of losing our father. But an equal in both body and mind.

"Perhaps not. But it is no business of ours. Do not worry yourself." He replied, slinging his gun over his bulking shoulder.

"One of them could not even look. He turned away." And as I said the words I turned back and saw them approaching behind us.

Rohan ushered me forward. "Get you inside and stop worrying about their comings and goings. Leave them be."

"Aye, and then you will pretend you are not curious. Are you not a little curious?"

He grew impatient with me. "No, I have no desire to know anything about them. They come here as outsiders and they live here as outsiders."

"One of them, he could not look at the land. He turned his back and would only look at the sea."

Rohan spat on the ground once more. "Perhaps they have never seen a whale before. Do you care? You do well to keep your mind on matters other than what these intruders may or may not be doing."

Intruders. Such a strange word. Had I not intruded also? Was I a product of this place? No. I had been given.

"What is it that you are afraid of? Our secrets keep themselves well. Not even Aunt Hannah will ever know, and she dwells under our roof!"

He grabbed me then, sharply and firmly so that I might not pull free. He pulled me close to him so that not even the wind could carry our words.

"Now listen to me!" He whispered viciously. "You know as well as I, where there are many eyes and ears so will many secrets be revealed! I promised to keep yours and keep it I shall. But I'll not tempt another revelation!"

There was hope only in silence. As he released his iron grip, I saw his jaw flex nervously. We would not speak of it again, and I would not trouble myself to care what the *intruders* were doing. I saw sense in his fear, and he was right.

We continued our journey in a mutual silence, but he knew he had my attention. As we neared the front door, he turned to me and gave me a fleeting look.

"Worry not." I reassured him. "I will hide myself."

The inevitable knock came as we finished supper. I stood within the shadows as Rohan went to answer the door.

He had taken on the role Daddy had left behind. He no longer waited for Mammy's word on things and now that there was nobody to please, he pleased himself.

Ewan watched him closely, always silently appraising him. I pitied him. He would never have that power. I wondered sometimes if he wished ill towards my brother.

But then the thought would leave as quickly as it had come, and there would be some camaraderie between them, even if it was not real.

As the white-haired man came into the room his eyes rested on my brother's frame. Yes, he had grown. Considerably. He was not done growing yet. I saw for a moment how others might view him. He could intimidate silently with a glare he had perfected in those dark times when he mourned our father deeply.

He gestured for Ewan to move from the table and offered our guest his seat. He came to join me in the shadows.

"I hope I have not intruded upon you this night." The white-haired man said, as Mammy came to pour him some tea.

Aunt Hannah was the first to put him at ease. "No, it is just that we are not accustomed to visitors. Please, will you have some tea?"

He accepted heartily and drank it down. Bethan stared at him as she sat by the fire, her little arm moving slowly as she stirred the pot. He smiled at her in that way a man does when he has children of his own of a similar age.

Unlike her brother, she was an open soul and smiled back longingly. She reminded me of Rohan before our Daddy died.

Everything was an adventure.

Aunt Hannah introduced herself and her children, and the white-haired man listened intently. He was glad to be indoors again; I could see it on his contented face. He did not like to be outdoors. He would not last long.

"I find myself without my host this evening. Is Mr. Gray well?" He asked then, noting Daddy's absence in the room.

Rohan picked up his knife and began to plane the blunt side against his hand absently. He was a wild boy and I knew he did it without knowing how savage it made him look. The white-haired man stiffened in his seat.

"Died. Last month. The fever took him." Said Rohan sharply, not taking his eyes from the knife.

"I am sorry to come to you at such a sad time, I offer you my deepest sympathies." The white-haired man replied nervously.

How strange we must have looked. The girl who smiled by the fire, slowly stirring the pot as she regarded our guest. The harsh boy who played with knives and towered above the other boy. The boy who would not come out of the dark corner. The women who lived alone, their husbands gone, and their children left to be forgotten. The girl with the raven black hair, the strange girl who stood by the water but would not go in.

"Thank you." Mammy said graciously. "May I inquire of your wife, Mr. Bishop?"

"She is with our children in England, awaiting our home to be built. She has expressed a desire for stables so that she might keep her horses. I had hoped to be rid of the great beasts, but she has a love of horses I shall never understand."

Horses would be something, at least. Our stables had only echoed of horses.

"What use have you for horses?" Rohan asked belligerently. Daddy would have been proud.

The white-haired man shrugged. "There might be little use for them. But I have a desire to keep my wife happy, and if that is found in keeping horses then I will not deny her."

Aunt Hannah sighed at the romantic notion. "You are a good husband."

The white-haired man smiled politely. "I'm afraid I have been an absent one, but now I will have the chance to make things right. We shall have all the time in the world on our little piece of Eynhallow."

Rohan laughed under his breath, a mocking hiss that made Mammy glare at him with unease. But she did not berate him.

"Is that what you plan to do here, Mr. Bishop? Have all the time in the world? You do well to remember this piece of Eynhallow will not flourish alone. To survive here, you must work for it."

But the white-haired man was undeterred. "Such wise words for one so young, how old are you young man?"

And there he was. The boy beneath the broad shoulders, lingering and waiting to resurface.

"Fifteen." He said sheepishly.

The white-haired man nodded. "I could use a strong arm. I will pay you well, if you would be willing to join my lads?"

Would he rescind? Would he take his own words, chew them and then spit them out? The offer was tempting. But would he work for the outsiders he hated so? Ewan shook with white rage beside me. He would have gone to work for the white-haired man. But he would never be asked. Rohan did not even consider it.

"My work is here. I cannot be spared." He said, rising from the table and leaving the room.

Mammy was quick to defend him. "Forgive my son. He still grieves."

But the white-haired man shook his head, unoffended. "He is a boy in a man's world. Speak not of forgiveness."

She nodded in thanks and slipped awkwardly into the seat Rohan had left behind. Picking up his knife she placed it into the folds of her skirt, as if the sight of it unnerved her. She feared for Rohan, that much I knew. He would not speak of his grief. He would not acknowledge the pain. He was courting an anger he could not control, and she knew it well.

"Tell me of your sons, Mr. Bishop." She sighed, gesturing Ewan to come out from the darkness.

Only when he was certain Rohan would not return did he step forward and come back into the fold.

"My eldest are here, they have pitched our camp on the land. I have my best lads from the factory too. A factory I no longer own, I might add. I have sold it now and intend to invest in some livestock and other such ventures. My youngest are well, finishing their schooling before they shall join us here."

Aunt Hannah's interest was piqued. Civilised conversation such as this she had craved since leaving the mainland behind.

"You must implore them to come here. We can brew more tea, if they are weary and in need of some home comforts."

But they would only judge us harshly. People from the mainland always cast their eyes upon with judgement and scorn. They thought us strange and backwards. Perhaps we were, but affairs of the mainland mattered little to us. We had not been to church. Mammy was afraid to cross the waters without Daddy and had kept her faith by praying by her bedside with the wooden crucifix on the shelf.

"Aye, I will pass on your hospitality. They have worked hard today. Although, I don't doubt one of my sons will be in need of some home comforts." And he looked troubled at as he spoke. "The youngest of my elder sons. I had hoped he would consent to stay with us, but he already wishes to leave. If I were not paying him so handsomely, perhaps he already might have."

Aunt Hannah shrugged. "It is simply an aversion to solitude. He will adjust, in time."

"That is my hope. I had thought buying this land would bring my family together. But I find Caleb unwilling to comply. But I am not getting younger, I have watched him grow. So, I will find some contentment in watching my little ones grow."

Aunt Hannah was utterly drawn in by his mesmerising voice and enchanting charisma. The white hair, above all else, was what set him apart. I wanted to remind her that he was a married man, but he was relishing in her attention.

I listened as we were regaled with tales of his youngest son Nathan and the horses he loved so much. His daughter was the same age as Bethan, and her name was Ophelia. Named so after the damsel from one of those Shakespeare tragedies.

And then he spoke at length of the literature he loved. But it was lost on my Mammy who clutched her bible closely, and my Aunt who had tried to immerse herself in culture but had never achieved that ideal she had wanted for herself. She had given me a book once, The Canterbury Tales, and even now I had not completed reading it.

It was growing dark when another, less expected knock, resounded into the room.

Rohan appeared once more, and Ewan instinctively moved from the table. But Rohan did not acknowledge him and instead went straight for the door.

Standing in the fading daylight was one of the men I had seen coming off the boats. He was tall, fair haired and bore more than a striking resemblance to the white-haired man. But it was his troubled face that struck me the most. He pulled his cap from his head and wrung it between worried hands.

"I am sorry to interrupt." He said, eager to step inside but distracted by something down by the water. "But I must speak with my father."

His English voice was exquisite. I wondered if all English men sounded so. Even when they were distressed, their voices flowed so beautifully I dared not speak in my own Orcadian way.

The white-haired man calmly rose from the table. "What is it Victor?"

"It's Caleb. He will not stay here a moment longer. He says this place is cursed and that we must not build here. He is trying to launch one of the boats, I have tried to stop him. But… you know his temper… I could not!"

Mammy dropped her bible. The sound of the thud resembled my heart as I stepped out of the dark corner of the room and into the light.

"He must not go out onto those waters!" I cried, and the white-haired man nodded.

He did not know quite why, but I knew he recalled the night we had prevented him from setting sail after dark. He would not question it, even though it was obvious some sinister force was at play and it was this which broke my heart.

How sinister could they be? If I was part of them, would I not also be sinister?

The human within could not allow another to be taken and without regard to my shoes or shawl I ran down towards the shoreline. I cared not who followed.

Rohan reached to keep me indoors, but he was not fast enough to catch me. I heard his voice call after me, ordering me to remain here.

He followed me, his familiar steps closing behind me. I knew he would make me go back and so I pushed my feet to carry me faster.

The land beneath my feet crushed between my toes and soiled the hem of my skirts. I heard others calling my name and another name I could not recall.

I had lost all balance as I reached the water's edge. My breath was gone. My head dizzied and my feet weary. I could feel blood as I stood upon the rocks and I knew I had cut myself on one of them. But it mattered little as I watched those great wide sails raised into the dark sky.

They know he is trying to find his way home.

The voice of the great whale penetrated all else and I had mere moments before they would find me.

"Are they going to take him?" I asked breathlessly.

There is many a finwife, looking always for her human consort. He will throw himself at their mercy.

"I will not let them take him, I cannot!"

You, who are Finfolk blood, would meddle in these things?

"Aye. I am not finwife. I would rather become Finhag than take what is not mine!"

Be it as you wish. But this one is not like the others...

"Is that prophecy?" I asked, but he fell silent. I knew he would speak no more to me this night.

The wind had picked up. One moment it blew the hair around my face into my eyes, the next it brushed it all away. It seemed not to know what direction it came in. The sails moved, threatening to break its ropes and knots.

I moved towards the boat, the red moon giving light behind me. It had grown dark so quickly, it was an ill omen.

I saw Rohan and the white-haired man and his son approach from the other side of the shore. But I would get there first.

The boat was ready to sail, it majestically bobbed in the shallows of the waves. From the prow came a long wooden plank that extended onto the shore. I saw the blood for the first time as I stepped upon it but disregarded it. I could not feel the pain yet. Voices came from onboard, low and angered voices of men that were fighting.

"You crazy fool!" One of them spat, as I crept onto the vessel, I went unnoticed.

He was a small man, with heaving muscles that had no place on such a short frame. But despite this he still came up against the bigger man, who was packing things into boxes. The other one stood by, watching them. Shaking his head in dismay, defeated.

"Who shall be the crazy fool when I have returned to the Mainland and you are left here to rot? I tell you I have an ill feeling of this place!"

I could not make out their faces in the moonlight, but their voices were fierce and unafraid of one another. It was as if neither wanted to argue but it had come to pass that they must.

The man standing by stepped forward and placed a hand on the small man's shoulder. "Simon, come. He has made his choice."

"No Isaac, I've known him since birth. Not one day has he been a fool. I'll not allow it now! Oh, where is Victor?!"

"You think my brother can stop me? It is true you have known me since birth, so you must know he is no match for me."

Simon laughed mockingly. "In brawn, perhaps. But if it were a battle of the wits, I'd put my last penny on Victor any day. Have you not the sense to see with? It's just an Island!"

The bigger man came out of the shadows and into the moonlight. He was shirtless and sweating. His great body was heaving with each breath, his muscles contracting in a way I'd never seen before. His fair hair was dirty and fell about his face, resting on his shoulders.

"There is more to this place, mark my words." He said with a heavy heart as he turned and looked upon me for the first time.

Be still, world. Stop your shifting.

Align the stars so that I might recognise the sky and cease this falling down.

Was it the boat that swayed, or I on my feet? When his eyes sought out mine, I could not look away and they bore into me like a wild animal.

I had not the wit to run, nor hide. He terrified me. But it was not a fear of threat, no he did not threaten me.

His stare was unfathomable. Intent and rested solely on me. He did not move, and nor did I. Not until I felt the sharp dig of fingers as they bore into my skin and the distant voices break into my reverie. They pulled me from this moment and unwilling, I stepped aside. I watched the white-haired man and that son if his approach as Rohan pulled me back.

"Caleb, what are you doing son?"

The white-haired man's voice was soft and sad. But his son did not hear him. He did not see him.

"Are you leaving?" He asked again.

Voices were hushed as the wind. Or perhaps I could not hear them. My heartbeat pounded over the sounds of them talking and mumbling. It pounded so fierce it was like drums within, drowning out all else. Those wild eyes kept mine, suddenly it did not matter that we were being watched.

Rohan held me tightly, the skin around his fingers turning a dark shade of blue. He would repent of that later, when he would realise how harshly he had handled me. But for now, he clutched me so tightly I could not protest.

There was no pain. There was nothing save for the drums and those eyes. I was so afraid of him.

"Caleb, will you speak to me boy!"

Only then did he look at the white-haired man. Briefly he noted his chest was bare and in the company of strangers. Somehow it mattered little now.

"I... I know not what I do..." He mumbled, stepping back as if compelled by unseen forces.

"No matter. Put your shirt on, and we shall get some sleep. On the morrow it will be as if this never happened."

The white-haired man handed him the jacket from his own back.

Isaac, the unassuming man who had stood aside to watch the others fight slipped it over Caleb's shoulders. It was as if the life in him had been snuffed.

"Sorry Father, I am sorry. I… I thought I wanted to leave. But… I will stay. Of course." He said absently.

Simon held his hands up in praise. "Thank the lord!"

The white-haired man turned to me, appeased. "Thank you, Finola." His eyes turned towards my brother. "And Rohan. I am sorry we have disturbed your evening."

Rohan nodded. "I'll get my sister back to the house now. If we are done here."

"No." Caleb said, his voice still distant and far away in dream. "She came to tell me something, what was it?"

"She came to prevent you from leaving. These waters are treacherous after dark. If you still insist on leaving, wait until first light. That is all." Rohan snorted.

"And it seems he has heeded your warning, young Finola. Thank you." Nodded the white-haired man, clasping his son on the shoulder good naturedly.

I could smell his wanting. It invaded me and I was powerless against it. *No, you must not want me. It is not real. You must not look at me so…*

"No, it was something else." He said, confused. As if he had slept a thousand years and woken in another place and time.

All of them turned to me expectantly. Even if I could find the words, Rohan would never have allowed me to speak them. His protection was starting to hurt me. His grasp too tight.

"It was nothing else. You have seen the whales. They are likely to capsize your boat in the moonlight. She heard that you were leaving and wanted you to know. There is nothing else!" Rohan spoke for me, slowly edging me off the boat.

Caleb's voice softened. As if he had forgotten something which had been dear to him but was no longer so.

"Finola, is that your name?"

I nodded. I could feel Rohan's chest at the back of me, my hair catching in the buttons of his shirt. He held me too closely. I could not shake his body from mine and his need to keep my secret unknown.

The white-haired man noted Rohan's grip and seemed aggrieved. "Now, I say, why not loosen your grip there? She has done nothing wrong."

The little man Simon smirked in the darkness. "Has she the wit to speak?"

If I had ever possessed a voice, it had deserted me. I could not deny that I ached to see the skin that was now shrouded in the white-haired man's jacket. The fire within my belly burned desire, I knew what I had done. I had bound his fate to mine, and he would hate me for it if he could.

Finblood pulsated through my veins. The nectar of it calling to him. *Be mine. Whether you will or no, you shall be mine.*

I wanted to despise the sight of him. Those wild eyes did not leave mine, even when I would have taken out my own to prevent the sight of him. But I could not. This was not flattery, a young girl who was glad of the company of a handsome man. This was not Nathan Munro. I could feel this tangible thing, blood and sweat and desire. There would be no peace for either of us. Finally, I came to know my curse.

"Aye. She has, but maybe you frighten her. There's not been others here in a long while. You'll do well to remember that."

Rohan grumbled, his warning seemingly appeasing his own misplaced sense of danger.

Simon rolled his eyes. "Friendly around here, aren't they?"

"Come Rohan." The white-haired man interjected. "Let us not fight. Caleb has decided to stay, we shall impose on you no longer. Take your sister back and we shall return to our camp. Perhaps, when we are all here together, we shall live in harmony?"

But Rohan sneered, a look that was all too much like his Daddy. "I do not like the way he looks at my sister."

Nothing was said. The other men could not deny what they saw but could not prevent it either. Instead, my brother pulled me onto the shore and as he led me away, I saw Caleb standing on the prow watching until we were out of sight.

We left them in the boat but a part of me remained.

Bethan was sleeping soundly in the cot beside my bed when I returned. Her curls neatly wrapped in hair rags, her innocent face at peace.

In the dim lamp light, I slipped off my clothes and inspected the darkening bruises. He did not know his own brute strength, my poor brother. But it was not that which caught my eye in the dim reflection of the window. I had not seen myself as others might. In the dark glass, the flame of my bedside candle casting shadows across the room, I saw myself.

The black raven hair hung over my breasts, covering them from view. But they were there, as I brushed my hair aside, I could not contain my breath at the sight of them. These were the breasts of a woman and I felt alive, as if death had been more a part of my life than living had been. I touched them freely, my hands running down the contours of them. But I did not imagine my own hands. Those dirty ones, the ones that wiped sweat from that heaving chest. Those were the hands I imagined.

And I knew the real victim of my curse was me. My desire was more real than anything mystical or legendary. But his was implanted by the call of the Finblood and he would never want me otherwise. I could not bring myself to sleep. I waited for morning in the hope it would bring some change.

Chapter Nine

THE FOLLOWER

T he milk had soured. I could smell it as I entered the kitchen and my heart sank, I would be expected to fetch more. But not before I had slipped out of the house to witness the sunrise.

Within these small hours there was escape from drudgery and memories of a man who had planted only the seed of curiosity.

I would force myself to look away from that cross. Revulsion of God was not the reason, but Mammy thought it so. I did not quash her presumption. My face was drawn on that paper within, there was no way to say if it was not.

But sometimes I would ache to look upon it to see what subtle differences there were. To see which parts of myself were within her. Only on the outside, surrounded by sky and sea could I forget.

On this morning I was suitably distracted as I made my way down to the shore. The morning dew was cold on my skin. I was surprised to see those boats still moored, tethered to the land by rope. Breaking their necks carrying supplies on their backs, there were three men moving amongst the sand and water.

Child of the morning... Said the great whale, unexpectedly, as they came into the bay.

"So it would seem." I sighed in response, as the blood of the sky streaked across the horizon.

Will you not come to us this day?

"I would love nothing more. But I will not go into the water and you know that perfectly well."

The spray from his back made that most comforting of sounds. I closed my eyes against it and allowed myself to imagine the water taking me to them.

Dearest Finola, know you not why we come here?

"To see your beautiful Finfolk and bask in these waters, is it not?"

Mankind does not see all it is meant to. That part of you will remain. But your Finblood has begun to flow. See with your Fin eyes. Why have we come here?

My Fin eyes? I could only see with the eyes I was born with. What mythical eyes were these?

"Speak not in riddles, whale! Always riddles and questions unanswered! You infuriate me."

Always you return. Because you know why we are here, do you not?

Did I? Had I doubted myself so much that I had known and somehow forgotten? What folly was this? What did it matter to me the reason that they came here? It was enough of a joy to me that they came for no reason at all.

"It matters not to me why you come. But you give me great comfort, when you do not speak cryptically. So, I will take comfort in that and question it no further."

Ah, Finola. You are not ready.

The birds came in from the rocks, diving towards the water as the whales headed back out to sea. Inside their dizzy squawks I saw their words in blinding colour. They told me to wait.

"Yes, I have waited!" I said to them as they landed on the water and waited for the fish to surface. "Worry not about that. I am waiting still."

The sky was turning blue. It was time to turn back. But I would not make it there alone, standing behind me, his arms folded securely, was the little man I had seen once before.

Upon his folded arms were pictures of women baring their naked breasts. Suddenly I felt an overwhelming urge to protect my own.

I pulled my shawl around me tighter and stepped back. His face looked at me peculiarly, as if he could not understand my presence. Had I ever renounced the solitude of this place? Now, as it was invaded, did I begin to feel that trespass. How solitude would have served me well now.

But there was none to be found, not even in the small hours as others slept. All was lost and I didn't like the way he looked at me with those disapproving eyes. He was a good inch shorter than me but built with muscles that could crush the heads of tiny sparrows and eagles alike. He frightened me a little and I did not want to linger in his company.

"Who might you be talking to?" He asked, puzzled, looking out into the empty waters.

"Myself. If I choose to. What business is it of yours?" I replied, scorned.

His eyes turned from disapproving to malevolent. "Well there's no need for such spite, I only asked."

I picked my skirts up and began to return to the house. His eyes followed me, silently and hungrily. Ah, yes it was hunger. A man such as he with breasts inked upon his skin. I would do well to avoid being in his company again. Not simply because he had seen me speaking to the birds, but because he made me feel sick within.

"Say, have you any milk to spare up at your place?" He called after me, following at my heels.

"No, it has soured." I said curtly and began to quicken my pace.

He stopped and I did not wait for him to speak more. I could hear all the creatures around me crying out my name. Their warning was clear.

Beware the pictured man! Beware!

Only behind the closed door of The Hylands did they silence themselves, but if voices could echo against air, theirs did. I began to feel a headache, like dark storm clouds brewing within.

If I could reach the house without speaking another word, I would be safe. I did not feel safe in his company, he unnerved me in a way I had never felt before. As if he wished me harm but would not inflict it yet.

He began to walk again and stayed a good pace behind me, those little legs carrying him over the terrain with difficulty. He was almost the same height as a child not grown. But everything about him was man.

"I don't suppose I could impose upon you to bring us some, when you have fresh?" He asked, politely enough. But his undertone was sarcastic.

"I shall ask my brother to bring you some." Ah yes, he would not like another altercation with Rohan.

He was aware of me, my body moving. I would have no choice but to strike him down dead if he touched me. The birds began to circle overhead, their warning crying out onto the wind. But none could hear it, save for me.

Some of them swooped to my defence, flying past the little man's head as he tried to gain on me. I stood and watched their wings fluttering, his arms arched against them. The pictures inked upon them lost under feathers. He cursed them, his eyes searching for me amidst the attack.

"What in God's name is this?!" He cried; his voice lost below the squawking.

I raised a hand, and their beady eyes saw it. They retreated, leaving the little man crouched like a child afraid of the dark.

"The birds behave strangely sometimes." I told him, as I watched them return to the rocks. "They cannot bear to see an injustice."

He was shaking. His arms still raised against invisible flocks.

"I shall do well to remember that." He swallowed, as if the threat against me had been forgotten. "It would seem they obey your command."

They loved me; I could feel it reaching to me from the sky. They covered me with a protection I could bear without bruises. I loved them in return.

"That would be absurd." I said, forming pictures within my mind which spoke to the birds in thanks.

"Yes, it would. Yet I find myself believing it could well be true."

Return me to the Eynhallow of my hatred. The dead land that spawned me and rejected me. That place that was alone at the end of the world, where none could find me.

"The whales would capsize our boats and the birds would peck at our heads. Even the people here would bite." Sneered the little man, looking towards The Hylands.

"Then go back to a place where they do not." I said resolutely, turning my back on him and continuing back to the house.

His laughter was low and mocking. "You think yourself monarch of this Isle? While Queen Victoria sits on her throne, do you sit upon yours?"

If there was a monarch of this land, then certainly it was not me. This little man, this vile creature, he began to enrage me.

Where once had been fear, it gave way to a very real anger that he would dare to follow me.

"Why do you follow me, little man?" I hissed, baring my teeth. "Your request for milk has been noted."

But it was not the milk he desired. Unshaken by his assault, I sensed his bravery return. Brandishing a furtive smirk, he checked our surroundings for prying eyes.

"Ah, bashful one, aren't we? I know many a girl your age would be glad of a fellow to follow their every move!"

Bashful would have meant I returned his attention. In some small form. But all I felt was revulsion and pity.

"I am not glad." I said firmly.

He raised an eyebrow. "Is that so?"

"Build your houses. Keep your horses and whatever else may please you. But do not follow me. Do not even speak to me."

It was a fair warning. My capabilities unknown, I felt the swell of birds ready to surge again. But what they could achieve from their violent onslaught, I did not know.

"Oh aye? And if I do not?" He tested me. "Shall you have those birds of yours peck me to death? Or those whales capsize my boat? Or perhaps you'll have the cows defecate on my shoes?" He almost laughed.

But it was I who laughed first. A rebellious mocking sound that broke the wind and silence. The cows? Such heightened beings would not leave their dreams long enough to know where it was, they defecated.

"Do not laugh at me, stupid girl!" He roared then, pacing over the uneven ground to face me.

He did not like to be laughed at. All the petulance and sarcasm gone; he met my laughter with venomous anger. I imagined him as a child, mocked by the other children for being much smaller. How much had he given of himself to become that bigger man? There was nothing left but a wencher and a drinker, and a broken soul who did not know how to walk away from insult.

"I shall have to teach you some manners." He spat, those sinewy hands reaching for my skirt.

Small, unassuming hands that had arms too large bearing over them. Oh yes, he would meet his reckoning now. In open fields, and cloudless sky, his sin would not go unseen.

I closed my eyes and waited for the onslaught that would surely come. Feathers and blood and broken beaks. Their voices came in flurries of pictures, too swift for me to understand. But I heard them come overhead and I would not be the only one.

Rohan knew their sound, when they had flown over the lifeless body of Nathan Munro. He would know that they signalled an omen. But would he find me? I felt hands upon me, but they did not grasp at me in urgency. He pulled at me, not in desire but in refuge. He pulled my body before him, seizing me in an iron grip. He was using me as a shield as the birds descended.

I felt the cool air from their wings grace my skin, but they did not touch me. Above the sound of the wind was a shrill scream that came not from me but from the little man beneath.

I opened my eyes. Birds came from each side, swooping down so that they might catch their prey. Some of them reached him, pecking pieces of flesh from his bare hands and arms. White feathers and blood. How swift would be his destruction? His or theirs? I felt his arms constrict around me, fighting them off. I heard some of them fall to the ground. *Do not die for me, precious birds! Do not bleed for me!*

"Have mercy! Please... Have mercy!" He cried, but his voice went unheard.

I could smell blood. White wings became red and I was never certain if it was his blood or theirs. I remained untouched, standing amongst the carnage with closed eyes and beating heart. He called to them to stop, his arms reaching to catch their wings but instead losing his balance and pulling me to the ground. I laid there until the world went black and not even the smell of blood could penetrate.

Birds flew overhead. Their flight blocking the sun. I stood within a ring of stones watching them, protected by the magic within. There was a dull sense of arms beholding me and voices whispering from beyond where I could not see. But they were not here with me, on this empty plane.

"No, no we must wait. She hallucinates. Soon she will know herself."

The largest of the stones faced the burning light, guiding it into the horizon. The birds had circled and come to rest, their burnt wings causing smoke to fill the air.

"I shall break his neck and throw him into the water to drown, the foul scoundrel!"

The sun died and sent its mark across the sky, the darkness encroaching. The shadows of the stones crept closer and I was aware of the fading light guiding me.

"I fear you may have already broken him. Caleb, he still does not move..."

Ancient ones that know my blood, they seek to find me here and come to worship. But I do not belong here. No, I belong beyond the shadows in another time and place. But where?

"If *she* does not move then all is lost. What is he to me? When *she* is here."

Oh yes, I am surely dreaming. I know that voice, it could seek me in Hell, and I would respond. The dark stones turned, their gray faces submitting to the night. I was safe here in these ancient dreams. But the arms which beheld me grew more solid as the sky turned blue. When I opened my eyes, I knew myself once more, and I forgot where I had been.

"Caleb, look at her eyes…"

Beneath the blue sky was a face that I knew as familiar as my own. I had kept it with me since the first I had set eyes upon it. His eyes were like the water and within them was an anger I could not fathom. He breathed hard; his cheeks flushed pink. I had not seen anything more beautiful til this moment. *Leave me here and I shall have my piece of Heaven. Do not move me, do not move him. We have collided.*

"All is well." He breathed, almost silently.

The air was moist and chill. Rain would come soon. The morning dew came from those falling locks of hair and ran onto my skin like tears. Bowed over me like shelter, his body arched to pull me from the ground.

Do not let me go. If your touch ceases, I will fall and none shall ever make me rise again.

On the ground lay the crumbled body of the little man, bloodied and bruised. His had paid a heavy price for his trespass. The scars would not heal. Forever he would bear them as a cruel reminder of his debauchery. The white-haired man smiled at me; the pleasant features of his face gave me comfort.

"Give her a moment." He said, taking my hand so that I might steady myself.

The birds had returned to the skies, their wounded feathers like a carpet of red and white upon the soil. I bent to pick one, its softness sticky with blood between my fingers. A few of them continued to circle above and then slowly returned to the rocks.

Everything had shifted and altered now. I knew, without being told, why the whales had come to these waters. Why the birds had come to my aid upon the land. They were our protectors. They lent their shape, so that we might take that form to guard our true selves. I would lament of it later.

The white-haired man stared at me expectantly, my body held between him and the beating heart I felt so tangibly within Caleb's hand.

"Do you mean to take me back to The Hylands?" I inquired, knowing my skirt to be ripped and my skin bloodied.

The white-haired man looked towards the billowing smoke of the chimney. "Would that displease you?"

I felt the pull of Caleb's arms around me as he moved me away, into the circle of his arms.

"Father take him to one of the boats and get him away. If I have not killed him, then there is time yet."

I took one last look before the earth moved away from me, and I was crushed against Caleb's heaving chest as he carried me towards the kirk.

He did not speak as he moved across the uneven terrain, taking great steps that seemed to remove all obstacles. I had not the energy to demand that he put me down, instead submitting myself completely to the scent of him as he held my head against his shoulder.

I was awakened truly, every other sense dulled. All I knew was his scent, the feel of his body against mine and the strength of him as he carried me towards the ruins.

I would that it were real. That I could have you for my own. Oh, sweet love of my aching heart. Be still, do not beat for him. He will only come to hate...

As we approached, he set me to my feet, and I felt myself mourn that he no longer held me close. His hand enclosed around mine, covering it completely. It was dirty and calloused, but still invoked within me that deep arousal that would not rest.

"What is this place?" He asked, inspecting the old broken walls. "The foundations are still intact. We should have built here."

"You cannot." I protested, from a place I knew not where, my voice speaking in urgency. "It is sacred."

"I dare say many a sacred place has other purposes." His free hand touched one of the broken stones, tracing the words that had once been engraved more clearly. "What does this say?"

I closed my eyes. "Favor i ir i chimrie, Helleur ir i nam thite, gilla cosdum thite cumma, veya thine mota vara gort o yurn sinna gort i chimrie, ga vus da on da dalight brow vora Firgive vus sinna vora sin vee Firgive sindara mutha vus, lyv vus ye i tumtation min delivera vus fro olt ilt. Amen"

The Lord's Prayer. In the tongue of the ancient Orkney Norn. Long faded but Mammy had taught it to me so well that I would know those words if I were blind.

"You speak the old language?" He asked, intrigued, his hand still clasped around mine.

"No." I confessed. "There is few now who do."

Suddenly his hand came up, tracing the blood that was not mine which ran down my face. Effortlessly he took a piece of shirt and ripped it until it revealed the bone beneath his neck. It flexed as he breathed, and I felt my own quicken. Gently he placed it to my head and began to wipe it away. It was too much to bear. I did not even feel the tears come, except for when they fell onto his caressing hand.

"Ah, do not cry. I do not know why, but I cannot bear to see it."

If you knew, then you would cast me forth and not look upon me again.

"Do not speak so, you cannot..."

He discarded the shred of cloth and took my face into his hands, with every intention to crush his lips against mine.

"Do not speak so? When I have dreamed of nothing else! I am not a man to woo or beat his oldest friend to within an inch of his life for any woman. Be under no illusion, I am more like him than many care to know! But... I know not what came over me..."

He was scorned. The blood in his veins pulsing wildly, sending him breathless. For the longest moment he held my face in his hands and regarded the detail of my face.

"If you are like him why do you not take me here, now?" I asked nervously.

He pulled away, as if the thought sickened him. Yet he was desperate. The conflict within was written in the eyes that burned into me.

"You think I would not? Do you tempt me?"

So easy it would be to submit to him. Had I ever wanted before this? Nothing seemed so significant. The sight of him here, his jawline flexing as he swallowed hard. Such little things I had never considered now drawing my attention in ways I could never imagine.

"If I tempt you then it is not of my doing." And it was true.

His desire did not come from his own heart. But was driven by my own, my own pulsating blood reaching to him to follow me.

"I think you could drive the most chaste man to madness with that face. You do well to live where no man can find you."

Once I had wanted nothing more than to be gone from here. Now the solitude is my friend.

"You have found me." I said, the words slipping from my lips before I could comprehend.

He stiffened beside me and the muscles and sinews in his arms tensed. For a moment he turned away, pulling those calloused hands through his hair. Desire was such a rich thing, full of longing and confusion. I had entered into it without knowing what would befall me. But how could I have known? I had known nothing til this moment.

"It would be at the end of the world where I would find you. I have been to many places and known many women. But here, where even God himself has forgotten, I find *you…"*

His voice curled around the word. Hunger and pain and from somewhere deep within I felt his desire pull at my own. The wind had changed its course, sending the rain above us.

But still we stood, disregarding it as it dampened our hair and ruined our pathway back to The Hylands. What will become of us if we remain here?

"You must not speak so…" I breathed, feeling the earth beneath my feet become unsteady.

With the land becoming a bog, I turned and denied myself my dearest wish. I could not bear to look at him in the rain. I could not conceal the wrong I had done to him, no more than I could conceal the desire to bear my soul. I had locked us both in a cage of white-hot longing, he would be my prisoner if I allowed him to be.

Ah yes, I knew it as I walked away, and his step echoed not far behind. Yes, he would follow me. He would follow me into the water and keep me young and beautiful as my beating finheart decreed.

But that which was human denied such instinct. I would not lead him there; I would not embroil myself in this wasteful passion that was not real. I would not take his heart, given freely or no. He would believe he gave it freely; he would offer it to me and beg me to take it.

"We must not meet like this again." I called to him as I pulled my feet through the cold and wet ground.

"I certainly hope not, I do not wish to find you in such… untoward circumstances… again."

He seemed to find no difficulty navigating the boggy peat, and soon he was at my side, finding my struggle entertaining. In the corner of his mouth was a smile he could not contain. It lingered on his lips, threatening to break into laughter.

I turned to him with my most melancholy glare. "Trust your initial feeling. This place is cursed, and so am I. So, shall you be, if you remain in my company."

He smirked. "I am damned for my sins; I am certain of that. But never have I longed to be cursed as this before. Curse me, if you will. But do not send me away."

"I thank you for your help. But I will speak with you no more. Go back to your father, he will be wondering where you are."

He watched me pull my foot from beneath the muddy soil, my shoe covered with the stuff. "Pig headed woman!" He spat coarsely, pulling me from the mire and back into the arms I had secretly longed for.

I was far too taken aback to protest. Pig headed? This was a revelation to me. Melancholy and strange. But never pig headed. When we came to steady ground, he laid me onto my feet. I was still deciding on whether I was insulted.

"Ah, don't be like that. Your anger only serves to make you more beautiful."

I peered at him through the raven hair, bedraggled and wet as it was. I was on the brink of showing him the palm of my hand but there was something in his face that jested with me. I could not help but smile.

He sighed slowly; his jesting washed away in the rain. "I was wrong. That smile is what serves your beauty most."

Already I was grieving the sight of him. That I would turn my back and walk away from him. Already I had begun to feel the cracks appear in the centre of my chest where I felt the hottest desire.

His face was searching mine for some answer, some response. But there he would find none. It was like a sickness washing over me, the grief of knowing he would never truly love me.

Do not seek for unrequited love. I shall bury it so deep not even the Ghosts will know its face. It will end here, in the wind and rain. It will wash us clean of this false desire. Do not follow me. Even in dreams, do not follow me…

"Not today." He murmured under his breath. "No… not today. Come, I will take you back to The Hylands."

In silence he led me back towards the house. I felt his brooding as he walked a few paces in front, conscious to look behind that I was still present but not too close.

Only when we reached the gate to the house did he turn to me and whisper a fleeting goodbye. I was bereft. Oh, the sweetness of him was all consuming. Nothing could have prepared me for this, I did not dare try to fathom it. I closed my eyes against the rain and recalled each movement of his lips, the way he smiled with one corner of his mouth and could transform from terrifying to jovial in a single heartbeat. The stubble of his strict jawline, and how it served only to make him more desirable. Those unflinchingly intimidating eyes, that bore into me as if he saw my true self but did not care.

Yes I had bound his fate to me, my desire had sung to him and he had heard my song. I would live in turmoil now, avoiding his constant presence and the temptation to allow his desire to consume me. For the first time I considered returning to the water. For the first time I had a reason to go. But tethered to the land, could I release myself from it? As I made my way up the garden path, I allowed myself a backwards glance at the sorry waves that whipped into a frenzy and I knew it was calling to me.

Chapter Ten

THE RING OF STONES

procession of lights snaked through the darkness, weaving their flickering glow into the distance. It seemed that I stood amongst them, moving towards the place of sacrifice.

Upon a great tor, where eyes of the world could view its great bounty, I looked across the land and waited for the sun to rise. All about me were whispering chants of a language I had never heard before. Their faces cloaked in dark robes, only their painted hands revealed themselves curled around ancient candles.

But I was not afraid and as the light of the sun flooded the land, I became aware of the ringed stones around us. High and imposing, I had been here before.

Once, in fleeting dreams that came upon me unwanted. Shadows shrouded me, the cold stone hiding the light. Painted hands moved me along the procession, until I was stood at the centre upon a table of stone. Barefoot and lucid, their chants became fevered until they reached a great crescendo.

Robes fell, taking the darkness with it. Standing before me were the naked bodies of men and women painted in strange colours, breasts adorned with the handprints of men and torso's lined with ancient symbols I did not recognise.

Ceridwen they whispered. *Felkyo.*

Still I was not afraid but moved by their apparent worship. *Foweer hing-hangers, An'fower ching-changers, An' een comes dinglan efter…* They sang in harmonious chorus.

The cow bells of old chimed in the air and I could smell that great scent of the beasts. They brought them into the stones, the spiritual beings that could open the doors from this world to the next. Their blood was spilled onto the stones that we might delight in the sacrifice.

Where am I? I know this place. I have always known this place and yet still I am lost. I am must find myself and return to my rightful place.

"Finola?" A voice called, as if planted on the wind, sounding over the rapturous chants. "Finola… you must wake!"

Blow out your candles, for I am gone…

Bethan's face stared down at me, her arms gripping my shoulders tightly. "You were dreaming."

More dreams to disturb my slumber. More mysterious demons to spite my only rest.

"I am awake now; you need not shake me more." I sighed, turning away from her petulant glare.

"I'm sorry, I did not mean to… Only that, you were speaking in a strange language. I was afraid…"

It would be her that witnessed my torment. "Be not afraid. It was just the madness of dreams."

She pondered this for a moment before uncurling the rags from her hair to reveal perfect ringlets that fell about her childish face.

"Do you think dreams are truly mad? I do not remember mine. Or perhaps I do not dream at all."

More mindless chatter, more innocent wondering. I could not fathom my own, what hope was there for her? Again, I was envious of her. To forget my dreams would be something.

"It matters little. Dreams are for when we sleep. When what we do is no longer relevant."

She raised an eyebrow of intrigue. "I was once told that our dreams are what we truly see. Do you think that it's true?"

"I don't know. I care not, now get you down to breakfast. Worry no more about dreams."

But I could not shake the vivid memory of lights upon stone. Voices speaking in chants and the desolate ring around me. I had not woken in time to ask the whales; the house was alive, and I would not go unseen. The pot above the fire was already boiling furiously whilst Aunt Hannah prepared some bread at the table.

Mammy was busying herself at the sink, her shoulders hunched over as she scrubbed something almost violently. Ewan had his nose in a book, sitting inconspicuously by the fire as Bethan tried to stir the pot beside him.

"Where is Rohan?" I inquired.

Mammy ceased her scrubbing. "Always tending to this, to that. But never sits to breakfast. You might know very well where he is."

Aunt Hannah shot me a pensive look, a look which told me never to ask again.

"He might have grown too large to go over my knee, but I am still his Mammy and he is not his Daddy. He has become so insolent. I did not raise him to be so. Aye, there's need of him. But he will not sit to breakfast anymore..."

She began to cry silently, the tears falling mutely. The sight of me did not ease her pain, it only doubled her over so that she could not look.

"I have lost both of my children..." She cried softly, dismissing her tears almost as suddenly as they had come before resuming her scrubbing.

Aunt Hannah rolled her eyes. "Ah, Mary. Such nonsense. Your boy will come to his senses when his grieving ends. Your daughter is right here. Do not be so maudlin."

But she did not recognise me. I was a stranger in the place of the little girl she once loved, and though it grieved me, I could not dwell upon it. She was lost to me as I was lost to her and there was nothing could be done to remedy it now.

"Your son makes a use of himself! Mine sits with his books and speaks seldom; I cannot remember the last time my son spent a day tending to the place as Rohan does!"

Her criticism bore deeply. I saw it in the clenched jaw and white knuckles that turned the pages awkwardly. But Ewan's face did not fluster or acknowledge. It was as if none of us existed in his world. Aunt Hannah stared at him expectantly, her hands on her hips.

"Ewan put that book down! Get you outside and fetch some water from the well! Lest you be at that book all the day!" She threw her apron at him, and it covered his book.

The spite was almost audible. Rising from his place he shuffled towards the door and for a moment I thought he might cry.

But he did not, instead he accepted his fate and went to fetch the water. I felt a shred of pity for him, that he had come here unwanted and remained a pawn of his mother's failings.

"Hannah, you must not speak to him so. Your son grieves as much as mine." Mammy berated.

But she was unrepentant. "No Mary, if he is to survive here, he must adapt. Like all of us."

She had done him a great disservice bringing him here. Where there was nothing for many, there was less for Ewan. I had barely noticed his presence in recent weeks.

Out at the well I was reminded of Daddy bringing in the water during a great storm, the wind urging him to abandon all hope.

For a fleeting moment I saw him standing there in the rain and snow, but it passed and all that remained was the dull sunshine that was hidden by clouds and my little cousin peering down into it as if searching for the bottom.

"You shall not find it." I said, peering into the darkness. "It goes so deeply into the land that it comes out the other side, underneath the sea where we cannot go." And I did wonder for a moment if I threw myself down the well would I end up in those enchanted halls?

It was as if he could not find his voice to respond. He looked away, as if it no longer gave him intrigue. There was not a spark in him that betrayed his interest, it was as if the lights had gone out. I had disliked him, that much was true. But now there was nothing but pity and sadness.

"I have hated this place. I used to live and breathe hatred of it. It was as if it was trying to kill me but would not relinquish me either."

Ah, there was that spark. The disinterest gave way to a softer look that almost gave way to those threatening tears. He opened his mouth to speak, and then closed it without uttering a word.

"I am not Rohan, or Aunt Hannah." I told him. "I too have dwelt in the shadows. You may speak freely with me."

He sighed heavily. "I am not Rohan, either."

"And neither should you be. We have no need for two like him." I surmised.

"But my mother thinks that I should be. She thinks that I should go hunting and fishing and tend the cattle and be large as he is. But I am not large, and I cannot tend cattle or hunt or fish. There is no place for me here."

"I dare say there is no place for any here. But we make one, nonetheless. I used to dream of the day I could leave and now I find myself bound to this place in ways you could never imagine."

His little face was starting to take on another shape. Dead eyes began to see, and he took note of my words.

"I was going to go south to Scotland. I thought maybe I could work in one of those large banks and become an accountant. My teacher said I had a gift at mathematics. Now I cannot remember when last I learned anything of value."

I imagined him in a black suit, carrying a bag and walking through streets of the Scottish cities I had never seen before. I could not vision the scale of the place. Only that Ewan had found his place there.

"Here is where dreams come to die. I shall die with them." He said mournfully.

The clamour of the door opening broke our conversation. Aunt Hannah began throwing old potato peelings at the clucking chickens that had been allowed into the yard.

"Where is that water?"

Ewan sighed heavily, looking at me only once before pulling up the pail. He handed it to his mother in such a way that half of it was spilled, sending the chickens into a frenzy. She cursed him as he went back into the house and then turned to me for absolution. But here she would find none.

"I don't know why you look at me so, I want only for him to accept his fate here." She shrugged. "I have heard about those workhouses in those cities he dreams so well of going to. They'd have us in one of those and then what of dreams? Better this than to take away all hope."

I could not bear to listen to her ramblings more. Aunt Hannah had become worse than the jabbering chickens, with their jumbled thoughts and nonsense.

"Waste not your time on him. He was spoiled by his father and still expects everything which has promised by him. Have you not better things to be doing?"

I turned to face her, expecting to see those hands on her hips, pointing at the work that needed to be done. But instead she paused to smile conspiratorially at the man standing by the garden wall.

"Good Morning. What can we help you with?" She asked, teasing.

Caleb pulled his cap to reveal that dishevelled hair that fell about his face. He wrung it in his hands, as if nervous.

"I'd like a moment with Miss Finola." He replied in those luscious English tones.

I could have killed her where she stood. That playful mockery I could not bear. She skulked away back into the house and left me feeling like I had been caught in the throes of a passionate love affair.

It was in my mind to reprimand him for coming to me like this, but I could not. He pulled a dirty hand through that hair and I was momentarily lost. How dare he come to me like this? I do not have the strength to rebuild my heart for each time I look at him it breaks.

"We have not enough milk to sustain us, and you. Perhaps this is something you should consider before building houses in places you cannot easily access!"

He stared at me implicitly as if I had just shot an arrow through his chest. "I did not come for milk."

"Whatever you came for, it's not here."

He cocked his head to the side, and I felt it pull at that place between my heart and my stomach where it felt the warmest.

"How can you know that?" He asked, suddenly suspicious.

There was something different about him this morning. Vulnerable and sweet. Had I ever been afraid of this beautiful creature?

"There is nothing for anybody here." I surmised.

His lips pursed in thought and I wondered what it would be know them. His eyes looked tired and red rimmed as if he had known no sleep and I was an enemy to myself as well as him.

I wondered what dreams had plagued him and if they had been as vivid of my own. These things I ached to speak with him of, they fulfilled each desire like a sadness that could not be slaked. I would never hold him in my arms, or in my confidence.

"You can send me away until the end of days. But I shall always return until you allow me to love you. You may curse me for it. But the true curse would be to never know you. You may call me fickle and tell me there is nothing for me here, but you have not known the thoughts and dreams I have had. They are binding me to you like sails to the wind. Tell me, I am not crazy? That you feel it too?"

You feel it because of me. Because I desire you, you will come to me like this and put your life in my hands.

"It is not for me to say if you are crazy, or not."

He was crestfallen. He would have one kind word from me, and I would give none. I hoped, in time, he would thank me for it.

"Why do you deny me? You will send me away a thousand times, but each will be a sweet moment between us until the next."

I could not disagree. These stolen moments were more fulfilling that a lifetime without ever having looked upon his face.

"You think I am a man for poetry and sweetness?" He leaned in, pressing his hands against the wall. There he was, the dangerous one I feared. "I do not care for women. They serve a purpose for me, and nothing more. They are easily kept, and just as easily they are gone from me."

His eyes bore into me and would not give me up. His lips twitching with every word. "Never have I given a second thought to a woman. Now I find myself consumed with thoughts of you."

And I with you. Where wild horses once ran free there is now only the wind but once again there is something beautiful upon this land. I would hand myself over willingly, if it were real.

I moved away from him, his eyes watching me as I put some distance between us.

"I have never known the touch of a man. What it may feel like to keep one, or have one gone from me." Ah, but it was a lie.

It was because of that one which had gone from me that I kept myself now hidden.

"You are pure, and I am not. But somehow you give me purity. I care not about my own virtue, my own heart. Take it, it is yours to do as you wish. I beg you to take it!"

He moved closer, climbing over the wall in one graceful movement. The muscles in his arms flexing and the size of him towering over me as he approached. That familiar lump in my throat threatened to choke me as his hands encased my face and lifted my chin to face him. I was powerless to stop it.

"Caleb no... You must not do this. You cannot know what you are doing..."

The sweetness of his breath was warm upon my skin. I tried to look away, folds of my hair falling over my eyes. But his hand smoothed it away and I could not stop the tears from falling at the sight of him touching me. I allowed myself to seize a stolen look upon him, with the promise that I would do so never again.

For the briefest moment my eyes met his and there it seemed that a veil of something I had no words for came down. I noticed the colour of his eyes, a deep blue speckled with green like the deepest parts of the ocean. His upper lip was fuller than the other as he parted them, breathing heavier now as he laid his head against mine. I barely felt his hands as they went around my waist and pulled me closer.

All was silence save for the drums within.

The beating of my heart sent my blood into violent pulses, screaming his name. How could this not be real? How could this tangible need not be borne of something natural? The human within me still lived. Perhaps it was that part of me which called to him and he came to me of his free will? I wanted it to be true. I had never wanted anything more.

"Finola Gray."

Mammy was standing in the garden, her eyes looking Caleb up and down. He moved away from me but did not take his hand from mine.

"Mammy?" I breathed, lightheaded.

She stared at me scornfully, the unspoken words telling me I should know better. His hand felt solid in mine and would not let me go, even if I had tried to free my grip.

"Mr. Bishop. Was there any reason for your visit today? Other than to see my daughter?" She asked expectantly.

He swallowed hard, that part of his throat that belonged only to a man flexed and I thought he would falter.

"No Mrs. Gray. I came only for your daughter."

She nodded slowly, the anger within her unfathomable face growing. But it was not him she was angry with and I would repent later.

"I see, well she has work to be done. As do you, or you'll be living without a roof above your head come winter. Be off with you now!"

She would wait for him to leave. As he went back over the wall, I could not deny my beating heart. I wanted to run with him.

"Now, get you to the stables there's milk to be fetched." Mammy ordered; her stare pensive. "You'll not be seeing him again."

"Shall I close my eyes, then?" I retorted, taking my leave of her.

It would have been foolish of me to stay. She no longer looked at me like a mother should. I would show her the same courtesy. She would try to keep us apart and for that I was glad. But not because he was wrong for me or because she cared for my welfare. But because our secrets would unravel once more.

The day was long and tedious.

As I milked the cows and listened to their quiet thoughts, I allowed my own mind to wonder. I pictured the ring of stones that I had dreamed of and tried to quieten the vivid memory of standing within it.

Through the gentle touch of my hands to the cow's udders I could hear the whisper of her soul. She asked me if I had lived before, but I could not answer. My flesh lived here and now.

I have known many lives and am content to have many more.

"I would be content to have another life." I sighed, "This one has served me nothing but sorrow."

A thousand years ago I stood amongst the people of this land not as a beast but on two feet. They called me a Healer and came to me when their spirit was sick. I was blessed with the touch of Ceridwen…

Ceridwen? "I have heard that name before."

She is the mother. The life force within us all. Some pray to her as Goddess, others as her child. You will come to know her again, in time…

"Have I ever known her before?"

We have all come to know her. Know you not that your kind are her kindred?

"I do not know much about my kind. I have asked the whales but all they speak is riddles."

She softly laughed. An ethereal sound that came from within and could not be heard outside the mind.

Whales are wise indeed. But have not the patience to explain their wisdom. They are here to escort you and nothing more.

Escort me? I glanced out of the broken barn door and out across the land towards the water. They would always tempt me into the water, requesting that I join them.

"They want to take me back to Finfolkaheem." I said, as if in dream, and it was not a question.

The cow grumbled, her patience for this tedious affair fast fading.

Child be not afraid. They await you, nothing more. They will guide you to that place when your heart desires and not before.

"Why is it that you should know this, and I am kept in the dark? Always I am in the dark! When will I know what I am and what I must do? Already I have Finblood within me, binding to me a human! And yet I am afraid, too afraid to go into the water. I will not leave Rohan…"

I pushed the half empty bucket away from me, thoroughly angered and unable to continue. The cow thought about it for a moment and then stepped towards me, her big black eyes peering at me through long lashes.

Rohan is not Finblood. He cannot make you stay. In time you will come to know your place. There will be no love in the world that could bind you here. You are what you are…

But it was futile. I was suddenly aware that my choices had been preordained. There would be no rest until my destiny was fulfilled.

The creatures of the water and the land and the sky, they knew my fate. The whales waited for me to return. The birds protected me from harm. The cows would give me spiritual wisdom, if they chose to. How could it be that they knew me better than I knew myself? They had been watching. Speaking amongst themselves.

"And what am I?!" I cried. "I dream of the ringed stones and know not what it means. They tell me that love will be impossible, that it will be nothing more than my Finheart calling for a human to drag into the water! The birds tell me to wait, but what am I waiting for?"

I kicked over the buckets, spilling the milk onto the ground.

"I tell you; I *do* love… I feel it in my bones and in my gut. He would follow me into that water, there we will love each other with none to say otherwise. But it will not be without consequence… will it? What the water will gain, so the land shall lose. Is it true? Is Eynhallow's day done?"

The wind whistled in through the cracks in the walls. Ghosts screaming to us that they remained. The cow closed her eyes for a moment before trotting out into the field without caring if I lived or died. Such was the nature of Cows and their incessant need to meditate and chew grass.

But it was more than I had ever been given before. She had taken pity upon me and spoken when no other would.

I sighed at the spilled milk and considered my own temper. Yes, I was angry. I had never been blessed with grace or patience, now when both were needed, I found myself shaking with the tempest of a fury that would not sleep.

I would have it so that I never need tear myself in half, but it would be the undoing of me. I was half human, a land dweller. I was half Finfolk, of the water.

The human in me would stay, but that other half wondered what lie beneath the waves. Waiting for answers instead of seizing them was becoming tedious. Every day was a constant reminder that I was lost between the two worlds that would someday collide.

I tried to remember being brought from the water to the land, placed in my Daddy's arms so that I might live amongst my human counterparts, but I could not picture it. I could recall nothing before the night of Rohan's birth, that which sealed me to the land.

For a moment I thought of his little hand in mine and the fingers curling around my hair as I soothed him in the dead of night. I would cry for that boy who was no more, but not today. Today I would clean up the milk and accept the things I could not control for what they were. Even the things that scared me and broke my heart.

The table was set for supper as the sun began to fall beneath the horizon. Rohan appeared in the doorway, dirtied and sweat drenched from his work in the fields.

It struck me that I had not seen him all the day.

He took his place and wiped his brow with a thick forearm that flexed his jaw at the smell coming from the pot above the fire.

"That does smell divine." He said, almost salivating.

Mammy was quick to cut his bread and plate his food, scurrying from one end of the kitchen to the other. Aunt Hannah waited by the window, her son nowhere to be found.

"I do wonder where Ewan is, never has he been later for supper for always he is here with his nose in a book…" She fretted.

Bethan put down her cup and eyed the door like a puppy awaiting its master. "It is impossible to get lost on this Island. I know, I have tried." She said stoically.

Rohan grunted through mouthfuls. "It is not impossible to fall into some unknown part of it though, I know. I have tried."

He had been sour this morning. But not for a moment did I think he would depart from us. No, he was too afraid, too weak. For a moment I felt a sickness wash over me, what if some misfortune had come upon him? For all he was, it was not much, he still felt like my cousin.

"I cannot sit here and wait. I must try to find him before darkness comes." Aunt Hannah said, pulling her shawl about her.

Bethan would have followed but Mammy placed a firm hand upon her shoulder. "No, little one. There must be one here if he returns."

But her eyes flew to Rohan, who begrudgingly put down his plate and went to get his gun from the doorway.

"He had better be sitting on a rock eating stale bread with a fishing pole in his hand, or I'll have his belly in that pot and we'll feast for a month!"

I watched Bethan curl away from him, disgusted and afraid of him as he slammed the door shut behind him. She ran to her room with tears in her eyes that did not come easily to her.

Mammy and I stood for a moment in the echoes of those who had gone before us, staring at the near empty room.

She cleared the unused plates and cups, standing them on the shelves before stirring the pot and slaking the fire. Anything but look at me.

"So, what must you do?" She asked, her body slumped over the fire. "Would you go and look for your cousin?"

"What good would I be? No doubt Aunt Hannah has got the Bishops to aid her by now."

Gripping the wooden spoon in her aging hands, she turned to me and pointed it at me ominously. "You know fair well what I speak of! Those damned birds, or the whales. They will find him. Now go…"

At first, I could not comprehend what she asked of me. Always I had hidden that part of me from her. She would not hear of my powers or listen to their potency but now she came to me bidding that I use them despite all else.

Her hands were shaking as she began to pray in the firelight, asking for forgiveness for what she had asked of me.

"Mammy…" I began, but it was futile. She would not hear me.

Chapter Eleven

THE LOST ONE

It was as if a distant memory came to me now as I watched the solitary torches move across the horizon. But it would not cloud my judgement as I went to the water lighted only with my knowledge of the ground.

Stars had already begun to appear between the moving clouds, the moon shining intermittently onto the water.

They would search for him in all the wrong places. But here, uninterrupted, I would know his fate.

The great whale came to me, as he always did when I called and though I could not see him in the black waters he made his presence known to me.

"I may not have much time. But I must know if a boy came into the waters today. You must tell me if he was taken." I whispered onto the wind.

Such a one as he would not make a Finwife happy.

"That is irrelevant to me now, please… You must tell me if he went into the waters!"

I heard the waters crash around his moving body, the vapour from his back spraying into the night sky.

He came but did not come. He is afraid of us.

"More nonsense. I should have known better. You hear my voice, but you do not hear my words. Why do you give me comfort and then take it from me?"

Clouds shrouded the moonlight and I knew he would speak to me no more this night. The birds had gone to their rest, the dark sky overhead empty of life save for the growing darkness and threat of rain.

I would find him blind, in the dark with only the sporadic moon to guide me.

He must have come this way but did not stay. I watched as the others searched the distant shoreline, but I was not drawn that way. The shadow of the kirk loomed and as I made my way over peat and bog, I felt the first drops of rain.

I would crawl on my belly if I had to, there was a sense that I was being called there. Like the old stones in that ring of ancient worship it seemed that a third eye had been opened. I could hear the animals. Could I hear the human soul?

This I would not speak of. Whatever ancient mystery had been awakened would have to wait.

The rain danced on the wind, light and cold. Twilight died and gave way to the pitch of black. I was alone and not even the sight of those torches in the distance could comfort me.

Ewan, where are you? If you are close, you must reach out to me…

But there was nothing but howling wind and crashing waves. I could have spited him. I could have cast him forth into that place he feared so much for consuming me this way. I wished that I had never taken an interest in him, that he had remained in the shadows and dwelt there without voice until his time was done.

But I could not reproach him, he had not asked to come here no more than any of us had. I could feel the wet and stick of the mud beneath me, clinging to my skirts and pulling my feet further into the ground. Each step becoming harder, until I could pull no more.

I almost laughed at the idiocy, of the memory of being carried over the bog and placed down onto solid ground. Oh, how I cursed those arms now for not pulling me out of the mire. The blood in me ran cold, as slowly I sank. Perhaps this was my retribution? For a moment I thought of Nathan Munro and that old haunting face of his. I wondered if his soul had forgiven me.

Finola Gray. You must stand…

I heard the voice come to me; a shy whisper that lingered only a touch higher than the wind. Such a voice as that, chanting almost, standing above. I lifted my aching head to see the entire herd of cows standing on the horizon, their shadows gathering around me. Their ethereal voices lifted me, above the land and sea, until I could feel not cold but warmth.

Fire brandished close to my skin, not burning but soothing. Did I fly above the world with my beloved birds? Or did I run across the land with the wild foxes I missed so?

Guide their lights... Bring them forth... She is weakening.

Ah, sweet songs. Take me with you to that place you go, when chewing grass and being milked, where is it you go? Shall I ever know? They would not leave me. Even now, in the falling rain, I was saved once again.

"Do you see him, Isaac?" I heard them call.

The cows dispersed, their beautiful voices drifting away, and I found myself waking from dreams that had come to me wide awake. Firelight flooded the sky and all too soon I felt a fool once again.

"There is something down here, bring that torch. I cannot see..."

I lowered my face against the revealing light. But I could not hide myself. My weakened body fell into his, all too soon my dreams of moving against flames became all too real. He held the torch above me in one hand and in his other he held me.

"Ah, you stupid girl!" He cried; his rain fallen skin dripping onto mine.

Yes, I had been stupid. But I was not done. It was not weakness that had trapped me, no. I felt it now as he held me against that hard chest of his. I was renewed. I listened to the hooves return to the open fields, and with them they had taken a part of my soul and with me remained a part of theirs.

For the first time, I had that same recollection I heard in their thoughts. Only it was my own recollection. Was this a part of them, leant to me as the whales had leant their shape to my kind? Or was it a part of myself I had yet to discover? As I began to regain composure, the pressure of my pulse against Caleb's wet skin became more than I could bear.

"Do you mock me?" I asked, moving away from his touch. "Always you mock me."

Isaac appeared at the brow of the small hill, shooing the cows away. I heard their annoyance in distant whispers and could not hide a small, almost indecipherable smile.

"Miss Gray? What do you do out here?" He asked, concerned, waving his torch before my eyes.

Caleb's grip advanced, I could no longer move away. It was as if he was protecting me from some unseen foe. But I sensed no threat. Since the little man's departure there had been no ill feeling. Save for when Caleb looked at me and I lost all my resolve.

"Go and tell the others. I will take her back to The Hylands. Keep looking!" He said authoritatively. Although Isaac was obviously older, he did what he was bidden.

Such was Caleb's ardour. He could invoke respect in any man, without having earned it. Much like his father, but more commanding in the place of his father's kindness.

"I do not mock you." He said to me, when Isaac had gone over the horizon. "But if you insist on continuing to be stupid, then I shall say so."

"Am I stupid that I wish to help find my cousin? Is that stupidity? Always it must be you who will find me, and not him then?" I asked.

He shook his head painfully, as if remembering the flesh of an old scar torn open.

"I am sorry for the last time. Simon would lust you. As he would lust a crippled maid or an old crone. The promise of breasts is all consuming to him. But he is gone now and yet here I find you troubled by yourself out on the moors again."

"Troubled? Is that how you see me?" And I was saddened by the tone in my voice.

I wanted him to see me as a leaf passing in the wind. As nothing more than a spell of rain on a clear day. To see me troubled, was to see me at all.

"I am perfectly capable of continuing my search. A little mud will not hinder much and, I am certain my knowledge of the land will ensure his safe return before your pathless ramble."

The air hit me as he allowed me to stand. Air, or spiritual awakening? I breathed in the rain and almost instantly I felt Ewan's heartbeat in the moisture. Or was it my own? Or Caleb's? I looked towards the kirk and remembered why I had come there.

"Your knowledge of the land certainly is something." He said, and I knew then that he mocked me.

Why is it that he must always find me in such need? I had never needed him before, why should I find myself foolishly needing him now? I was being blindly deceived by my own magic.

I did not offer a bold response. The wind picked up and sent my hair into disarray. The long strands of it swept off my shoulders and into his face. But he did not push it away, instead placing the locks between his fingers and touching it softly. I heard him breathe deeply, before the wind silenced everything else.

Even the wind shall make him touch me. Am I now powerless?

"Wherever you wish to look, I shall go with you." He said softly, lifting his torch above us to guide the way.

Any hint of mockery gone, something else invaded him then. He went before me, leading me towards the kirk like a protector against an old foe. But the dead stones were just echoing of a past long gone. None would hurt me here.

But then it didn't seem to matter, and I was simply touched that he angled his body around me so that if any should try to harm me, they would reach him first.

"The damn boy chooses a good night to run away." I heard him murmur, his face shrouded in darkness as he turned the torch towards the ruins.

"To run would be something. Here we only walk, and slowly at that." I replied, keeping my eyes on the horizon.

"This place is not part of the rest of the world, that much is clear to me."

He turned to face me then, the torch light throwing shadows across his glorious face. His jaw flexed as he swallowed, and I thought I would go insane at the sight of it.

"Perhaps you are right." I almost whispered, but the words were lost on the wind.

Without permission he took my hand. His skin was warm despite the cold air and I was glad of it. Part of me was scolded by his presumption that I would not mind.

But we had been here before and he was all too aware of my fading resolve. Perhaps there was a reason that I continued to find myself in these predicaments that required him to save me.

Whatever that reason was I could not deny that I was its victim too. Still I thought of Nathan Munro and those maddened eyes that bore into me like wildfire.

Sometimes I longed to stare into Caleb's eyes, if only to see if that same madness was there. But I would not allow myself such a pleasure. I was too afraid. Even as he led me into the broken archway of the kirk, I had to look away. His face was shrouded in darkness as he lifted the torch above us.

"We should shelter here until the rain calms. There is little chance of finding him in this…" He said, slightly pleased with himself, as he looked out into the stormy night.

The old stone was wet, and the moss was slime. But in the corner of what was once a place of worship we found some shelter under an old fireplace. The ground had given way to grass, but it was dry enough to sit upon.

I pulled my shawl about me tighter and watched as Caleb stuck the torch into the ground. I felt his body solid beside me, I stiffened against him as he came to keep me warm. The line of his arm rested against mine, leaning towards me ever so slightly. He pulled his coat around him tighter, but soon he began to shiver and not even the torch fire could warm our bones.

He was so big, so strong. But he was not stronger than the Eynhallow wind. Even in Summer, there were nights of desolate cold.

"How do you endure it?" He asked me through gritted teeth.

But there was no way to tell. "Winter has not come yet. If you cannot tolerate summer storms, then you shall perish here."

"I would gladly perish…"

He would not say more. Here in the darkness everything took on another shape. The imposing old kirk gave way to its Ghosts as they cried through the cracks in the stones. Wailing and sobbing, it sounded like a choir of the dead singing out of key. For all of Caleb's strength, here in this tiny corner of an ancient church he gave way to a nervous fear and moved closer and closer towards me.

"Tell me about England." I asked, wishing myself away.

He sighed thoughtfully and I was sorry that I had asked. But then his body softened, and it was as if we heard no more Ghosts.

"I care not for it. There I was just hired help at my father's factory. It was good work and I was glad of it. But never was there fresh air or sunlight. I think that's why he came here. For the air and light."

I tried to imagine the gloomy place he spoke of. But I could not. Not even in books or dreams had I ever heard of such a place.

"I lodged with Simon…" His voice stopped at the name, he waited for me to flinch.

"It matters not to me." I told him. "You have known him a long time."

"We lived in a house with a few of the other factory workers. My father always asked me why I did not continue to live with him, but I would not have the other workers know he was my father. Simon knew, and of course Isaac but none of the others. Always there would be this whore, or that whore coming and going. The boys liked to have a woman in their bed, and I was no different. But it was futile. They meant nothing to me. Yet they would always come to me. Always me. Simon would use me to find a wench of his own, because they would never choose him of their free will." He seemed to smile wryly as he spoke, the torch light igniting his face.

But I did not dare look, for fear that I would never take my eyes from him.

"But none of it matters now. The factory is gone and so are the whores."

He turned to me then, rain falling from the hair that hung about his wet face. "Tell me about Eynhallow."

But it was not as colourful as that. Still I found I could speak easily in the relative darkness, where my voice was bodiless. I spoke freely of the other families, and their demise. I spoke of my childhood friend, the only friend I had ever known, Jenny McAvoy. How I had missed her terribly in those first months.

And even now, when my mind was free of current affairs, I would allow myself to slip back and think of her and our childish games.

But I could not speak of everything, those things which were closest to my heart I kept there. I did not speak Nathan Munro's name. I would never reveal the true potency of what I had learned in that year we had spent here alone.

He was silent for a while, his eyes looking dead ahead into the torch flame. Neither of us noticed the wind had almost ceased.

"I wish we could have come here in those days. But perhaps without Hamish Munro's land we could not come at all. So, for that, at least, I am thankful. Perhaps it will be like that again someday."

But I could not shake those words. *Eynhallow's day is done.* It sent a potent shiver down my spine, which he mistook for coldness. He offered me his coat, but I declined.

"They had been here for generations, as had my Daddy's family. It was in their blood. To watch them die and leave, I shall never forget. We were not spared though; we were left behind. This is not a place to build memories. You do well to trust your first initial feeling."

"It matters little. That sense of foreboding seemed to all but fade at the sight of you on the boat that night. The way you stood there breathless and strange. Somehow I knew you had come for me and I must follow."

It was my finblood, nothing more. Do not forget yourself Finola. It is nothing more than the draw of your allure, the calling of your desire which brings him near.

"I came only to warn you about the waters at night. That is all."

He shifted beside me, raising a hand to catch the rain. It was nothing but vapour.

"And why should you care? I dare say you did only come to warn me, but why? What does my life matter to you? Would it have mattered so much to you if I had come to any harm? You had yet to meet me and yet you came to prevent me from leaving. You keep saying no to me. But here we are, in the dead of night. We shall find ourselves here again, no doubt. No matter how many times you reject me."

I began to despise his certainty. But it was borne from something else, not hatred or loathing but passion and wanting. How strange it felt to want to strike his face and kiss it at the same time.

"Do you think I could live with blood on my hands? Regardless of who you are to me?"

For a moment I saw it there. The blood which had already been spilt by my hands. But it was just the firelight dancing upon my skin.

No, he was not like Nathan Munro. He did not come to me with falsities and a craving for me which came from binding spells.

But did I dare to believe it? Had I enchanted myself? Why did he not take me here and now? He would laugh at me if I suggested such a thing. But not Nathan Munro, no he would have stared at me gravely until I had agreed to his false instincts.

Caleb seemed to come to me from somewhere else entirely. Perhaps fate and not enchantment? For a moment I dared to believe, but as swiftly as it had come, I allowed it to fade. No, he did not love me. It was not real.

"And who am I, to you? Am I a neighbour, friend? Or shall I show you what I would like to be?"

Suddenly I was afraid. His body became imposing. I was nothing but a trembling girl with no knowledge of the things which he spoke of. He would show me, if I allowed him. Of that, I was certain. Would he mistake my trembling for the touch of the biting cold? Or would he know I was afraid?

"You are Caleb." I replied through chattering teeth.

He sighed thoughtfully, in one smooth movement he took the torch from the ground and held it above us. It was as if I had not spoken, or if he had not heard me.

"The rain has settled. We should get you back to The Hylands. Perhaps Ewan has been found, or if we linger, they will send out a search for us also." He offered me his hand and he pulled me to my feet.

But he would not be there. Somehow, I knew it before we had even left the ruins. The clouds had given way to stars and the moonlight shone down onto the water like fallen snow. It shimmered and moved upon the water's surface as Caleb lead me back out into the night.

All was silent, save for the crashing waves and distant whispers of the creatures all around us. I would have let him take me back if it weren't for the low sobs coming from the darkness. Caleb heard it too, his natural instinct moving me behind his body. Slowly he moved the torch towards the shadow of the kirk, but there was nothing but darkness and air.

"No." I said, shifting myself to stand beside him. "Not here…"

The sobbing quietened for a moment and the silence tried to convince me I had heard nothing at all. It was a low, guttural sound. As if it could not be slaked. It came from a place of great pain and suffering. I followed the sound of it, almost silent as it was and found him sitting in a ditch behind the ancient stones. Crouched low, his head bowed into his knees, he did not see me until Caleb brought the light overhead.

How sad I felt looking at him. He was broken beyond all repair. Not even his eyes could deny he was done with this life, red rimmed and tired from crying.

I wondered if he had cried much, or if he had cried at all before this? It was as if his tears could form an ocean were, they not left to drop from his sodden cheeks. My poor cousin. Finally, I felt something for him.

"Ewan." I said, "Why did you not make your presence known?"

He resolutely bowed his head and would not come out from his hiding place. "I had no mind to. I am as well here as I am anywhere."

"Ah, boy! You'll catch your death out here." Caleb said jovially, trying to raise his spirits.

But Ewan seemed not to care. "Yes. Perhaps I will."

"If I do not return with you, what will your Mammy think? And your little sister? They are worried for your safety."

Again, he lowered his head, refused to acknowledge me. The defiance began to irritate me. I was wet and cold, and I had almost come to harm in my search for him.

"Hold the torch." Caleb said authoritatively, freeing both hands so that he could reach into the ditch and pull Ewan from his misery.

As small and timid as he was, he put up a bold fight. Kicking and punching the air as Caleb moved him onto the ground.

"How dare you!" He spat, trying to push Caleb aside so that he might return to the dark and muddy ditch.

But Caleb did not shift, no matter how hard Ewan pushed. I wondered how differently it would be if Rohan were here. A boy of the same age, yet his strength magnified. I had not realised just how weak he was.

"You'll thank me tomorrow when you have slept a good night in your own bed and wake to a good breakfast! Get you back home lad and stop this nonsense!"

Ewan's face softened. Anger soon became desperation. He would not go back, even if Caleb carried him there on his back. He would not go back.

So, we reached an impasse. Caleb would not take him against his will for fear of hurting the poor boy and Ewan would not follow us back to The Hylands.

But I could not return without him to greet Mammy's face imploring me to impose more magic upon myself. She could not love me anymore, even if she had wanted to. I was an abomination to her God; I knew she would hate herself for calling upon me to use my ungodly powers. She would hate us both if I returned empty handed.

"I won't go back there." Ewan sobbed; his whole body racked as he spoke. "I don't exist there."

"Then where do you exist?" Asked Caleb, his patience waning.

Ewan looked out onto the sea and beyond, as if searching for his place.

"Don't speak to me. I do not know my own voice. I have not used it for so long." He replied vacantly.

Caleb shook his head vehemently and sighed. "I have not the time for this. I was asked to find you, and so I have. I am done here. It matters not to me if you stay or if you do not. But I am not leaving Finola out here. Will you come with me?"

His hand reached out to me and I was overcome with temptation to take it. But I would not live with myself if I did. Ewan, little and weak as he was, had put up a good fight. I did not want to see him come up against Rohan, casting his eye upon him in that way he did.

Those were the eyes of a boy who had become a judgemental and angry man. Grief had caused both of them too much pain. But it had made Rohan a beast and Ewan a shadow. In my heart I could not take him back, and yet still I found myself wanting to.

"Take us down to the shoreline. I shall remain with him there until dawn."

We stayed within sight of the house, under the cover of night. Caleb sat upon the brow of the hill, his torch keeping an ever-watchful eye. He had asked me why I would go there, but I could not say.

There was a sorrowful urge within to sit beside the waves and be close to my comforting whales. As cryptic as they were, they were here to soothe me too with those sounds which did make sense to me.

I sat with Ewan by the water's edge and hoped somehow, he would feel it too. He did not speak at first, nervously playing with the rocks beneath us. His eyes would move from the black water, listening to the whales spit their vapour into the air. He seemed to have given up. There was no fear anymore, no recognition. Everything had slipped away from him. He was done.

I looked back at the firelight where Caleb sat and wondered if he could hear us. His silhouette gave nothing away. I could barely take my eyes from him. He would not leave me, but he would not encroach on this time with my cousin either. He was everything Nathan Munro had not been. I dared myself to believe for one fleeting moment that his love was true.

"Finola?" Ewan said, breaking into my thoughts.

He was looking at me with those sad eyes. In the darkness he looked like a child who had lost his way.

"Before we came here, Bethan would talk of those folk who live under the sea. She believed they were real and spoke of nothing but finding one. She said it was you who had told her the stories. Tell me, do you think they are real?"

I felt the edge of my tongue longing to speak the words. He would ask me this now, when I had more reason than ever to keep those legends to myself. But I could not deny that sadness within him. It made me want to comfort him, to give him something to believe in.

"Yes." I said quietly. "I have seen enough to believe so."

He sighed and turned away from me, staring out into the pitch waters. The rolling waves the only indication that it was there at all.

"What have you seen? Tell me." He urged.

He pulled at that part of me that seldom surfaced. That part of me that yearned to see another smile. He had been in that solitude with me, that much I knew. He had dwelt in that place where nobody looked at you, where nobody spoke your name.

When I looked at him, I saw nothing of the man he would become and only the child he had been. He had not been allowed to shine. Here he never would. I took pity on him.

"I dreamed of a ring of stones. Where the old people of this land would worship alongside the Finfolk. They say the Finfolk are the kindred of the old Goddess Ceridwen. Before they were driven back into the sea. I saw their flames of fire and cloaks, standing within the stones together. It seemed as real to me as you are now."

"Where is the ring of stones?" He asked, with no hesitance.

But I could not place it outside of my dreams. There was nothing beyond it, only darkness.

"I know not. It is only a dream, and I won't dwell on it."

But that was a lie. Oh, the lies I had told. How once I had felt guilt for them and now, they came so easily.

"Tell me the stories you once told Bethan. She has spoken of them enough, but she is no good storyteller."

I was nothing compared to the storyteller I had heard them from. But as I sat with Ewan on the dark shore it mattered little to me if he knew, or not. They were only stories. The truth was a thousand miles away from my lips. He listened intently, as his sister had. Waiting until I had finished speaking to comprehend what I had said. He stared at the moon hanging above the water and somehow seemed at ease. In the darkness I thought I saw him smile.

"Bethan is a romantic little thing. But I am inclined to agree that it would be quite easy to love such a creature. Perhaps the legends of screaming kidnaps were made from spurned husbands and wives who could not bear to speak the truth."

It occurred to me that I quite liked the way he spoke, and I wished that he had spoken more. He was eloquent and thoughtful. So much more than I was. He was wasted in the shadows and taken for a fool.

"And I would let them take me, if I was chosen. If there's any truth in the legends and I am made to slave away, then at least there I'll have some use."

He just wanted to be needed. Here he was overlooked by Rohan and his dominance. Beaten to submission by a passing glance. I wished he could see that side of Rohan that had all but gone, but there would never come a day Rohan would ever allow another to see it. He could not bear to smile anymore. His grief had become a permanent sneer and, Ewan was usually on the receiving end of it.

Where once there had been a playfulness, a willingness to be friends at the very least, there was now a void which could not be filled. Two boys mourning the deaths of their fathers in ways too different to reconcile.

"Maybe I'll go. Whether or not they will have me. There will be no Finhag's. Not because they have drawn a human consort into the waters to live with them and keep them young, but because they have found love."

I couldn't help but smile. "I think you are as romantic as your sister."

He did not reply, but instead leaned back onto his elbows and waited for the sun to rise. I had not seen him so calm, not ever. It was as if the years had passed him by and none of it mattered now. I laid down beside him but could not await the rising sun. I closed my eyes for a moment.

It would be the enchanting sound of whales that awoke me. Their voices lifting above the breeze to ease me from my slumber. Where once my cousin had been, in his place was a solitary pair of shoes and a jacket ripped at the elbow.

You already know what it is you are thinking to ask.

But I could not help shed a solitary tear. "Did he make it? Do not give me folly words and cryptic responses. Did he come into the water and make it there alive?"

He came into the water before sunrise and there we did guide him to the land beneath the sea. What becomes of him now, I do not know.

"It matters not. His fate is tied to those below now. Thank you..."

But I did, for a moment, wonder if he had greeted death. Whatever had become of him it would be a welcome to him, of that I had no doubt. I wished that I had known him better, but I could not repent now. I turned away from the water and went towards the house solemnly, carrying his coat and shoes in each hand.

Caleb slept at the brow of the hill; his torch extinguished. He had remained all through the night, keeping a watchful eye until he could keep them open no more.

Ah, such a sweet sight he was. As he slept there was a serenity upon his face.

Untouched by the troubles of the world, in sleep was where he was at peace. I had no mind to wake him, but as I stood above him his body began to sense my presence and he stirred.

Slowly his eyes opened, looking upon the land as if he could not remember why he was there. Then he looked upon me and all seemed to make sense once again.

"Why do you carry his coat and shoes, he will have need of them." He said, clearing his throat of the deep breath of sleep.

A lie would have to be told. "He will have need of them no more."

Caleb stared at me, his eyes reaching for parts of me I hoped were hidden better than wanted them to be.

"Where is he?" He asked.

I pointed towards the sea. "When I awoke, he had taken one of the boats and gone to the mainland."

He jumped to his feet, still a little unsteady on them. He looked down to where the boats sat upon the shore. He counted them; I knew as he scanned the line of bobbing sail masts.

"All of our boats remain, which did he take?"

I shrugged and hoped he would ask no more. "A small boat of ours. It matters little, I must go and tell my Aunt."

He nodded, but his eyes remained on the boats. He would not question me further, but I knew something perplexed him. He escorted me to the garden gate and there he sighed heavily as it became time for us to part. He opened the gate for me but lingered there. I was afraid to pass in case a small part of me should brush past him and I would be forced to face him.

"Would you like me to come inside?" He asked sheepishly.

I could not have him bear witness to my lies. Somehow it mattered to me that I did not show any of part of me that I did not like to him. I did not know what I would say. His body so close to mine was at best a marked distraction, at worst a tool to make me only speak faithful to the truth.

"No, my Aunt will be hysterical. She has already lost her husband, her home. She will not bear the news I bring."

It seemed that he still lingered, even though there was nothing left to say. I broke the distance between us and went into the garden untouched.

"Finola?" He said quietly, "I would ask, only I have never asked before of any woman, or girl… May I call upon you again sometime?"

He was calm and somber, as if he had not slept at all. A burden had been lifted, something tangible had changed. But I could not say yes, or no. Instead I silently walked away, and his eyes stalked me up the garden path to the door. For a moment I thought he would stay, but as I made my way inside, I knew he retreated. He would come to me again regardless.

Lucie Howorth

Chapter Twelve

THE OTHER HOUSE

Τ he screams pierced the morning air. The defiant sobs cut through me like broken glass. She was not hysterical; no, it was something else. She would have struck me across the mouth if I had spoken another word. I wove a lie that ran so deep, it sealed my fate as a sinner.

I watched as Aunt Hannah fell to the ground, unable to stand with the magnitude of her loss. Her tears did not come at first, only a blindness of despair that kept her from speaking a word.

Rohan carried her to a chair and placed her at the table. She stared at it, as if she didn't understand. It was not her that screamed, that came from somewhere else. From her place by the fire, a childish shrill like a Banshee in the night.

Bethan ran to the door; certain she would find her brother there. She called me a liar, part of me was afraid that she knew what I was. But when the screams subsided, she thanked me for trying to find him and fell into my arms in a fit of exhaustion from crying. Her eyes were red rimmed and tired, there lay my greatest regret.

Mammy, in her own way, let me know that she knew of my lies. But she would not question me. Instead, the distance between us was cemented in her unwavering silence towards me. In those first days after Ewan's departure it seemed the darkness would not relent. That we would dwell in this purgatory until the day of judgement.

Aunt Hannah waited for him to return, sleeping in a chair by the door. Bethan spoke of him as if he had died, trying to imagine him elsewhere without her was too much and Mammy told her not to speak such folly.

That she was certain somewhere in the world Ewan had found a place for himself.

Only Rohan seemed not to care. He took great delight in no longer having to share his space or goad the poor boy into picking up a mucking spade. For him it was as if Ewan had never been and it did not go unnoticed. So began a silence between Aunt Hannah and Rohan, one that seemed to have lost no love between the two. Even as we sat by the fireside it was as if there was a torment that could not speak its name. Misery had been bred once again and even though summer gave way to autumn, I found myself avoiding The Hylands.

I watched them build a ruin from rubble. Every day the new house began to take shape, standing defiantly where another once stood.

But it was as if I could only see the ashes. Around the perimeter they built a dry-stone wall to mark their territory. Their piece of Eynhallow that did not want them any more than it had wanted any of us.

Isaac was a strong man, lifting and carrying stones that seemed larger and heavier than he was. Victor Jnr would watch closely, marking upon a piece of paper what had been used and what needed to be replenished.

It struck me that he was not a man of labour, but more numbers and figures. But when the occasion called, he would pick up his tools and do what needed to be done. The white-haired man was older but did not tire as he should have. His determination pursued a life which would bear no fruit. But always I would be distracted by the sight of Caleb, shirtless and breathless as he dug the trenches of new foundations.

Once I thought he saw me, his eyes catching mine as I stood watching them from afar. But then he looked away and it was as if he had not seen me at all.

He did not come to me again. I waited for him without knowing, feeling a sullen ache within that I did not know had a name. At night I would lie awake, sleep evading me as I thought of the sweetness there could be in the world because he was simply within in it.

How many days had passed? Nine, ten? The more of the house that was built, the less of me there seemed to be.

I busied myself with the mundane tasks that seemed to keep us from rotting into the land, but I was not present. I was elsewhere.

The birds came and sat by my window, allowing me to take their soft wings between my fingers as I slowly caressed them. Bethan thought me strange and would not touch them, afraid they would peck at her.

She was not the child she once was, full of wonder and easily enchanted. Eynhallow had finally broken her spirit with the loss of her brother's presence. I feared she would suffer a fate much like Rohan's. Where once there had been a happiness unslaked, now there was only a bubbling sadness that threatened to spill over.

She watched me closely, unknowing of the dialogue between the winged creatures and I. Always she would stare hungrily to touch them, but never reach out to them. I found myself turning my back on them all, seeking solace in the birds and the cattle. In the hours before dawn I would retreat to speak with the whales, who never sought to give me a straight answer but still they remained a better source of company than all else.

For a moment I could forget that something tugged at my heart, that something gnawed away at the very core of my existence and only when I glanced at the other house was, I reminded of my heart's dearest wish.

It began as a slow and sinking feeling whenever I went out into the garden to find he did not wait for me by the wall, or the front door. But as the days passed, it conspired to overtake my entire body. Even in the hours I tried to sleep, I was haunted by the sight of him in my waking dreams. I could not close my eyes for fear of falling into those dreams of sleep that seem so much more real to me. I would wake in a blind panic, wondering if today he would uphold his last request.

Why had I not accepted? Why had I walked away without giving him the word he had longed to hear? I ached now to say yes to him. Somehow it mattered little how real or enforced it might be.

If I had brought him to me under Finblood pretences I would still have him now. Perhaps I had woven a spell so deep I caught myself in the threads of it. I missed him so much it no longer mattered.

The human parts of me still hoped that it was of real love which he had come to, but each day there seemed to be less of her and more of that girl I barely knew.

I must strive to know more, to know the truth. But I was a coward and would not ask, for fear that I would bear the Finhag's fate or become the feared kidnapper from the sea. Nothing made sense anymore. I wondered if it had ever made sense.

Rohan was bringing in the crops, his silent moves between the fields and the house went almost unnoticed were it not for the heavy footfalls up the garden path. I appeared in the doorway and handed him a cup of water, he took it from me gratefully and for a moment I caught a glimpse of the boy Rohan.

"I am almost done. What is there for supper?" He asked, in that deep voice I sometimes forgot was now his.

"A little chicken, and bread. There is some eggs too." But in truth the chicken had been tough and tasted foul. I had not wanted to kill them, but even in death it seemed they served little purpose.

Rohan nodded, disappointed at the prospect of another sorry meal. "I must go to the mainland before winter."

My blood ran cold. Winter would not only bring that bleakest of seasons back to Eynhallow, but the reality that we would serve it alone. The white-haired man had said they would return after Winter to complete the building which could not be done in the bitter cold. He would return to his glorious England and take Caleb with him.

"You are not yourself." Rohan said, handing back to me the empty cup. "You give too much thought to matters of the heart, you do well to abandon all hope where that is concerned."

Surely, he could not have meant that? "And what experience have you drawn that conclusion from?"

He stared at me sourly, as if he needed little reminder there were no women here that he could pursue.

"Watching you stand and watch them, it grieves me. That you would lower yourself, to be so brazen about it. You told me that you would hide yourself from them, but you have not. You throw yourself right in the path of their wondering, they will wonder about you someday make no mistake about that."

And if they did, it would be a revelation to me. "I wonder about myself, even now." I confessed. "The hearts of men, perhaps they will know the right questions to ask. Perhaps when they ask, there will be one who knows the answer to reply."

The thought horrified Rohan, who sighed and placed a tired hand to his aching head.

"Have we not endured enough here?"

But I was not done yet. "And yet we still endure it. For what purpose? If you had any sense about you, you would get you to the mainland and find yourself a good woman. You are young yet to have your pick of them."

He smiled wryly. "And Aunt Hannah? And Mammy? Would they be inclined to believe I had gone to a better life too? Perhaps I will go into the water and see what fate awaits me?"

He was teasing me. "You would berate me for giving them a better hope than the truth? I am not that cruel. He has yet to confirm a sinister fate. I fear Nathan Munro's end may have been of his own doing. I need to know the true nature of these… people. Legends and stories hold no truth."

He placed a hand upon my shoulder and nodded. "You speak to those whales that dwell in the sea, have they not knowledge of the… people under the sea?"

I almost laughed. The thought of any whale speaking truth in a way I could understand was unheard of.

"Whales are not the most forthcoming of creatures. They have the knowledge but cannot convey it as easily as that. The cows speak more fluently. When they are inclined to do so."

His forehead creased; his eyebrows raised. "The cows? What do they know of matters beyond their own land?"

But how to convey the deep spiritual lives of such beasts? Those who had lived more than once and recalled each life?

"There is one of them, who often speaks with me. The others are far too concerned within their own thoughts to give much notice to what happens around them. But one of them told me of a life she had once lived as an old healer. They worshipped within a ring of stones beside the Finfolk, before they were banished back to the sea."

I could see that he did not comprehend it. Always he had taken me at my word and never questioned. It did not matter to him.

"Aye, well best we do not speak of it more. We are no longer alone here." He looked out towards the other house with disdain. "You do well to remember that."

And so, he returned. The sour and angry man that had taken that boy's place. I sighed for the memory of him and watched as my brother returned to the fields. But I could not shake the incessant need to unveil the truth. I would tread the path carefully under the cover of darkness. I was glad to be away from Bethan's childish sleep talk and the glow of the candle she insisted on keeping by her bedside.

Mammy and Aunt Hannah had not yet retired, instead they sat in the parlour by the fire speaking of their youth and all which had befallen them. It had become a nightly ritual to expel their deepest regrets before bed.

They were growing old with a sadness shared, for that at least I was grateful. The woman who had raised me as her own would not end her days alone. I could ask for no more than that. I came to their bedroom door and opened it slowly, the moonlight flooding the wooden crucifix I had come to retrieve. Grey light sending the shadows of it across the floor and towards my feet as if inviting me to take it.

On silent feet I went towards it and took it from its place. I dared not look as I took the scroll of paper from within. It sat within the folds of my skirts until I heard the sounds of Mammy and Aunt Hannah retreating to bed.

When all was done, with the house sleeping deeply, I made my way out and down towards the water. The night was cold and clear, the stars coveting the night sky like droplets of light to guide spirits on their way.

She was a stranger to me. This woman's face so much like my own, yet I could not remember her. All I knew was that Daddy had loved her completely, without any hesitation or fear. She had kept him prisoner, whether she would have intended it or no. Perhaps she would have done him a kindness by taking him back to Finfolkaheem with her. Instead of rotting away on this Island to raise a son who would become an empty vessel with a woman he could not love entirely. Such had been his life; in the end I could not deny him a peaceful death.

I did not miss him as I once had. Consumed no longer by grief, but in its place a serene knowledge that his time had come. My only regret was that in those last days he could not bear to look at me. But even that was something I had come to accept and understand.

As I took the scroll out and unbound it, even in the pale moonlight I could not discern my own face from this. Even with the subtle differences that made her what she was and I only half of that.

"I send this to you in the hope that you will find it." I whispered softly, placing a length of thread around an adjacent rock so that it might sink into the depths. "I must know who I am…"

It was the only piece of her I had. As I held it in my hand, I was reluctant to release it. But there could be no other way. Still I clutched to my humanity like it was teetering on the edge of an eroding cliff. I hurled it into the sea with an unsteady hand, watching it reach the waves and go under.

You are tempting fate… Came a voice from below. *Do you know what it is you ask?*

"I have barely begun to ask."

The whales were swimming close by, I could feel their presence like a slight breeze upon my skin. But I could not see them.

Return with us, Finola. You shall have your knowledge.

"No, I remain here. Still you would ask that of me? When you know."

But why do you remain in a place that no longer wants you? They asked, their voices reaching out to me like arms for an embrace.

"Tell my mother to come for me. If she has word from Eynhallow she will come." And as I spoke the words, I hoped that they were true.

I felt a blind panic rise within my chest, turning my thoughts back towards The Hylands and the other house. My heart bled. I could not bear to listen to the whales and their ramblings tonight, or their incessant requests. I could not give them an answer they desired any more than they could for me. They would save me; I was sure of that. When I had need of them most. Therein lay the comfort they gave me, but that time was not yet.

And so, I turned my back on them and retreated further inland, spurred by the panic rising within my chest. Oh, how it beaten hard and fast sending my head light and my vision blurry. I did not dare look back in case my request had been granted. As much as I had wanted it, I was afraid of it.

Within the newly erected walls underneath open roof and night sky were the tents which had become home to our new neighbours. Two of them sat side by side, a fire burning embers between them. They had built a grand fireplace, much bigger than our own.

I felt a stab of envy for a moment, imagining this place in its entirety. They could not envisage the desolation here. This place had been built for those who had never known true sadness. They would come to know it; of that I was certain. The curse upon this land fermented and matured, and now it sucked the life from all of us. If they were untouched now, they were blessed indeed. But it would not last.

The four men had retired early, their lamps sending shadows upon the canvas around them. The unmistakable shape of the white-haired man sat with a book in his hand as another form lay sleeping beside him. In the other, the lamp was dim. Two men sat at opposite ends, laying down cards in succession. I stepped away; afraid they would sense my presence.

Why had I come here? To torture myself further with notions that somehow, I could shed the reality of who I was and gain Caleb's heart without driving him insane?

I could not deny that I somehow felt conditioned to be close to him. I could not stay by the water to be questioned by creatures who had never known the land. No more than I could return to The Hylands amongst those who had never dwelled within the sea. Here was my sticking point, my greatest reason to stay.

"Ah! Another good hand! I'll not play against you when the stakes are higher!" I heard Isaac say, throwing his cards down.

The shadows were faint and as I stood listening, I feared mine was evident to them as theirs was to me. I was still claiming too much courage to make my presence known.

"I wouldn't take another penny off you, lad. I've had a month's wages from you before and there's an end to it." Caleb replied jovially.

It stabbed me. Had he not known a moments unrest since last he saw me?

"That was not a fair hand... I was drunk! You may as well have waited until I slept and taken it from my pocket then." Isaac recalled, it tasted bitter in my mouth.

Such happiness they must have known.

"No, no… *Simon* would take it from a drunk man. I won you soberly and in good faith. I cannot help if I have better luck." And for a moment, I thought I heard him laugh.

"Have you heard word from Simon?" Isaac inquired; all joviality gone.

Bitterness turned to sore anger.

"No. Nor do I have any desire to. What word could reach us here, even if I had welcomed it? No, it is done between us."

The sweetness of his words banished all other thought. If there had been anger and bitterness, it ceased and there was only the instant gratification that he spoke so low of someone I also despised.

"You have known him a long time. What is she to you? That you would banish him from your presence for good?"

I wanted to speak. To let them know I was here, that to speak freely would mean that I heard them. But curiosity was never my friend. I stepped forward, letting my feet carry my sense of longing with it.

"If I could tell you, old friend, I would. But there's little words to say what manner of feeling I have for her."

My breath caught in my chest, tight and uneasy. Somewhere a creature cried into the night, for a moment they stopped to listen.

"Have her and be done with it, Caleb. We leave here in three days. Surely your craving will be gone on our return. Perhaps then I shall have my old friend back. Instead of this whisper of a man."

The shadow of Caleb's body moved. He shook his head vehemently. "No Isaac. I'll not treat her like a whore. I would frighten her, then she might not look upon me the same ever again."

Isaac sighed. "And it would matter to you? Or is it that large brother of hers that keeps you from taking what you so obviously desire?"

From somewhere within the vehemence, Caleb laughed for a fleeting moment. A beautiful, guttural sound that brought a smile to my own lips.

"Her brother? He is of no consequence to me. I have come against brutes the size of him before, if not larger. No, it is not that. She would have me stay away from her, so I have. But it will do little good. I fear I have already somehow bound myself to her. I have come to her and she has sent me away each time. If she does not come to me in three days, then I shall not return at all. I have... missed her."

Speak, stupid girl. Raise your voice! Tell him that you have come, and he will never need fear again. Unbound yourself to him, Finblood and Human blood alike! Let him follow you wherever it is you may go, forget all else. Be not afraid of this man. He is not driven insane by spells, but love. It is true, he loves you from a place untainted by legend and yet you still do not speak!

"What can I say to you? That might make you see sense. She is a feckless girl! A beautiful one, but feckless nonetheless! Of all the women you've known in England, you would stay for this one on an Island nobody wants? I, for one, will be glad to be rid of this place. What has changed since that first day? You would not even stay to see the job finished and then…"

Caleb's head fell into his hands. "Isaac, you are as dear to me as my own brother, but do not seek to fight with me. There is not a woman alive who could hold my attention the way she does. To stay away from her has taken strength I did not know I had. She came to me when I had need of her most, when I did not even know I had need of her. So, you may return to England. But I cannot be where she is not. I cannot sleep another night's rest without my head being filled of her!" His voice heightened. The white-haired man turned his head away from his book and the younger Victor stirred at the sound of it.

"This place is cursed. I have known it always, yet I would lay my soul down for it just for a single look from her! I am tortured by her, because I torture myself by not standing by her door! The sight of her standing on that hill, the black hair in the wind, I am in pain because she does not come forth! Do you see?! I love her Isaac. I love her so much I can't be myself without her. She *is* me… If I had gone back that first day, I would spend the rest of my life with whores and women I do not love, she would be here, waiting for me always."

I do not want to know who I am. I take it back! There is no truth I desire more than this. Return to me what I have given to you, I shall forget all that I have desired, save for him. I shall go back to the house and place that damned piece of paper back into the crucifix where it had always belonged. I shall not meddle in such things! What does it matter to me now? I will not become whatever I am meant to become. I will not go back to that place. I will not care another day and I will live in purgatory between the two worlds because I shall be with him. Give it back to me, I call upon no one!

But there was nothing but incessant waves, the expanse of sunrise spilling over the horizon. What had I done?

Chapter Thirteen

THE THIRD DAY

sickness took hold. Flesh was cold and yet burned like a fever, but I did not shake or tremble. I could not move my own bones, their very existence within my own body seemed to ache within.

It is foolish to go about in this weather, under the cover of the cold moon, and not expect to take a sickness.

Aunt Hannah made me sit by the fire and drink broth until I could no longer keep it down. I had never felt so delicate and that I might break at any moment. I was aware of dreams lingering on the periphery of my mind, as I sat and watched flames dance, I thought I could see those hooded figures standing within the ring of stones. Each flame that licked became a torch, held high above hooded cloaks in the dead of night.

Mammy was too afraid to come near, crossing herself when she thought nobody could see. Ah, how it pained me to see her so. God had finally consumed her. With little else in her life to tend to her senses, it seemed religion had become more than her daily bread.

I was aware of the time slipping from me. But I could not shift myself away from the fireside. My body betrayed me. It renounced me and punished me for the act I had performed and shunned.

Ah yes, this was retribution for desire.

I thought of Caleb and his words that had altered everything, I fell into a raging despair that paralysed me. I tried to clear my mind of such things, but still I could barely move. Every twitch sent ripples of pain through each sinew. All I could do was will him to come to me. To hope that he would hear of my predicament and come to inquire of me. But as each day the sun set with no sign of him, I began to lose all hope.

"Strange, don't you think? She does not have the fever. But yet her skin burns, and she will not move. I am afraid we will need to return to the mainland Mary…"

I heard them whispering by the door. Aunt Hannah, her voice hushed, unaware that my hearing was untainted.

Mammy sighed heavily. "We have not had need of the mainland for a long while, I'll not go back there now. She will heal of this, whatever it may be."

Her faith was unwavering. But it was not for me, but for herself. Her unwillingness to return to Evie.

"And if she takes a turn? What then? I'll not have another death on my hands! So help me God. We must know if she is dying…"

Perhaps I was dying. Perhaps this is what it felt like to slowly die after all.

"Mary? Why do you do nothing? She is your only daughter!" Aunt Hannah urged, her voice becoming hysterical.

Both of the women came into the room, one of them a picture of calm as the other worried and dithered. Mammy hastened to the door and out she went without a glance in my direction. Aunt Hannah stared at me pitifully, before coming to place another blanket upon me.

"I do not think your poor Mammy is herself. Do not think ill of her. She is perhaps mired with worry so much that she can't bear to look upon you like this. But have no fear, I shall care for you. Will you not get up and walk a little for me, Finola? For your Aunt Hannah?"

Would that I could. Why could they not hear my screams? I was silently fading away.

"You poor thing." She crooned, pressing the blanket into the sides of the chair I had sat within for days.

Her pity was unwanted, and I could not look at her face.

Who are you? You are not my Aunt. You are a relative of the woman who raised me. How is it that you come to me now and show me tenderness for the first time? If you knew what I had done, what I knew… You would hate me.

I had hours to think of it as they slept. They did not move me from the chair, afraid I would cry out again in agony. They had brought Rohan to me, to try and lift me but his mere touch had reduced me to muffled screams. If I had cried out with my untainted voice, they would have spoken of it on the mainland. But I could barely speak to converse, less convey my pain.

This was not a fever and not knowing what ailed me perplexed them so. Except for Mammy, who knew it was something unholy.

Instead, Rohan kept vigil by my side as all else slept. He kept the fire burning and boiled some water for hot tea that he would put to my lips and urge me to drink.

Swallowing was like taking those embers from the fire and trying to consume them. But still I could not fully convey it, so he brought me more tea and I was forced to endure it.

"Finola, you must tell me what I should do." He said quietly, as he curled a large hand around mine.

Do not presume that I am aware of what needs to be done. I am at the mercy of whatever this is.

He tried to smile, but it appeared as a grimace upon his lips. He had begun to grow his facial hair; I noticed the specks of red in it by the dim light. It leant more age to his appearance. I began to wonder if he had ever been a boy but had always been this man I saw before me now. He had not yet turned sixteen.

"Please Finola. Mammy says that it is not an illness any human could endure. Aunt Hannah has spoken of taking you to the mainland so that a Doctor can examine you! I do not know if I should allow it. What if they discover something? I will not let you die here, but I cannot risk your secret either. You must tell me what it is I am meant to do!"

Let them come and take me. Tomorrow there will be nothing left of me. It will be too late…

My secret was a burden to him. He would keep all others at bay to save me from having to reveal it. Perhaps death would relieve him of it and his life could begin once again. I would never be able to consolidate the two parts of me. I could feel my bones melting away from within. I had no choice, but it let it end me.

"Please Finola…" He begged; his bloodshot eyes boring into me. "You are to me whatever a mother is."

He began to cry. Unashamedly and with a quiet sadness, he let the tears fall onto his cheeks.

"Are you dying?" He asked, and I could feel my own tears as tangible as his, but they did not spill.

If I am, then it will be as it should. Already I forget myself...

The burning skin turned inward, like flames licking my blood. I tried to recall Rohan's face as he sat beside me speaking in hushed chaos. But the face before me was like a stranger. Oh yes, I knew him somewhere in the corner of my mind but for this moment all faded away. The room sank into darkness, taking the fire with it.

"Finola! Speak to me! Oh god no… Come back! Come back to me…" I heard the voice call, but it was bodiless and carried no weight within this world.

A thin veil of darkness shielded me. It was not around me, but in front. As if I could touch it. From somewhere beyond I began to feel the presence of another.

"Finola Gray, remove your cloak." They said to me authoritatively.

The darkness receded as I pulled the hood of the cloak back and greeted the moonlight.

The procession ran before me and I found myself a part of it. Within the ring of stones, I stood as one of them. Their torches licked the night sky and filled the air with smoke. I felt the warmth upon my skin, welcome and soothing. If I was in the land of dreams, it had never seemed more real to me.

No longer did I stand on the periphery, looking in. But I was within it somehow, feeling the cloak about me fall about my shoulders and my place in the back of the procession.

All the pain was gone. I could barely remember the agony in my bones and the paralysing ache. Here it seemed I was nothing more than a passing wind through the stones. As the others removed their cloaks, I became fully aware of myself.

Their faces were beautiful and drawn as if they knew the secrets of the world but could not reveal them. Some with white hair and the bluest eyes that shone like the summer sky. Others with red hair, their pale skin like marble statues carved by nature. Beside me were the raven-haired ones, black as night with sinuous stature above all the others.

The men, bare chested and glorious, held sickle knives in their hands bound with a vine I had never seen before. Their skin was painted with symbols which bore no meaning. The women let their hair fall about their naked breasts, carrying in their hands a single wreath of herbs that smelled sour and sweet all at the same time.

I sensed the ones in boar skins, their shadows entering the ring to stand beside us. They smelled entirely intoxicating to me and yet I could not bring myself to look upon them. They were smaller, their essence not of this world. They were entirely human, awaiting to take their place in worship beside the Finfolk. I knew, as a person knows these things without ever having them confirmed that I had died.

"Welcome." Said that same authoritative voice.

It came from the centre of the stones. From moonlight shadow it came towards me, all eyes turning towards me. I was blinded for a moment as the form eclipsed the light but as it came closer, I saw the cloak fall to the ground.

Before me was a painted chest and a loin cloth which barely concealed any modesty. But I found I did not care. I diverted my eyes with little effort towards the eyes of the man before me. He was raven haired and taller than the others, his strict face in stark contrast with the long flowing body which was his.

"Where am I?" I inquired, but my voice seemed to become lost amongst the silence. Still, he acknowledged and heard, tilting his head towards me.

"You have been here before, have you not?" He asked, his lips remaining still.

I knew these stones somehow.

"I recall it somewhere." I gasped.

He smiled benevolently and from the folds of his cloak he gave to me a piece of paper.

"I believe this is yours." He said, revealing to me that memory I once had of my mother's face.

I looked at the paper and wondered what it was doing here in this dream like place that shared no space or time or reason.

It had not been tarnished by water. It was as if it had gone from my hand to his and back to me in a moment.

"Where did you find this?" I asked, afraid of the answer.

There was something about his face that gave me comfort. The others revered him and stood around him listening to his every word and in turn they listened to me.

"One of the guardians brought it to me. The one in this picture, she is who you seek?"

I once thought I did. I had thought long about her face. Now, when somehow it seemed within my grasp, I renounced it and longed for something… someone else.

"She is my mother." I whispered; afraid the truth would bring about something I could not endure.

The man nodded knowingly, his long flowing fingers taking a strand of my hair so that he might look at it closer. I could not deny him. Something told me he was someone of importance, who I should revere and be honoured of his company. Something in the way all others lingered on his every movement.

"I know this." He said, this time using the speech of his voice so that all around us might hear. "And I know you, Finola Gray of Eynhallow."

He was warm and engaging. I was utterly spellbound by him. The way his body moved within the wind, not against it but as one with it. His long raven hair was taken into pieces and bound in that same vine I had no name for. There was a power radiating from him that was so tangible I could almost see the aura of it around him. I wondered if he were a Ghost, here to take me to my final resting place?

"Who are you?" I dared to ask.

He smiled again and somehow his face became familiar to me.

"My name is Astala. I am high priest."

His name sent a shiver of silence through the procession. But it bore no resonance to me. I tried to place this strange and beautiful man in my memories but there were none. He seemed to understand my reluctance, and it only served to pull me closer towards him.

He leaned towards me, the facets of his skin becoming clearer. It was not like any skin I had ever seen before. Glinting in the moonlight were scales like that of a fish but concealed within a glow that almost shimmered like moonlight on the water. As he turned his head, I became aware of every feature. The glorious fish-like skin and hiding within the strands of his tightly bound hair, just behind his long and sleek pointed ears, were two breathing gills that moved with each breath he took. So hidden and small as they were, I was inclined not to notice at all had he not forced me to see them. I reached behind my own ear, small and human as they were, and felt nothing but the smooth human skin there.

"Am I dead?" I inquired.

A high priest to pray over my body? Perhaps this was the path I would walk to that after life Mammy had prayed so hard for? There was no way my body could have sustained that pain which was now a distant memory.

Astala, the high priest shook his head. "No. You are not dead."

"Then where am I? And what is this place?" Of course, I was alive. I began to feel the ache of panic rise within my chest. "How did you come to receive this picture? And what is a guardian?"

Yes, I was afraid. If I was not dead, was I lost within a dream? The white-haired ones and the red-haired ones stared at me as I tried to retreat. But the raven-haired ones encircled me, their shining bodies moving into the moonlight.

"Be not afraid." Astala told me, holding his hand up in command. "You are amongst Kin."

I searched for my mother's face amongst those around me, their raven hair all coming together as one in the dark wind. They struck me with their brilliance and beauty. Each of them bore the same shimmering scales within their skin, some of them bound their hair in vines and others allowed it to flow free. But all of them were tall and sinuous. I had grown taller, but still they towered over me. For once I longed to renounce my humanity. For a fleeting moment I cursed the ugly reality that I would never resemble these creatures entirely.

There was something human about them. But if ever they were mistaken for one, it would be the most beautiful and perfect of mankind. Though taller and graced with skin that reflected moonlight, I could see how they might walk the shores unnoticed if they were shrouded by their cloaks. If I had ever been called beautiful, it was because of them.

"You tell me not to be afraid. But how am I meant to feel no fear when I do not know where I am or how I came to be here?"

They conspired silently. Their eyes exchanging knowing looks. When they were done Astala nodded and they once again rested their eyes upon me. It seemed to me that they had decided upon something with which I had no part of. If I was not dead, then I wanted to be gone from here.

"Very well, Finola Gray. We have little time. You must listen carefully. You, who are Halfling, daughter of my daughter. I have guarded you well. But now I see it has come the time that you must know who you are. So, I have brought you here within a dream, to the stone circle of Finfolkaheem."

As if it had never been before, I began to see the ripples within the moonlight. It shone down on us bold and bright, from the surface and down to the depths below. But surely it was a sky? It felt as if I were within a world much like my own, and not at the bottom of the sea.

"I was never certain of which parts of you would remain human..."

I looked towards the boar skins, the human consorts, their lives tied to this place as their hearts were tied to the Finfolk.

"Where is my mother? Tell me!"

His face contorted at my anger. He wished I would quieten, I reminded him of *her*. Daughter of his daughter... So, he was my grandfather? He looked young enough to be my brother.

"Do not be vexed." He said, raising a hand to my shoulder. His touch was cold and sent chills into my bones. "Their fate was one they chose. As will yours be."

They chose their fate? Who amongst them would speak out about the legends? None would ever leave their companions long enough to return and tell of what became of them.

"I fear I have no choice." I confessed. "Every day I am less as I once was."

"I have been watching you all your life. With the help of the guardians, I have known your every move. From the day your mother returned you to the land to this moment now."

It seemed he knew more about me than I knew about myself. This bothered me. He commanded my respect and had probably earned it with many heroic exploits in his mysterious life. But to me, in this moment, he was nothing but a dream like spectre who had invaded my mind without invitation.

"I don't understand... I don't understand any of it! Where is my mother? Is she here?"

Their faces washed with sadness; it was as if I had spoken ill of her. Astala, his otherworldly presence dimmed somewhat, looked over his shoulder into the distance. Yes, I could feel the wind.

There was air and smoke and wind down here, surely none of it could be possible? It made little sense to me. I was beginning to feel sick with the disorientation.

"Calm yourself, there is much we must speak of. I fear there is too much to say of this moment. But know this... The time has come for you to take on your next form. I had never been certain if you possessed the ability to shift but I have been sent word that you have taken a fever. Fear not, it is the pain we have all felt before taking on the form of another. It will fade."

I was suddenly reminded of that former pain. The excruciating heat within the bones.

"What form? What will I become? Please, tell me if my mother is here? Will she not speak with me?"

It grieved him that I continued to ask. "Your mother is not here. Time enough for all of that will come. But for now, you must return to your body and become what you were born to become. Finola, daughter of my daughter, I shall see you again my little one."

His voice revealed within me something long dormant. Things within that I knew to be true but had been a mystery to me before. I was on the cusp of learning some terrible truth, of that I knew when I had asked for my mother.

But entwined within was something else, something far beyond anything I could imagine. I closed my eyes against this strange and sublime place. The ancient rock turning to shadow, the pale forms moving away from me. It was as if I ascended and as I broke the surface, I was faced with a pain so intense, I could not even scream out my agony.

I opened my eyes. Cold, hard stone beneath me. Warm flesh above me.

Rohan's voice penetrated the eerie silence of my vision. He called my name in urgency and fought to keep me upright.

There was nothing solid of me. The bones within had burned to nothing. All that remained was a sense that if I could just keep my heart beating all would be well. I writhed and slithered within Rohan's grasp. I heard his voice pitched deeply somewhere in the distance, calling my name over and over.

I was aware of myself close to him, but I was removed. Whatever body I was within was no longer my own. Ripples of pain reached through even vein, every sinew until I knew nothing but the brilliance of a white light around me.

Rohan stepped back, blinded. The light coveted me, filled me and renewed me. Where once there had been pain there was a feeling of numbed elation. My body moved but I dared not look. Bones, blood and flesh resigning themselves over to a magic which was greater than they could withstand.

I was no longer afraid.

The beat within me told me I was still alive. There was a flash somewhere, perhaps it came from within, like lightning. It appeared the worst was over. I opened my eyes slowly, aware of the smell of the fire burning below me.

Below me? As smoke rises, I see it. Every piece of dust, every spider's web intricately woven within the beams. Yes, it is below me. The old wooden table that has sat within that room since before I could remember was below me. Cups and plates and a loaf of bread sitting upon it patiently. I could not fathom this familiar place from up high. It made little sense to me. Somehow, I yearned to be higher and yet here I was amongst the rafters.

"Finola?" His voice was a sound that came from the corner below. Muddled and backwards, at first, I did not understand until a half-forgotten memory forced its way from the back of my mind to the forefront.

Rohan looked towards me. His eyes wide and the black centres flooding the white.

What is that sound? That sound so like wind... Where does it come from?

"What in God's name?!" He cried then, cowering away from the sight of me.

It was then I became aware of it. As I tried to use my voice to call his name there was the sound of an ugly squawking coming from within. The low, cutthroat sound came out clear as a bell. A demonic call that came from the pit of my stomach.

I hear the ocean above the wind. It is never so clear as it is to me now. I hear voices coming from beyond the house. Mixed words that make little sense above the crashing waves.

"Come down from there, do you want Mammy and Aunt Hannah to find you?!" He whispered violently, afraid to come any closer towards to me.

It occurred to me that something was very wrong. The sights and smells of this most familiar of places were all different. Rohan had never looked upon me with fear before.

As a child I had protected him, of late it had been him who had been the one to protect me. But now it seemed to unravel before me and neither of us could be protected from what had happened here.

"You must stop that incessant flapping!" Rohan roared, his arms finally reaching out to me.

As he came towards me the ground seemed to come up with him. It was as if I was amongst a land of giants, where the most ordinary of things towered above me. He fought with me for a moment as I tried to evade his grasp. I saw the kitchen window in the corner of my eye, half open and somehow large enough to crawl through.

The glass gleamed in the morning sunlight. Red sky reflected within it and there in the foreground was the most beautiful black raven I had ever seen. Deep black eyes set upon a noble black feathered head, they stared back at me as if somehow, I should know myself.

For a moment it was as if I had met another like myself and was greeting them. But as I flexed the pitch-black wings, I knew it was myself who I confronted.

Rohan calmed as I regarded myself, steadily approaching as I considered flying out of the window. In his hands he held something, at first, I could not make out the colours. My bird eyes saw so much of it, in vivid detail. I recalled every grain of dust, every chip in the wood. It was not until I noted the white collar that I realised he was carrying my clothes.

"If you're going to fly out of the window, then do it now. Do not wait." He said, folding my clothes up and stuffing them into one of the cupboards behind the pots and pans. "You must find some way to change back, but do not return until nightfall when I can bring you your clothes without being seen."

At first it was as if I was a child taking their first steps. I encroached onto the windowsill and opened my wings out to greet the wind. It pulled me into the air and took me, at first it appeared as if the land below was falling but it was I who spiralled upwards.

Eynhallow was a sombre picture from above. Sitting within the sound like a petulant child. It did not want to be part of the other lands and shunned the coastline. Through a bird's eyes everything became so clear and daunting. With each movement of my strange wings I could feel the cold air beneath me carrying me. I never wanted to come down. If I could remain within the clouds I would never have to return to my misery.

And all the while the birds told me to wait… As they came towards me, circling me and following behind their words came no longer in vivid pictures but in clear and striking speech that I could understand. Outwardly their squawking was prettier than mine, their wings a contrasting white. Arctic Fulmar I had heard them called once by Daddy. But not I. I was pitch as night to their day.

She's here… quickly, tell the others…

They came to me in flocks and I met their eyes in flight. They welcomed me. Word began to spread that I had come to them and they had been expecting me. Their whispers carried down the wind and soon I found myself surrounded by every bird who lived upon Eynhallow.

I cast my bird eyes upon the boats that sat upon the rising shore. The foam of the waves licking the rocks and people moving against it. From above I could identify their every step. The white-haired man and his wide gait, moving between the two boats carrying things from one place to another. Isaac and the younger Victor standing by the water speaking in hushed tones as another man walked away. It was this other man which caught my attention.

I know you… I would know you if I were woman or beast or bird. Yes, I will know you still.

There was something about him that saddened me. The wind was coaxing him towards the waiting boats, but he stood against it looking at the lonely house on the brow of the hill. Perched upon the chimney, I watched him regard the flock of birds that circled ahead. They had come to see me and were now retreating back to their nests. For a moment I thought he spied the solitary raven, as out of place in this dying vessel as a snowdrop growing amongst concrete. But he seemed not to notice and continued his vague stare at the house.

You seem so worn, so defeated. Do not be sad, for I find myself wishing for anything but your sadness. I am here and I shall not leave your side.

But the words were a forest of dead trees within my mind. They did not grow. But rotted instead for I could not speak them. I could only watch as he despaired.

"Caleb, boy! Will you fetch the rest of the tools to your old father?!" Called the white-haired man, his voice crisp and clear as if somehow, I was stood amongst them.

He hesitated for a moment, his eyes resting on the window which was mine.

Look at me, if there is only one more thing you do in your life then look at me!

"Lend me some strength boy, I am tired." The white-haired man said, placing a loving hand upon Caleb's shoulder. "It has been a task greater than I anticipated. After winter I shall bring more workers back here with us."

Hear my voice. In this guise or some other, hear me! Do not leave me to perish here without you.

"I may not return next spring." Caleb said, his voice low and abrupt.

The white-haired man tightened his grip. "What is it that grieves you, my son?"

That I have not come to him. That I have not thrown myself at his mercy and declared myself. If my wings could carry me to you in my human form I would come down from this rooftop and let my presence be known.

"The world has changed, Father. I fear it will have altered completely on our return to England. Time moves not as it does everywhere else in this land."

And it was a portent that sent a coldness to my bones.

The white-haired man smiled. "Ah, you are right. One of the many reasons I chose this place. Here we have all the time in the world to please ourselves. Time is seldom used for things which make me happy, but here I may use it at my leisure. I may watch my children grow and my grandchildren born. In time, I hope to see the youngest of my elder boys happy."

He could not say a word of comfort. Somehow his happiness was tied to something beyond his own grasp. The white-haired man clasped his son into a warm embrace before leading him down into the boats which would take him from me.

Soon it will be too late, and I shall pluck each feather from my body to rid myself of this curse. I wish not for wings but for arms and skin of my human flesh. I wish not for this body, this mystical prison I have found myself within. I am not a bird; I am not a raven! I am a human girl and I love you! Caleb do not go where I cannot find you! I shall not send you away more. I shall not resist whatever temptation this is! I shall sin until I can sin no more for one touch, oh the waves may call you to their breast and carry you away, but I shall remain! Be still and await me. I do love you and I will come for you!

But I could not. The bird which flew above and rested on their deck was just a simple bird. They did not see me, did not even remark about the strange black raven which had never been seen on this land before.

Instead they packed their boats and prepared to set sail. Aunt Hannah and Bethan appeared at the shoreline, handing them food and water for their journey.

Mammy waved from the doorstep, too pious for a real goodbye. I watched them all, allowing this tragedy to unfold. I flew as far as the wind could take me, following their boat out onto the open waters until I could no longer make my wings carry me further.

He did not look for me. He did not raise his head in the hopes that I might have come for him. He could not. He would not. The bitterness of winter was already in the air. I felt it the higher I climbed. I wished for it to strike me down. But instead I drifted back and waited for the inevitable breaking of my heart.

Chapter Fourteen

THE SNOW

hen I returned to my human form I had forgotten how to live within it. My time as a bird had been brief but yielded a newfound set of emotions incapable for a human.

And so, I cried heavy tears, racking sobs that would not be silenced.

Rohan found me naked and alone in the barn, my old bones still slipping into place. He brought to me my clothes and some water to drink and I shall never forget his face when first he looked upon me.

Relief tinged with fear.

Had it truly only been a day? Somehow it had felt much longer. Like I had been without my body for weeks, even months.

Physical pain gave way to something which made me wish for the pain of broken bones burning within to return. Closing my eyes, even for the briefest of moments meant that I had to endure pictures of his face that haunted me. Watching him over and over in broken images as he went across the water and far away from me.

When finally, I found the strength to return to the house I was greeted with a suspicious silence. Mammy cared not to know of my miraculous recovery. Aunt Hannah on the other hand, berated me for not saying goodbye to our neighbours.

At night when I cradled tears upon the edge of my lashes, Bethan would sigh thoughtfully beside me but had long learnt to keep her silence.

I felt a prophecy had come true regarding her fate. She had lost herself, but barely seemed to notice. On the cusp of womanhood, she had grown into a beauty which was all her own tempered with a sadness that made her all the more alluring. She had arrived here with all the promise of a world that existed outside Eynhallow.

I hoped, of all of us, she would be the one to return.

And so, we fell into another winter. Another bleak sufferance that brought hunger and desolation.

But the cold did not bite as it once had, and the wind howled though I seemed not to hear it.

Thoughts were consumed with the unrelenting wanting of something I could not have. A regret gnawed away at me that threatened to eat me whole. Of all the things I damned in the world I now damned myself for not going wherever that boat went.

For not taking my wings across the water.

I paid no mind to the meagre food put in front of me, shifting my plate towards my brother who ate his share and mine heartily.

Mammy spoke under her breath of my ungrateful nature, but I no longer cared what was in her mind. Her regard for me had faded into nothing but passing words and snatched glances of disapproval.

I wished I could fade into the background for everyone else. But the eyes upon me were everywhere. From the eyes in the sky to the watchful stare of my brother who waited every minute of every day for me to shift once again.

He said it was a fear born of watching me that day in unspeakable pain, my body slipping away from him and into something else. I tried to imagine what he had seen but blurred images chased all rational thought. I was slowly going mad. I welcomed it.

Madness would shadow the intolerable nights where I would wake in sweat on cold nights that took my breath away. The candle I refused to extinguish would burn to nothing before morning light and I would watch it fade into a pool of molten wax and a burnt wick.

Bethan's sleep was deep and serene, I envied her. Hers was a misery of temporary residence. She had known happiness once and would know it again. I wondered why I should give so much thought to her, she was a non-entity to my shallowed life. She existed on a plane beside me but ceased to touch any part of me in any real way. But that was about to change.

The snow began to fall in earnest in my 18th year. I had never seen such a blanket of white. It covered the shore and the hills and the ground below. The white-haired man's half-built house became lost in flurries and it settled upon the half built roof. It was a testament to something that would never sit well with me. As I recalled the words of the great whale who knew our fate.

Your house will not hold…

I shuddered and would not look at it. I turned my back on anything that reminded me of the things I had lost. There was a need to think of Caleb and I would find myself forcing my mind away from him.

And then would begin the dreams of a man with skin that shimmered like the scales of a fish. Raven hair in the wind, all of them standing together. In waking moments, they would invade my thoughts and I wondered if I would ever have rest from these things which haunted me.

I longed for the mindless chatter that Mammy and Aunt Hannah shared. The snow brought with it an eternal talking point. They wondered when it would cease, how much of it would fall. They lamented the last time the snow had been like this, during their childhood on Eynhallow. It quite excited them.

But Rohan cursed it, his feet red and sore from walking the fields. In the end the snow had a defeat over him, and he could no longer step outside. His shoes were saturated and hurt his feet and it took three days to dry them by the fire. We ate salted fish and stale bread until I could feel a sickness growing within me.

If I had known any winter before, then hunger had been a friend. This was exile at its core. Prisoners in our own home. Tensions mounted, suddenly the allure of the snow no longer held any sway with us. Even Mammy and Aunt Hannah became tired of it and prayed for the day it would thaw. The things which I had been trying to avoid crawled into the forefront of my mind. All I could do was sit and think about Caleb and how he was faring in England. In the dead of night, I would try to run from dreams of the ringed stones.

"You know, I really don't like Rohan anymore." Bethan said, as we prepared for sleep.

She rarely spoke at this time, but our confinement had been so complete that nothing made sense anymore. I had become used to the silence of our bedtimes, but I was glad she had spoken. It was a welcome distraction.

"He is angry to be kept indoors. He will become more pleasant in the springtime." I told her, feeling the tangible annoyance my brother felt as I built a fire in the corner of a room in the tiny fireplace we had tried not to use until it became too cold to survive the night without it.

"He is always angry about something. It is not that. Only that now he looks at me differently. His eyes follow me, as if he could eat me up. You don't think he would, do you? He is not *that* hungry?"

I could not place his eyes, or what they had been watching. I had been too consumed with other things.

"That is absurd." I sighed. "Whatever would make you think that?"

She quietly shifted her skirt down, the entire garment falling at her feet. Although I did not look at her directly from the corner of my eye, I could see the body of a woman slipping into her nightgown. Her breasts were round and full, her hips creating the perfect shape that would please a man's eye. In that moment a feeling of horror came to me. My mouth became dry at the mere assumption and I prayed that I was wrong. In the place of the child that had first come here was now a burgeoning woman. The only one upon the island that Rohan could cast his eye upon without true sin.

"He is your cousin. He would never hurt you." And in that moment, I hoped that I spoke truth.

Bethan shrugged. "I shall never understand men or boys. They are stupid creatures. Benjamin McDonald was a stupid boy and Rohan is a stupid boy too."

She was fourteen years old. The gap between them had been bridged. He had become a man while she was still a child. But no longer was it so. For a moment I wondered if she did not like him because she could not articulate her feelings. But how could I judge when I was no better?

"Perhaps he is but pay no mind to him. Come spring he will be outdoors again, and you'll not have to see him until supper time."

She sighed in a melancholy way that I recognised. The horror within the pit of stomach churned and I wondered what would become of them. It was inevitable, of course. One so obsessed with the romance of love, locked away on an island at the end of the world with one who had never known the close company of women other than his mother and sister. It seemed foolish to me now that it had not occurred to me before.

"It is very hard to pay no mind to him, is it not? He is so… big. Always he sits where I am trying to cook or wash. Today he insisted on sitting by the fire as I boiled the water. The big lump that he is."

So, the coil had already begun to unravel. I had not seen nor heard a murmur of their furtive glances and stolen moments. Where had I been?

"He cannot abide to be indoors." I reiterated. But I knew it was a poor excuse for what I suspected was something else entirely.

"I am beginning to tire of the indoors myself." She replied absently, climbing into her side of the bed. "Perhaps I shall try to go outside tomorrow."

But it was unlikely. A blizzard raged outside, white frenzy as if the sky was falling down. In the dark we could not see it but in the air, we felt it. The glass pane of our window had frozen solid and not even the warmth of the fire could reach it. If Daddy could see this winter even, he would not have kept us here a moment longer.

"I would not try to venture out there. I dare say there's enough snow to bury all your feet and half your knees. I do not know where the grass ends, and the sand begins anymore. So, I'll not trust myself until I do."

She gave this some thought and then retreated into our familiar silence. A storm raged; I gave some thought to the creatures who must endure it outside. Their fragile lives were battling against the elements and as the wind whistled through the cracks within the stone, I concluded there could be only one to come out victorious.

It was not yet morning when the wind died. The eerie silence was enough to pull me from a dreamless sleep, aided only by the monotonous humming of the storm outside. The fire was now embers and as I lit the candle beside me, I caught sight of my own breath in the dim light. Pulling the blankets around me I turned to make sure I had not pulled them from Bethan, but there was only an empty space where once she had lain. She stood in the doorway; her shadow almost indiscernible against the darkness.

"Will I go to hell?" She whispered, lingering in the cold.

Her voice was low and faltering. I could not see tears, but I knew that they were there.

"What is it Bethan? What have you done?"

In the candlelight her shivering body took on another worldly form. The long white skirt of her night gown almost ghostly.

"I have sinned."

She would not come to me. She welcomed the cold as punishment and backed away as I offered her blankets of warmth.

"Speak not of sin, foolish girl. Come back to bed. In the morning we shall talk."

But she would not. "No, I cannot speak of it. To speak of it would rub salt in the wound. No, I shall not speak of it."

"As you wish. But come back to bed, you'll catch your death."

A brief, yet maddening laugh escaped her lips. "That would be *something.*"

I could barely tolerate her in daylight. In the dead of night, she was infuriating.

"Aye, and you'll have it someday. But until that day will you not come back to bed?" And I resolved that this would be the last time that I would ask.

She reluctantly came and laid beside me. But I was certain she did not sleep and, in some part, neither did I. For I knew to be true that which she would not speak of. That it had come to pass, this horrific thing that churned my stomach to sickness.

, It was a sin that would not sleep. A self-inflicted wound that was open and bleeding and would not stop. When the snow did not thaw, but instead turned to ice we found ourselves at an impasse. It was decided that Rohan would kill one of the cattle and we would smoke the meat and preserve it in salt.

This did not sit easy with me, I implored him to choke one of the chickens instead. Yet another winter had claimed them, not by my hand but by the unrelenting frost. All that remained were some snow-covered eggs that we would save for when the starvation became unbearable. So, for the first time in fourteen days we found ourselves parted from Rohan and for one of us the wait for his return was almost intolerable.

I could not berate her as she sat by the window. I could not say to her that it was wrong. I knew what it was to love another and miss their presence. But hers was temporary and mine could not resolve itself. That old envy peaked for a moment, I found I could no longer look at her. It was an envy tempered with my own regret.

Perhaps it was not obvious, the way she moved against the window in the parlour. It gave the best view of the fields; on a clear day you could see miles out over the island. She paced the length of the room, unintentionally giving away her nervous disposition. Something had tangibly changed, soon it would come to light.

But this was her secret, I had no place to question her. When Rohan returned, blood soaked and dripping wet she let out an audible sigh. She had gotten her dearest wish to fall in love. If she had been sorry for what she had done that first night she had gone to him, she would never be so again. With reckless abandon she went to him and gave no apology for it. Theirs was a simple thing, born of necessity and inevitability.

But it seemed not to matter to either of them. She took his jacket from his broad shoulders and her touch slipped down the contours of each arm. Aunt Hannah hushed her out of the way like a nuisance and Rohan's eyes sparked in vexation. But neither of the old women noticed. I would have liked to have known a love such as this. Although forbidden, it seemed to me that it came as easy to them as breathing. There was something incredibly human about it and I could not understand it.

I ached for Caleb in such a way that made it impossible to think of him now. In buried memories of him sitting beside me in the pouring rain I could recall each feature of his face in perfect detail.

But as I tried to imagine him as he was in England, there came nothing but a sadness that burned like fire. I wondered if I would ever be able to reconcile that part of me that had kept me from going to him that day.

I despised myself for it. I spurned this blood within and would have seen it spill from my veins than endure this pain again. I would welcome the physical agony of the shift a thousand-fold over the constant reminder of what I had lost. If I thought I could find solace in anything I no longer sought it out.

I was afraid of shifting again without warning, in a place where I could be seen. The snow meant that I could not go outside to speak with my animal guardians. This was something I both cursed and welcomed. When finally, it began to thaw, I was almost sorry to see the white diminish.

Chapter Fifteen

THE BALLARD OF ROHAN

My brother was a silent and brooding creature. As far removed from the boy he had once been as a snowflake to a flame. His grief was gone but in its place was now a dark figure that could not revert to who he once was even if he wanted to. But in stolen moments there became a glint of what he could have been. If pleasure made him smile, I could not deny him this small happiness.

And so, I kept his secret, distracted prying eyes from it. Mammy noted the change in him, but only seemed pleased to see some of the darkness fade within. Aunt Hannah was a foolish onlooker. She sensed the shifting tide between her daughter and her nephew. But only a half suspicious eye was cast upon them. For the reality was something she never dared imagine could truly happen. As had I at the beginning.

But as the winter died it had become abundantly clear that if we survived another like it a new madness would take hold. None of us would surface from it unharmed. Perhaps the fact that we had survived it brought new meaning to our lives. When it became hospitable enough to withstand the biting temperatures outside, I ventured out and reacquainted with a part of myself I had begun to almost forget.

I saw them scurry off towards the barn, hand in hand. Rohan and Bethan, in their furtive glances over the breakfast table had been anticipating this all morning. So, I took my leave of The Hylands and went to the half-built house which had somehow stood against the ailing weather.

One of the walls had come down in high winds, but only because it had not been protected properly. But the rest of it had managed to battle onwards and greeted the spring as a friend. The ground was soft from melted snow, but the brick had resisted the slide. I wished that the white-haired man could see it now. That he could stand here with me and admire what he had tried to do. It was only in the back of my mind, in a half-remembered dream, that I recalled the voice of the great whale prophesying the end of all things.

It was a voice I had missed. As I looked across the waves I wondered if they would return this spring. The waters appeared empty without their sleek bodies rising from the waves and gently going back down. Of course, I knew that not to be true. When I turned my back on the sea, I wondered which eyes would be following me across the shoreline and back towards my human life.

Like a tether that could snap at any moment, it seemed that I soon must come to a decision about which path I must take. I could not hang on much longer in this half-life. The birds asked if I would join them once more, but their requests were greeted with a resounding silence. I was not ready to submit myself completely. Although I had given myself over entirely to that shape, I clung to my human form like it was a rock enveloped in a sodden moss that threatened my meagre grasp.

When I returned to the house, all was quiet and dim. A broth boiled slowly above the fire and there was bread on the table. Aunt Hannah sat idly and stirred the broth, a pastime Bethan had long grown weary of.

"Where is that daughter of mine?" She inquired, as I appeared in the doorway.

"I did not see her." I replied, quite lying with no conscience to feel guilt about it. I had long since absolved myself of that.

"Ah, she has an empty head of late. I fear the winter has robbed her of her senses."

Had it not robbed us all of something of ourselves? I was quite certain I had lost an aspect of myself. But what, I was still unsure of.

"She laments her brother still. Of that I am certain. I fear it shall meddle with her sanity before long. I will think of Ewan only as a boy and not as he might be now. Or else I shall crumple to the ground and not get up. But she imagines him elsewhere and it does her no good."

"She'll find peace someday." Was all I could say.

A semblance of hope for her in the wake of dark days. Aunt Hannah was to me as a picture that hangs on the wall in one's home. It was always there, always present. But it never changed anything, only on the surface. But in the long run, always it could be replaced. She was Mammy's sister and what Mammy was to me now was less than a hanging picture.

"Peace is for the dead. In my experience of the living, there shall be no peace until that day. You think there is peace here to be had? Mr. Bishop is a fine man, but a foolish one. Though I dare not say it to his face, I am glad to have others for company here, I do wish to tell him to flee this place and not harbour such folly dreams of having a good life here."

It struck me that I had not conversed with her much, even during our incarceration indoors we had not taken the time to speak. I felt sorry for her, now more than ever. Here was a human I would never understand.

"Where is Mammy?" I asked then, not to inquire as to her whereabouts but to ensure I could be gone when she arrived.

"She went to the barn. But that was some time ago…" She ceased to stir the broth and raised an eyebrow, as if something had occurred to her suddenly that she had not given thought to before. "She should have returned by now."

A sudden dryness to my throat clutched at me. A dread that would not be slaked.

Oh, forever I have wanted a secret unknown, I shall reveal all of mine to save Rohan's. My little brother… What have you done?!

His protests came low and hushed from behind the barn door. As I came to it, I heard them speaking in rough tones. Three voices, speaking in unison. I had begged Aunt Hannah not to follow, but she would not be coddled. It was with a heavy heart I opened that door and prayed for it all to somehow blow away.

Rohan, his half naked body shrouded in twilight held a hand against his face as I let inside the dying sunlight. Bethan, her modesty protected by a half-laced gown sat upon the hay with a tear ravaged face. Standing against them was a trembling old woman, her fists clenched so tightly the blood had run cold and white. I could not see her face. Nor did I want to.

"What goes here?" Aunt Hannah breathed, confusion soon turning to realisation. "I say, Bethan, what goes here?"

But she could not form the words through racking sobs. But they were not sobs of regret or apology. The fierce look in Rohan's eye only served to place their stance as one of rebellion. They would never be sorry.

"I shall have your sins in my pocket, son." Mammy said, in a strangely calm voice that only thinly veiled her true rage. "I swear upon your father's bones. I shall not leave this to rest. On the morrow, I shall take you myself to the church and there will you repent!"

He spat on the ground and wiped his mouth with a grubby hand. "Aye, and you'd hold it above my head for the rest of my days."

Aunt Hannah stepped forward, pulling the door closed behind her as if others could hear her. But it resisted the pull and swung open, revealing them in all their shame.

Bethan quietened her sobs. In the cold light of day, it was as if they could hide no more. Aunt Hannah stared at Rohan, his bare chest rising and falling with deep breaths. She went to him slowly and began to beat upon him, raining blow upon blow that he could not feel. For a moment I thought he would strike her, but instead he stood resolutely and allowed her to take out her rage upon him. She roared into his defiant face, the very blood from her veins spurting forth into the whites of her eyes. I had never seen such hatred, such spite.

"You brute! How could you do this? You are an animal, a monster!"

It was then that something peculiar unfolded. From somewhere deep within, Bethan found the strength to dry her tears and pull Aunt Hannah away from an unharmed Rohan. She gasped, a sharp intake of breath, more of heartbreak than shock. Then she watched, as we all did, as Bethan took her place beside Rohan. None would ever remove her from it.

"Bethan? What is the meaning of this?" Sobbing uncontrollably, Aunt Hannah allowed Mammy to pull her back.

"Need there be a meaning?" The young girl pleaded, suddenly appearing much older than she had ever appeared before.

Of course, she was more woman than I. She knew that thing a woman comes to know when she has lain with a man, that I had yet to become initiated into.

"He is your cousin, child. Your flesh and blood." Mammy said sharply, keeping her sister at bay. "And you are but fourteen years old. Do you not see the sin in this?"

I recalled the night she had asked me if she would go to hell. This had not come about without much soul searching. Each of them was now resolute as they stood together, willing to defend their love at all costs.

"It is not unheard of, is it not, mother? That cousins are allowed to marry? I know this to be true, because Benjamin McDonald once told me that his mother and father were cousins and there is no sin in that."

Rohan placed his large hands upon her shoulders, willing to pull her back into his arms should either of them protest.

Aunt Hannah broke free of Mammy's grasp but did not approach. Instead she stepped back, shaking her head uncontrollably.

"We have been fools here!" She cried. "What good could ever come of this? When Seamus died, it was the end... the end..."

Mammy tried to console her, but she would have none. "And I have been the biggest fool of all. To come here, to bring my children here. Now my son is gone, and my daughter has been... Defiled! By her own cousin."

I saw the words cut through Rohan like a knife. He closed his eyes and swallowed hard.

"I myself am only seventeen, Aunt Hannah." He reasoned. "Do you forget that?"

She regarded his size. "You have been a man much longer than she has been a woman. See… she is yet to become a woman!"

"And is that your grievance? That I am older? Or that I am her cousin?"

She was cornered like a defenceless mouse against a house cat. It appeared that neither, or perhaps both were her grievance.

"It matters not." Mammy interrupted. "We must decide what is to be done now."

Bethan turned and clung to Rohan's chest as if they would somehow drag her away at any moment.

"I'll not be parted from him." She said resolutely.

"I see. Tell me, how long has this been occurring?"

Rohan stepped forward, pinning a terrified Bethan to his side. "If there is blame to be placed, then you must place it on me. I am a weak man. I swear I never once looked upon her, not once, before winter."

"And you think this rids you of any wrongdoing?" Aunt Hannah spat. "Do you dare to justify yourself?"

"I justify nothing. I cannot expect someone who has lived on the mainland to understand."

He turned away, picking up his shirt and covering his bare chest. Aunt Hannah looked to Mammy; whose face seemed to take on a sadness.

"I begged your father. Always I begged him that one day we might leave this place." Her eyes drifted to where I stood in the corner. "I blame myself. What sort of man does not seek the company of a pretty girl? She is the only one he could cast his eye upon."

"You behave like Judas!" Screamed Aunt Hannah, turning her rage and disappointment to any who spoke against her.

"No, I do not condone it. But there is no help for it now. See, how could it be avoided? They have only each other."

With Mammy's change of heart, Aunt Hannah turned to face me. Her solid eyes bloodshot from tears, and her skin pale as snow.

"Did you know about this?" She demanded.

Bethan pleaded with me silently, her face desperate and nodding slightly. Rohan seemed to have absolved himself with Mammy's words. She would punish him, of that I was certain, but she did not hold him accountable. That was all the acceptance he needed. She would pray for him until the end of her days, regardless.

I saw no reason to lie. "I knew."

If there had been any colour in her face, it drained from her. She stepped back in horror, the lines of her age seemed to deepen. For a moment, she seemed older than Mammy.

"I've seen them. Those children born of incest. There might be no law against it, but a law which is made of man cannot transcend what God decrees. He has shown me what comes of it. Some of those McDonald children did not live long enough to know the sins of their father or mother. They weren't... born right. Do you not see?!"

She did not speak again. Instead, there descended a strange understanding that she would not spend another moment in our company. Betrayed and abandoned, she walked away and left us to pick up the pieces. Mammy had Bethan follow her and promise to make amends. But it was too late for any of that. Rohan stared at me, awaiting my judgement as he put his shoes and coat back on.

"It is better this way." He said, "Better this than bearing secrets. We have enough of those..."

"I do not begrudge you your secrets." I said, on the verge of offence. I had asked for none of this.

He dropped his shoe and stared at me incredulously. "Have I begrudged yours? I simply meant that now I am free of mine, perhaps yours will remain."

"You will not be allowed to rest." I reasoned. "This is only the start of it."

He shrugged and picked up his shoe. "Then so be it. I'll endure it. Have I done such evil, Finola?"

"There is greater evil in the world, I do not doubt. But Aunt Hannah can only see the sin, not that two people have come together when there is no other to turn to."

"Aye, and think you that the only reason? I would pick her out of any girl on the mainland. I would pick her, even if she were not the only one to pick. It is true, perhaps, that my eye only turned to her out of need. But then she picked me, too."

I did not doubt that he had loved her and loved her still. The way his eyes cast to the ground, fearful and fierce at the same time. He had nothing to fear from me and he knew that. Yet he would defend this love, no matter the cost.

"I have punished myself. I have pushed myself to the brink of madness with it, I am not absolved of this. If I have relinquished my place in Heaven, then so be it. There is no place for me anywhere, without her now."

The sun rose a little earlier every morning. Golden light spilling over the horizon, flowing into the room at an hour I was not accustomed to. Some mornings I would close my eyes against it, torn between relief that winter was over, and the impending doom of what spring would bring.

When the whales returned to Eynhallow I welcomed them with tears of joy which came to me unexpectedly. I wanted it more than ever. To know that side of me I had run from long enough. A third eye had been opened and it would not even blink for fear of the darkness. They waited for me. I resolved that I would not keep them waiting for much longer.

"I feel we are losing you, aren't we?" Rohan said to me, as I stood by the garden gate at sunrise.

I smiled ruefully. "Never that."

"You remain here like a caged bird. Winter has been too long; you have not been yourself since that day…"

Perhaps it was true. But I had given little thought to it, instead consumed by a longing that remained even now.

"A caged bird? Do you see my shackles, brother?"

He placed a hand upon my shoulder and pulled me into his embrace.

"I have been a little selfish. It has been my secrets that have troubled you of late."

I could feel his heart softly beating beneath that heaving chest. "Have you softened, then?"

He laughed and the sound of his laughter was sweet to my ears.

"Perhaps not as much as Mammy would like. But enough to admit my faults, aye."

I recalled for a brief moment the babe in my arms, the squealing thing that would not rest.

"Then there is hope for all of us, even if we are damned." I sighed.

He tightened his grip. "I loved you first, never forget that."

And there he was, the little boy I had held in my arms. A wondrous face watching mine, both of us trying to decipher the other. I remembered it as if it had been yesterday, clear in my mind. There was no doubt that he spoke the truth. Because I had loved him first too.

"How long did you know?" He asked me, pulling away from me slightly so that he might look me in the eye.

He was serious and brooding now, fragments of his present self-marking their territory.

"Always." I replied, "I think I always knew."

He nodded, as if that much should have been obvious. "And you did not come to me?"

"It was not my secret."

"It matters not now. It is a secret no longer and I care not what any other save for you thinks about it."

He awaited some confirmation. His eyes probed me expectantly.

"Do I have your blessing?" He asked, "I'll love her regardless. But whatever people say, it will matter not to me. Except for you. It matters a great deal to me that I have your blessing."

I could see his face, young and innocent, sitting by my side by the fire. His little hands reaching out towards the flames, my own hands pulling him back in warning. *No Rohan, you mustn't get too close. The fire will burn you…* And without hesitation he had heeded my warning. Taking in each word as law.

"Of course, you have my blessing."

Fear turned to joy, every crease of worry upon his face unfolding. He sighed in relief, his large shoulders falling as if a great weight had been lifted.

"And now you must listen to me. Promise me something?" He did not wait for me to respond. "It is for me that you remain. Aye and for Caleb Bishop. I am not a clever man, but I am not stupid either. Think you he will return? That which is not set in stone must not be waited upon. Do not remain here for me, Finola. I have found a companion to spend all my days with. I shall not be alone. You must not worry of what may become of me. I fear for what may become of you, if you stay here. Already there has been too much waiting. I have not rested properly since…"

His voice caught in his throat; a memory that had haunted him stuck there. "Well. You know what I speak of. I thank God every day that it was I and no other with you that day."

I had wondered when this day might come. If I had been stood before a mirror and seen myself for what I truly was, still I would not have been prepared for it. Standing before my brother now, on this red sky morning, it was as if I saw myself within him.

And I could not hide. It gave me a small comfort to know that he would have Bethan by his side. But I was afraid for myself. I had not given it much thought, instead I had buried it. Unable to admit that the real fear was not for what I might leave behind, but for what lay before me.

"Say something, Finola." He urged.

I knew what it was that he said to me. The pain in his worried face told me it was not easy, but necessary. He would push me if he had to.

But I could not find the words. What words could there be for what he was asking of me? The sky was already turning blue, the wind dying to a fractured breeze to mark the beginning of a warmer day. The house had begun to stir, and we would not have much more time together.

"I promise." Was all I could say.

He nodded. All too soon he was gone from me, his long slow strides taking him back indoors. Back to his own struggle. There, where the land met the sea was mine. My struggle and the two fates had never been destined to collide. My entire life, no matter how I tried to avoid it, was leading me down a path in the opposite direction.

But what if Caleb returns to me? And I have bled my meagre heart for nothing? When all could be replenished? Then shall Nathan Munro's death be in vain. Then shall Ewan departing be for nothing at all. Before all else I must know… If his love is true then I am not fated so ill. I am not Finhag. I am not afraid to go into the water.

Lucie Howorth

Chapter Sixteen
THE LETTER

Mind troubled by the emptiness, I heaved my corrupted memories towards the window and almost felt feathers beneath my skin. It was a fleeting shadow of something I once felt, and then it was gone. I was about to learn my fate. As white hair came ashore and looked towards my unchanged house, I felt the fire burn within and wondered if I would have breath to move myself from where I stood.

I had not slept, destroyed by what Rohan had said to me and disturbed by the shifting beside me as Bethan crept away from our bed to his. One day we will reveal the truth, but one of us will die before we get there. I prayed hard that their love would not cause it.

And I am nothing. Just a breath once exhaled where I stood, by winds long gone. If they had love, then they were the lucky ones. All I had was bitterness and fear. It grew like an illness as boats emerged on the horizon, one after the other in succession over the waves.

Aunt Hannah appeared in the doorway, her demeanour dishevelled as she carried water in from the well outside. She looked at me expectantly and sighed in dissatisfaction.

"Have you the wit to greet our neighbours?" She asked breathlessly. "See, they return!"

She hurried away, spilling water as she rested the pail upon her bony waist. But it was not me she was dissatisfied with. It was herself, the reality that she could not keep Rohan and Bethan apart. However clandestine they were. We all knew what occurred once the candles went out.

I made my way out into the garden. If my body had not felt as if it were my own before, I feared once again I would be transformed where I stood and taken by the wind. I checked my bones, my skin. Nothing shifted, nothing moved. Except for the relentless beat of my heart that seemed to thrum so loudly I feared that others would hear it.

The white-haired man appeared at the gate and was greeted by Mammy and Aunt Hannah as if royalty had come to Eynhallow. Behind him stood his eldest son, the one who shared his name. Victor was unchanged, winter had served him well. It had served them both well. The white-haired man had not aged a day. The lines around his eyes creased in that familiar way as they sought me out, and finally he smiled upon me.

"Ah, here is the beautiful Finola." He said kindly, so kindly that my heart almost broke. "How well you look."

And yet, I do not feel well at all.

He had called me beautiful, as if it was now reserved for him to do so freely since our last summer in his company and because, he was old enough to be my father.

"Welcome back." I replied shyly, allowing him to take my hand in greeting.

He nodded slowly and sighed, as if the journey had finally claimed his strength. Mammy ushered the two men inside, where freshly caught fish was laid out for them and a broth bubbled upon the fire. Rohan's absence was politely noted, there they greeted Bethan in much the same way I had been greeted. She was called beautiful and much was made of her sudden growth. Aunt Hannah grimaced, but not a word was said.

"Come, sit to the table and tell us of your journey. You must be weary." Mammy urged.

They tucked into the fish like men starved. Victor, taking it within his hands, forgetting all sense of propriety. Perhaps they felt no need for it here. I wondered how different it would be in their own home. The elder Victor gave a disapproving look and the younger picked up his fork. A grown man and yet he still looked to his father for approval. He was not so different from a boy I once knew.

"I shall not lie; I will not miss the journey. With that in mind, I have brought more men to work the land. I was foolish to think that the four of us could do much and with Simon leaving us so early on, I did not anticipate such a heavy workload."

I thought they would blame me, but their eyes did move from the food on their plates. It was a passing comment, but one that made me sick to the stomach. Or perhaps it was something else.

Where are you? Why do they not speak of you?

Victor cleared his plate and thanked Mammy and Aunt Hannah wholeheartedly. "I have dreamt of good food for days. I cannot say my father is an equal when it comes to cooking. I shall be glad to have my wife here, when our son has grown a little more."

The white-haired man smiled, a broad beaming smile that revealed all of his well-kept teeth.

"Ah yes, there is much to be said about that. The poor lad did not have the best of starts. He came into the world with his cord around his neck. We feared the worst, but I am happy to say that my Grandson is as healthy as can be."

I could feel the rush of congratulations in the air as Mammy clasped her hands together in praise of her God who had apparently saved the poor child. They all thanked God; I was left to watch them out of the corner of my eye. My attention drawn elsewhere. I watched the boats skim the shoreline, three of them in all. The largest I had seen before, but the other two I had not. I counted the faceless bodies as they came ashore, some of them jumping over the side and others waiting until the wooden gangway had been placed upon the sand. There were five in the water and five still on board.

"Ah, what a beautiful name." Mammy said, demanding my attention. "Don't you think so, Finola?"

They had all turned to me, my absent mind noted. "Forgive me, I was distracted."

Of course, Mammy was the first to roll her eyes. "Always distracted this one. Her mind is never set on the task in hand, it is a wonder she gets a thing done!"

The white-haired man smiled politely. "Were we not all distracted during our youth?"

He was defending me. I had done nothing to deserve it. I suddenly felt ashamed of myself. Raven hair covered my face as I bowed my head. Finally, Mammy seemed pleased.

"Mr. Bishop's Grandson. We were speaking of his name. They have called him William, as your Daddy was named also."

But I could not imagine the child which the name belonged to. William was a name for men. But I acknowledged it with a nod of agreement and tried to keep myself within the room.

"I do look forward to meeting the rest of your family." Mammy lamented. "I dare say it shall do us some good to have neighbours once more."

The white-haired man nodded. "I dare say it shall do us some good too. I seem to grow ever wearier of the towns and cities in my old age."

Somebody speak of him! Has his absence been noted? Does he come ashore with the others? Does he come ashore at all? Speak his name just once, I would beg out loud if I could! Do not keep me in this purgatory, there is a sickness which grows with every passing moment.

"I met with Hamish Munro as we passed through Evie. He is looking well. He asked if I would pass on his regards to you. The church has mourned your absence. He asked if you will not consider returning there?"

Aunt Hannah sipped her broth thoughtfully. But Mammy was resolute.

"It is not for me to say for anyone else. But I shall not go back to the mainland without..." She crossed herself, as if speaking of him would somehow bring a curse upon her.

"I have often considered it. But I dare not travel the waters alone with my daughter." No, she would not speak of why. She would not dare to have Rohan follow them to the end of the earth. I had counted ten men.

Ten more pairs of eyes to watch us. She would be content with that to keep them apart. But if she thought it might, she was a fool.

"Then you must come with us. We shall make the journey once a month, once we have made our place here. Church is something I do not like to miss, but I am sure God can see I am building a place for his sons and daughters."

Oh, do not speak of church. Do not speak of anything more, I cannot bear to hear it. Hush your idle tongues and idle talk and let me crawl into the ground to die. Have I not endured enough of winter cold? Did I survive just to be sat at a table to listen to gossip? They must know what it is I crave? Is the pain not etched upon my face? Do I not writhe in agony?

"Tell us of your other sons and your daughter." Aunt Hannah said then, their voices suddenly drowning all else out.

I held my breath.

"Ah yes, my little Ophelia and Nathan. They do very well indeed. Although I do think the anticipation of their new house is becoming a little too much for them. Ophelia asks her mother daily when it will be ready. We tell them it will not be much longer, and I hope we speak the truth!" He erupted into laughter, but it did not last.

His smile became something of a frown. A real sadness overcame him.

Whatever it is you must say, then say it. Say it before I strike you down where you sit, and they shall drive me into the water whether I will go or no!

"Caleb is also well." He said, but the words were fallen and glum.

He did not elaborate. I was forced to endure their formalities until a knock at the door brought an end to the welcome. A man appeared in the doorway. His stride was bold and long, he clutched a cap between his hands that he pulled from his head as he entered. He filled the doorway, his head bowed as he came through. I was astonished to discover that somewhere in the world there were others of considerable size. Out of curiosity, I wondered if he equalled Rohan.

Oh, but this man was not a brute. He was sheepish and polite as he requested that Victor and the white-haired man return to the half-built house.

"Ah, Silas. I have kept you waiting too long." Apologised Victor, instructing his father to stay seated. "No, I shall go and speak with the lads. Stay here father, if these fine women will have you?"

They were flattered enough to agree. The white-haired man was treated to more hospitality as I sat there on the fringe of hysterics.

"I think I shall try to find Rohan. If one of these workers should come across him, I'm not certain their welcome will be as warm." I lied and they knew it was a lie.

But I cared little. As I took my shawl from the hook behind the door and rushed outside, I did not even look back to see their faces watch me go in disappointment.

I called after Victor. His companion, Silas, was the one to turn first. His eyes speculated, as if he had seen me for the first time. But Victor did not turn.

"Do not think that I will not come to you again!" I spat, suddenly overcome with venom for his ignorance.

Silas tried to edge away, but Victor placed a hand upon his bulking shoulder.

"I cannot give you what you want, Finola." And the words were filled with regret.

Who was he to presume what it was that I wanted? If he was trying to shame me, then it had the desired effect. Suddenly I felt such a fool. They would know me for a fool, as I stood there on the verge of tears, showing them my deepest vulnerability.

Silas appraised me. "This is Finola?" He asked.

Victor nodded and a queer look between the two men was exchanged that I did not fully understand. When Victor finally turned to face me, he had managed to compose some kindness for me. But I did not want it.

"You have come to ask word of Caleb?" He asked.

But of course, he already knew. It was as if they all knew.

Outsiders! Who are you to claim this land? It will not be claimed by those who have dwelled here before and will not be claimed by you! Who are you to come here and presume? You do not know an inch of my soul; you do not know sorrow! Do not look at me, do not lay your judgement at my feet! You are not worthy. You will perish before you know one day of happiness here. The land will not allow it! Fools, all of you!

Perhaps it was a curse borne of anger. Perhaps it was nothing more than my misguided inner mind telling me to leave them be and spend my days wondering always. Either way, they saw something burning within me. Had I begun to cry? No, the tears retreated inwards and would not show themselves. It was something else.

"Come Victor, one such as her is a rare breed indeed. Give her word!" Silas said, his eyes still appraising me like a lamb to the slaughter.

"He got a minister's daughter with child. He married her four days ago. He was given leave to come, but his wife would not allow it."

Precious fate! Take me from this place and cast me into an abyss where none shall find me. Tie a rope around my neck and throw me into the endless space below. Anything... But not this.

I roared. I scratched at their chests as I longed to take out their hearts as mine had gone before them. I begged for the ocean to turn and drown their damned heads until their last breath was stolen.

But it was futile.

And instead I stood captivated for a moment, wondering if I should move or remain. They remarked amongst themselves that I did not look well. Their hands were on me then, but I could not feel them.

"Finola, are you sick? You must sit... Silas, fetch some water!"

No, no, no... not water. I'll know enough of that soon enough. It is not water I require.

"I did not want to give you such grave news." Victor said to me, once Silas was gone from our company. "There was nothing could be done. I swear to you... If ever there was a marriage of convenience it was theirs. Perhaps not on her part, but entirely on Caleb's."

Does he offer me comfort? Does he dare?

"I had no idea. I thought it fickle... You should know, Caleb... He is not an honourable man."

Perhaps it was hysteria, but I could not stifle the crazed laugh which escape my lips.

"Think you I did not know that? For all he was, he was not with me. He has found some honour, then."

Silas returned, and they implored me to drink.

"I do not know. It was not honour for which he married. Nor was it love, or any other redeeming quality. But more the fact that our father took pity on the girl and she was willing, I dare say more than a little. He arranged the wedding; everything was done in secret. By the time it came to pass, there was nothing Caleb could do to stop it. For all that he is, he would not see our father humiliated. But I fear the cost was too great."

My smiling friend, who held a knife to my back. A kindly face who looked at me sweetly and sneered in secret. Ah yes, I had known the white-haired man to be kind. Perhaps it was this kindness that he had bestowed upon some minister's daughter also.

But it was a bittersweet thing for me now. His kindness towards her, had stabbed me through the heart.

"Victor, this girl is delirious. You must go and check the tools and brick, but I shall take her back to her house."

I was lifted willingly into Silas's arms. He was not like Simon, not like Isaac either. In his arms, I felt a safety that would become clearer to me as Victor made his was back down towards the boats.

"So, you are Finola." He whispered gently, as he placed me firmly back onto my feet.

I was no more delirious than I was a clucking chicken.

"Yes, and who might you be, Silas?" For a name never quite spelt out the character of a man. That much I had learnt of men, if nothing else.

"A friend."

From his pocket he pulled out a crisp white envelope. Folded in the middle, it had obviously not been removed from its place since it had been put there. He handed it to me quickly, urging me to keep it hidden.

"Caleb took me into his confidence, before we set sail. I do not know why he chose me."

But of course, he chose wisely. I could see this man's tenderness laid bare upon his very face.

"Perhaps because I am already married. I am not a threat."

I recalled Isaac's words. How he had encouraged Caleb to have his way with me and disregard me just as wickedly. His oldest friend and yet he could not trust even him with this task.

"But if I may be so bold, I can see why he would want to bring word to one such as you. Miss, if you pardon me, but word of your beauty has reached all of us. I dare say it is driving him mad, that we are here when he is not."

He would excuse himself, but he had captured my attention.

"Have you known Caleb long?" I inquired, as calmly as I could muster.

"Since I came to work at Mr. Bishop's factory. Never spoke much with him, always he was with undesirable company. I had my wife and son to provide for. But we spoke a little, here and there."

"You know, then? He has told you everything?"

He bowed his head. As if the things he had been told he had no right to know. But they were Caleb's thoughts to tell who he wished, and I had no right to encroach. I was sorry I had asked.

"I do not know if it is *everything*. But he came to me on the eve of his wedding to confess himself and to give me this letter. He spoke of Finola, the girl on Eynhallow. He spoke of how you spurned him."

But he was quick to retract what he had said, his hands calling out to me in forgiveness. "I mean not to insult you, but he was not quite himself that night. Nor has he been since he first came here really."

I needed not forgiveness, there was no insult he could offer me that could change a thing. I had spurned Caleb, over and over. There was not a single drop of untruth.

"Perhaps this is my punishment, then. For sending him away from me. I thank you, Silas, for bringing this to me."

He bowed graciously and left me with nothing but the wind in his wake. He offered no other word, no agenda. For a moment I was humbled, until a sick vision overtook all else. Of Caleb stood in a church, the round swelling belly of his bride stood beside him. *Why, Caleb?*

I did not go back to the house, but instead I stalked away as silently as I could towards the kirk. There, underneath the broken arch where we had sat together in the rain, I opened the envelope. In that cleansing moment, I knew that the very act of leaving me had already proven his love was true.

My Dearest Finola,

It is my greatest wish that this letter finds you well. I have begun to write this a thousand times already. I have never had to put my heart upon a piece of paper. But there is little else I can do.

I have built my life on mistakes. But none I grieve as much as the one I made on the day I left your shores.

What foolish notion I had upon that day I can barely remember now. I waited until the final hour and when you did not appear, I allowed myself to leave out of anger and spite. I did not take my eyes off the shores, until it seemed the whole Island disappeared before my very eyes. It was too late to turn back.

Even as I write this, it takes every ounce of strength I have not to come back to you. To stay away from you, to be apart even as I slept under the same stars was like tearing my own flesh from my bones.

There is nothing left of me. Because I am a weak man and I do not deny that I wanted to forget you.

Every waking moment consumed with regret that I had not tried harder to win your heart drove me to insanity, and reunited with my old life, I lost the fight against old demons. Such a man as I am, with such wicked things at his disposal, to be as far away from you as I am now there was no other medicine. No other way to rebuild the broken pieces I had left behind.

Forgive me, Finola. I have sinned against my own heart and there is the greatest sin of all. I shall burn in hell for this and this alone. For all other sins are insignificant to me now.

My father has told me I am to be married on the morrow. The bride shared my bed but once and scarcely for a moment. I was a heartless bastard towards her, but I did not pretend that I would be anything other than a fiend. For a moment of madness, I shall repent for a lifetime.

She is with child and I am to believe that I have fathered the wretched thing. I cannot say otherwise. Her honour is intact, whereas mine leaves little to be desired. Was she not the daughter of a minister, I may say some other fool had gotten her with child?

But I cannot place blame on any but myself. My father thinks she is a good match for me, and he has convinced the Minister, and any other with a wagging tongue about my conquests.

I believe this is my punishment. For whatever I have been before, the sorry excuse of a man I shall be forever more.

But for a few sweet moments I was neither.

Every moment spent with you was like the darkness receded. I would have courted you with such grace that every hand I had ever laid upon another would be washed clean.

I remain here because I deserve to perish for what I have done. But not a single moment goes by that I do not think of you and our stolen moments. I pray that you did love me, behind every single reproach.

For I have loved you since the very moment I saw you on the boat. Barefoot and beautiful. I shall love you until my wasted heart is no more.

Forever Yours,

Caleb. Xxx

Chapter Seventeen

THE DEATH OF MORNING

I no longer counted the days. All of them seemed to merge one into the other. The passing of time held no interest to me and neither did all else.

My mind was dulled with a numbing sensation, unable to think of times gone by and unable to think of times ahead.

The past bore too much pain and there was no future in which I could see myself now.

When I turned nineteen, I rebuffed any acknowledgement of the day. Nineteen years and I was no closer to that all-consuming fate I had been promised.

I was a woman now and none the wiser than I had been as a child. Except for that part of me that yearned, I would not allow it to be felt. My discontentment was swept under the carpet in favour of the illness growing within Hylands walls. Where a love had blossomed, so had an intolerable hatred. What came of it ended another chapter in our lives that I was not displeased to close.

Heartless, or perhaps because my heart was already broken, I could not bring myself to mourn greatly on that crisp spring morning.

The sun had barely risen. Dew fell down the windowpane like rain, dripping from the moss that hung from the roof tiles. It was warm and the breeze was soft, and I could not bear to greet it as I pulled the bed covers over my head and tried to forget, that another day had come.

Bethan had not returned from Rohan's bed, which was unusual for the hour. But I was restless and stifled and couldn't remain in bed where thoughts tried to claw their way back into my mind. I met with Bethan in the hallway, who smiled sweetly as we passed each other.

"You must not leave the hour so late." I told her.

But she shrugged and seemed not to care. "They are not fools."

The house was steady and still, as it seemed to always be before any had risen. The foundations seemed to sigh in relief, before the onslaught of what we might bring to the brick and mortar.

It had been nothing but putrid bile and evil tongues. When the door was closed, so began the campaign of spite and mistrust.

Aunt Hannah, away from her God and her church, had not been able to cope. The loss of her son, a toll so great she had barely grieved, had somehow shifted into a great loathing for the daughter who had now betrayed her. There was no rest for her while their love lived. Ewan became a martyr in his absence. Spoken of as the perfect child who had never dishonoured his mother. Perhaps he may have brought dishonour, if he'd had the presence of mind to stay by her side. Mammy would not speak of what she knew occurred. Perhaps from blind ignorance, or because her sister's wrath was enough.

I went to the well to fetch water for the pot above the fire, thinking of nothing in particular as I watched the pail go down into the murky depths.

It was then that I saw her. I knew that she was dead. There is no look that the living can give with eyes so wide. Only the dead can hold a gaze so deep and yet so empty. The blue of her lips had begun to take away the colour of her face and she clutched eternally to the grass beneath her.

I cannot go inside and take news of her death into the house. I cannot shift her body; I cannot bear to touch her. I must scream and scream good. Then they will come running to me and see for themselves what I have found. Then I am cleansed of this great responsibility.

And so, I stood beside her lifeless body, screamed until the throat within me cracked and tears came from the sheer sound of it.

When they found us, I was sufficiently traumatised. But in truth, I felt nothing. Bethan, who had already been awake, came first. Followed by Rohan, who was still shirtless and unshaven.

"Ah, lord no!" He gasped, pulling Bethan away from the sight. "What has happened here?"

Through senseless tears I shook my head. "I found her like this."

Two breathless men appeared at the garden wall, upon seeing Aunt Hannah their hands flew to their faces. One of them turned away, unable to look. The other could do nothing but.

"Jesus Christ, would you look at that…" Said the man who stared, brazen and unthinking.

Rohan put Bethan aside, reaching for the man in one great stride. He dangled on the end of Rohan's grasp.

"Ay, I never meant no offence!" He cried, trying to wrangle himself free.

But Rohan's grip was absolute. "Speak one more word. I dare you."

He would have, but the scolding in Rohan's voice was a warning he would be wise not to ignore and he knew it, as Rohan slowly let go, he kicked back and ran away, afraid to even look back. His companion stepped back, both retreating from the scene about to unfold.

When Mammy caught sight of the body lying on the ground, it was as if the heaven's she spoke of heard her and the rain began to fall.

Rohan moved her from the garden, wrapping her body in sheets and placing her on the bed away from sight. But I could feel her in the house. She was still here, not quite departed. She would grasp onto her faded life with every part of her soul, but it was futile.

Hour upon hour crept by, as darkness fell, I thought I could hear the faint laughter of acceptance. But perhaps it was only the wind. There was no other sound. Flickering candles danced in the drafts that escaped through the old stones, the fire threatening to burn to embers as we sat in silence. Bethan had quietened her sobs in Rohan's chest, but Mammy had not shed a single tear. Only her vacant stare betrayed any grief. I felt guilty that I had not shared their bereavement. Perhaps Rohan was right. Was I becoming lost?

"What must be done now?" Bethan asked, her voice broken from sobbing.

The sound of it broke the silence. A strange, unexpected sound that roused a thoughtful sigh from each of us.

Mammy threw another log into the fire and stoked it until flames began to rise once more. But she offered nothing more.

"Speak Mammy, it will do no good to let it fester. Am I not living proof of that?" Rohan said, his affectionate gaze resting upon his cousin's face.

She shook her head, strands of grey hair falling about her face. "She'll not be buried here. That would be a cruel thing indeed."

A knowing look was exchanged, from Rohan and Bethan and then to me.

"No." Rohan agreed. "There is none here who did not know of her dislike for this place. No, we shall take her to the mainland to lie with Uncle Seamus."

There was a unanimous silence that screamed a regretful reluctance to make that journey.

"I wish that I could send word to Ewan." Bethan lamented; her belief still locked stoically on Ewan returning to the mainland. "He would want to know if mother died, wouldn't he?"

Her eyes shot to Rohan, who soothed her gently. "When we return to the mainland, we will have word put out. He will find out, one way or another."

And there it was. That conspiratorial look that was reserved for that most deepest of secrets.

Do you ask me to send word? To that place where I know he dwells? You think it is as simple as all that? You have too much faith in me, brother!

"I will keep watch by the fire tonight. Mammy, you must take my bed. Bethan, will you remain with her?"

He had left little room for her to disagree. I knew it was to meet his own agenda.

"I think I shall retire now." Mammy said then, vacating her seat slowly and without purpose. Bethan holding her arm as if at any moment she would fall.

The moment they were gone, Rohan closed the door. As if that old door could keep out our whispers. It was sheer ceremony, a hope that we would go unheard. His jaw flexed nervously as he came closer to me. Pushing the hair away from my face, he placed his lips beside my ear and spoke in hushed tones.

"You know what it is that I ask of you."

My cheek brushed the side of his as I rose upon my tip toes to whisper back. "You think I have that authority?"

"You must try, or she will! She will ask where her brother is, and they will think her mad. If she is to believe he went to the mainland, then he surely must have been seen. It does not sit well with me, to lie to her. So, the best that I can do is anything within my power to bring him back to her! Do you understand?"

It is true, then. My darling baby brother. You have found one dearer to you than I. One that you will protect now and forever, above all others. I shall be a pawn in your endeavour to keep her safe. Perhaps I have lingered too long...

"Yes." I whispered, pulling my face away from his. "I understand."

Guided only by the moon, I made my way down to the shoreline. The half-built house was alive with men coming and going from their boats, torches fading into the darkness as they retired for the night. They unnerved me; their movements so close to my own. I wondered if any of them had the same morals as that damned little man. If they did, I vowed I would cut them where they stood if they tried to touch me again.

Perhaps it was the secrecy of my being there by the water and wanting to be concealed that made me think such barbaric things. I had not touched upon these magical things during the freeze of winter. A part of me was now afraid that I had lost touch with it. For a moment I stood, dazed, watching the moonlight slip between the waves. The tide was receding, and I knew I did not have much time.

"If you are there, then hear me."

The ominous wind picked up. Somewhere, a bird cried into the night.

"I have not forsaken you! I beg you, hear me!"

There was a lull, a quiet moment where the wind receded and all else was still. Not even the birds made a sound. All was silent and still. Until the waves broke, crashing together as a heaving body lifted above the surface. Sparkling in the moonlight, he came towards the shoreline. But no further than was allowed. Tears pricked at the corners of my eyes. Perhaps for the fact I had doubted myself, or perhaps because he still came to me.

What is it, Child? Why are you crying?

But the tears fell onto lips that could not hide their smile.

"Because I thought that you would not come to me."

I am your guardian, Child. I will come to you always.

"Yes. I have known this, yet still I have doubted it. But we will speak of it another time. For now, I have come to beseech something of you."

The whale lingered before me; his fin just visible against the moonlit waves. He was considering something.

"I would not ask. Only that I have news for my kin under the sea. Although I suppose he is not my kin more."

The boy speaks of you as his Kin and highly he does speak of you.

"Then you have seen him, then? Can you get word to him of his mother's death?"

He was considering something. Whispers I could not hear, but were there, nonetheless.

He knows the one who gave him birth has passed.

"That cannot be..." I was troubled by the thought. "How did he come by this knowledge?"

He dwells in the house of your grandfather. He who sees all.

Knowing this gave me a bittersweet comfort and yet it uneased me still. Vague memories I had suppressed burned like virgin candles. The man with the raven hair, the skin like the scales of a fish.

"I implore him to return to Eynhallow. His sister grieves much and has need of him. If indeed there is one who sees all, then he will allow it."

That will be as it will be. But he will not be the boy you once knew. You will find him changed.

"As you have said, it will be as it will be." And it was true.

It mattered little to me if the boy I had once known returned, or a changed man in his place.

Then it shall be done.

Lucie Howorth

Chapter Eighteen

THE TRUTH

I called his name in the darkness and when he heard me, his arms found me when no other could. Nothing in life could ever be as sweet as this beyond sleep. Even with eyes closed, I knew these arms. They had carried me a thousand times in sleep. Even in memories buried so deep I could not remember them in the waking hours, here they abandoned my cause and came to me, setting fires within.

There was still a shadow of him in the place that he had left behind. When the darkness gave way to light, I saw his face. Then sleep would become my enemy, even his name would be lost in dreams. I would force myself to wake, too afraid to stay in this beautiful hell. *Caleb*...

But it was nothing but a dream. A foolish yearning that came to me when I no longer had power over my thoughts. Alone in my room, it was cold even in the spring, the room filled with mist that had come from the sea.

A thick mist it was this morning, giving my mind other things to think of. The sun was fighting behind it and would break the seal soon. Dawn had not yet fully broken, and dew was still collecting upon the windowpane. Even my hair was damp, stuck to my cheeks with tears I had shed in the night. I damned myself for it and wondered when the oblivion would stop.

Perhaps it had only been a few minutes, perhaps it had been longer. The haze of awakening began to lift, and my mind placed firmly those feeling to the back where they could be numbed. They would return to me again in sleep, I had no doubt of it. But now I was awake and the battle to keep heartbreak at bay resumed.

I passed the room where Aunt Hannah's body lay. Swiftly moving beyond it as if being so close to death would somehow impart itself upon me. I passed the room where Mammy and Bethan lay, their exhausted sleep still undisturbed.

Even as I came into the kitchen on silent feet, I found my brother asleep in the chair by the fire. Even in misery their sleep was undisturbed. All of them in sweet unconsciousness.

I would not linger to see them awaken, stirring from uninterrupted slumber. The mist crept in from every crack in the old house, threatening to invade the very air we breathed.

Outside it was no better. The thin veil of light that would fight to the death began to bleed through, giving subtle shapes to the land beyond.

I would know my way regardless.

The sound of the water could not be mistaken. As I carefully stepped between the uneven ground, I was secretly pleased with myself when I finally reached the shoreline. The sand was cold and moist, and the tide was high. I shivered against the cool breeze that seemed much colder in this strange mist. The boats sat ominously, bobbing around in the swelling tide, the sight of them too ghostly to stare at for too long. The men would not resume their work until the mists receded. If they did not believe this place was cursed before, they would surely believe it now.

Strange even to me was this mist. I had never seen it linger so low into the land. It brought with it a coldness that was of winter, so had no place in the burgeoning spring. I felt the skin upon me rise in little bumps and my teeth begin to chatter.

Somewhere from beyond it seemed voices began to chime. Perhaps it was but one voice? I could see none of the men come to their boats, but perhaps they were shrouded in mist? This voice knew my name. As it seemed the sun would break though, so it seemed the voice came closer.

"Show yourself." I whispered, suddenly afraid that I was no longer alone.

Where the sun began to show itself, there in the mist before me came a spectre. Light began to dissipate the foggy air, the shape of something I could not define coming towards me.

Yes, I was afraid. I was reminded of the angels Mammy had spoken of when I was a child. I closed my eyes against the awesome sight. I did not want to see; I did not want to know. I would let them do as they would. If it were of this world at all, if it were not imaginings of my broken mind. I regretted that I had asked that disembodied sound to show itself.

"Finola, open your eyes." Said a bemused voice, that was familiar and yet so very different from anything I had ever heard before.

It was as if it had never been. As if the land had never known a day of mist. Clear in the sky, the morning sun burned above a pale shade of blue. Not one single cloud lingered. I almost drew back in real fear, until I saw before me the reason for such strange magic.

"Ewan!" I breathed, the sight of him bitterly overwhelming.

Not the Ewan of my memory, though. Gone was the pale and sickly child. Gone was the pallor and grey. Gone were the timid eyes and stark reluctance. Here, before me, was a boy who had grown into his own skin. True, he would never be large. But it would not suit him to be so. The differences were subtle and yet so alarmingly different. Dressed in a modest tailored suit, I wondered what artifice this was. Had he not come from the water?

"Enchantments." He said, noting the direction of my eyes as they scoped his appearance. "I will tell you everything you have need to know. But first, will you not embrace me, cousin?"

Perhaps I was relieved, perhaps I was still a little afraid. I allowed him to take me into his arms and hold me there for a moment. The scent of him was not right, the suit felt as real as anything made by my own hands, but the rest of him was almost like a dream. He smelled of salt and weeds and it was not entirely unpleasant. I almost took a deep breath of him into me, before he pulled away to appraise me.

"You are well." He said, but it was not a question.

He was entirely confident, with a broad smile to match. If I was no longer afraid, I was certainly made nervous by this creature before me. His eyes no longer seemed to recognise darkness. They were bright and hopeful. I almost cried for what he had become. He was an overwhelming sight.

"Speak Finola, it is certainly a good thing I am here, is it not?"

And it was. But here in this moment I could not see beyond that goodness. He was a shiny new penny. Unspent and untarnished.

"You have come from Finfolkaheem? The whales sent word to you?" The words came out panicked and rushed, I almost brushed his collar to see if it were indeed real.

He nodded slowly. "I have. I will tell you everything you have need to know in time. For now, I will be content to play my part in whatever façade you created for my absence and I shall pay respects to my mother and sister."

My heart sank. I felt a little regret that I had not given them a real façade.

"I could not give them much. I told them you went to the mainland. Whatever else you wish to say, that will be up to you."

He nodded solemnly and gestured towards the house. "Come. Let us get this business out of the way. Then you and I shall speak freely."

So rich and smooth were his words. He had never spoken much, if at all. To hear him so now was a true testament that the pain I had caused had been justified. Had he come to me a broken man; I'd surely have let a wicked thing happen.

He went before me towards the Hylands, regarding the half-built house. The men were staring at the sky, puzzled. Ewan was amused. A brief and quiet laugh escaped his lips, I had never heard him laugh before.

"What would they prefer? To witness the strange boy dressed in his Sunday best emerge from the waves, or a deep mist to shroud such magic? I dare say they will be scratching their heads regardless."

It had not occurred to me that the mist had served such a purpose. For a moment I felt foolish, uninitiated. How wrong it felt that Ewan should know more of this land than I.

"Before you go in, there is something more you should know." I said, as we stood on the doorstep.

He raised a protesting hand and laid it upon my shoulder. "Worry not. If I received word of mother, do you not think I did not receive word of Rohan, too?"

"Then you know? Are all our comings and goings known?"

He smiled, and it was kind and pitying. I could not bear it, that he should pity me when once he had been the most pitiful of us all.

"I will see my mother now." Was all he said, before opening the door and leaving me to stand wondering.

He spent a few precious moments by her bedside before his presence became known. The shrieks of relief and happiness resonated through the brick and out to where I stood in the garden. But there was one who did not make a sound and when he came to stand with me outside, there no relief or happiness to be found.

"The wanderer returns." Said Rohan, with a deep sigh.

"Do you not owe me thanks for it? It is what you asked of me."

I was annoyed that he did not appear happier. I had done this for him and no other.

"Aye sister, I owe you a great many thanks and thank you I do. But that does not mean I am glad to see the pathetic creature back here."

"I think you will find him a changed man."

Rohan shot me a look of reproach. "If I find him a man indeed, I shall greet him as one."

I wondered what made a man. If there was a defining moment, or a measure of their character? Or perhaps it was the size of their manhood, or their stature? Was it the clothes they wore? It seemed to me that there was a fine line between men and boys, and it was not something age could define.

"Such folly. Be glad of it for Bethan's sake, now might they go to the mainland with their sanity intact."

"You mock me?"

I had not meant to. "No, I do not mock you. But whatever idea you had of them trying to find Ewan where he could not be found is now no longer a concern."

"And will he be returning to where he cannot be found?"

That I did not know. But I did not doubt his sincere tethering to that place now. It would be a fleeting visit. But one I suspected would change everything.

"I think he will return. He is not of this land anymore."

A fact which became more apparent as we sat to the table in the kitchen. Ewan, in his smart suit, sat patiently as he waited for Mammy to bring his supper. Rohan sat in the chair by the fire, sharpening his knife while smoking Daddy's old pipe. The two of them had shook hands and greeted each other well. But there was little else to say and for now each seemed happy to tolerate the other. Rohan would let him have this moment, if only to see Bethan smile.

Ewan had made the decision to leave on a whim, he let it be known, as he spoke fluently within Hylands walls for the first time. Upon his return to Evie, he had sought solace in the church and subsequently found himself an apprenticeship in Kirkwall. He worked in the home of an accountant, who was now retired and wanted a young heir to his business down in Scotland. He was happy, healthy and above all, he was where he wanted to be. How he had come to hear of his mother's death was not asked and it was only presumed that Ewan's visit was perfectly timed. For that at least, there was no lie.

But I could not deny there was an unbearable anticipation to hear the truth. They sat until the small hours, mostly speaking of mundane things. The half-built house, and the men who had come this spring to complete it. The long winter of snow that had come before that and how glad they were that Ewan had not been here to witness it.

As ever I sat compliantly, my thoughts not quite present and witnessed their conversation. Offering a little of my own, but not enough to fully become a part of it. Rohan was silent, brooding by the fire, occasionally stoking it with a blackened poker. He only lifted his head to acknowledge when he heard his name spoken.

"Rohan?" Ewan said expectantly, his hands spread upon the surface of the table as if he was about to stand. Instead he leaned back slowly and let out a tired sigh. "Have you given it much thought?"

His eyes shot to me, as if he should know what Ewan spoke of.

"Marriage." I said quietly, "He wants to know if you have given much thought to marriage?"

Rohan dropped the poker into the fire, the handle falling into the dying flames. He cursed himself and wrapped the sleeve of his jacket around his hand to try and fish it out without burning himself. Once he had managed to pull it out, he threw it down into the fireplace and cursed once more.

"You're not her father, Ewan." He spat.

But Ewan was not perturbed. "I think the lack of either parent gives me the right to ask, cousin. I am her brother. I am her elder. There is no other now who will speak for her."

Rohan's eyes burned anger. Ewan had never dared speak so and I had known he would not take kindly to it. I wondered, for a moment, if the two of them would finally come to blows.

"You think she has had need of you? I say to you that you are not her father and you remind me that you are not only her brother, but my cousin also? Think you we have not tortured ourselves enough with that fact? Aye, I'll marry her. But only if she will have me."

He was not so fluent with his words and Ewan was aware of that. Did he get pleasure from seeing Rohan belittled? I began to taste something bitter in my mouth and I did not like it.

But Bethan did not seem to notice. In that moment, there was nothing beyond Rohan. There was that stab of envy again. For her, every possibility life could offer was handed to her upon a plate. Even here, where I had been certain she would perish, she had found the love she had dreamed of all her childhood.

She went to him and buried her face within his huge chest, losing herself there for a moment. I could not bear to watch. She was fifteen and had been offered a marriage of love. I was nearing my twentieth year. I had not so much as known a lover's touch.

"Of course, I will have you. There is no other I would have before you." Bethan said, her arms wrapped tightly around her chosen one.

Perhaps he had not anticipated to come up against a love he could not understand, but Ewan's mouth twitched nervously as he nodded in agreement.

"Then it is settled then. I shall see to it that you are married the day after mother's funeral."

Mammy had not spoken much in the passing days. I had forgotten she sat silently in the armchair near the door. As she slid from it and went towards the fireplace, she shook her head diligently.

"Aye, I dare say you mean well. But there'll be no weddings while my sister is still cold in her grave. I'll not have it."

This seemed to worry Ewan, who took in a sharp breath to protest. But instead he sighed deeply and considered his words more carefully.

"Aunt Mary, I sympathise with your loss. I have lost my mother, but I have little time before I have to return, and I would like to see my sister married. Have they not been sharing a bed?"

Mammy's eyes widened. As if she had not noticed the comings and goings within her own household, for the first time realising what might have been occurring. She was no fool. But there was no doubt she felt like one now. I wondered if he was here simply to belittle all of us. Would I be next?

"That is not for her to say. Have we not gained the right to govern our own laws here? I doubt even the eye of God casts itself upon us now!" Bethan said, defending that which was dear to her.

Mammy crossed herself. "Bethan, there's an end to such talk! God has blessed us and will do so until the end of days. If your brother would see you married, then married you shall be. I shall pray for us and on the morrow, we shall set out for the mainland."

She would not say another word on it. It was not what she wanted, but she would not argue. She was tired and known too much sorrow. She did not often change her mind, but when she did, I knew she had given up.

I wasn't entirely certain I cared much for this person Ewan had become. His confidence seemed entirely arrogant and without sympathy. He had not cried for the mother whose apron strings he had clung to as a child. He did not grieve her as he had the father who had died before her. I was not certain that I was in the company of the same person and as the night grew late, I found myself watching him suspiciously as he bid his sister goodnight. Rohan inclined his head in a polite gesture, but nothing more. The crackling of the fire grew more pronounced as the conversation that had dominated the evening ended. When it was just the two of us, I watched the veil slip.

For a moment, he seemed to allow himself to mourn. Burying his face within hands that would not show his grief. Then it was as if nothing had happened and he composed himself valiantly.

"Will you take a walk with me, cousin?" He asked, gesturing to the walls around us. "I would prefer not to speak where my sister might hear."

It seemed absurd to me now that she should be the only one who did not know the secret that bound us all together. She would think it terribly romantic and keep it locked within. But something told me now was not the time to digress. Ewan was staring at me and it was not pleasant.

"Where do you suggest we go? This land is no longer solitary. Or would you prefer one of those men from the mainland to hear us instead?"

He smiled in agreement but paid no mind to what I had said. "We shall not be heard. That I can assure you."

It was not yet fully dark. Red sky bled into the sea as the sun went down. Silhouettes of birds flew ahead, their voices in pictures flooding into me like forgotten pieces of a book I had once read. They seemed to like Ewan and told me not to be afraid.

As we made our way behind The Hylands and away from the half-built house we passed the kirk and went further towards the other side of the island. The side I rarely went to, where only Rohan would often go. There was no shoreline. Only rocks that stood like towers in the water. Here, it seemed, we would stand together and watch as red turned to black. There was something peaceful about the water here. The waves did not breach as they did upon the sand. Instead it lingered in pools, slowly encroaching like a caressing hand. I was reminded of a day long ago when Daddy had brought me here to watch the sun go down. He sat me upon his knee and spoke of nothing in particular. But it was of little matter to me, I was a child and in that moment I was complete.

Ah, Daddy! How long have you been gone? Have I truly not noticed the turning of time without you? I wish to hear your voice again. To stand here with me and watch the sun. I wish to see your face and speak with you of nothing in particular.

"Why have you brought me here?" I asked, more abruptly than I had meant to.

"This is where it all began." He replied, "This is where you first came to be on Eynhallow."

"Why is it that you should know all of this and I do not?"

He shook his head. "Because it is my task to know this and when I am done so shall you know it too. True, I have come to pay respects to my mother. But there is another reason I have come. The time has come for you to know the truth of your birth, your people."

And you are to be the one to impart this wisdom? I should cry, if it were not so important to me. I have waited for this; I have fought for this. Now I am to be told when there is no fight left within me, when I have tortured myself endlessly?

"How did you come by this knowledge?" I asked, but I was not sure I wanted to hear the answer.

"Perhaps I should start with the knowledge itself and then may I tell you how I came by it."

There was only one thing I wished to know. If there was anything else, it would be just as well.

"Nathan Munro. Tell me of Nathan Munro."

Ewan's face fell. It was as if he was almost sorry to hear me speak his name. It was true then. I had been the cause of his untimely death.

"He was a threat. It was his intention to alert others of your true birth, once he had discovered what you were... what you still are. They had no other choice. It was not their intention for him to die. They tried to initiate him into their ways, teach him things he could not learn from mankind. So that he might one day keep their legends fair. But he did not want to learn. So, on the day he escaped it was too late to save him. I dare say it was a kindness that he died. He would have been forever haunted by the things he had seen. He did not want to embrace it; he did not want any of it. So, you must not blame yourself for his death another moment longer. He brought it upon himself."

Sheer relief flooded through me. Veins pumping harder as I tried to accept that which I had been told. It made little sense to me, even now as Ewan took my hand and bade me sit so that I would not swoon. I allowed him to see me cry and it seemed, for a moment, that he was crying too. But when I wiped the tears away, I saw that he was once again composed, his eyes fixed on the dying sun.

"There is so much for you to understand. I still have much to learn myself. I think, perhaps, I am not the right person to bestow this upon you. I have made much of being forthright when it comes to Bethan and ensuring she will be taken care of when I am gone once again. But I have not fooled you, cousin. You see a bumbling idiot before you and you would be right."

"You are not the same person you once were." I said softly, still choked by tears. "Perhaps you still doubt yourself, but you are no bumbling idiot."

He seemed thankful for my estimation. Perhaps he needed to hear it in order to continue. He did not feel worthy, almost unfit, to be the one here with me now and yet, in some small measure, I was glad that it was him and not a stranger.

"Will you hear me, then? I will give it no justice. I am no great storyteller. I can only give what I was bade to give. But it is what it is."

I nodded slowly and looked away. I would hear him.

"You fear the Finblood, do you not?" He asked, without hearing my answer he nodded. "I have come to tell you that you must not be afraid more. Legends are told to protect and preserve truths. The same can be said of the Finfolk legends. The legends are great, but the truths are much greater. I do not even know where to begin…"

He shook his head and then smiled, as if all the world were nothing but an illusion and we were nothing but spectators. I could tell what he was thinking. I had seen him overwhelmed once before; on the day he was brought here. But there was something absolutely positive this time. There was no sadness, no dread. Only a look of pure admiration and love.

"You have heard the legends, of course. The tale of the Goodman and his three sons banishing a great monster from this land, a shapeshifter who had stolen his wife? They say he reclaimed Eynhallow as revenge and now the Finfolk can never set foot back upon their Hildaland.

For those of us initiated in the truth, we know that there never was a Goodman and he did not have three sons. Perhaps there have been many men who lamented that their wives were taken by forces beyond their control. But they were never taken by force as such, screaming. They were never driven by the force of the Finblood.

They were never compelled, never made to love their consorts. It is a love they have spoken of in legends. That the Finfolk call to their human consorts, binding them with their own desires. Still they speak of it. Mankind being dragged into the water, against their own will. Following into the water as if in a dream, compelled by the love of the Finblood."

"Is that not the way of it?"

Ewan cocked his head to one side. "For thousands of years it was believed and with good reason. For indeed, they can enchant with one fleeting glance but no further than that. The race of men are selfish, their spirits tainted by greed. Whether they would be good people or not.

But regardless of that, the Finfolk found themselves drawn to humans in a way that could not be avoided, the humans, they were drawn back. But as with any tradition, a man could not leave his wife without reason. A woman could not leave her husband without reason and so came the legends of horrific kidnappings.

The Finfolk rising from the waters to take their chosen spouse down into the depths to live a life of slavery and doom. Would that not be better? For some it is more tolerable than the knowledge that they went by choice."

"And what of those who do not take a lover?" I asked meekly, thinking of the man my Daddy had been. Waiting, always. "What of those who do not go? But spend their lives waiting?!"

"For those I cannot say. Whatever their reasons, they are their own." And he was sorry he could not say more.

It was etched upon his face in the dying sunlight. As shadows cast strange shapes across the rocks, I wondered if he would suggest that we move. But instead he remained, watching the waves as if at any moment one of them might encroach, he would welcome it. The flesh of his bones no longer belonged on land.

"There is a richness of life for the chosen ones. A love bound by the ages, a millennia to hold your beloved in your arms. Legends to hide the indiscretion of it. If I had been chosen, it would be well indeed. But I was not chosen, I was thrust upon them and accepted by them regardless and for that, I am eternally grateful."

I could not fathom the years which had gone by, so few as they were. Let alone wonder of all the things which lay ahead in thousands of years to come. To hold my beloved in my arms? For a moment, it would do. For a thousand years, it would be more than I could ever dream of.

"What happened to you, Ewan?" I quietly asked, as he paused for thought. "On that night... when you left us?"

He turned his head poignantly. There was a fire lit within. He smiled and it was a sight to behold.

"Ah, there is the secret which nobody knows." He said, winking with one eye in a playful fashion that was entirely unlike him. "I have spoken much of false truths. Of things which have not befallen me. But here I may speak of it and tell you the real truth. I have longed to tell you of this, ever since it happened. I almost thank my mother's passing for giving me a reason to come back. If only for this, to fulfil my wishes and that of Astala."

And there it is again, that name I have heard before.

"I almost did not go. I almost went back to The Hylands, to tell my mother that I was sorry and that I would never leave her side again. But the dread of it and the direction of my feet said otherwise. I wondered, for a moment, if I could swim to the mainland. I had heard stories of those who had tried to swim to France. There was every chance I could make it and if I did not, I would drown gladly. But they knew me. As soon as I breached the surface, they knew the real reason I had come. Even if I had not known it myself, they did. The whales. The guardians."

As if they had heard his voice, one of them broke the surface close by and sent their spray into the air creating rainbows in the darkening sky.

"I do not pretend I have any power of speech with these creatures. I am only human. But in that moment, I knew that they meant me no harm and I allowed them to lead me down... and when I could feel my breath leave me I prepared to die. I was certain it would come. I closed my eyes, felt my body cold and empty. When I thought it would come, at that very moment it felt as if I had been reborn. There is no need for air, no need for breath. Yet there is both in abundance. Down there, in that place, it is as if the water hangs within the sky and we are below. Safe and protected. They brought me to the gates of Finfolkaheem. A great hall of gold and silken weeds." His eyes broadened as he checked my eyes for any glimmer of recognition.

"You have been there, have you not?"

"Not purposely." I replied. "Tt was so long ago now; I barely recall it."

Perhaps he did not want to push me. Something told me he knew that I was not being truthful. Perhaps he knew the memory of that place did not simply leave a person over the course of time. I did not want to remember it. I had not been prepared and they had not shown themselves to me. The mere thought of it was strange and daunting. Yet I remember that feeling of peace and calm. I had belonged.

"Well, you'll come to know it again soon enough. The gateway, as it is called, it is not a gate as such. More a veil between this world and theirs. A place of great importance. When I came to it, I thought all the places in that strange land would be much the same. But banquet halls of gold... there is only one. When you pass through it, you will know it as nothing more than a waiting post. Where they come, where they go, where one world meets the other."

Where Nathan Munroe was hiding...

"It is where the whales took me and could come no further. But it was as if they had sent word before us, I do not know how. In the halls of the gateway there he awaited me. I shall never forget it. I was afraid of him to begin with. It would have been foolish of me not to have been. But then he laid a handout and placed it on my shoulder. He knew my name; he knew why I had come, and he promised that he would not turn me away if one day I promised to fulfil a purpose he had foreseen. At first, he did not let that purpose be known. He took me to his home, he clothed me and fed me and taught me the ways of the Finfolk. The other humans, the consorts, they said it was because I had known *you*. That because I had come from that place where you dwell, he had welcomed me as the family of his Granddaughter. You know of who I speak, do you not?"

The man whose skin glowed like the scales of a fish. The man whose raven hair flowed freely in the strange wind. The man who had brought me to the ring of stones. A dream within a dream…

"Astala." I breathed. "My grandfather."

Ewan nodded. "He is a great man. The greatest I have ever known. High Priest of Finfolkaheem. He is the one who all come to for guidance. They look to him as a leader, but he will never see himself as one. The other tribes chose him and, he has been their High Priest for many of our human lifetimes."

I had nothing to say. For my meagre experience of this other world, I found myself dumbfounded. If I had spoken, what would I have said? Tangled his grasp of the truth with my fathomless questions? He seemed lost now, as if he would lose his touch if he stopped. Ewan, his boyish face, was gone. There was a man who had to make sense of what he had been told, for my sake and his own.

"There are three tribes. Astala is from the house of Raven. The oldest of the tribes. Black hair, dark eyes. All of them share the bloodline of the first Finman and Finwoman, creatures created in the likeness of the God and Goddess to live upon the world and not in the heavens. The house of Babel came a little later, their white hair and blue eyes in stark contrast to the Ravens.

Descended from those in the house of Raven who did not bear the darkness in their hair or their eyes. Then came the house of Teine. They came from both houses, Raven and Babel. Distinguishable only by their fire red hair. It is a history all humans must be taught and know by heart. If they are to live amongst the Finfolk. It was one of the first things Astala taught me, at first, I wondered what he meant. They do not live in houses. The tribes do not live together, but all tribes live as one. But it is what it is. That is how they distinguish each other. You are of the house of Raven, unless you did not know that already."

There is another part of me which is human. Do you forget that? I must not forget… I must not forget! Tell me whatever it is you have come to tell and I shall listen. But I shall not relinquish all of me!

I was afraid. For many years I had been searching for the answers and now that I had them at my disposal, I was unsure if I wanted them. I thought myself a fool and I was certainly behaving like one. A speechless mute who would not look her confessor in the eye. Ewan was patient and humble. Perhaps he did not want to be the bearer any more than I wanted to be the receiver.

Say something, you stupid girl! He will think you have not listened; he will think you an imbecile if you do not speak soon!

"Mother…" Was all I could say. "Where is my mother?"

He shifted backwards. His entire body moving away from the words I had spoken. I forgot that I was afraid and tried to keep him from turning away from me entirely. Now I was angry and afraid in a whole new way. Why did nobody know where my mother was? Why was her name banished? Why had she quarrelled with Astala?

"I demand to know, Ewan! I have little use for truths about legends if I do not know who my mother is!"

He was holding his breath. Tears rimmed his red eyes and threatened to spill out and down his flushed cheeks.

"Aye." He said finally, breathing in and letting the composure take him. "I dare say you do deserve to know who your mother is."

But he would not tell me. If I had extracted the things within his head with my bare hands, this he would not offer me. He looked down into his lap, admitting defeat.

"I am not the one to tell you these things. I have not given any of it the justice it deserves. Astala should be the one to speak with you and he has sent a court jester to do a king's job. He said that it did not matter, that coming from me would sweeten the blow and you would return with me to complete the transition you started on that day you shifted for the first time."

He must have seen something in my face that I did not convey. Horror? Fear? He shook his head vehemently and moved closer once again.

"I am sorry, Finola. You must do what it is within your heart to do. I have tried to bring you answers, answers which you deserved long ago. But I am lacking as a messenger. If you wish to stay, I will not say another word."

He was wrong, of course. How could I have been given this news any other way? If he had sung it to me in a sweet voice it would still remain the same.

No, I was glad of what he had told me, and I sensed that there was more to come. But he had lost the will to continue. Perhaps I should not have asked about my mother. Perhaps he did not even know what happened to her, or even her name. Or even if he did, he would not tell. I felt a warmth in my heart that things I had once feared now came to light.

Like sinister shadows in the night giving way to daylight, appearing as nothing more than mundane things. I softened towards Ewan because of it and folded up the thought of my mother, then tucked her away to the back of my mind where she had lived from the very moment, I knew she existed.

"There is one more thing I will know." I said, as light heartedly as I could. "The stories of the Finhag. Are they true?"

He allowed a brief smile to brush across his lips. He stood, his face darkening in the twilight. I took his hand as he offered it to me, and we stood for a moment to watch the sun slip beneath the horizon.

"Finhag's of legend, there are none. A Finwoman will not suffer and age if she does not take a human consort. But, as with anything that lives, everything has a life span which eventually is snuffed out. The legends of Finhag came from the youth and beauty of the finwomen who claimed their consorts. Jealousy and spite, the human wives left behind spoke of the ugliness that would come if they did not take a husband. It is no different than the spurned husbands left behind, spreading stories that do not welcome the truth. But we do not deny them either, for they safeguard the

Finfolk way of life. Fear not, Finola. Finhag's welcome their form as they grow old. A thousand years can be a long time to live."

It would be a thousand years until I understood what it fully meant. But now I was a little closer, at least, to finding out. It was strange to me that my only regret came from the least significant part.

That I had not cursed Caleb into loving me. That his love had been as natural as the turning tide.

When Ewan would have spoken more, I bade him quieten. I had heard enough. As we made our way from the red sky and back towards the house there was a pitiful silence resonating from him. Perhaps it had been cruel to give him this task. He was exhausted and so was I. I went to my bed and slept without dream.

Lucie Howorth

Chapter Nineteen

THE FUNERAL AND THE WEDDING

tanding in the church I felt the chill of the rafters come down around me. I could have slept on my feet. It had been an arduous journey. One that I had endured by keeping my head low and not daring to look at the shrouded body, that lay at my feet.

It was something I could never become accustomed to. I prayed I would never need do it again. When we arrived on the mainland it was far too emotional for Mammy, who stayed by the boat as Ewan and Rohan carried Aunt Hannah to the church. I asked her if she would come with me, at first, she sat and stared at Eynhallow as if it would not await her return.

"This is the furthest I have been from your Daddy in twenty-three years." She said solemnly, before turning away and allowing me to take her.

There was a little haste in burying Aunt Hannah. Her name would be added to Seamus' headstone at a later date, but as I watched the earth fall onto her modest wooden box there at least was some witness to her resting place. I wondered if I would ever return to pay my respects. As I stood and watched her lowered into the ground, I had my doubts. Strange the solemn tone that prevailed, now as I stood in that very same church, we had said goodbye, we stood in the presence of that very same God to witness the marriage of Bethan and Rohan.

Pious Mammy nodded in agreement with every vow spoken, her hands clasped tightly together as she clutched a leather bible. Ewan, his face unreadable, stood behind Bethan at the altar. Ever shadowed by Rohan, he seemed to be sobbing silently as his shoulders moved in that subtle way. I pretended that I had not seen, I did not want to know what manner of thoughts plagued him. We stood in the church at his request. It was not without a bitter taste that I watched Bethan's euphoria unfold.

Dressed in her mother's wedding dress, clutching a small bunch of flowers at her breast, the dress fit her perfectly. Long white sleeves of lace poured down her arms into a ring of pearl around her elbows. Frills of lace hid the bosom that sat round and profound above the tight corset. Trimmed in more pearls, the dress met the floor and spilled out into a train that curled around her feet.

Her hair was pinned inside a white bonnet that betrayed the slightest hint of the array of curls inside. But it was hard to feel spite, even as I studied every inch of that dress in search for some part of it that might have made her look a little uglier, to see the exaltation in Rohan was enough to feed my guilt.

I could not begrudge them this. I could not feel that old envy in the face of my brothers unending happiness. This was his conclusion. There would not be another destiny for him save for the one he carved out on this very day. Ah, there it was. The real root of my envy. That I wished that I could be the one to stand in this church with my love and promise to love him til the end of my days.

Self-pity was unmeasurable and I berated myself for feeling it. But when it was all done and the rapture in their eyes was coveted with happy tears, I could only congratulate them and hope that a similar fate awaited me, in whatever form it may take.

She would not part with the dress. Standing in the churchyard, the people stopped to watch them fawn over each other in that way only a newly married couple does. We gathered for a moment to speak of the beautiful service and when Mammy suggested we get Bethan out of that dress and back to Eynhallow, her face betrayed the sheer horror of giving up this perfect moment.

"I have been married for less than a minute and you'd have me back on that island without so much as consummating it!" Bethan roared in hushed tones, the well-wishers gathering by the church gate looking on.

Perhaps she was not as empty headed as I had previously thought. The power which came with being Rohan's wedded wife was already being put to use. Mammy, knowing her place as head of the house were over, submitted to the younger girl. But not completely.

"You speak of consummating things as if you have never consummated anything before." It was a spiteful tongue she spoke with.

Bethan stepped back in defeat. But with great care not to draw any attention to himself, Rohan took Mammy by the wrist and leaned down to whisper into her ear almost silently. What he said to her I will never know. I could not hear the words spoken and I never asked him afterwards. But the colour from Mammy's face seemed to rise as she listened. Her eyes widened and the lines upon her face deepened. When he was done, he dropped her wrist like a rotten fish, and she bit back tears of sadness and rage. Almost as if it had never happened, Rohan addressed us all with a triumphant smile.

"Today is not for remonstrations. I'll not have another stern word spoken. I wish to take my bride and show her off, for when I am home there will be little chance for that. See how beautiful she is! Come..."

The small crowd that had gathered by the gate were more than happy to yield this chance for gossip. Rohan spoke with the farmers Daddy had once broken bread with, inquiring of their families and speaking of his joy on this day.

But their judgement was cast upon Bethan's tender age, and without speaking it aloud I knew their thoughts turned to the fact that they were cousins. But Bethan seemed not to notice and allowed the local girls to pet her dress and admire the lace. They gave their condolences too. For a moment it seemed her joyous mood would fade, but then she looked down at herself once more and suddenly it seemed not to matter that her mother was dead. If only for the moment.

But they would not speak to me. I would have nothing of value to say and both of us knew it. Awaiting by the graveside of his parents was Ewan, like any mourner he would not be disturbed. I stepped away from the mindless chatter and went to his side, firmly in the shadows where it seemed we both belonged.

"Have they not had their fill of this place?" He said wearily, bending to touch the freshly returned earth.

"Let them have a moment more. When she is back at The Hylands she will find the place her own. There she'll stay until one day she finds herself back here at the wedding of her own children. Much like the old woman."

He stifled a smile at the sound of me calling Mammy an old woman.

"I always thought she would be the one to leave. Never for a moment did I doubt it. But I was wrong, now I shall be the one to leave."

Standing up firmly, dropping the earth between his fingers, Ewan stared at me as if he had not heard me right.

"Then you have chosen? You will return with me?" He said eagerly, like a child awaiting praise.

Perhaps I had not known the choice I made until I spoke it aloud. I could wait forever and become as one with the stone and stand still, ancient like the kirk for all the time. Or I could embrace the inevitable.

"There is nothing here for me now. My brother has a wife, he has no need for a sister. The man I love is hundreds of miles away with a wife and child on the way."

"Then we shall return tonight. When they sleep and not before. I'll not have a goodbye."

He did not say more. Perhaps I would have one goodbye. But not yet. For now, I was content to watch a rare moment of happiness unfold. It would be this pleasant memory I would take with me.

There was no sadness. Only anticipation. As we made our way across the water, chasing the sunset, it was as if I had never been undecided. It would be a destiny fulfilled, a moment of great discovery. There was little else for me to achieve here. Save for sufferance and defeat.

I had come full circle.

I recalled those days of desperate longing to leave, coupled with the fear of doing so. I was sorry that I had remained so long, sorry that I had waited for something that was never meant to be. Daddy had known it and Mammy too. Perhaps this was why she had distanced herself, made herself a nobody.

Or perhaps I was searching for what was not there, it was indeed true that I was no longer a daughter to her but a nuisance.

The wind picked up. Somewhere in the sky a gull cried, in the middle of the Eynhallow sound our inconspicuous boat rose and fell between the tidal waves. Ewan kept my gaze whenever I looked up from the horizon. He seemed to need confirmation with every passing moment that I would not change my mind.

It would have been so easy to. Just to disregard the things I had come to know. But with his constant gaze locked upon me, as if I would disappear from view, I knew it would be foolish of me. I allowed myself to look upon the bride and groom, sitting beneath the white sail in an embrace that would not quit.

There is time for you yet, child... Came the voice so sudden and so clear.

Eyes averted towards me as I moved to peer over the side of the boat. Close by, but not too close to touch, a great whale moved against the waves. His body moved smoothly in parallel to the boat, keeping a perfect rhythm.

"Time?" I whispered into the folds of my shawl, low enough that none would hear me. Save for him.

Simple hearts can love in simple ways. But your Finheart beats differently. There is time for such a love.

He knew what I had been thinking. I wondered if he had always known what I had been thinking but chosen not to address it.

He followed us closely, the contours of his body keeping perfect time with our boat.

"Do you know something which I do not?"

There are a great many things I know which you do not.

And I rolled my eyes at my own stupidity for asking such a vague thing.

"Is that so? And do you know what I have decided, then?"

He cruised a little further away, as the boat navigated through the roughest stretch before we would reach the shoreline, he could not come much further.

That is for you to say. I only speak of the things which I know that you do not. Decisions of yours are things which you know, and I do not.

Perhaps then he could not read my thoughts. A higher intuition, but not the ability to read my mind.

"You do not speak of the things which you know, for if you did perhaps then I may have come with you sooner."

But come with me you shall. When the time is right.

It bothered me that this beautiful creature should be so certain of the things I had barely had time to wrap my consciousness around. As we neared the shoreline, I watched him break the surface once more before going where I could not see.

When the time is right, Finola Gray... his voice echoed before breaching where I could not hear.

The deep sea swallowed him. As the boat reached land, I was distracted with the need to continue speaking with the great whale. But the wind upon the water was gone and sound carried much easier. He would come for me soon enough; we would speak of many things. But not in this moment. Rohan cast his eyes upon me, a triumphant smile putting me in my place.

Whatever watery lullaby possessed me released its grip. For a moment we looked at each other, him and I. It was as if he was letting me go. My dear brother. The words he had spoken to me before had held no weight. He could tell me he no longer had need of me, but truly I never would have let that be enough. No, this was confirmation. He did not have to tell me. Stood at the precipice, he would have pushed me. When he looked away the deed was done and there was little else to consider. It was almost as if I was already gone.

I was weary and sick. Somehow the telepathy between those creatures and I would take the very essence of me.

As the boat came towards the shoreline and glided into the sand, I awaited the pit of stomach to calm with the motion. There was not a single rock or plant out of place. But I greeted it anew. I think, for a moment, I smiled. As I stepped onto dry land it seemed that finally I knew how ingrained I was within this place.

Mammy sighed heavily, pulling herself over the side of the boat with great difficulty. Even with Rohan to aid her, she slipped onto the shore like a seal pup with a broken flipper. Nobody spoke. There was a collective silence of tiredness, sadness and anticipation.

Perhaps the anticipation was only on my part. But I felt it, nonetheless. I was glad that none of us spoke, for if we had then I would not have heard that desperate voice calling out to me from beyond the horizon.

Faint and almost lost on the wind at first, I thought perhaps a creature that no other could hear desired my attention. But when eyes and ears turned in the direction from where it came, I knew that it was as real to them as it was to me.

I knew that voice. I had heard it once before. As he came bounding towards us from the direction of the half-built house, at first, I was alarmed, until I saw the momentary smile upon his face.

"Silas?" I inquired, as he boldly approached in that way one does when they have spoken intimately.

He caught his breath for a moment before pulling off his cap to reveal a head of messy hair. He tried to pull it down, almost nervously, but it had a life of its own.

Rohan was quick to step forward, his bride still firmly held in his other hand.

"Forgive me, Miss Finola. I've been watching for you since first light." He breathed, wringing the cap between his hands.

Rohan raised an eyebrow. "We have been to the mainland to bury my aunt, as I am sure you are aware. What is so urgent that it could not wait?"

Ah, I would miss that protective wit. He had learnt some manners of late, but the brute was still simmering under the surface and even deeper so, was that little boy. But here stood the man and I felt pride.

"Mr. Bishop... Senior. He was sent word from his wife in England that their youngest son had been taken ill with the fever. He had to leave in haste, at sunrise this morning. He does not know when he will return. He implored me to ask that Master Rohan, him being so strong, that he might reconsider his offer to come and work on the house? He will pay handsomely. That if Master Rohan would oblige, it would be all the better for us to have someone who knows the land so well in our company. You see, building isn't going as well as we had planned. There's been subsidence and when the snow thawed it got damp within the stone. I dare say we could not complete it, without Master Rohan."

Bethan released Rohan's hand and sent it up to her throat. "Oh Rohan, you must do it."

Of course, he would. Not at their request, but at hers. Mammy inquired about the little boy; the son who had been taken ill with the fever. But Silas shook his head and said that there was nothing else he could say.

"May I ask who it was that sent word?" She asked then, "It so seldom reaches us here. When I was younger it was as if there was no need of us in that world beyond."

He was nervous and would not answer. His eyes shifted uneasily from Mammy and then to me.

"Our messenger was a member of the Bishop family. He is speaking with the younger Mr. Bishop at present but has said that he will call upon you tonight."

And as Silas walked away, I dared to hope of who it might have been. But only for the briefest of moments.

As I sat to supper and pushed the food around my plate, I was bitterly aware of the arrival that would come. Mammy had grown weary and retired to bed, closing the door behind her to spend the first night alone without any companion beside her. I knew it wouldn't be long before Rohan took his bride to rest. Still our messenger had not come. What would they want with us, anyway? It was not our business to know their purpose here.

"You are not with us tonight." Said Rohan, his voice travelling across the table.

I looked up to meet his smile. It pitied me.

"I am weary." I said, laying my plate aside.

"As am I." He replied, rising from his chair and taking Bethan by the hand. "Tomorrow you will be with us though, won't you?"

Such a sweet lie, to escape my lips and tell him what he wanted to hear. But I could not. For I did not know if I would be here tomorrow.

"I'll always be with you."

For a moment he seized my gaze. He would stay and ask me what I meant. But he knew and there were no words. Instead, he turned away from me and went to his marital bed and that was the way I wished it to be. No goodbyes. No sorrow that would eat away at me.

Ewan had been mostly silent, slipping back into his old place as easily as slipping on an old pair of socks. He did not look comfortable there and I knew he longed to return to Finfolkaheem. When the room fell silent and all the doors were closed, he took the plates from the table and began to eat whatever was left.

"It will be a long while before you have another meal. Better you eat more and fill yourself." He said between chews.

I wasn't quite sure what he meant. Perhaps they did not eat in the same way. I could not eat more, regardless. The pit of my stomach churned, and a sickness escaped my throat. It burned and I could have swooned. But I managed to keep it down.

"And then shall we go?" I asked, swallowing the sickness like bitter regret.

His eyes went towards the window and the encroaching darkness.

"Not yet. Before dawn. There will be enough light to guide us and still remain shrouded. There'll be no magic for us this night."

"Is that so?" I asked, "Must there be organised conjuring?"

He rolled his eyes at my assumption and continued to dip the bread into the meat sops.

"You may have the gifts, but I do not. If I speak to the guardians will I be heard? Will they send word that we are to return? Yours is the only voice they hear. I am but human. Not even a consort at that. No, we shall return under our own steam."

"And what is it, to be a consort? Why should it matter?" I asked, he placed his food down and sighed regretfully.

"They are chosen. They have a place amongst the Finfolk. I was neither chosen, nor did I earn my place. I was given my place to serve a purpose and I am painfully aware that I must earn it each and every day."

I did not ask which purpose. Already he seemed gravely distracted. He ate swiftly and when he was done there was little else to pick at. Regardless of when my next meal would come, I was not hungry anyway.

"Are we to sit here then, until dawn?" I asked, still weary and in need of sleep.

He thought about it for a moment. "No, sleep if you must. I will stay here and wait for the right time. I could not sleep, even if I wanted to."

Muffled laughter and delight came from the room next to my own. There was no desire to try to sleep beside that.

"I shall remain with you." I said, "And wait for the right moment."

I wondered what the right moment would look like. Would it be the striking of the clock or the squawk of a bird? Would it be the beating of my heart or the sound of the wind?

Ewan drew into himself, contemplating what was to come. By the fire came the sound of crackling wood. Above the drum of wind and muffled love. A trance of sorts came over me as I eyed the licking flames. A half-forgotten ache crept in and I saw the face of the reason I had remained.

I have tried to forget. I have thrown your image into the fire and watched you burn and still you haunt me. I have built walls around you. A fortress of great magnitude to keep you at bay. Still you come to me and taunt. I have no power over you. Not here, nor when I sleep. Nor when I am awake. When I am gone, I shall remember you still and there will be no peace for my heart. It would be just as well if you had died. For then the peace of when I shall see you once more would give me shallow comfort. But not in this life. A life that will stretch forth beyond yours. A life that will remember always the promised kisses you never gave to me and the regret that it was I who made it so.

Lucie Howorth

Chapter Twenty

THE FORGING OF FINOLA

he stench of dead fire filled the room. Not even the embers burned now. Somewhere in the distance a bird cried, the sound carrying across the wind and through the stone of The Hylands.

It was not yet dawn.

Red threatened to spill across the sky but was not yet ready. Ewan slept by the cold fireplace, curled within his own jacket on the floor. All else was silent. Nothing stirred. Not even the spent lovers in the room beside me. Nothing else moved in the world, so it seemed.

For a moment I sat spellbound, wondering if we had lingered too long. There was a peaceful calm in Ewan's sleeping face. Undisturbed and without thought, I had not the heart to wake him. Perhaps when the sun began to rise, I would let him stir. But not before.

I was haunted by a dream that had come and gone. Still dazed by sleep I felt a quiet longing in my heart that couldn't remember where it had come from.

Slowly I looked around me at all the things which remained the same. The stone fireplace, unchanged since childhood. The wooden table in the middle of the room, scarred by Daddy's cheese knife that he had plunged into the grain after a good meal. The fish hanging above the fire, waiting to be cooked and eaten. That old door that hung within the frame like an old man clinging to his walking stick. Why did it seem that I had said goodbye a thousand times and yet here I was memorising each tiny detail? Had I ever wanted to leave before? Had I ever longed to be parted from this place so fiercely?

The wind came through the cracks in the house, whistling softly in that familiar way. Ewan stirred for a moment at the sound of it, lifting his head before drifting back into sleep. My heart rose and sank in that moment. I realised there was a mix of dread and adrenaline coursing through me. When he did wake, then it would be time.

The sound of the water encroaching onto the shore called to me over the wind. It was a distinct roar that I could not ignore. With great care not to make a sound, I pulled my shawl about me and crept out into the early morning darkness. The ground was moist with dew and the air was crisp and fresh. Faint shafts of red light peered over the horizon, sending the white clouds into the sky as blackened shadows.

I made my way slowly towards the water, certain that if I remained here, I would no longer be afraid. If I stayed indoors, I would doubt myself. Out here I was reminded of the choice I had made. The dream which haunted me could fade away into that dull part of my mind that seldom bothered me during the waking hours.

But today it did not. Today it burned like wildfire until I found myself sobbing on the rocks. Today I purged of my love. I wanted for him to see me like this. I wanted him to see what I had become.

For I had been nothing before and now I was less than nothing. Over my biting sobs there was no sound, no light. I buried my face into my hands and let them come. Whatever had been locked inside me spilled forth now and I had not known how much would come. I cried without thought or regard. I had no control over it now, the tears came unbound and suddenly I was aware that I was not just crying for the love I had never known. But for the father I had lost. The mother I had never known and the one who had abandoned me. The winters of struggle and the secrets which had been kept from me. The truths which had been just as harsh.

I cried for the brother I had loved as dearly as if he had been my own child and the lives, we would have in worlds apart. I cried for the stolen years of my life which I could never retrieve. I cried for Eynhallow. The island itself was crying out to be left alone and still it was being trespassed upon.

For all of these things and for reasons I could not say, I cried helplessly and fiercely into the folds of my shawl until my gut began to ache and my throat began to burn. Each tear that streaked my cheeks was a sign that I had hung on for too long.

I had buried my soul so deep that I had not known the shape of it. The taste of salt upon my lips was all that kept me warm. Everything else was cold and wasted. Racking sobs came from me in surging waves, each one more violent than the other.

I remembered my Daddy. I remembered his face as it was when I was a child, to that moment I watched the life leave him. I remembered the night Rohan came into the world. When a storm so great raged outside that his cries were almost silent. I remembered the sweet boy and the morose man and what he had become now. I remembered the other families before their demise. The other children who littered the fields with their laughter and how not even an echo of them remained.

I remembered being the only ones left and the solitude. I remembered Nathan Munro. His face staring down at me on that fateful night. His eyes burning into me with hot desire that I could barely contain myself. His body upon the shore...

I remembered Mammy, her body becoming frail with the burden of religion and the loss of those she had loved. Her face as she turned away from me, never to look upon me again. Each winter of desolation. I remembered the rise and fall of the tide. I remembered those golden halls under the sea.

And then I remembered him. The pale moonlight as I saw him for the first time. That moment of pure clarity as his eyes met mine and his eyes each time, I would send him away. I hated myself for being foolish. I hated myself for every moment I could have had that I did not take. For every kiss which was mine that I returned with nothing but refusal. Those tears were the most bitter of all and I did not like the taste.

It seemed as if every memory I had become one and when I could cry no more, I gave in to sheer exhaustion and laid upon the ground waiting. It was wet and cold, but I felt neither of it as I breathed hard and watched the air turn it into grey swirls of mist.

I closed my eyes, shut out the reddening sky. I allowed my dreams to take me to wherever they would, I was done being their prisoner. He came to me and clutched me to him tightly, his arms carrying me to wherever he wished to take me. I felt his arms so resolutely. Tightly bound about my body, clutching me so tight I could almost feel the pain.

Ah yes, this dream is what I have cast forth for too long. This dream is everything I have wanted and not dared myself to think of. I shall let him carry me and hold me and when I awake and find him gone from me, I shall cherish the sweetness of such a vivid untruth and take it with me as a memory I could never have. Hold me close, if you will. It is but a dream, a dream...

"Sssshhh..." His voice said, the sound of it more familiar to me now than it had ever been. "Sssshhh my love..."

The sea crashed somewhere in the distance. Wind came in from the same direction, the birds stirring as the sun crept over and spilled into the water. I could feel myself moving against it, more tangible, more real with each step.

"I am sorry..." He whispered softly, a hand moving the hair from my face.

This was no dream. The air was fresh and crisp as it had been only moments before. The sound of feet stepping on moist ground was so distinct. If I dared myself to open my eyes... If I opened them and saw him...

"Finola, my love. Open your eyes." He said then, as if he had known.

I had cried enough. There were no tears left. But when I opened my eyes they came from somewhere. Not sobs of regret, but quiet droplets of something I had no name for.

He was not the Caleb of my memory. He was changed. The hair which used to flow down over his beautiful face was gone, for reasons unknown he had cut it short and kept it neat. The rough stubble had grown into a beard of sorts. But the eyes which bore down into me were the same. I would have known them even if he had changed beyond all recognition.

The arms felt the same, his embrace still the same mixture of desire and urgency and restraint. For one still moment I took in the sight of him, then allowed myself to be consumed by venomous anger. I struck him once, cold and hard across his jawline. He turned his face away but did not buckle with the blow. I had probably not struck him hard enough, or perhaps he had been expecting it. He did not release me, and I was glad.

When he turned back his face had not changed, as if he had felt nothing at all. Instead, he disregarded my obvious anguish and placed me on the ground silently. His hands still clasped gently around my shoulders, he allowed me a moment to find my balance before taking it from me completely.

If I had known in that moment what it was within his mind, perhaps I would have prepared myself better. As much as anyone can ever be prepared to be kissed for the first time. He clasped me harder, his hands crushing my arms as he pulled me in to him. He turned his head slightly, too swiftly for me to protest. It was as if he was never in any doubt that I would. He brushed his lips against mine, softly at first, those eyes probing me for the briefest moment as if asking for permission. Then he kissed me harder and with fierce conviction. Whatever small part I had in this kiss, I savoured it. He pushed his body against mine, his mouth opening and showing me that nothing else mattered. How surreal that I should be here in this moment of unexpected bliss.

On the cusp of something more spectacular, I didn't want him to let me go. I didn't want to let him go. His hands went from my arms down towards my waist. Even closer to him, I could sense his kiss becoming more urgent, more fervent. Before I could submit myself to him completely, I felt his body shift away. In a cool, swift movement he pulled apart from me and stood breathless and apologetic before me.

I was not spent; I was not done and would have had more from him. He could not give me this sweetness then take it from me.

But he would not have it. He wanted to, that much I knew. The eyes could not hide the hunger. But it was as if he suddenly remembered himself and shook his head.

"Where have you been?" I breathed.

His face rested against mine, but he would not kiss me again.

"Purgatory." He whispered. "But I was saved. I found my way back to heaven."

His lips trespassed briefly between the strands of hair that fell about my face. It was as if none of the tears mattered anymore. I felt as if I would never shed another tear as long as I lived.

"Why?" I asked, "Why have you come back?"

His hands circled my face, lifting it to meet his eyes.

"Do not pretend that you do not know why. Could there ever be any other reason than you?"

Why in this moment? Why, when I had given up all hope? You come to me now, when I am done with this weary world? There was something keeping you from me...

"And what of your wife?" I asked suddenly, stepping away from his embrace.

His face fell. But he made no attempt to stop me from parting myself from his grasp. His kiss had thrown me off course, but now I regained my composure. I remembered the sight of him leaving. The letter I held in my hands that brought news that he would never be mine.

"I swear." He begged, careful not to come too close. "If I could erase everything from the moment, I stepped onto that boat that took me away from you I would give my soul to do it. I was a weak fool."

Still I could not blame him. I had never given him any reason to remain with me. Yet he was standing here before me and it was more than I deserved. If I had broken his heart a thousand times, he had broken mine only once.

"My brother is sick. His mother needed to send word to my father that he must return. She does not think he will survive. I do not wish my brother any harm, but it presented me with a reason to come back that would not put any stain on my father's reputation. A hundred times before I had thought to come back, but I stayed because I deserved the punishment. I was always told it would be a matter of time before I got some poor girl with child. I never thought that it would come to pass."

It tasted bitter in my mouth as he spoke the words. If I could have spat it out, I would have. But I had to swallow it.

"And now you kiss me as if you are not a husband or a father."

His eyes shot to the sky and he breathed deeply. "I am a husband. That I will not deny. But in name only. I have not laid with my wife since the day I got her with child. The marriage remains unconsummated. I might have been weak once, but I was not going to deny my heart repeatedly."

He shook his head woefully. "But I shall not be a father. She is no longer with child. It did not form properly and died before it could be born. Poor thing, she almost died herself when she lost it."

He seemed genuinely heartbroken about this. For a moment I thought he might break his composure. But when tears formed at the corners of his eyes, he bit them back and in one brief moment it was gone.

"I am sorry for your loss." Was all I could say.

But he pushed the words away as if they meant nothing. He didn't want to hear it; he had heard it a thousand times before.

"Do not be sorry. It was my true punishment. For what I had done to my own heart, and yours."

He spoke of punishment, but who dealt it? He was consumed with it. For every action, every decision he had ever made he spoke of a punishment that he must endure. If I was to leave now, it would be punishment indeed.

My heart began to sing to me. A doleful song of a love ripped apart. I was done with this dying land. But standing before me was a reason to remain. All the definitive answers fled from me. The choices I had made that had been so definite suddenly seemed open to negotiation. There was a calmness that ran through me. This choice had been made once before and I knew the consequences.

A death bed in years to come would yield the secrets of a love unbound. He would speak of me to his children and how he had remained on the edge of the water for the rest of his days, seeking me within the waves. Or I could allow him to follow me. I had chosen him; of that I had no doubt. But first, he had to know the truth.

"Worry not about my heart. It will beat long after yours has ceased." I murmured quietly.

His eyes watched me as I turned away, seeking the dull warmth of the rising sun. He would have taken my hand, but I placed them at my breast to feel the thrum of the heart which beat there. It was strong and fast, and completely his.

"You cannot know that." He mused, slipping his arms around my waist to watch whatever it was that I watched.

"I know it as certainly as I know that at any moment the sun will rise over the water and this land will be washed in daylight."

He pulled me tighter to him.

"Yes. We shall be here to see it, together. I swear there will be no other sunrise for me if I do not have you."

The resistance of his arms as I moved slowly away was hungry and wanting. The mere sense of his touch would throw me off course. There could be no going back, even if he would hate me, there would be no going back.

"There will be no more sunrises if you *do* have me." I said, turning to face him as the morning rays peaked over the horizon.

"Where I am going, I am not even certain if there is a sun to rise or fall."

His face was a mixture of confusion and sadness. Then it seemed that all expression escaped him. His eyes wandered off into the distance as my voice carried on the wind.

"You speak as if you are leaving." He mused, "Why does it feel as if at any moment I shall lose you?"

I felt the sting for him. That old ache that was unhealed that was surely to come for him. I could not change it for him, any more than I could change the wind or the rising sun.

"You return to me on a strange day." I said. "There is little time…"

He would have asked me something. A question. But instead we watched the sun rise and when there was enough light to guide our way, I turned to him. Behind us, as silently as he could muster, Ewan had appeared.

"So, you have chosen him?" He asked softly, ready to accept whatever I would decide.

Caleb pulled me away, as if Ewan somehow posed an unseen threat. I had forgotten that Caleb had been there on that night, when Ewan had gone into the water. It was too late for fear, too late for memories.

"I have." I replied, and Ewan nodded.

But Caleb did not understand. He grasped me tightly, the white of knuckles bearing down into my flesh.

"What does he mean? You have chosen me? For what have you chosen me?"

I dug the fingers from my arms and made him stand away from me.

"You cannot begin to understand what I am asking of you."

He seized me again and pulled his mouth close to my own.

"You cannot begin to understand that you could ask anything of me, ask it of me and it shall be yours."

Ewan sized him up cynically.

"You would do well to remember that, where we are going." He said matter of factly, approaching the water with a smile upon his face.

"And where is that?" Caleb asked, sensing a danger that was not there.

To a place where nothing will make sense. To a place I do not know, a place I could not dream enough of to say if it were fair or dark.

To a place that will be heaven, or hell, as it chooses. To a place where regret will be too late before you have even got there.

"Sometimes." I said to him, "It is better not to know."

Winding his hands around mine, he lifted my fingers to his face and there I caressed him silently. His eyes, threatening tears that he would not let spill, searched for the answers I could not give.

"So be it." He finally said and he nodded towards Ewan.

Chapter Twenty-One

THE GATEWAY

The peace I had known, sometimes during chaos and other times when there was nothing but darkness, was shrouded in blindness. There was no peace anymore. Not from hurt, not from anything. I would never reconcile the two halves of myself. They would never live side by side. There would always be the part of me which lived upon the land. That part of me that lived in sweet ignorance and dreamed of a life far beyond the shores of Eynhallow. I would never be able to find it within my heart to let that girl go.

She had come so far and would serve as a reminder when all else seemed lost. I had reached out to that part of myself and found that even the strange and silent younger Finola gave her blessing for me to go.

As I took that first step into the water, allowing the cold tide to touch my reluctant skin, I knew that something tangible had begun. Before me, out there, I heard voices singing in joyous unison and it was not fear which gripped me.

Instead it was the knowledge that I had been here once before and I was going home.

The great whale appeared and told me to go to him. I released my shawl and loosened my dress.

Wading out fiercely into the water I had avoided, the cathartic feel of the tide against my body brought tears to my eyes and a reluctant smile. I threw my head back, the red sky flushed with bird's overhead. They squawked and chanted and whispered in their beautiful colours.

They did not tell me to wait today.

Ewan was already ahead of me, the clear image of him growing fainter and fainter as he approached the waiting pod of whales.

He did not turn to see if I would follow, he did not seem to care if I did or not. When the moment came, he submerged underneath and was gone. I knew what I had to do, and I must do it swiftly. But I would have this moment, this was mine and mine alone. The finblood coursing through my veins diluted whatever humanity was left within me. I could feel it burn and fill me.

Something was happening. Something I could not control. I pulled and scratched at the dress that clung to me, ripping it from me with no regard for the naked body underneath.

I could hear a voice calling to me, from the land or from the sea, I did not know. It told me to stop, to put my dress back on, but I couldn't. From the corner of my eye I saw an old woman standing on the brow of the hill, her arms waving wildly and her voice trailing on the wind. She would come to me now and I would turn back to her and she would ask my forgiveness.

But it was too late for that. She wielded a sorrowful form and perhaps she sought me out for another reason. I would never know otherwise. She wasn't my Mammy, not by blood nor by choice.

If I was naked, then it was my choice. If I was here, then it was by blood. The subtle consciousness that remained gave way to the sensation that I could no longer feel the seabed, there was nothing beneath my feet. The bitter cold of the water numbed everything else and when I could finally look back and see the shoreline, it took my breath away.

There, his naked torso just visible above the waves, stood my love. He watched me curiously, as if he had begun to follow and then somehow stopped. He watched me, as I watched him. Did I float aimlessly, or continue?

He moved slowly, his body reaching forward until he was by my side. He was afraid and timid. I had never seen his strength diminished so. But through it all, he looked to me and waited for what would come.

Beneath us, shadows danced. I could hear him, his voice clear like a bell and the mighty weight of his body reaching upwards. When he broke the water, for the briefest moment, his eye caught mine. Black and reflective, I saw my face within it and knew that he was here for me. Caleb reached for me, his hands brushing my waist and gripping it tightly.

"No, do not be afraid…" I told him. "He is my friend."

There was not time for incredulity, or questions. We were already gone. I placed a hand against the whale, and his skin was soft and firm at the same time.

"Go ahead." I urged, placing Caleb's hand on the great piercing fin that invited us to ride.

He was utterly frozen but did as I had asked. There was a longing to ask what was happening, but he never uttered a word. He had come this far without question, but now the time had come where there could be no coming back.

The whale lingered a moment at the surface, allowing us to trace our hands across his great body. How had I stayed away from these creatures? How had I ever remained on the land without knowing this touch? I could feel his heart, his soul. He would not speak in riddles anymore, but in languid sentences in a language I had not thought I'd known. I wanted to convey this joy with Caleb, but as I looked over, I saw the sheer terror in his eyes.

Tell him, child… He must come of his own accord. The whale broke into my thoughts, his voice ringing out above all else and yet, the outward silence had not been broken.

"Ask me." I said, "Ask me whatever you would ask of me."

His breathing was low and quick. When he spoke, it was in rushed tones that required deep breaths between the hurried words.

"No… I go wherever… you go."

It was never going to be an easy task. But he would come, he did not need to know where or why. He would come because it was where I would be, and it was reason enough. I looked at his face in the red morning light, clinging to the great beast which came to guide our way.

He was not afraid of what would come after, only that the water was cold, and the whale seemed all the more fierce up close. He was not screaming; he was not being dragged to a fate untold. He was mine and I was his. The lives we had touched would go on, as would ours.

It was a simple thing, so simple that when I took a final look upon the Eynhallow shores I was not sorry to say goodbye. Mammy, her shadow quiet now, still stood by the water's edge. I knew she was sorry, that she would remain there long after I had gone. But somehow it mattered not. If I had once dreamed of leaving this place, it was only because I was bound somewhere else.

Eynhallow's day was done, perhaps not for those left behind. But it was true for me. If ever the day would come that I ever set foot back upon those shores I knew I would not find any trace of myself there. Perhaps not even a trace of anything I had ever known. But still, I was not sorry. This fight was won, and this song sung. She would be the one to lament now and if God listened to her she would find comfort. If not, then that would be hers to bear.

My final thought was of Rohan. Not of the man who slept soundly in his bed at the side of his wife, but the screaming babe who came into the world with thunder. The sinewy look of his newborn face and the tiny hand which had gripped mine and never let go. For him I would shed tears, but here I could not taste them as the salt of the sea encroached. It was for him I had stayed and even as I looked my last upon the sky, I knew that for him a goodbye would give me cause to remain forever more. If he was angry with me, he would understand in time. I closed my eyes and saw his vivid smile; on the lips of the boy I once knew. When I opened them again, Eynhallow was gone and there was nothing but the murky depths and the beating of my own heart.

A beat which softened the closer we became. A beat which dulled to a sullen drum as we sank further and further. Down here, there was no need for breath nor a heartbeat.

Both ceased, both inched between life and death. I was aware of the whale by our side and the icy hand within mine. Yet somehow neither made sense to me. My memory had served nightmares of a face I had thought long forgotten. Within a garden, in a place far, far away, I found myself trying to remember that face, but it was another time, another life.

The golden grasses, the colourful weeds that I had no name for, all of them remained the same. It was I who was changed. I who came here with the knowledge I had lacked before. Through the garden we drifted, the glowing water ushering us forward through fantastical visions of great halls and things which perhaps were not truly there at all. I was aware when the whale began to drift away, the current taking him higher and higher. He did not say why, but somehow, I knew that he could come no further. We would be alone when the moment came. Whenever that moment would come and whatever would happen.

A joyful rapture and a haunting song began to creep in. A sense that we were not alone and fearful golden gates. Etched into the ocean floor, glistening between shafts of light that peered down from the surface. Blind to the naked eye, but there if you knew where to look for them. Drawing me in like a moth to a flame, those gates called to me and they knew my name in fluent languages unspoken for thousands of years.

They opened without command and the darkness took hold. Wherever Caleb was, his touch had gone. Could it be that I was falling without him? Spiralling past those great golden gates and into the abyss alone? He would curse me for leaving him behind.

Searching frantically for his hand, for any part of him, I knew that to try would be futile. This darkness was quick, and I was never certain if I was surrounded by water or air. This world did not exist under the ocean. Underneath the water there was nothing but rock and solid ground. The ocean was a gateway, a passing veil between that world and this. I knew it, as much as I could have known, as I passed through the spiralling darkness.

Perhaps the two places lay side by side and the water was nothing but a fairytale. If there was a way back and surely there must have been, it was far from my grasp. It seemed that I rushed through an empty space with nothing to hold on to. I began to wonder, as much as I could when all my senses were taken from me, if I was going to make it.

The distant sound of running water came to me like dreams. The distinct sound of it falling over solid ground. I felt my body once more, the darkness slowly receding towards a heavenly light. Is this what it was to die? Had I somehow got lost along the way and given myself over to the heaven I was promised?

It mattered little. Wherever I was going, I was hurtling towards it too quickly to care. I could feel air bubbles rise from my throat and out into the pale water. When I took my first breath, it was not death which greeted me. Clear blue water lies ahead, but I was above it somehow. The flow of the fall took me and plunged me into the depths below.

A waterfall?

I wasn't certain of it until I emerged. The air was cool and fresh, and it hit me like the first winter snow. But more than that, *it hit me.*

Deep, uncertain breaths came to me as I spat out the water that had somehow made its way into my lungs. But I was breathing. For a moment I had forgotten that down here, there shouldn't have been any air at all. Nothing made sense. Not the clear cascading water which emerged from the high rock face of overbearing mountains that lie above me. Not the pool of clarity below, which was so clear I could see the water grow dark as it went down and down towards an end, I wasn't sure was even there. Not the queer wind, the way it blew cool but the light above was unseasonably warm.

Not even the colour of the sky made sense. How could I be below the sea? Birds flew overhead. Clouds moved on cool breezes. I had found myself at the source of a river which stretched out over green pastures that lulled in the bright new sunlight. The sound of falling water was relentless. A loud thrum to drown out all else. I quickly realised I had been thrown from the top of it and from down here it seemed like I'd been spat from the mouth of a great snow tipped mountain. It spurted forth from a precipice that appeared like a great scar within the rock. There was no way back up, not even if you could scale the rock. The water moved in one direction.

I looked about me, above and below. A speckle of fish flitted beneath me, silver scaled and shimmering in the sun. They shot down into the dark depths where the light could not touch when I moved my feet around them. The pool was surrounded by a luminous moss, old rocks were drenched in it and seemed to breathe as the light moved around the slimy green slithers. Fields of different colours rolled out before me, trees that sprung from the ground climbing higher than any I had ever seen before. Their branches swayed in the wind but did not rustle like the familiar sound I'd heard before. They hoo'd almost like a mother singing a lullaby and in the far, far distance, where the sky met the land, I saw the jagged edges of more mountains laying in shadow.

"Finola, of House Raven?" Spoke a soft voice, so soft it almost sang. Quiet and yet, I heard it over the drum of falling water.

I looked up, shafts of sunlight peering down behind the form which stood on the moss-covered rocks. After my eyes adjusted, I noticed someone offering me hand. Painfully, I became aware that I was still naked.

"Who are you?" I asked, aware that the water was so clear they had probably already seen all that there was to see.

He straightened up. Wearing only a cloth to cover his manhood, I shied away from the sight of him standing by the pools edge. His black hair fell back into curls pinned back with fish bone, I noticed it in the wind. He looked amused, his face twitched into a half smile that was both mocking and endearing.

"My name is Catesby." He said, proudly. "I was sent to find you and bring you to the house of Astala, your grandfather."

I suddenly became aware that it was only him and I, realizing that I had somehow lost Caleb somewhere along the way.

"I brought someone with me, he was with me at the gates but..."

Catesby raised a hand to silence me. "The boy came before you. He has been taken to the House of Consorts."

Already I could feel the fringes of tears come upon me. This place, in all its glory had exceeded my expectations. Not even in dream had I imagined that it would be like this. I realised, suddenly, that I was completely uninitiated and unprepared. I looked up towards the pounding waterfall and wished that I could grasp the cascading water and climb back up.

"When can I see him?" I asked, wondering if this was something I ought to ask or demand.

The boy called Catesby moved, the sunlight from behind him blinding me until I raised a hand against it. His skin was not like I recalled, from dream like visions half forgotten, it did not resemble scales of a fish. His ears did not point, his body was not tall and sinuous but firm and muscular like... a human.

"You will not see him again until he is initiated. Human consorts must learn our ways before they can be allowed to exist alongside us." He said, firmly, leaning down to offer me his hand once more.

I decided my dignity was probably misplaced here. I allowed him to pull me from the water and surprisingly he did not look at the places I thought he might. From behind a rock he handed me a simple cloth made from the same fabric he wore; I had no name for it but it felt soft on the inside but rough on the outside as I wrapped it around me. He handed me a fish bone clasp to tie it off, only then did he allow himself to look at me.

"You're human." I said, with a hint of presumption. "Have you been to the House of... Consorts?"

He was still amused by me; I could tell in the way that smile of his cocked to the side of his lips again.

"No." He replied wryly. "I am not a consort."

He began to walk down a pathway I hadn't noticed. The ground was soft beneath my feet and I sensed that he wished me to follow.

But I couldn't. I remembered a whale, a flock of birds, a little boy standing in a doorway crying for me. Memories did not come to me like they once had, all of them seemed to be locked away in a part of my mind I could not access.

Something had happened to me in that darkness, something I couldn't put my finger on. Something had changed, I had changed. Here I was not the strange sullen girl from the abandoned isle. Here… I was nothing.

"Not nothing…" Said Catesby, as he turned and gestured me to follow.

I raised an eyebrow. "I beg your pardon?"

He was only an inch or two taller than me and yet when I approached him, he seemed to tower over me. Every part of him was sculpted in bare muscle and even though he was small in stature, every part of him seemed to flow one part to the other.

"You are not nothing here." He repeated. "We've been waiting for you to return for a long time."

His eyes were familiar somehow. Brown, warm and entirely like eyes I had looked into before. I realised I had probably spoken out loud, but all I could hear was the chattering of my teeth as a cool breeze hit my moist skin.

"What are you?" I asked, without thinking of the words before they slipped from my mouth.

His smile faded and he looked to the ground. "I am like you."

Yes, he was. I knew he was the moment he said it. He'd heard my whispers the way I could hear the animals back on Eynhallow.

"Come." He insisted then, turning his back on me to go the way he came. "You will know everything, in time. But for now, I have been given the task of introducing you to White Mount."

I raised an indelible eyebrow. "White Mount?"

"You did not think it would just be one place, did you? Is your world not made up of many?"

Foolishness, evidently, had become my friend.

"Follow me. Everything you see from the mountainside to the horizon is White Mount. The home of Astala..."

The moss-covered pathway leads down from the river and into the lullaby trees. Tall and unlike anything I had ever seen, they flowed upwards with trunks thicker than the foundations of houses. Vines twisted around them, reaching up towards the canopy above. The forest floor was soft to the touch, as if the ground would swallow you if you stood too long. He moved quickly and with purpose along the shaded pathway, expecting me to follow with equal speed. But here, the air lingered cool and light.

A dizziness took over, and before I could go any further, I felt myself fall to the ground. It seemed that everything around me was trying to take my breath. The wind, the air, the very leaves upon the high trees above. Maybe I imagined it, maybe I wasn't here at all and it was simply another vision to trick my mind. If I opened my eyes, would I be a bird again?

"Stand." Said that quiet voice. "You must stand."

His arms came underneath me and helped me up.

"I can't..." I protested.

"No, you must. If not now, then never." He insisted, placing an arm around my waist.

"What's happening to me?" But the words were jumbled, I was never certain if I had spoken them aloud.

I felt his hands around me, his voice somewhere in the distance. Trees passed by and rocks and moss and yellow eyes in between watching from afar.

It's just a dream. When I awake, I shall be within Hylands walls? Mammy will be reading her bible by the fire, Rohan and Bethan keeping vigil by the gate awaiting the brother that went in the night. The half-built house, a house of bones waiting for skin and the men trying to build it, with false hope. It will all be there, when I open my eyes.

But it wasn't.

PART 2
THE YOUNG PRIESTESS

Lucie Howorth

Chapter One

FINFOLKAHEEM

My grandfather's house was etched in stone at the foot of the mountains. The outcrop of rock overlooked the land, sitting within a great lake that formed from the passing river. I was dropped at the foot of the open door, a curtain of pearls moving aside as faceless forms came running towards me.

I was taken to a white room that sat at the top of the winding towers carved from the mountain itself. I could feel their hands upon me, some of them probing my breasts and others pulling back my hair. Their voices, although clear, seemed far away. I lingered somewhere between asleep and awake, but somehow, I was not afraid.

"She's been gone too long." I heard someone say.

"She was never meant to linger this long…" Said another.

And then nothing but silence. The more I breathed, the more I began to see. Blurred vision became clear. I was not in a white room. I was within the belly of a pearl. The smooth texture of the walls resembled white waves, the light casting shadows of deep blue.

The bed was nothing but some sort of animal skin, suspended from strange fibred rope. A window had been carved before me, flowing out across the fields of green and brown and yellow. Water seemed to fill every part of the landscape. Rivers, lakes and beyond it seemed that waves crashed somewhere I could not see.

How long I had been there, I could not say. But when I looked down, they had dressed me in a gown of silk and adorned my hair with pearl. I had already begun to forget the things which I thought I never would. It was only then that I began to feel fear prick at me.

"You're awake." Said another voice, this time closer and familiar.

I turned to see Catesby sitting on a chair made of fish bone. I had not noticed him before, not known he had even entered the room. Or if he had ever left it.

"How did you get here?" I asked, but I was greeted once again by that half smile.

He still wore that cloth about his loins and nothing else. But for him, there seemed to be no shame in it. He came over to the bed and looked at me intently as if searching for something in my face.

"For a moment I thought you were never going to wake up." He said, stoically. "They said it would take time for you to adjust to the air we breathe."

"They say a lot. Who are *they?*"

"The elders. I'll take you to see Astala, if you wish? He will tell you everything."

I looked down at the gown they had dressed me in, the fine material of it clinging to my body like a second skin.

"Why does he not come himself? Why does he keep sending you to bring me forth?"

He noted the anger in my voice and seemed disappointed by it. Gone was his mocking face and in its place was one of a scolded child. I was immediately sorry for what I'd said.

"He can't be in many places at once."

"I presume this is one of many things I'll be told when the time is right."

He sensed my frustration. I knew it as he shrugged and urged me to go with him. I slipped down from the bed and noted the fluid movement. Like water… here everything moved like water.

"I don't want to see Astala." I said, pulling down the silk that had hitched around my knees. "Take me to the House of Consorts."

Already he was shaking his head, those black curls of his coming down around his eyes.

"You ask something I cannot give."

As I approached him, he backed away. As if being close to me would somehow get him into trouble.

"Why not?" I asked, stopping dead before he was backed against the smooth white walls.

"Because he has not been to the stone circle, he hasn't been initiated. I have already told you this."

I had known a stone circle once. Somewhere in my mind I remembered seeing them gather around a ring of dark stones, red hair and white hair and black.

Some truths had been revealed, but others kept hidden. All of it centred around the mysterious grandfather who seemed to hold the key to everything.

If he had wanted to see me, he would have come to me already instead of sending his messenger to watch over me. I would not go to him, I resolved, until he came to me first.

"Then, take me to the stone circle."

This seemed to please him more than my previous request. For the first time he smiled without a hint of mockery, both sides of the smile reached his eyes.

The hillsides were coveted in a strange heather. It smelled unlike anything I had ever known, indistinguishable to anything on Eynhallow and so pleasant that my breaths were long and deep.

Down by the riverside it grew over the banks, snaking into the water and changing colour underneath it. From hues of deep red and purple, it turned blue and green and yellow. I followed my companion in the direction the river flowed, from the mountain house of my grandfather and down into the vast open spaces below.

Where groves of trees came and went, it seemed that we were entirely alone until yellow eyes peered out at me from within the vines and branches.

"What are those creatures?" I asked, pausing to spot one of them a little closer.

As I inched towards them their little eyes closed and scurried away.

Catesby turned to see what had gained my attention. He waved a passive hand and rolled his eyes.

"Nothing but parfois. They live in the water but come out into the trees to mate. They never make themselves seen, but they see all."

"But what are they?" I pushed.

He didn't understand the question. "They are what they are."

"Not dogs. Not cats either?" I clarified.

He cocked his head to one side, his brow furrowed in confusion. "What is dog and cat?"

It occurred to me that whatever a dog and cat was to me, a parfois was to him.

"They are what they are." I sighed, and somehow it saddened me that it would never make sense to either of us.

I wondered why Catesby had come to me and no one else.

As he led me across the sweet-smelling heathers, through mires of clear water, down into the valley below the mountainside I watched as each step he took was a knowing one. He knew this land, as I had once known a land far, far away. I wondered if time moved as it did here.

How long had I been gone? Days, weeks? Did they mourn me? Or had I been gone so long that their mourning had ceased?

The light didn't seem right here. There was no sun to rise in the east or set in the west. Just a phosphorus glow from somewhere above. I'd barely had a moment to mourn it myself. From the moment I arrived there had been a succession of mysterious things I could be told and others I could not.

Catesby, for all that he was, seemed happy to tell me about little creatures with yellow eyes. But for anything else, I would have to wait.

Down in the heart of the valley I could see the ring of stones come into view. It stood within a glade, the deep sloping hills surrounding it dotted with homesteads made of wood and mud.

They were queer little things, like green and brown domes with smoke billowing from the top. Catesby stopped as we approached and pointed to one that sat at the edge of a great forest that began at the far end of the valley. It was the biggest one of all, made from the bark and vines of the trees.

"You see that one?" He asked, smiling broadly.

I nodded.

"That's where I live."

He seemed proud of the dwelling. To me, there seemed nothing spectacular about it. Perhaps there was not brick or cement here, only the primitive surroundings at their disposal.

"Tell me, why were you sent to me?" I asked, entirely out of the blue.

I had not meant to ask. I had already thought that I would ask later, when I had learned all there was for me to learn, but it struck me now that he lived in this place not at the great mountain castle of my grandfather but here amongst the trees and valleys.

"Because Astala asked me to." He confirmed, avoiding my eyes.

"And do you do everything which Astala asks of you?" I probed.

Once again, he seemed uneasy, as he had been when I had asked about the House of Consorts. Perhaps he had been told what to tell me and what not to.

"Of course."

Frustrated, I stopped dead. "Are you his servant?"

His hands curled into fists. I straightened up as he inched towards me, fire in his belly.

"They told me you were a quiet one. That you didn't speak much and when you did little of it made sense. What makes you so bold now?"

I could have cried at the memory of that girl. She stood at the foot of the water, looking out. Always looking out. Here it was like she didn't exist.

Here… she made sense. Here she was a child with inquisitive eyes. Why hadn't I cried yet? What kept me from crying?

"I'm sorry." I managed to say, between the menagerie of thoughts. "I didn't mean…"

Catesby's face fell. For a moment his eyes met mine. His look was sorrow and something else. He wanted to tell me everything but *couldn't*.

"Forgive me." He uttered. "I forget that you are new to all this."

In silence we went down towards the stones. Whatever reason he'd been sent to me, I resolved that I was glad they had sent him and no other.

These stones knew me. I had been here before in strange dreams, standing with my grandfather and the others. There seemed to be little difference between the dreams and the reality of it. They were cold and hard to the touch. They were stones, like any other. In this world and the one I had departed. Standing in a ring, Catesby sat by the edge and let me walk into the middle alone.

"I've been here before." I confessed.

He nodded, shifting onto his side and lifting one leg so that the cloth covering him barely covered him at all.

"This is a sacred place. We come here to pray and to think. If you were going to be anywhere in any form, it would be here."

I recalled the shadows, the strange collection of forms who had stood by the edge. The humans.

"When I was here it was like a ritual was taking place. They held torches and stood around the stones with their red and white and black hair. Over there…" I pointed, "There were humans."

Catesby nodded. "Perhaps it was a Solstice. Or when the moon is at full and we gather to pray to the Goddess."

I looked up. It seemed that there was no moon to pray to. The sky was a strange mixture of the sky I had once known, and the surface of a clear ocean. His eyes followed mine upward, his finger pointing to something I could not see.

"Give it time." He said softly. "Soon your eyes will know what to look for."

Why hadn't I cried? Where were the tears for what I'd left behind, for the man I loved? I'd been so fiercely distracted, so focused on what lay ahead that I'd forgotten to think of what had come before. I looked at Catesby, he was nothing more than a stranger to me.

His familiarity had come unbidden and I had clung to his presence like a babe to its mother. He was playing with a small sickle knife that hung around his cloth, toying with the blade silently as he brooded by the edge of the stones.

I do not know you. Yet, I feel as if I should.

"Do your eyes know what to look for?" I asked, and the question pricked at him as he dropped the knife and stood erect.

"Of course." He said, clearing his throat. "I was born here."

The revelation came as somewhat of a surprise. "Were you?!"

He looked at me from the corner of his eyes, as if he had revealed more than he should. He had said that he was like me. Maybe I had presumed too much.

"Yes." He murmured, coming into the ring and sliding down the flat side of the stone before him. "In that very place I live now."

He sat with one leg propped up, not caring if his cloth moved this way or that. It seemed to me that my eyes naturally averted to his and no other part of him. It had nothing to do with modesty, or perception of politeness and everything to do with the fact that I had no desire to look there. It seemed that the lack of desire was shared, as I recalled his disinterest in those parts of me as I emerged from the waterfall pool. For the first time, I had been laid bare without the fear of my own blood.

"You have never been to…" I faltered. "Forgive me, I know not what to call the place I come from."

"Eynhallow." He sighed, "No. I have never been to the other 'Aheem."

"The *other* 'Aheem?"

He placed his hands palm up before me, in one he created a fist and in the other he spread his fingers.

"Here is your world." He said, waving the open hand. "And here is ours."

Carefully he curled his open hand around his fist. "One abounds the other. Perhaps we are side by side, perhaps truly we dwell within some place at the bottom of your waters. I do not know. But you call our world Finfolkaheem, because this is where the people of Fin exist. We do not call your world… Humanaheem…" He laughed softly at the absurdity of it, "'Aheem is just a word for a place, a home, somewhere to be. Your island was Eynhallow, but there was a world beyond it. As it is here."

"And what do *you* call it?"

He shrugged. "Where we are now is just a ring of stones."

"Is this something else I must wait for?" The words came out more impatiently than I'd anticipated.

Always I must wait. My father had made me wait, when I had my hands around the truth it still evaded me. I was utterly alone. There was no bible to hold, no brother to protect me, no silence within the wind.

There were no whispering words of comfort from familiar creatures in sky, field or water. There was no way of knowing if Caleb fared well, or if he wondered about me as I did about him.

Suddenly I didn't care where I was or what any of it meant. I felt a very real, very fierce anger begin to bubble beneath the veneer. I had excused myself long enough beneath the veil of my hair, keeping myself to myself amongst the town folk on the mainland. I had been punished, made a slave to my own instincts. I had loved, and I had lost. But what use was any of it if I was always to be coddled like a child without wit?

There were stories in those yellow eyes, I'd seen them, and I knew they wanted to be read. I could not hear them in the same way, but whatever gift I'd been bestowed it had transcended the arch between that world and this. I did not need another to tell me this truth. It revealed itself to me the way any natural thing occurs. In the same way that it occurred to me that

Catesby had been sent to keep me from speaking words I should not speak, for discovering things I should not discover and most of all, to keep me from going wherever I was not meant to go.

I had not yet seen another soul, save for blurred half-memories of fabled elders speaking over my half dead body. I wondered if they saw me and hid themselves from view. Or if I had simply been blinded from the true nature of things? I would not let them see my anger or feel it. But I would know it was there, like all the secrets and lies. I would have my own.

"You ask too many questions."

No, I ask the wrong questions.

He seemed to grow impatient with me. The way he smiled, the way he saved that smile for when I said the right things, it was as if he was pleased when we could speak freely. For those things he wouldn't say I would bide my time. I had come this far.

We stayed at the stone circle for what seemed like a very long time. Here it felt as if I could keep some resemblance of myself. I didn't speak to Catesby again and he made no effort to speak with me. This seemed to please him even more than speaking of the things which he could, in the silence, he began to pick up disregarded rocks at his feet and carve things I could not make out into them with his knife.

At opposite sides of the circle it was hard to make out anything other than the tan coloured cloth around his loins and the mass of black curls around his head. I had decided I would sit as far from him as I possibly could. Partly to see what he would do, partly because I had begun to sense that being alone was not an option, no matter how much I yearned for it.

Was I a prisoner? Of my own free will? He would not tell me, even if he could. He was a pointless emissary, as I closed my eyes against the sight of him, I willed the tears to come. He would not see them from here, falling down my cheeks.

I have cried a thousand tears and now when I have need of them most, they have gone. There is nothing I want more than to cry for whatever it is within my heart which bleeds. Why do I not cry? Even when I have bid the tears to come?

The sky began to shift. The relentless glow began to dim and the shapes and colours darkened. There was no specific moment, no moon to rise and no sun to set. It was as if the sky was a candle, snuffed out by a breeze. It was hauntingly beautiful, the shift between night and day. There seemed to be a twilight of sorts hanging in the sky, where shadows were cast but enough light remained to guide our way. Catesby looked up, his body stiffening. Perhaps he had fallen asleep, perhaps he had noticed the coming of night. He looked over towards me and whistled a high-pitched squall from his lips. His head of curls moved as he nodded towards the direction, he wanted me to come. Reluctantly I went, crossing the stone circle as slowly as I could. My cheeks were still painfully dry.

"Come, I'll take you back now." Catesby muttered, scattering the carved rocks that had gathered around him.

I noted a few of them had taken on the forms of various fish, other birds. They were intricate and should have taken days of work to make out the likeness he had achieved in a matter of… however long we had been here.

"For what purpose?" I asked, he sighed at me in that way I was now accustomed to. "You know more than you care to share, you brought me here when you could not take me elsewhere and you kept me here until now… why?"

For the first time he looked me directly in the eye. "I will not disobey my High Priest. He is good, kind and gives me no reason to question whatever he asks of me. He bade me stay with you until night and so I have."

"He has not been good, or kind to me. He continues to give me reason to question." I spat back, and there in the back of my throat I finally felt that lump which came before tears.

He heard it; I was certain. He heard my voice break upon the verge of those god forsaken tears. His hand came up slowly, reluctantly and he placed it upon my arm.

"He has been more kind to you than any of us."

There was something in his voice. The onslaught of night sent shadows across his face, somehow it seemed he was comforting me.

"It does not feel as if I have felt much kindness in this life." And there it was again, that lump upon which I must choke.

"In *this* life?" He clarified.

Were the two truly different, one from the other? The blood which pumped aimlessly through my heart had not ceased, I had not died.

This life of mine was still mine, still ongoing.

But perhaps there had been a rebirth? Perhaps when I fell from that mountainside waterfall, I had been spurted forth into a life anew?

This flesh of mine, this hair, these eyes… these memories within all belonged to me and yet, the two had already begun to seem as if they would never ever reconcile within me.

"I'm afraid." I confessed; Catesby's other hand came to rest upon my other arm.

"I know you are." He almost whispered, "But you have nothing to fear."

I felt the first tear began to fall, softly and slowly and salty.

"What if I do not love him, if you keep him from me, will I remember to love him?"

Catesby smiled, a slow and deliberate smile sent to tell me that I was afraid of something which would never come to pass.

"You do not forget how to love."

The second tear came, more quickly than the last, fell down my face and rolled down onto my neck.

"You do not know…" I cried, letting each tear come.

His grip tightened. Why did this grip seem as if I had felt it before? It was firm and sure, but soft and comforting at the same time.

"I do know!" He said, in a whisper, "I do know, Finola!"

I shook my head against his comfort though. He spoke of things he knew nothing about. He had never been to the *other* 'Aheem. How could he know what the world beyond was like? How could he know what I had sacrificed?

"Nathan Munro." He said then, "That damned fool, Nathan Munro. The ones who came from another Island, to Eynhallow. The one who came with you, I know all about him... and them."

I squirmed out of his grasp. "No... no, you must understand... the guardians..."

He was afraid now. His eyes began to look around for prying watchers. I had not seen another living soul, why should he look for them now? He knew that I would not hear him, that I had gone beyond the anger and frustration to a place where I no longer wanted to know.

The tears came now, flowing uncontrollably. But I did not cry for the things which I had wanted to, I cried because I had forced it upon myself and now had little control over it. I backed away from him, didn't want to hear any more fallacies or mysterious reasons why I couldn't be told the truths which I deserved.

"No." He said then, "You can't understand."

His presumption sent a rage into my belly, firing within and sending my blood to boil. I wiped the tears from my eyes and glared at him with a darkness I had not known I possessed.

"But you will." He added, raising a hand into the air above him.

He held it there for a moment as if he meant to strike me. But he brought it down swiftly and carefully, the air rushing through my hair. I closed my eyes; his hand was nowhere near me. The sudden rush of air had not come from him, but *behind*.

The grove of trees that surrounded the stone circle began to rumble. A low thrum that began to sound like rain as the leaves began to shake. Green leaves, long and sharp that extended from deep brown and orange barks and vines. Then, from the colours came the white. Flocks of them rushing from the canopy beyond, into the sky and all around us. They landed on

Catesby's arms, shoulders, one even sat comfortably on top of his head. They fluttered around, their wings caressing me but never getting close enough to land. I looked through the flurry of white and over to the face that smiled through.

When their wings settled, each of them scattered upon rocks, upon the ground, upon Catesby. They were the same birds that lived upon the rocks on Eynhallow. The same birds that had saved me, that had told me to wait.

"How can this be?" I cried, reaching out to touch their snow-white wings.

"They are mine. They tell me all their secrets. They told me when you were coming, they told me everything before that."

"Is that why Astala sent you?" I asked, resting a careful hand on the head of a curious bird that had landed upon my shoulder.

Catesby shrugged. "Yes, and other reasons. Come, I'll take you back now."

He raised a hand a second time, at this command they fluttered back into the trees and were hidden once more.

I followed him back up the mountainside, through trees and mires and riverbanks. The white castle carved from stone was illuminated now, the windows shining out over the land. A fire burned bright atop one of the high towers and cast a shadow of itself over the surrounding water. When we reached it, Catesby offered me his hand and helped me to step onto the pathway that lead through the lake and up toward the castle gate.

"I go no further." He said, stepping back.

I found that this made me sad, a little afraid. "No, you must come with me."

He shrugged at the sentiment but gestured me on. "No, I have to get back now. But you'll see me again, I promise."

For a moment I wasn't sure if I should thank him, or embrace him, or simply walk away. He smiled that smile that was not mocking, that met his eyes and made him sincere and then turned to leave.

"Thank you." I called, after he was too far for me touch.

Lucie Howorth

He turned once and then he was gone.

Chapter Two

FINBLOOD

The causeway was as smooth and clear as a glacier, reaching out from the rocks and through the water towards high pearl white gates. The water lapped at the edges gently, on the breeze I could barely feel. There was an intimidation which came with walking across it, as the outcrop loomed ever closer, its high towers and fires and ornately carved windows looked out. I still had to breathe deeply to know I was still alive.

For this place was surely a dream? The fissures of the land seemed to melt one into the other. Colours and textures and elements all seemed one.

As I approached the gate, it opened effortlessly like wind had taken flight within the ivory structures. There atop the stairway that lead to the entrance was a figure I had seen once before.

I became aware that I was alone. Caleb was nowhere in sight and every other living creature I had ever loved seemed to exist in a realm too far to touch.

The air didn't reach my lungs quite right; I was still faint and not sure if consciousness was fully intact. The pathway glowed beneath my feet, the clear stone beneath casting strange colours from the sky above. I anticipated that it would all look quite ordinary once my head was in the right place. But something told me that wasn't so. I wondered, as I placed one foot in front of the other, if I would ever fit?

Astala's face came into view. Benevolent and smiling. He wore the same loin cloths as in previous visions, entirely unchanged. A small sickle knife hung at his side; his long hair braided down his back to reveal his breathing ears.

I wondered if I would ever not be perturbed by the subtle shine of his scaled skin. Would it always grab my attention so? His hand reached out to me, long fingers that webbed so slightly and so subtly. He felt cold to the touch, but soft and sure like the skin of the great whale who had guided me here. When finally, he had me within his grasp I looked up into his eyes and there I saw the whole world.

"Finola." He breathed, his body pulling me in towards an embrace I hadn't anticipated.

Of course, my body flowed into his, I put my arms about him as a dutiful grandchild should. But still, he was a stranger to me and the odd way his body felt meant that I tensed mine against him. I had hoped he wouldn't notice.

"Do not fear me, Child." He soothed. "You are back where you belong now."

He shifted to the side, bodies appearing from behind. The entrance was not brick, nor wood, but the same pearl rock that adorned the room I had awoken in... was it the night before? Time shifted so slowly here, I noted that I must not lose track of my days.

The walls had strange vines climbing down them with beautiful blossoms bursting down the green stems. Ornately carved stairways that flowed into the entrance cascaded down.

Dwellings were not as they were back on Eynhallow. With walls of stone and chairs and tables and doors. The people who seemed to appear from nowhere came from what looked like tunnels, but as I arched my eyes to see closer, they were not tunnels, simply one room turning into another.

"Cousin."

I turned and there before me, was the first familiar face I had seen in what felt like an eternity. Dressed in the loins of the Finfolk, Ewan was smiling broadly.

It was hard not to contain my astonishment. "Ewan!"

He good-naturedly nodded. "It is good to see you here."

"I saw you only a day ago... Didn't I?"

He laughed, a laughter that was still new to me. "Yes, a day ago, dearest cousin."

He was jovial, almost on the fringes of happiness. There were lines in his face that had never been there before from expressions previously unknown.

"This is also your cousin…"

Ewan stepped aside to let a tiny girl step forward. She had the raven hair of my family's bloodline and the formidable piercing stare that reminded me of a picture I'd once seen of a woman I'd hoped to call mother. She wasn't a Halfling though; her blood was pure.

"Hello." I said, unsteadily, my mouth suddenly dry.

She smiled. An enchanting smile. But she did not offer a word to me, instead she ran to Astala and hid behind his long form.

"Now, come on Elodie… Greet your cousin properly."

He ushered the tiny one forward. But I had lived through many forced introductions. She owed me nothing.

"It's fine, I am a new face." I reasoned.

Others came forward. An Uncle who bore a striking resemblance to Astala, his name was Esson and he was my mother's brother. His wife was a beautiful finwoman who stood by his side, lowering her head to me in a solemn greeting.

She was not from the same house. Her hair was purest white, her eyes the deepest blue. But the rest of her was all Fin, pointed ears hiding those breathing gills behind and skin of tiny scales. Her name was Elora of house Babel. All of them were nothing to me. I had hoped to feel a tinge of emotion. Something to prick at the reasons why I had come here.

These beings of dream were still ethereal, their strange bodies not human, not anything else I could quite describe to one who had never seen with their own eyes.

They were beautiful and flawless and languid in each flowing movement. The women were dressed in flowing simple gowns of white, of material that caught each curve of their lean figures. There seemed to be no seams, no stitches. Yet each distinguishable from the other.

Elora's hair was adorned with a single jewel that hung down towards the middle of her great piercing eyes. It was the deepest blue and caught the light when she turned her head. She was silent and timid, her daughter seemingly sharing the same quietness.

But Esson was more forthcoming. The next in line for the title of High Priest, as sure of his place as anyone I had ever met. Astala seemed strangely aware of every move he made, as if he watched to ascertain something. There was pride there, of sorts. But there was another feeling too and I sensed it. I wondered if Astala knew it too.

"Where is Catesby?" He asked, a look of disappointment flashing across that deliberate face. "Damn the boy!"

I wondered why it should matter. Why Esson placed a hand on his father's shoulder and almost seemed to laugh at the prospect that Catesby should be present and yet wasn't.

"He bade me come here alone." I uttered.

Astala, for all that he was, looked upon me kindly.

"Of course, he did." He sighed. "That boy has human tendencies. He takes his tasks as literally as they are set out for him."

"Why should he be damned?" I asked, the numbing sense of nothingness dulling the reality of how out of place my words sounded.

Perhaps Astala was the one who made all the decisions of who should be damned, therefore was not to be questioned? Even Esson, who had appeared almost arrogant a moment ago stepped back and let his true place be known.

"Child, there is a third eye to see with and yours is still closed."

His lithe hands clasped my face. Close up I could see the way his skin danced in the fading light. He was too young to be my grandfather. My heart began to race, his breath was warm and his lips too close as he kissed me softly on the forehead.

"But that is why you are here. Soon, child... all your eyes will be open."

He was gone almost as suddenly as he had appeared. Perhaps he possessed the ability to turn into air, perhaps it was something only he could do. But the others did not dissipate, they remained. I felt a chill in my bones, that something wasn't quite right.

Life was a meandering lane of questions. One revelation leading to another. This life, previous lives. Perhaps there was no end to the turmoil of wondering who I truly was? All I wanted in that unforgiving moment was Caleb. These people were keeping him from me.

"It will not be forever." Elora spoke, finally and softly. "Your love thinks of you in return."

It struck me immediately that I was not safe. Not even my own thoughts were kept locked, not from her. She did not look at me as she spoke, instead her eyes looked beyond as if she heard something, or someone out there in the land as far as the eye could see.

But Esson was looking right at me.

"Our gifts, as sparing as they are, all differ one from the other." He said, his eyes moving adoringly towards his wife. "Hers are unparalleled."

"Because she is able to hear the thoughts of others or because this serves some other purpose?" I asked, his lip curled at the insinuation that she was anything other than spectacular.

"What is it you fear of us, Finola? We are your family are we not?"

Are they not?

"Perhaps it would be remiss of me to expect you to understand my fear." I replied, flippantly. "But I appear to belong neither here nor there."

I had forgotten that Ewan was still there. It struck me that even with his newfound confidence he still knew when to stand in the shadows. Perhaps it was something that would never leave him, perhaps there was hope that I'd never lose myself. Perhaps it would be something to find myself first.

"I felt the same, I did not come to know where I belonged until I faced my fears. There is joy to be found Finola, if you will open yourself to finding it." Said Ewan, attempting to comfort.

But I was inconsolably closed. I wondered if this strange land had the power to withdraw anything from me other than fear.

Time was a bountiful commodity here. It flowed one second, one minute, one much like the other. The light never really left the sky, but night was distinguishable from day, nevertheless.

My room remained the one I had found myself in, in the tower overlooking the land below. Often, I would stand by the oval window watching the strange sky change colours.

Astala sent things he thought I might like to fill the empty spaces. But the void was never filled. Not with boxes made of fish bone, gowns of different colours in that material I couldn't name. Not with jewels to adorn my head, or with furniture that resembled the things from the other Aheem.

Astala himself was an enigma. Always spoken of, but rarely seen. It seemed that others were always doing his bidding, but when they were given their biddings, I did not know. He was always present at the breaking of night; at the meal we ate in the room which had no roof.

Vines which gave birth to berries adorned the walls and grew out and above. A great white stone sat in the middle of the room, circled with chairs made of whale bone and ivory. There was no head to the table, no propriety. We ate from simple bowls with our hands. Fish, meat, the textures I had never tasted before. Berries and fruits, I had no name for. Their tastes sweet and unknown. Each day he would ask how I fared. If I was healthy, if I was happy. If I was content. Always I would answer the same. Always I would ask where Caleb was. Always he would tell me that he dwelled in the house of consorts, nothing more. I was free to come and go as I pleased, yet strange eyes always seemed to be watching.

The Finfolk of the valley were farmers and fishermen and, in the village, where Catesby lived life seemed simple and lived on a breeze.

They lived in huts made of vines and plants and earth. A great fire was lit each morning in the centre of the village, on a plain that overlooked the rivers. It was used to smoke fish, to keep warm or to sit by and simply be enchanted.

The Finfolk with human consorts seemed in abundance here. Living side by side, the Finfolk and their humans and their Halfling children. They were beautiful in nature. Here their strangeness did not seem so… strange. They were quiet, thoughtful and always in search of something to keep them occupied. There were no schools, no books. Education seemed to be something passed down and taught in everyday things which still seemed superfluous to me.

Esson did not like it when I went into the village. He spoke of our house as if it were royalty, we were to be revered as such. Perhaps arrogance and other such human qualities were not lost upon these people. I wondered if they knew my aching heart was bleeding. If they understood my basic human need for the man I loved?

Days ticked by like the flowing tide and each one brought me no closer to Caleb. No closer to anything. I started to wonder if I would have fared better on Eynhallow, in the same turmoil of not knowing. At least there I had something familiar to grasp on to. It was an empty feeling to forget where you were each morning and wonder why you were there each night.

Elora knew, I was certain her silence screamed of my uncertainty. Each time our eyes met over that great white stone I knew that she knew my plight. Yet still, she remained silent. Offered nothing in the way of comfort.

These Finfolk were not warm. Their blood was invariably cold, I discovered. They could love, but not endear themselves in ways that humans could and yet I sensed their passions in the fields, in the waters, in the way they took things which were plain and ordinary and turned them into something precious.

They kept their rituals closely, firelight ascending through the valley and mountains around the ring of stones each time a human came from the house of consorts to live freely. Each time a child was born. Each time a man married a woman. Astala would lead each procession, closely followed by Esson and Elora and their child Elodie.

At times I saw Catesby's face lingering behind, even Ewan attended. But always he stood away from the others. I did not dare to ask why. Perhaps this was the reason I feared the night, feared the morning. I did not ask enough questions; I did not force my curiosity. I floated on a similar breeze and it was becoming far too cold, like the winters I thought I had left behind.

"Something troubles you."

Solitude of the heart. My body aching from every bone, every sinew. Perhaps the dreams of a lonely isle which plagued my vague sleep. I couldn't say.

"I see it in your eyes, child."

Astala was chewing a piece of meat, the rest of the flesh in his hand pointed towards me. He seemed aggrieved, almost as if he was offended that I wouldn't confide in him over our meal with others present.

"I am fine, Grandfather." I mumbled, certain that Elora could hear my unspoken words.

Astala put his meat down. "You mourn for the man you came with, I may not have the gifts of my daughter in-law here, but I know this to be true."

I swallowed my food and it almost choked me.

"Perhaps you will permit me to see him. Just once…" I meekly asked, the food sticking in my throat.

But Astala gravely shook his head.

"I cannot allow that Finola, you know this. Not until he is initiated properly."

Nobody else spoke a word. Nobody offered a way of comfort.

"What of this initiation?" I continued, already emboldened by the fact I had nothing left to lose. "I came here uninitiated, did I not? Am I to be accepted because I have your blood and blood alone? My whole life I have had nothing but people who profess to love me keeping things from me as if I have no right to know them. My father told me a woman who did not give birth to me was my mother. My grandfather tells me I cannot see my love until he is initiated, neither of you do me any grace or courtesy."

The corner of Elora's mouth began to curl upward, her eyes remaining solely on her food. Almost as if she silently wanted to agree with me but couldn't say the words. Esson did not seem to notice, his attention burning into me as he awaited Astala's reply.

"Your human is to be initiated so that he can live amongst us completely, as if his blood were ours." He said, almost bemused.

"You speak of blood as if it means nothing. Has your blood not taught you anything, then? Are you still bitter at the secrets which were kept from you? Ask me child and I shall give you the answers you desire. But you have made it this far, have you not?"

The lump in my throat dissipated as I swallowed hard, my hunger completely gone.

"Aye, and I dare say I'd still be lingering in purgatory had you not sent my cousin to me. Why do I still feel as if it is you who could rid me of this feeling, and choose not to, Grandfather?"

Astala moved away from his chair, pushing his food into the middle of the stone. The fluid movement of his body as he rose almost struck fear in my heart.

"You have not been treated well, child." He simply said, almost mournfully. "I shall see to it that you are never mistreated again."

As he left the room, only my eyes watched him. I was struck with this enormous feeling that perhaps he was not a bad person. Perhaps his burdens were greater than any of us could imagine. For the first time I began to see why others fell silent around him.

"You do him a disservice to think that he would keep anything from you, that he would freely choose to keep your human from you." Esson said, once the room was emptied of Astala's presence.

Elora's face fell at the sound of her husband's voice.

"Am I to know of these things?" I too stood from my place. "Surely I am to be somehow initiated myself?"

Esson did not look up from his plate. "Your initiation began long ago."

I would have plagued him with questions, but I was well used to hearing these meaningless explanations.

"Perhaps it did, Uncle. But as with everything I am the last to know."

I was surprised to hear such reproach in my voice. Esson barely lifted his head to address me with his eyes. The meat on his plate held more interest.

"Forgive me, I have lost my appetite." I sighed, moving away from the table with less grace than I could muster.

My heart was pounding in my chest. My palms wet and warm as I curled them into fists. I resolved there and then that I did not like my Uncle. He was repugnant and arrogant and rejoiced in the suffering of others. The only person he spoke highly of was his father. As for him, my heart was still undecided.

"Don't be vexed, Finola." Ewan said, in a vain attempt to resolve my ill feeling. "Be happy. You are where you belong now."

Was I?

"I used to hate Eynhallow." I confessed. "I used to hate the stone walls of The Hylands. The stupid cold winters and the boat to church every Sunday. I used to hate the mud on my broken shoes and the wind through the cracks in the doors and those godforsaken foxes."

My eyes pricked with tears at the memory. "But at least I knew it well enough to feel hate. Here... there is nothing."

He could not argue with me. Instead he looked towards Esson for some resolution and I knew that I had lost my cousin for good. He wasn't a slave to humanity anymore, he was a slave to the Finfolk. The saddest piece of the puzzle was that he preferred this fate to the one we had concocted for him that wasn't true. As I turned my back, Ewan winced as if in pain then he returned to the shadows where he belonged, no matter where he dwelled.

Astala was standing outside the room, a long arm stretched out against the wall as if he had been waiting for me. I longed to be alone, but his great piercing eyes bore into me. They were not human eyes, more slanted and deeper, with stories untold. He still intimidated me.

"For a moment, I saw a vision of your mother where you sat."

He wasn't berating me. But he wasn't happy that I resembled her either. Was nobody going to rejoice that I shared her face?

"Where is she?" I asked, certain he would point me in the opposite direction.

"I cannot offer you any comfort, Finola. When I tell you that I do not know where your mother is, I tell you the truth. But perhaps, if you will permit me, I can offer you something in her place?"

He had not walked with me yet. Not accompanied me anywhere. He walked at a slower pace to accommodate me; I could see it in each careful stride as he led me away from the mountainside. I could see the scornful image of my uncle at the gates as he watched us go, but I didn't care. It did not matter, human or otherwise, there would always be people I didn't wish to be around.

The sky was darkening as we made our way down into the valley. Soft hues of blue turned to violet, swirling above like ripples on a lake. Astala spread his fingers to feel the grass below as we walked through it, caressing each blade. I could see the little eyes of the parfois looking out from the growth, their curiosity almost as intense as mine. I still didn't know what they looked like, what manner of creature they were. They were far too timid to come out into the open. I didn't dare speak. Astala seemed happy to simply walk, it occurred to me that perhaps I had more in common with the parfois than any other being here.

He had a peculiar smile on his face. It was young and carefree, and I still wondered how this man could be my grandfather. Esson seemed to be the same age, but perhaps there were centuries between them. I didn't dare to imagine how old Astala truly was. He stopped before we reached the village, where the river forked from either side of the mountains and became one. In green fields of long raised grass, he turned to me and sighed so gravely I wondered how a moment ago he could have been smiling.

"Are you happy here with us, Finola?"

Happiness was something I had no knowledge of. Perhaps I had felt it fleetingly once or twice, but it had never lingered.

"I don't know." Was all I could say.

Astala wasn't satisfied with my response. He raised a hand towards the village and all the people within it.

"I want you to be happy here. I want you to know the blood in your vein's pumps in all our veins. You are with your people."

I wanted to believe it. I wanted to completely hand myself over to this place and all it had to offer. But a lifetime on a barren isle had taught me not to expect the sun to come out after a rainy day.

"How am I meant to be happy if I do not know where I am?"

Astala nodded. "I know your father kept much from you. It was a great injustice. Perhaps you would have been with us sooner, but I am too old to dwell on what has passed. I am old, Finola and there is still much to put in place before I die."

He didn't wait for me to answer, even if I could have said something, there were no words left. It had not mattered before, nor did I feel that it mattered now what I said. Things would be as they had always been regardless.

"And I have served you no better. But I do not want to be as your father was. I do not want to leave you in the darkness, wandering alone. I think, perhaps, there was some wisdom in your words tonight. Why should you not be initiated? Why should you not learn our wisdom and histories? I had thought that they would come to you naturally but even I am not too proud to admit when I am wrong."

He seemed sincere to the point of regret. I wondered what things he had seen, if his heart had ever broken, if he knew things which could only be learnt through hardships. He would not convey, but for a brief moment it seemed that perhaps this was one of those things.

"What could you learn sitting to feast with my son and his silent wife? Esson tries to be a good man, but he will not teach you. I had thought perhaps Catesby would have been some service to you. But he is slow to reveal anything, that boy. It is true that I asked him not to reveal too much too soon. But my reasoning was sound. I did not wish to scare you."

"Why did you send him to me?" I asked, perplexed by Astala's tone each time he mentioned Catesby's name. "Of all the people here, you send a boy from the village?"

The breeze turned cool. The raven hair that ran down Astala's back picked up as his eyes went towards the homestead nearest the forest. The one where Catesby lived.

"A boy from the village." His voice was distant, almost as if it pained him to say the words. "No, my child. If ever there was a boy who did not know his place, then it is him. He is much like you, Finola. It took him a long time to know who he truly was. But it cannot be denied. You will both be given the same fate, in the end."

I looked up to see my grandfather so grieved he could not keep his eyes on the horizon. He looked down at me in return, the fluorescent sky above glowing red.

"Why do you say that?" I asked, for the first time I was given a straight answer.

Astala smiled. "Because he is your brother, Finola."

Lucie Howorth

Chapter Three

FREE AS A BIRD

y brother was a tiny little pink thing that wriggled in his blanket. My brother cried in the night and kept me awake until dawn. My brother was an eager little boy who played with wooden soldiers by the fire. My brother was a brooding man who wouldn't speak a fine word about anyone. My brother was Rohan. I did not know if he was alive or dead, but when I thought of him, I imagined him at the table in The Hylands with Bethan at the fire and their children playing with those same wooden soldiers.

Perhaps Mammy sat in the chair, old and frail. Perhaps she was long gone. I was never certain how long I had been here, but I knew time moved differently. Perhaps a moment here, a mere breath, was more winters than I'd ever known back there.

Regardless, I knew who my brother was. Or had been. Catesby was no better than a stranger and yet, I wondered about him. I wondered why he chose to live in the village and not with his family. Why he chose not to tell me on that first day that he was my brother. But most of all, I wondered why our mother had returned me to the other 'Aheem and left him behind.

I stood by the fire in the heart of the village, the revelation still turning in my mind. Astala had returned to the mountains, to his white castle carved from stone. I repressed my anger; I always had pushed it to the pit of my stomach. I felt as if my body would give in under the burden. The flames danced freely in the fire before dispersing into the air. I envied them because I was tethered to the ground.

I could see Catesby's homestead beyond the glowing flames, smoke billowing from the chimney into the trees and beyond. I felt rage bubble underneath the surface. I had never been the master of my destiny. I never had any control over my life, as if it were somehow not mine at all. I envied my brother. Even if he was dead now, I envied him still and his human life.

I didn't know where I wanted to be, neither here nor there. To go back would mean to exist on a breeze before being snuffed out like a candle. To remain would mean having everything I ever knew snuffed out anyway. I could feel the tears come unbound. I remembered these tears; tears I had cried only once before. Tears that wracked my body and shrieked outwards from my throat and threatened to kill me.

They heard me and came out of their homes to see what that awful sound was. Here, I was not alone. Here there were many people to hear me. I could not stand on a shoreline and be unheard. But I no longer cared. I felt arms on me. But not the same arms that had saved me last time. Not arms I recalled. Not arms I wanted. They pulled me away from the fire and when I looked up, I saw eyes that begged me to quieten.

"You do not get to hush me!" I screamed, pushing him away from me. "I am not a puppet! I am not a slave! I am not a pawn!"

Catesby stepped back. His arms raised in surrender.

"Forgive me, I meant not to harm you."

I felt a prick of remorse. "How is it that I am driven mad here? I was driven mad there too. Am I to be mad forever more?"

Catesby shook his head. "That's the curse of the Halfling."

Only then did I hush. Only then did I let the tears cease and the last of them fall onto my lips.

"Curse? Why would anyone wish to curse us?" I asked, tasting salt as I spoke. "All this talk of things I know nothing of, speak to me of things I know! I beg you, give me something!"

His eyes fell to the ground, then he noticed the people who had gathered to see my grief manifested. He ushered me into his homestead, there he sat me in front a fire I could call my own.

It was a simple place. Completely unlike the castle carved from stone, with its whale bone and pearl. Here there was mud and wood and clay. Catesby had drawn crude drawings on the curved walls, images of fish and seals and birds. There were meats hanging on hooks above, his bed was not a hammock but a nest on the floor. But still, he seemed proud of it and offered me water to drink.

I couldn't help but stare at his face. Those black curls that fell about his eyes, it all made sense to me now. He was as lost as I was and this... this place was his to call his own. No matter where he was, he could close the door and be here. It was to him what The Hylands was to Rohan.

Yes, he was my brother.

"I am sorry." I apologised. "I feel I have been unfair to you."

The water was ice cold and quenched a thirst I didn't know I felt. Catesby drank a dark ale, the froth dripping down the side of the bone cup. It smelled off to me, but he seemed to relish the taste. Part of me was offended that he had only offered me water, but perhaps he knew well enough that I wasn't seasoned for such things. He wiped the froth from his mouth with his hand and sighed in satisfaction at the taste.

"No more than I, with you." He surmised, taking another deep swig. "I suppose I am free to tell you everything now, or else why would you be here?"

I drained the water. "I know nothing of supposed freedom. But I do know that you are my brother."

Catesby closed his eyes and let the empty cup drop from his hands. He seemed distressed, racking his hands through his hair.

"I have longed to tell you, but I was told not to. The Elders... Astala, he... He wanted you to find out these things for yourself."

"It matters not to me. Who tells me what, who makes the decision to keep things from me? Whatever their reasons, I care not. I have only ever known honesty from the one person I cannot be with. Everything else will come as it will. I have grown used to it."

It had to not matter. Or else the rage would come again, and I would be consumed by it.

"Tell me a tale, then. Tell me everything on the tip of your tongue."

He would need more ale for it. He sank another cup before pouring another, this time he offered me some. I disliked the scent of it but accepted anyway.

"I do not have a tale to tell. I was born and now, I am here. I have always been here."

His eyes were glassy and downcast. He stared into his cup as if the story belonged in there instead of his mouth. If only he could drink it down and tell it.

"You must know who your father is." I said, he visibly winced in pain.

"Of course, it would be a cruel thing indeed not to know who your father was." His words sounded bitter.

"I spent most of my life believing my father's wife was my mother." I shrugged, "Perhaps that is more cruel."

Catesby shook his head. "I never spent a day with either of my parents."

It struck me that she had left us both behind. Any preconceptions were dashed in that moment. I wanted him to know that I was sorry.

"Tell me, Catesby. Tell me everything you know. I have a right to know." I begged, "I swear, I'll do whatever it takes. I'll never ask another foolish question again."

There was a hint of reproach in the way he tried to smile. Which of us had been dealt the kindest blow?

"I was born here, as were you. On the same day."

My breath caught in my chest. Not just my brother, but my twin. I began to feel the essence of his suffering like an unseen wave that resonated around the fire.

"Then your father is my father." I said, it wasn't a question. A realisation that made me sick to my stomach. "He never knew…"

"What could he have done even if he had known? The birds tell me all their secrets. I saw him in their memories. I saw him watching for mother, driven mad by her absence. I saw him holding you in his arms, every day growing more and more like her."

"And so you saw him grow sick and die? And all but abandon me towards the end?"

He hid his disdain behind the cup of ale. "She tried to take us both to him. But she did not succeed. I used to wonder, as a child, what it might have been like to be the one she took.

Lonely and exiled. Strange and misconceived. Do not wish for what you can't imagine. No matter how you may try to. My poor brother, more blood to me than the brother I had known. How I have felt the absence of you without even knowing.

"Why did she try to take us both? What could have driven her to do such a thing?"

Catesby's eyes caught mine. Burning red through the fire between us, he was scorned and angry but underneath that simmered a feeling that I knew I shared with him.

"She would not take William for her consort. She quarrelled with Astala for a very long time. She longed to be in the human world. But Astala would not allow it. It was her intention to take us to Eynhallow, to be with our father. All of us, together. But Astala found out about her plans and took me in the night. But he could not reach you. He begged her to stay, but she refused. Where she went after giving you over to him, it is not known. Finfolk have not been in the other 'Aheem for a very long time. Mankind have forgotten."

There was fresh turmoil in my heart. "But, why?! Why did she want to be in the human world?! This makes no sense. To separate us so... To leave us both... Why didn't she want father as her consort?"

He was angry with me now. I had sworn not to ask more foolish questions. He glared at me in firelight. In his face was torment and things which he had resolved within long ago. A bitter regret that he had taken me in and given me pity. I was certain he wanted me to leave. But I found myself not wanting to go.

"I can't say what was in her mind. How am I to know why she did what she did? I only know what I know because that is what Astala told a child who would not stop asking where his mother was. He hushed me to sleep with stories about how he saved me in the dead of night. His arms carrying a squawking baby, my cries awoke my mother who in turn grabbed the other baby who was silent and sleeping. He asked her one last time not to do it, but she had disobeyed him. He swore to her that night that no happiness would come of it. She had broken his heart and one of the most basic laws of the Fin."

Of that, I knew nothing. But there was something I did know. Something I could offer him. I was tired, I was exhausted. But in that moment, I felt of use. That I had a purpose, if only for one breath.

"On Eynhallow, they told stories of the Finfolk. Terrible stories. Finmen emerging from the waters and dragging a human wife down into the depths. Beautiful finwomen turning into hags if they could not find a consort. The story of a man and his three sons tricking a great shape-shifting creature to his death so that no other Finfolk could ever set foot upon the land again. I spent a long time thinking that these stories were the truth. Everyone did. I thought when Nathan Munro died that it was because of me. My father's wife, she made us read the bible endlessly. So that we would never hear of the Finfolk, never go down that path. But I think perhaps it was fated for Nathan to die. It was him who told me the stories. It was him who set me on that path."

Catesby shook his head. "It doesn't matter now. Stories we were told as children. All that matters is that you're here now."

But my curiosity was still piqued. I folded it away like dry linen and extended my hand towards my brother. He took it gratefully and finally smiled without a hint of anything beneath it.

"Why don't you come back with me?" I asked, "Why do you stay here and not with your family?"

He dropped my hand.

"No, my place is here. This is where she lived. This is where we were born. As soon as I was old enough to take care of myself, I returned here. I never saw eye to eye with my uncle."

It was not hard to see why, so I did not ask. This place was warm and simple, not completely unlike The Hylands in the way it made me feel.

"Perhaps I will stay here then, with you." I suggested.

The wind whistled in from the outside. The smell of flowers and earth along with it. He never announced his comings or goings. Instead, he just appeared when and where he would as if this world was his and his alone. But it was not frowned upon, and never questioned. It was as if he dwelled nowhere in particular, the white castle in the mountains was just a place to hold what was closest to him. Astala, High Priest, stood before us in the dim firelight.

"The decisions of youth." He sighed, his skin strangely glinting as flames licked the air. "How I wish I could take the turmoil from you."

It didn't seem to matter to Catesby that he was there. But I was used to courtesies being extended whenever someone came to the door uninvited. It was strange to me that there seemed to be no ceremony outside the ring of stones. Manners differed, but it was still odd to me that he had not made us aware of his presence. I felt as if he had perhaps been there the entire time, just waiting.

"Finola, what is your wish?" He asked, "Would you stay here with Catesby?"

I didn't know how to respond. Supposing Catesby didn't want me here? He had not said otherwise before we were interrupted. I decided to answer his first question and ignore the second.

"It is my wish to be taken to The House of Consorts." I said staunchly. "It is all I have ever wished."

Astala closed his eyes in thought. Catesby looked at me as if I had asked for the one thing he could not and would not give. This house of Consorts seemed impenetrable. I imagined people going in as feckless unknowing fools and emerging as the great and wise initiated. It troubled me that I did not know what occurred there, I had a great curiosity.

To me, everything I sought to know existed in that one place. Everything I could hope to be. The one thing I had come to love the most. Perhaps they had hoped that I would forget. Perhaps that was why all the humans were taken there, to see if their fin lovers forgot about them. If they did, were they cast out to perish? For certain they would not be allowed to return. I remembered a boy who had tried once. It would drive me mad if he did not send me there.

"Such a thing has never been granted before." Astala began, opening his eyes as if he had done with his thoughts. "It is a place for the chosen humans to become more than what their humanity allows. To live amongst us *as one*. A tree can only bear fruit if it is planted in the precise place at the precise time it is meant to. But what if it wasn't? What if it was planted in dirt that was not fertile enough to help it grow? You have been planted in the wrong earth, Finola. I see that now."

I began to feel as if he were relenting. I knew that I was not alone in that thought as Catesby began to open his mouth in wonder.

"Grandfather, she is half-blood!" He announced suddenly, "You can't mean to send her there?!"

I felt the bitter stab of betrayal. What did it matter to him if I went there or not? Why did he wish to see my heart bleed out before him into this dying fire? Astala put a hand to Catesby's shoulder, and I could see the breath rise and fall from his chest in quick succession.

"How do you dare?!" I spat, rising against my newfound brother. "Why would you oppose it?!"

He didn't seem to understand why I was angry. He was taken aback.

"Forgive me, Finola. I meant only that it is a place for humans. You are more fin than they will ever be, you have not need of it."

Of course, I forgave him. There was nothing to forgive. He was as much in the dark as I. His life here meant that he knew all there was to know. But my life had not been here, and he was wrong, I was not more fin than they would ever be. I had come here as human as they were.

"Catesby, I am not like you. I am not wise and powerful. I do not know what this blood within me means. I have lived a life of unknowing. I am not going to learn, unless I am taught. Who of you here can do that?"

His eyes went to Astala, who did not need to speak the words. "The House of Consorts." He agreed, nodding. "So, you will go there."

I could not sleep that night. My mind was filled with thoughts of Caleb. His face, his eyes, his voice. Things I had fought hard to keep vivid in my dreams. Things I had thought of which had not yet come to pass.

In my dreams he was standing on the brow of the hill overlooking the sea. Always I would come out of the door at The Hylands and walk down the garden path towards him. His scent would carry on the wind, the smell of whisky and something which was all him and nothing else. Then he would turn and see me, a smile appearing on his face as I came towards him.

Sometimes I would reach him and let him take me into his arms, other times I would awake and feel the sweetness of the dream fade. But tonight, I could not close my eyes and imagine it. There was only him, his lips and tongue, my incessant need for both.

I sat by the window in the tower and somehow, I could smell that whisky on the wind. I wondered if he knew I was coming. Or if he had forgotten me. Winter did not seem too apparent here, no seasons to make the world change. I tried to imagine the cold winters touch that had kept us apart, but it slipped from memory.

I knew I was going to see him again; I knew that by dawn I would be on the road to where he dwelled, nothing else mattered. Whatever knowledge awaited me, whatever awakening it mattered not in comparison to seeing his face again.

Sometimes I asked myself why I loved him so. What magic it had been that drew me to him? Why him and no other? The wenching, merciless, lying fool.

Unaccountable sins were on his head, if there was a God to hold him accountable for them. He was a man of animal instincts, on that good fortune I hoped he fared well amongst these people.

Perhaps he was as bound to this place as much as I had been. Our fates tied, one to the other, for all time. I could hear his voice whisper in my ear, he was close to me. I knew that time had not changed a thing. My heart began to beat like a drum, a vicious thrum that spread throughout my entire body. I had never known what excitement felt like. But I knew, as much as I could know, that it was that which I felt.

A soft knock broke me from my reverie. I looked towards the closed door and wondered who was on the other side of it. It was not Astala, he did not knock for anyone. As I moved from the window, I let the beat in my heart quieten. Elora's face was shadowed in veil and she moved quickly inside as I opened. I had never seen her quite so animated. Always she seemed to be silent and transparent. Her face was drawn in anguish as she moved the veil aside. Her voice low and deliberate.

"Finola, you must leave for the House of Consorts tonight…" She breathed heavily, "Do not delay…"

It made no sense to me. "But, why? Astala has said I will go at first light with a convoy to take me."

Elora shook her head, silver white wisps of hair falling about her face. "No, you must make your own way there. Esson means to sabotage your journey. He thinks it wrong that a granddaughter of the High Priest should go there. He intends to bring you back, if you will not, he will bring you back in chains."

"I thought you were a peaceful people." I said, "Ewan, when he came to get me, he told stories of your great enlightenment."

Elora shook her head. "I hear their thoughts. All of them, even Astala. He thinks I cannot, for once I told him that the thoughts of the High Priest were beyond my powers. Whether he still believes that, I do not know. But I hear them, all of them. Ewan is nothing but a pawn within a greater plan."

Her words did not make sense, but the way in which she spoke them invoked great fear within me. She took my arms in her hands and squeezed them tenderly, her eyes locked with mine desperately.

"Finola, you must promise me that you will go tonight." She begged, pleaded.

I was suddenly terribly afraid. "How will I find my way?"

Elora turned me towards the window, her fingertips digging into my flesh with urgency. Her long slender finger then pointed outwards, over the rolling pastures and rivers towards the mountain peaks that covered the horizon. The greatest peak of all was white tipped and razor edged. It seemed a thousand miles away.

"The house sits at the base of that mountain. Where the source of the river spills out, just as it does on this mountainside. They are twins, this mountain and that. Only this one is basking in sunlight and warmth... that one is blue and cold."

Her words sent a shiver down my spine. "Like Winter." I whispered.

She paid no heed to my words. "Follow the river, and when you come to the fork keep going north. You cannot get lost that way."

It made no sense to me. If Esson had taken issue with me leaving for the House of Consorts he should have made quarrel with me himself. How could I go against my grandfather, my High Priest? How could any of us? I began to wonder how many conspired against him. I felt sick to my stomach and stepped back, away from Elora's grasp.

"And if I leave? Then will Astala find me gone and be angry with me." I reasoned, stepping further and further away.

Elora began to shake her head, as if she didn't understand my reluctance. "Better that than to fall at the hand of your uncle."

It seemed absurd. "Is it his intention to kill me, then?"

She almost laughed. Her thin red lips poised to smile. "You are the image of your mother, Finola. There is much of her within you, even if you do not know it. He sees that, do not think that he does not see her when he looks at you."

"And of what consequence is that to me? Did he wish harm to my mother?" I asked, my heart beating so rapidly I felt faint.

Elora did not look at me. Instead, it was as if she had given up.

"You may heed my words, or no." She sighed. "I come to you even at the risk of my husband finding out I have betrayed him. There is good in this world, but do not harbour delusions that there is no bad. Astala is a good man, he has fought many wars to bring the peace you see here now. But he is unable to enjoy this peace he has wrought. He knows what Esson is and so keeps him close."

My mouth was dry. I didn't want to know what Esson was. All I knew was that I didn't feel myself around him, my being felt compromised. His eyes watched too deeply; his words cut too coarse. His eyes never smiled, and his wife remained silent. If I knew nothing else, I knew that he was the bad in this world.

"I loved your mother." Elora said then, her eyes filling with tears. "She was my sister; in every way you can be a sister. If I do not take care of her daughter, then I have failed her."

I was being pulled both north and south. I could not deny that she had come to me in good faith, to put me out of harm's way. But I had come to see that my grandfather was a man who possibly did love me. In his own way, perhaps from afar. These strangers were still yet to crawl under my skin. My trust remained on a lonely isle in a different time and place. I wanted to believe that I was going to be ok, that all my decisions had led me here for reasons that would someday become clear to me. In truth, I did not know what to do.

"You come to me with riddles. Every breath I take is mired with revelation; I am thankful for that. I have ached for that my whole life. But I do not understand what I am meant to do? I am not like you. I will never be like you."

Her hand came down against my cheek, the scales within her skin soft and cool.

"Go to the House of Consorts. Find your love, be with him. Astala will know why you did not say goodbye. When you return you will understand. You will be whatever it is you are meant to be."

It did not sit well with me. This often-silent creature coming to me in the dead of night, speaking words she was too afraid to speak in the daylight hours.

As she slipped away gracefully without a sound or breath, I was left wondering how I could ever move like that. But more than that, more than anything was a sense that I'd been given something to hold onto. Of all the things I did not know, of all the things I was yet to learn I had forgotten all the things I already knew, which they did not.

If magic was all they knew, I had to remember there was a burning humanity in me. I'd known desolation and cold, and starvation. I'd known hate and love, all the shades in between. If these Finfolk had emotions on a spectrum I had yet to grasp, I pitied them if they had never known the gratitude of receiving a new pair of shoes on their birthday.

Or the first thaw of spring after a harsh and long winter. Or the look of disappointment in their father's eyes as he draws his last breath without ever seeing the woman he loves ever again.

I remembered a small fox contemplating his life on an isle that was not his home. He was starving and alone, I'd fed him the last remnants of food I had. I was that fox and Elora somehow was me. Perhaps between magic and humanity, there wasn't much difference to be found. For certain there was rage and indignant distaste for change. There was a familiar look in my uncle's eyes that was entirely human. It was envy and wrath and turmoil. He hated that which was not like him and strived to bring forth the downfall of it. I had seen how Astala overlooked this and loved his son regardless. If he could accept the failings of his children, why did he not accept those of my mother?

Perhaps he knew deep in his heart that Esson was a bad seed, but had tried to plant him in the right soil? It struck me that Astala was a gardener and this land was his to plant and seed and toil.

But how could he be as benevolent as that if he had favoured his son?

Even to the extent of allowing him to undermine his word? He had decreed that I was to go to the House of Consorts. If my uncle were to sabotage that, he would be going against the word of his father. I had seen the bond between a father and his son, I had never understood it. But there was one thing I did understand, one thing I had always known.

My brother had always loved me, in the face of any adversity his hand had always been the one to seek me out. His little hand in mine and later, my little hand in his. If I could count on anything in this strange and uncertain time, it was my brother. My eyes went down towards the glinting firelight of the village down in the valley. He was not Rohan. He would never be Rohan. But I had need of a brother, and he seemed willing to be one.

I stepped onto the smooth window ledge. There was a breeze in the air, soft and cool and it fanned my hair away from my face. I could not see that there was any other way.

Like the parfois looking out from the shrubs, I knew there were eyes on me. Of devious plots waiting to unfold, in their grasp I felt nothing but pity for their misplaced rage. I'd been long on a lonely isle with only my reflection to guide me, I needed nothing more within than what I already had.

But Caleb was there. If there was no other sweet knowledge than that, I would go there. I did not have the wisdom to transform at will. But I recalled the breaking of bones and searing hot pain. I let my gown fall out onto the breeze, the wisp material carried lightly and easily. I closed my eyes and thought of the birds. Wings flocking to my defence, the breeze was theirs and theirs alone.

Which aspect of my blood would come into play? I clung to humanity like a babe to their mothers' breast. But not tonight. I called upon memories of a boat sailing away, my love on board bound for where I could not follow. Black as tar feathers in the place of skin. Watching from above, crying inside because my bird eyes could not shed tears. If I stepped forward, just one step would I fly? Or would I fall to my death below?

The breeze wasn't cool anymore. It was warm and comforting. Or was it? I wasn't even sure that I could do it again. I dangled a toe over the edge. I dared myself to jump. I wanted to jump. Perhaps I didn't even care anymore if I lived or died. My heart became a thrumming locomotive, beating unbearably fast. I could hear the sound of it above the moving water below and the wind above. I wasn't whole, I was suddenly split into tiny pieces that pulled me out of the window and beyond. I let my body pull itself apart and when I opened my eyes, there was no window.

Lucie Howorth

Chapter Four

THE JOURNEY BEGINS

atesby knew the birds. They flocked to him and remained there, not out of obedience, but because they loved him. My naked body slumped to the ground, exhausted from the flight. That old pain coursed through my veins; I could taste blood on my lips.

The birds landed on Catesby's roof, pecking at the crude wattle and daub. The sound was deafening and yet, all I could hear was the sound of my own heart steadying itself against the form it had just taken. There was a physical element to this magic, one that I still had not mastered. But I felt overcome regardless, because I had thought that I would die. My body was still shifting as he came out into the night, dragging me into the homestead by boneless arms.

"Have you lost your wit?!" He spat, placing animal skins that smelled of tanned leather across my shoulders. "You are not initiated yet; you could have killed yourself!"

My voice was still shaken, breaking on each word I spoke. "I have shifted before."

Catesby shook his head, raven black curls falling about his disappointed eyes. "I dare say you have. But still, I doubt Astala would be pleased to know you've flown down here without caution or care."

"I doubt Astala would be pleased." I agreed, "But I do not have time to lament."

I could feel the sky changing, and dawn approach. With it, an omen I did not want to face. If what Elora said was to be true, it would not be long before I would be hunted and found.

"You have quarrelled with our Uncle, have you not?" I asked, pulling the skins about me as if it were stitching me back together.

Catesby's lip curled in distaste. "No. I have managed to avoid defending myself against one such as him. Why do you ask?"

I did not have time to delay. "He means to prevent me going to the House of Consorts."

But Catesby did not seem too perplexed. "He is far too idle to plot such a thing. He values Astala's favour, above all else he looks to Astala for his blessing in all his dealings."

It did not seem untrue. I had seen the way boys looked at their fathers, silently demanding their approval and feeling constant disdain without it. Why should the Finfolk be any different?

"He is always observant of me. I know he watches me with disapproval, I do not know why. Sometimes I think it is because he hates my mother, I look so much like her. So they tell me."

Catesby shrugged, watching as the last bone cracked into place, his face grimacing at the sound of it.

"I would be interested to know how you came by this knowledge. Who told you what he intended? It is true that there is no love lost between our Uncle and I. It was his casting of judgement that I did not like, but there was never a quarrel between us. Give me the name of your informer."

I lifted my head towards the heat of the glowing fire. The crackling wood sounded eerily similar to my bones, but now that my body was whole again, I could feel the warmth on my skin. I was naked and Catesby had seen me naked, I did not care that underneath this second skin I was still naked. The sins of the God on Eynhallow were a folly down here, shame seemed to be something completely unheard of. But there were other things, things that transcended the veil between the two worlds.

"Elora came to me." I whispered, my voice low against the sound of the wind and fire. "Urged me to leave before Esson came for me."

There was a story I had not heard. A story about my mother.

Catesby had lingered in doorways, much like I had. The things he had heard remained with him, ever inward and never repeated.

Until now.

He asked me solemnly if I would tell him about our father, I promised him that I would. But first, he had a story about our mother and the woman who had loved her like a sister.

"Babel blood has always been... unpredictable. They are impulsive and spontaneous without forethought. Of all the houses... bloodlines, whatever you will, Babel would be the one that I would put at the front of an army to fight a great battle. All of our greatest warriors have been white haired, so when there is one such as Elora with her talents of the mind, she immediately caught Astala's eye. He wanted her for his son's wife and of course, it would come to pass. Mother was always a cautious one, so they say. Raven blood is strange, we are not impulsive, we are not the greatest warriors, but sometimes our wit helps with holding a sword."

I was completely drawn in.

"We are thinkers, we are fortunate in that of all the bloodlines we are the ones who can change our physical form, in order to better understand our own minds. These things are very rarely reconciled. The impulsiveness of the Babel and the cautiousness of the Raven. Yet they did and indeed they were friends."

The races of mankind came in a host of glorious colours. I had never witnessed the full spectrum. But once I had seen a man in Evie, his skin was pitch as night and his hair like the darkest wool. He came from the other side of the world and spoke in a beautiful language I did not understand. He lived in the village for a short time, while the boat he arrived on was fixed, and then almost as suddenly as he was there, he was gone again, and I never saw another face such as his again.

The races of Finfolk, it struck me, were not measured by skin but by hair. Yet, despite it all, they were one. Catesby was a formidable storyteller. Perhaps even captivating me more than the first time I had heard tale of the Finfolk.

"When Elora married Esson it was not a marriage of love and she sought our mothers counsel in those early days. They would laugh and joke, and Esson grew jealous of their closeness as would any husband, I suppose. Of course, Elora knew his thoughts. But still she preferred to spend her days in the company of our mother instead of her new husband. I heard them talking one night, Astala and Esson, about the last time Esson had spoken to our mother.

He told her that if she did not let Elora go he would forsake her forevermore. For all that our uncle is, mother did love him, and she did not want to hurt him. So, she went from this place and Elora did not forgive her. They said when she returned, she carried us in her womb and that Elora was angry because she was still yet to conceive a child. There grew a great wickedness between them thereafter, so I am not sure which part of Elora came to you tonight. The part of her which loved our mother, or the part which hated her."

In that moment it did not matter to me. If my uncle plotted against me, then let him come. If his wife despised my mother so much, she would put me in the path of danger then let her.

Catesby seemed to wait on my reaction, his eyes pleading with me to say something. Of what he had said, I had nothing to add. Jealousy was not an emotion I'd had the opportunity to know well. So I could not relate to this sort of hatred. Instead, I gave him what he wanted.

I painted a picture in my mind of the table in the kitchen, my father peeling fish with his knife and Mammy stirring the pot on the fireplace. My little brother playing on the stone floor with wooden soldiers while Mammy made me read verses from The Bible out loud. That had been the way of it. After all the others had died or fled, when it was just us on that lonely island waiting to die or be saved.

I spoke of Rohan the way he had been as a boy and the man he became after father died. There was a hint of regret in the way Catesby nodded, that he had not been the brother I had grown with. I shared in that regret. How I would have liked to have had a brother of my own age. Who had been with me in the womb and beyond? But I could not spend too much time on that thought. He was with me now, our stories kept us bonded.

"What is a fox?" He asked, his voice breaking into my thoughts.

I had forgotten what I had been speaking about, somehow his question sounded odd. I tried to recount what I had said and remembered that I'd been speaking until my throat had gone dry.

"It is..." I could not help but smile at the memory of asking what a parfois was and his answer was perfectly sound. "It is... simply, a fox. A creature with four legs and a long nose and fur the colour of rust."

He could not imagine it, but it did not matter. Dawn was fast approaching, and I had a decision to make.

"Esson has not come for me." I noted, "Perhaps he has tried to and failed."

Catesby drew a long breath. "Or perhaps he did not try at all. It would not be too difficult to find someone who had very little places to go."

Be that as it may, I knew where I had to go. I would go there alone if I had to. But I was still afraid. Fear had been my shadow for all the years I could recall. Yet, I had conquered it. Perhaps someday fear and I would become friends and all the days of my life would have some meaning.

"I cannot trust a soul. Can I?" I asked, and the realisation was more than I could bear. "These people have more faces than they care to show. Humanity is cruel and unkind and desolate, but there's evil here too and it looks like spite and jealousy and abandonment."

Catesby stood, taking a large hunting knife off the wall. He sheathed it to his side and checked the smaller sickle knife that never left him.

"Stay here. I'll find you some clothes and gather some food. We leave at first light."

Which was precisely the time I was meant to leave.

It did not seem to be of any consequence to him anymore, spite and jealousy and abandonment. He was quietly wise, rarely giving a glimpse into how much he knew of the way things were. Yet he was as a cold morning breeze, perhaps never being where he was meant to at the precise moment he was meant to be there.

I knew Astala despaired with him, but it was becoming clear that it was from a place of affection. When he returned with a garment made with bone clasps and the colour grey, I noted that he had grown breathless. His eyes were wide and perilously deep, throwing the dress at me with such aggression that I almost fell back. He turned and began to fill a burlap sack with dried fish and berries as I slipped the dress over my head and clipped the bones together at the shoulder.

"What is the matter?" I dared to ask, noting his sudden haste.

"Firelight at the ring of stones." He said sternly, "The Elders are gathering."

I didn't understand. My heart began to pound with all the ferocity of a locomotive, my skin feeling the prick of heat as panic began to rise from the intensity in my chest. I dared to lift the curtain and look outside, torches winding their way from the village towards the ring of stones. The sound of distant song and drum flowed down through the wind.

"What is the meaning of it?" I asked, afraid that I already knew.

Catesby had a look of indignation. His eyes squinted; brow furrowed as he stared at the winding procession.

"War." He breathed. "Sometimes it's war. Sometimes it's nothing more than failing crops or the direction the fish swim in. But I have not seen them gather without warning unless..."

My hand flew to my open mouth. "What is this madness?!"

"I do not know. I last saw a procession like this as a child, when Astala was betrayed by his brother."

My lips quivered. "What betrayal do you speak of?"

He looked into my eyes, as if all the world was going to spin and take me with it. "He knew where our mother was."

They found me in the village, their torches of fire thrust into my face as they shouted my name one to the other as if I would somehow disappear if my name was not called.

Catesby watched as they took me with such force, I did not see whose hands I passed through. When they brought me to the stones my body ached and throbbed from rough hands, I was angry.

Esson stood there. By his side was Elora, she did not look at me. I inwardly screamed at her to say something, knowing she heard me. But she remained silent and I knew her stance was to be by her husband's side when there were other eyes upon her.

Her betrayal was the worst kind, aimed towards the husband whose side she stood by and to me, who she had come to in the night knowing he would never allow it.

Behind Esson stood three people I had never seen before. Two of them were female, with long red hair. The other was male, his hair black as night. All three of them tall and lean, with a strange look of benevolence. Yet I wasn't certain kindness was what they would show me, Esson did not share this look. I noted one of the women appeared older.

She had begun to stoop, the light in her eyes had dimmed. She was the first to step forward, pulling Esson back with an authoritative hand upon his shoulder. She carried a staff in her other hand, the willowy white wood held her frame as she walked, she gripped it with hands that had begun to show age. Perhaps these were the Elders so often spoken of.

Behind them a small group of cloaked figures stood close enough to protect them, though I could not see their faces, I knew some of them were human. Something in the way they were smaller, less intimidating. The entire gathering seemed vastly out of place. As if they had gathered too quickly, with too much haste to appear at the stones.

"Catesby, what say you?" She asked, in a high-pitched voice. Her eyes remained with me, even as she spoke to another.

Catesby came forward, stripped of his knives and stood by my side.

"It was Astala's bidding, no other." He said, with more confidence than I thought he had. "She comes to us from the other 'Aheem. She must learn our ways and there is no other way for her to do that."

The woman nodded thoughtfully, her eyes never leaving my face.

"It is quite unlike our High Priest to make such a decision without consulting with us first. This is not the way of it. She is House Raven, not a consort."

"I am nothing!" I cried, "All I have ever been, is nothing!"

The woman seemed perplexed, as if it were utterly impossible to be nothing. She took a sinewy hand and placed it on my cheek. Her skin was cool, the tiny scales moving against the smooth human skin of my own. I wondered how old she was, her eyes were strangely blue and milky and unlike the eternal youth I had seen in every other finman or woman.

"Your love is not ready to receive you, child." She soothed, "If you were to go to The House of Consorts what do you think you would learn? Other than that love is the greatest distraction of all?"

She was not my friend. I shied away from her touch and looked at the faces around me. I wasn't certain what they waited for.

"Where is Astala?" Catesby asked, sharing my uncertainty. "Where is my grandfather?"

The corner of Esson's mouth curled upwards. "His presence is not required. I can be here in his place."

"Is that so?" Catesby's hands began to curl into fists. "You dare to go against his word and bring the Elders to counsel without him? Finola has done nothing wrong. She does not deserve this."

Without him I was a caged bird. My heart sang for him and feared for what they would do to him for such insolence. I wondered what the Elders thought of Esson. If they truly supported his claims, or if they had been duped into sharing his thoughts with lies and deceit?

I could feel a change in the air, as if the pretense was not quite right. Almost as if half the people gathered here did not know why they were present, and the others were not sure who or what had brought proceedings.

The old woman was of higher ranking than Esson, but he felt his cause gave him reason to stand in Astala's place. There was an air of stupidity to him, I wondered how he could claim to be there in Astala's place to oppose Astala's own words?

"You think I have need of the High Priest, boy? I remember a time when his father was young, long before any of you were thought of." The old one cackled, her eyes remained with me, always with me. "I anointed him with my own crumbling hands, forever will he remain underneath my touch."

She was decidedly irreproachable. I found myself falling into the trap of finding her almost agreeable. She had begun to take on the form of the fabled Finhag. But age had not dulled her spirit. She was not ugly, her appearance only served to promote her formidable word.

"Even so." Catesby added, "I would still like to see my grandfather."

The old woman sighed, a short and dissatisfied sound that came from deep within. The other red headed woman came forward, she was younger and not quite so vocal. Without saying a word to any other she pressed her mouth against the older woman's ear and whispered things no other could hear.

For the first time she looked away from me and closed her eyes as she listened to the quiet voice beside her. When she was done the younger woman stepped back, those old eyes returned to me.

"You are the child of Nim and her human consort, are you not?" She asked bluntly.

I could not raise my voice to speak. Catesby nodded in my place, without looking away the old woman acknowledged with a raised hand.

I had never known her name. Somehow this fact choked me until my throat threatened to cease all breath. She had only ever given my father one name, he had never been certain if it was meant for me, or if it was hers.

"I do not know. If you please, I never knew my mother's name." I managed, between sobs which threatened to strike me down.

"A human consort who never returned with her. Who raised Finola as human, on Eynhallow ground?" Catesby said, still fighting my cause.

Esson dared to approach, his manner one that I did not care for.

"She is not ready to be received, did you not hear her, boy?!" He spat, "And even if she were, what place does she have amongst those humans? Never in all of our history has a halfling been to the House of Consorts."

This was his fear. Of all the things in this strange new world, he was afraid that his place might be lost. To have one of his own in a place he did not see fit would mean to bring about a change he was not ready to submit to. He wanted to be High Priest. But my fear was growing that he wouldn't make a good one.

Catesby did not seem to be scared, even though fear tugged at my heart. He stood almost as tall as our uncle, even that human part of him that made him smaller seemed not to matter when standing right against wrong.

"You are a fool if you don't see." Catesby said, his breath verging on laughter. "She is more human than any of us half-bloods will ever be."

What could he say against the assault of truth? For a moment there was a flash of condemnation, almost humiliation that he had brought all these witnesses to the stone circle to see his downfall against a simple boy.

I began to feel as if it were becoming too voyeuristic, that it was wrong to say these words where others could hear. The man who had come with the raven hair still had not spoken, nor stepped forward. I could see the look in the eyes around me. If any of them had ever been certain of what they had come for, perhaps doubt had begun to set in?

"Esson..." Said the old woman, casting a disparaging glance. "When you came to me with your concerns I listened because for centuries that is what I have done. I have listened to a thousand words from a thousand tongues and seen wars raged and lovers torn asunder. My word has brought strife and relief in equal amount, think you that I am without sight now that I am getting old? I see your bitterness, oh yes, and the ones you aim it toward."

There was a pause, a moment where I thought perhaps, I had seen the raven man before. As the breeze took his hair from his shoulders, I wondered if he had ever been to the white castle in the mountainside and perhaps passed my way? He did not look at me, it seemed as if he almost refused to. But it did not go unnoticed. He was familiar somehow, but where had I seen his face before?

"I beg you, Mother Teigne, it will bring shame..." He seethed, "She will be despised by those who wait upon their consorts until the appointed time."

Oh, what shame did he speak of? Did he dare to pretend that he gave care towards my welfare now? If there was any shame, it would not be mine. I knew, then, that his only care was for a shame on the descendants of the High Priest. Himself and his own. There seemed to be no limits to this shadow within him.

I had never met anyone like him. His eyes did not meet mine, they never had. I had thought his disposition not to my taste, but I could have tolerated it. I would have learned to avoid him, where possible. Stayed out of his way. Surely if I were not under his feet then he would be the better for it? Was shame worth putting his position with his father in danger?

Mother Teigne, it seemed appropriate to call her, perhaps she was the oldest of her house, her bloodline. She was not my friend, but I was starting to see that she was nobody's friend. Certainly not my uncles.

"Be that as it may." She said, leaning on her white staff. "She is the daughter of Nim, Granddaughter of our High Priest. Shame or no, she will remain what she is."

Esson seemed defeated. "And what of her love? You said yourself that he is not ready to receive her."

Mother Teigne nodded, her old grace had not left her yet. "There is one other thing to consider. The High Priest is not here, and it is true what the half-blood boy says, you have called us to counsel without him. We come here of our own accord, to listen and heed what is said. But I must consider this an attack on your father's word, for he has spoken without our counsel before. In times when only his word is needed."

Esson did not react at first. Elora recoiled behind him, at the sound of the thoughts of others in her mind. Was I in immediate danger? Or was I to be set free at any given moment? I could not gauge the atmosphere now, or what turn events had taken.

I thought they had come here to serve Esson's purpose. Everything now seemed so unclear. Esson grabbed Elora's wrist, preventing her from moving away further. She gasped, not afraid of his touch but surprised that he had touched her so with prying eyes to see. Mother Teigne looked as if there was something she did not like the taste of in her mouth.

"Enough of this." She announced. "I have borne witness to some folly in my time, but none so as this. Esson, child, as much as it pains me to call you the son of our High Priest, the son of our High Priest you are. Close as he keeps you, be under no illusion that it is to temper your dark tendencies. We gather here to pass judgement, on whom, it remains to be seen."

Then, he stepped forward into the torchlight. The raven man who had been silent all this time. He placed hands upon Esson's shoulders and rested his forehead against him. It seemed as if time stopped and the torchlight fell away and all the darkness and silence carried all around us until I could see the man in his true form. His face altered and Esson drew back in horror.

"Father!" He exclaimed, "What sorcery is this?!"

The only one who did not seem to exchange a glance of confusion was the old woman. Astala was everywhere at all times it seemed, how could there ever have been any doubt that he would not be here for this moment? I felt foolish that I had not trusted my own intuition to begin with.

"My son." He said gravely, "Why do you insist on this?"

Esson was still too shocked to display a response. His wide eyes fixed solely on Astala's true face.

"Did you not think that I would hear of this?" He asked, "Why do you act against me so?"

If he had waged a war against his own brother who had betrayed him, perhaps Catesby had been right to predict another.

"Father I act only to protect the ways of our people, our bloodline." Esson stammered, his voice aching to pick up the strength to speak with conviction.

Astala shook his head. "No son, that is not the way of it. I have already lost one child. I have fought hard to keep you at my side."

I could feel the curl of Catesby's hand around mine, the gentle pull as he brought me back to his side. The direction of the breeze changed; the torches seemed to dance with it. I was reminded of a girl standing on a stony shoreline watching the candles go out in windows on the horizon. I missed the way the breeze sounded between old stone walls. I missed the boiling pot above the hearth fire, the bed I shared with my cousin.

"Grandfather." I choked and he turned to face me. "I would like to return to Eynhallow."

Perhaps it was a dream that I had suffered in a sleep which had lasted too long? I was ready to awaken now. In that old bed, endure another harsh winter of darkness and solitude. I wanted no part in this. If there was going to be a war, let them fight it without me. I was not beyond abandonment myself, perhaps I was not so different?

"You are afraid, Finola?" Astala asked, his sincerity not marred by his anger. "And if you were to return? What then?"

I tried to imagine. The guardians coming to me always in their quest to have me back in the water. What if they had forgotten me? What if Rohan had forgotten me?

"I want no part in the wars to come." I confessed. "I know not what to fight for."

Astala seemed taken aback that I had asked, his shadow in the torchlight seemed to paint the face of a man who wanted to crawl into despair but couldn't. I wondered what he had seen behind those blue eyes. But part of me didn't want to know his truth. It was too much to bear.

"And then shall I call Ewan to come and show you the way? You will go back to Eynhallow as incomplete as when you left. If you do not know what to fight for, there is no place for your heart not here nor there. My beautiful child." He placed a hand upon my cheek and stroked the tears that had fallen. "I knew a girl once. She was glorious and powerful and held more grace than I could muster within myself. She is within you. I have seen her quiet strength and courage. You are a bird without wings, you have already fought to come this far."

I remembered Caleb saving me from things that tried to hurt me. His arms carrying me in times when I could not carry myself. I had not felt strong. I had not felt courage.

"No Finola." Elora said, breaking free of Esson's grasp. "It was you who carried him. You must go to him."

He was insulted by her boldness; in response he took her hand and pulled her back into the circle of his embrace. I could see that she did not want to be there, but would remain, nonetheless. She had my pity and she knew it.

Astala shook his head.

"This grieves me, there is no balance to how much this grieves me so." He sighed, "Esson, my son. I had hoped one day that you would come into your own and be at peace with whatever troubles you so. I had thought a wife such as the one you have would have brought you joy, especially when the child was born. Elodie, I fear, will grow in your shadow."

"We are not gathered here for me." Esson said through thin lips. "We are gathered here for her."

His eyes rested upon me, as did all the others. I still stood by the fact that I wanted to go home.

"Call Ewan to come." I breathed, "I have made my decision."

How could I stand to be here? I could not bear the confrontation.

"You sadden me, child." Astala said, "It need not come to this."

I looked at the ground and wondered if I stood very still would I take root and become like a tree? If I were a tree, I would be nothing more than a vessel for the wind to travel through.

Esson did not have the power to make decisions for me, neither did the Elders. None of them decided where the trees would grow. Seeds would live on a breeze and land wherever they may to make the ground their home. I did not wait for their blessing, as I began to walk away, I wondered where my feet would take me. I heard their voices behind me. Esson's sounding out in fair warning that I would be damned, but I had been damned already. Mother Teigne asked me where I was going.

"Am I not free to leave?" I asked, "There appears to be no hands upon me anymore."

The old woman nodded. I thought I saw a hint of a smile.

"Those who laid hands upon you will be dealt with accordingly." She sighed, as if the entirety of the farce had left her old bones exhausted. "You are free to leave, child."

Esson pointed a long and ominous finger. "She isn't going back to Eynhallow."

Astala's hand moved slowly, yet quick enough to force his son into submission.

"I have fought too long and too hard to see this land torn apart again." He lamented, a sorrowful gaze emanating from him that should have been a weakness, but within him, it was a melancholy strength. "My son conspires against me; I had not thought that I would ever know that same betrayal again."

If he was placated, it did not stick. Esson was breathing too hard, his eyes burning wide and the corners of his mouth trembling.

"One day you will know what I have done to keep this land at peace, father. Mark my words, they will feast on their anger at a half blood of the High Priest's bloodline dwelling in the House of Consorts."

I wondered if his prediction were true, or if it were the ramblings of a mad man. Astala seemed to weigh this for a moment, only a brief and fleeting moment.

One of the cloaked figures stood forward, as if he had been silently called for. Pulling down the cloak of his hood, Ewan's face was drawn and sombre and entirely reminiscent of his former self. Of course, he had been there the entire time and for a horrifying moment I wondered if his had been one of the hands that had forced me to the ring of stones.

"You think I do not know the hearts and minds of the people, my son?" He asked, almost pityingly. "Do I not serve them as they serve me? I had feared for an age that my son would not follow me. Not once have you come with me to the places I go to when I am not here. Not once have you sought to gain the knowledge a High Priest needs in order to serve and be served."

Ewan took something from the folds of his cloak and handed it to Astala. Esson did not seem to understand the meaning of it. Instinctively, he stood back.

I was certain of one thing in that moment. I did not understand the ways of these people, there was doubt in my heart that I ever would. It seemed to me that Esson had brought me here to right a terrible wrong he had perceived. There was no doubt in his mind that I did not belong in the House of Consorts with enough conviction to betray his own father. But the sting of betrayal seemed to linger on Astala's mind, I began to wonder what had become of Astala's brother.

Mother Teigne raised her old hand and the younger woman nodded. She retreated from the circle, the figures in their cloaks following close behind, save for Ewan, who stood resolutely still. I wondered why they were leaving but knew better than to ask. All I could feel was Catesby's hand curled tightly around mine and it was that which I gave my attention to as the stone circle seemed to become strangely smaller, until there was only six of us remaining.

"You are not fit to stand in my place when I am no longer here." Astala sighed heavily, "I have known this for many years, yet I had hoped that by keeping you close you might somehow come to know that piece of you that might perhaps one day become High Priest."

Esson was not finished. "If I am not like you, perhaps then I will be a High Priest to serve in ways you have not even begun to imagine."

The words were bitter, even I could taste them. But Astala did not react. Instead, he placed a small and intricately carved dagger at his son's feet and bade him look at it. Esson seemed to know the meaning of it now, but I did not.

It was a beautiful thing. The blade was sharp and curved, almost like a crescent moon with a shine to it I had never seen before. Almost as if the reflection of the strange sky above dwelled within the steel. The handle was made of bone, adorned with one deep red stone at the hilt. I could have sworn it had been cut to resemble a beating heart.

"Will you not see things as I do, father?" Esson asked, a little gentler than he had previously spoken.

"I did not come to this position because my father held it." Astala said, "I came to it because I was chosen out of all the others to serve the High Priest of my youth who had no son of his own to teach. He was a good and kind man, but he did not hesitate on the battlefield. When sacrifices needed to be made, he made them with courage and sorrow both at the same time."

For the first time, I began to see some fear in Esson's eyes. Uncertain, perhaps, of what this meant for him. He picked the dagger up slowly, in a curled fist that held it tightly. Elora began to cry, silently and almost as if the tears were for something only, she could hear. The silence was deafening.

"There will be none left to follow you, in the end." Esson said, calmly and almost as if he knew it to already be true. "Too many of your kin have been driven away."

My breath caught in my throat. Catesby must have felt it in the way my body tensed. Instinctively, he pulled me further back. But I would not go.

Astala sighed gravely. "One day, my son, it will all make sense."

Esson took Elora's hand. Somehow her sobbing had ceased, and she was once again poised and unreadable.

"I will not rest." He foreshadowed, slipping the beautiful dagger into the hair bound at the top of his head. "I will not rest, Father..."

As he retreated, pulling Elora behind him, I wondered if the stones knew how to circle in and become smaller or if it just appeared that way as we stood, only four of us now.

"I am sorry for what you have witnessed here." Astala seemed to gather his strength in a series of breaths that seemed to renew his resolve. "I am, perhaps, as weak as he thinks me to be."

He went over to Ewan, sure to make certain their words were hushed and in secret. I was too distracted to care what they spoke of. Catesby leaned in, creating our own hushed tones.

"That has never happened before. I thought blood would be spilled!"

He sounded breathless, almost as if he had been holding it in. Perhaps there was a level of tension I had not perceived?

"What do you speak of?!" I insisted, but Astala was already approaching.

Out of the shadow's cloaks appeared once more, the old woman walking heavily by the younger woman's side as if they had perhaps been there all along.

"You knew this would come to pass?" She asked, in a withering voice that already knew the answer.

But he did not acknowledge it. He somehow seemed older than he appeared for the first time since I had ever laid eyes on him. Bending a long and sinuous knee, he knelt to greet me and with hands which were older than I cared to imagine, he held mine within them. I could feel all the worlds collide in his touch, perhaps every realm which ever existed was flowing through the palm of his hand. There was a power within him, and I was overwhelmed by it.

"Why didn't you kill him?" I asked, I knew that I was crying.

"I will not take a blade to my blood again." There was a pitch of untold sorrow as he spoke. "He carries it with him now."

He held me within him. I could feel his essence pulsing through my veins. He had known a loss so great I could not bear it. It felt as if he would be ready for another war at any moment, but there was acceptance for the pain that had passed. Somewhere deep within it hurt, but he had already sacrificed himself for the greater good and would continue to break parts of himself up in order to keep everything else whole. I had never felt such love. It was the only word I had for it. He was showing me his love.

"My little one..." He whispered softly, the feel of the scales upon his skin against my own a strange and familiar comfort, "Go and be free. Go and be whatever it is you have need to be..."

I looked at Mother Teigne. She was smiling. Yet there was sadness here. She raised a withered hand and made a sign of a crescent moon upon her brow with the tip of her thumb. Astala released me, took his love with him and yet, it remained with me. I could feel the warmth of his touch still upon me. For a moment I wondered if he had indeed transferred some sort of power to me, as my heart was racing far too fast.

"Where will you be, Grandfather?" I asked. "What's going to happen now?"

But all he could tell me was to go and be free. So, I did.

Free. It was a word I had often used and yet it had lost all its meaning. I wondered what would happen if I returned to Eynhallow. In the cold light of day, I knew I had been too rash to think of it. I had made too many sacrifices to give up now. I found that my feet were taking me further and further away, I did not question it. It occurred to me that I did not want to belong in that white castle. I did not want to sit at that table. I did not want to dwell on that mountainside. I did not want my days mapped out for me.

I don't think I fully understood the implications that morning that I walked into the water, of what walking away would bring about. But it meant little there in that tiny moment when I did not look back. I did not know where I was going, but somehow it did not matter. I had spent so much time fighting with myself I did not have the energy to fight with another.

If I went to the House of Consorts, or if I did not, where was the harm in walking away to wherever I may? Was I a prisoner? Of course, I was followed. But not because I had to be. I don't think his feet knew what else to do either. Our steps were mirrored now, I was glad he travelled a weary road with me. I knew that Astala would continue to watch over me, as he always had. There was little else I needed to know in that moment. I made my way out of the ring of stones, Catesby followed close behind.

I felt the wilderness of Finfolkaheem like a newborn child felt their first breath of fresh air. I went to it screaming and uncertain. The forests were deep and unrelenting and in shades of green I had never seen before. The strange fluorescent light above shone down through the leaves and shadows danced on the forest floor bringing it to life. The sounds of the creatures sang out in unison as chords of day and night played out. Sometimes they were doleful, and I felt it prick at my heart, other times it was nothing but joy. There were Finfolk who dwelled in the forests, I saw them in their homes that hung high up in the canopy above. But they did not call themselves Finfolk, it was a word used by humans and these tree dwellers were the most shy and timid of all.

"But why do they not call themselves fin?" I had asked one night, when our fire was dying to embers.

"Because they do not live near the water." Catesby had replied, emptying his cup over the flames as if to demonstrate.

"Greenfolk, or Treefolk." I murmured, on the verge of sleep. "How beautiful…"

They did not like to leave the safety of their woodland homes and kept themselves entirely separated from the Finfolk who lived by the mountain valleys and rivers. I did not think they were grateful for our presence as we passed through, but they did not deny us passage all the same. Finfolkaheem was as large and imposing as any world might be. I could not quite grasp the geography of it, or if there would ever be an end to it.

"Are there countries, like in my world?" I enquired, as often as I could, when the day was ending and our nights by fire began.

I wondered if Catesby ever grew weary of my questioning. Sometimes he appeared quiet, as if he wished that I would keep my mouth closed. But then he would smile and indulge me once more.

"I do not know what a country is." He would tell me, and I would be reminded that his knowledge of my world was as little as mine of his. "But there are many different places, each of them with a name, some of them I have never seen before myself."

"Then we must go to them all." I said excitedly, "I spent much of my life on a tiny bit of land, never seeing much else."

Catesby nodded thoughtfully. "And oh, how I would love to see that land."

I could not think of it. To see him standing by the gate at The Hylands. The sorrow of that false memory tore at me, and I chose to bury it.

"Did Ewan not tell you?" I asked, certain that my cousin would have been more than happy to indulge him.

"No." Catesby had said flatly. "Ewan is there to serve Astala, for whatever purpose he sees fit."

I knew he had accepted his place and cherished it. Perhaps it was one of the only things I did understand. Our fireside conversations touched on many subjects, as the days went by and our travels took us further from those mountains and valleys, I began to see a side of my brother I had previously not seen.

He was child-like in his enquiry, his eyes widening at each new place we encountered. We passed a village that sat by a great lake, or perhaps it was an ocean? The homes not unlike the ones from Catesby's own. These people were open and welcoming, unlike the Greenfolk who did not bother us. Many of them were House Raven, with black hair falling down their long lithe backs. But there were a few of Babel and Teigne. It was a little Raven boy who saw us first, his little fin legs running towards us as we approached the village.

"I have heard of this place." Catesby confessed, "They call it Seohl Bay."

The boy was young, as he grew closer it occurred to me that he was no more than five or six. If I was to hazard a guess in human years. His oval blue eyes gleamed in the sunlight, tiny scales on his skin glistening as he ran. His black hair was still short enough that it sat snugly behind the points of his ears, which moved very slightly with each breath.

"Are you *her*?!" He asked, breathlessly.

I exchanged a look of confusion with Catesby, who smiled kindly at the boy before whispering something into his ear that I could not make out.

The boy's face lit up with elation. "I will go and tell my father." He simply said, before running back the way he had come.

Chapter Five

SELKIES

"What did you whisper to him?" I enquired, with a raised eyebrow and narrowed forehead.

"No matter the size of the world, news will always travel faster than we do." He replied, placing a cool hand on my shoulder.

"Did you not think that your return would not be met with inquisition?"

I had not given it much thought. I'd been kept within the mountains and my own assumptions. I was readily awakened to the reality of myself when I saw them coming out of their homes to see my face. They were elated and curious and did not hesitate to bring us into the village with all the celebration of someone or something far above my station.

The village was spread out against the shore of the ocean-lake which went on for miles and miles. It seemed to me that it far surpassed even the sound that surrounded Eynhallow.

The huts were not round, but square and fairly resembled the sort of home that I was more familiar with. Outside they hung skins and meats, tools and clothing. The centre of the village burned a fire, a little smaller than the one from Catesby's village and all around it sat tree stumps and carvings I could not decipher.

There was no white castle in the mountainside, nor a ring of stones to worship within. It was just a village by the water, nothing more, nothing less. We were brought to the centre to sit by the fire and offered fish and root vegetables in crude wooden bowls that were smooth to the touch. I took the food gratefully and wondered what I had done to deserve such hospitality.

"So, you are Finola?" A voice asked, breaking through the many who had gathered to sit with us.

The little boy appeared, holding the hand of a much older man who I ascertained to be his father. His hair was black and long, as tall as many of the fin were, he seemed to be taller still. He bore a scar beneath his left eye, that seemed to have healed too deeply. It was silver in colour and streaked across his face like a star across the night sky. But it was not ugly, and it did not make me want to look away.

"I am." I confirmed, putting down my bowl.

He bid me continue to eat and took his place to sit beside me as I chewed on salted fish. His eyes appraised Catesby boldly, it seemed as if he already knew who he was and did not need an introduction.

"News of your return reached us a moon ago, but we had not thought that we would ever find you here." Said the scarred man, throwing sticks and dead grass into the fire. " My name is Amund, this is my son who shares my name. But we call him little Amund, until he grows larger than me then perhaps, I will take his place."

He laughed good naturedly and patted the boy on the head before he lost patience with our conversation and ran off to go and play.

"And you are the son of Nim?" He then asked, as if Catesby's place proceeded his name. "I saw you once, when you were a small child, with your grandfather at the ring of stones."

I liked this place. I could feel the warmth of it like the sun on the first day of spring on Eynhallow. We were joined by many more who gathered by the village fire, some of them talking amongst themselves and others leaning closer to hear what Amund said. I had not grown used to the crowds, or the feeling of being around others. But here it felt as if I could stay in their company all night. It was strange. I was not afraid, and I did not hold myself inward, as the light began to fade and darkness prevailed it only served to ignite my soul further. I found myself feeding off their joviality. It was as if it were a completely different world from my grandfather's place, it did not go unnoticed.

Catesby came to sit at my side, a plump dark coloured fruit I had no name for in his hand. He offered it to me.

"You are happier here." He noted, urging me to eat.

I took a bite and sweet water spilled down the back of my throat. Far too sweet for me, I was accustomed to salted fish and dry bread. I handed it back to him and he laughed at me, as if my tastes were far too bland for this realm.

"I wish that I had come here first." I sighed.

"There is no other way." He lamented. "The gateway has always been at the foot of the mountain."

It did not matter to me. A wish was but a wish, a silent longing and nothing more. If I knew nothing of anything more, I knew enough of silent longing.

"Ah yes, the gateway…" Amund interrupted, turning himself away from whatever had been holding his attention. "I have heard of how it spits you out of the mountainside into the water below."

I could feel the darkness of it still and the strange vastness of it. Catesby put his hand in mine, I wondered if he had known my thoughts.

"Tell me, Finola, what do you make of our world?"

He had asked an impossible question. As it was becoming clearer that there was more to it than I'd previously been offered to see.

"Ask me when I have seen all of it." I replied, deciding to take another bite of the sweet fruit in rebellion of my old tastes.

Amund shook his head, wisps of red in his black hair falling about his scarred face. "I am near to seven hundred of your human years and I have yet to see all of it myself. Your world seems to me much smaller. There was once a human consort here in the village, she was brought by one of the fishermen who saw her walking along the shore. They had many children and their children's children still live here in Seohl to this day. She was wise as she was beautiful, I was just a young one when she was already grown but I remember her stories which I have passed to my son also."

I remembered a girl who had sat on the ground overlooking Eynhallow sound, listening intently to stories of the people I sat with now. In love and enchanted and still spellbound by the romance of it. But the truth was far from what I'd been told. I still held some bitterness towards Nathan Munro. It came as a surprise that I should recall him now, when I was most happy and content.

"I have never understood it." I confessed, "This land is shrouded in mystery. We shroud it further by folklore and myth. But it seems to me that humans have been coming here and Finfolk have been going there for far longer than the mind recalls."

Amund nodded in agreement. "It is so. But there are many who do not condone the marriage of the two and for good reason."

Catesby's hand flexed in mine.

"We tell our stories to protect what we have." He reasoned, and again Amund nodded in agreement.

"Yes, boy." He said affectionately, "But do you think it has always been so? The House of Consorts was created to initiate and teach mankind about our ways. But there was a time before that. When there were no stories, no folklore. When the fin would walk the land of the human, the Hildaland and it was neither here nor there. The veil had not slipped quite so far, one from the other. Our human consorts moved freely into our world.

But man does not live as long as fin. Humans, they are quick to be born and quick to die. Take another human wife, or human husband. Finblood can only be diluted so far. This land was becoming full of half-bloods, our kind were dying out. Astala decreed that times must change. He created the gateway at the bottom of the sound, the only way in and the only way out. The humans spread their folklore of the Goodman and his three sons; we became monsters on our own land. But it did not matter, finblood began to flow again and for many years we enjoyed the peace of mind which comes with knowing our half-blood kin would grow at our side. Until you, that is."

His eyes rested upon me. "Mankind is bitter when there is a door which was once open to them suddenly closed. As the ages go by there are fewer consorts, but that is not to say that we do not welcome them now. They may be fewer, but it is because of that that they are fiercely loved. Never forget that, Finola."

The hour was growing late, but nobody seemed to be tiring. I could hear the faint sound of a flute being played somewhere on the other side of the village fire. The muffled sound of a drum, but I could not see the music being played. A hollow whale tooth passed down to me and it was filled with a drink that looked black and sticky. I gave it a veritable sniff, and it was not pleasant. I passed it to Catesby without bothering to taste, and he took a long, deep swig. Amund seemed pleased by how much he had drunk and took the rest in one quick sip.

"We are not so much different, finblood always pumps more strongly through the heart." Amund said, passing the whale tooth on. "Which is why you will live longer than your human blood allows."

"I had heard it told that a human who has the heart of a fin will have their life extended somewhat." I said and it completely eluded me as to where I had gained this notion. "Is this true?"

Amund smiled, a broad and meaningful grin that was wise and experienced. "Somewhat." He agreed, he said no more on the matter.

That night I did not sleep. The village was alive with song and story. The fire did not burn out until the sky began to turn once more; the sounds of morning began to seep through the last of the merriment.

Amund offered us a place to rest, in his place that sat snugly between the shore and the land behind. Seohl Bay was, I discovered, a great fishing port. It was the home of those who chose to take the form of the seal.

Legend called them Selkies, but in truth they were nothing more than shift forming Finfolk. Like the Greenfolk, the Selkies had their own way of living. They were merchants of the water and their village had prospered.

Amund took great pleasure in telling us the story of the Selkie. Living as seals in the water and shedding their skin to become human on land.

Perhaps the way it had got lost over time, but it seemed to me that it was the other way around. It did not matter to me; I was grateful for their welcome. It was the warmest I had ever received.

Amund's place was like home. There was a table fashioned from wood in the middle of the room, it was the closest thing to Eynhallow I had seen. Above was a ladder leading to sleeping quarters, it was there I laid my head on a bed of skins to sleep the day away.

I awoke with my hair in a tangle. I could taste it in my mouth. With no concept of the time, I felt my body try to regain its strength. I was weak and could not open my eyes. I had been breathing deeply and felt the dry bitterness in my mouth and I craved water.

Muffled voices sounded from down below, but I could not hear their words. I had not slept so deeply for so long. It felt as if years of broken sleep had come to me all at once. My head was still somewhere else as I tried to open one eye, and the blurry vision of a body sleeping beside me came into view.

Little Amund slept soundly at my side, his bottom lip moving with each breath. I watched him for a moment, his fin skin almost changing shade with each tiny movement. I had grown so accustomed to it I barely noticed it anymore. The physical differences did not seem so apparent. The tips of his ears pointed out more fiercely than mine, the shape of his eyes more almond. There were gills behind his ears where there were none behind mine and his height would soon surpass any humans.

But in this form, asleep, where there is no other pretence, it struck me that somehow, we all must dream. Of what, it did not matter. But regardless, we all could dream. I hoped his were happy. Which was a revelation to me. I'd never met anyone new that I'd wanted to care about before. But I did, I wanted to care. Not just about little Amund, but my grandfather and my brother too.

I raised myself up and pulled my hair from my face. The smell of cooking fish hit me, and I was suddenly ravenous. I heard Catesby down below, his voice familiar to me now even when I could not see his face, I would know his voice in the darkness. Endless hours of listening to him by firelight had engulfed me.

"What if you are wrong?" Catesby said, I inched closer to the precipice.

Hanging slightly back so that I couldn't be seen I was pressed against an old door again, listening to words I had no right to hear. I had done this before. In another life.

I heard Amund move around the table. "I am very rarely wrong, boy."

Catesby didn't respond and my need for water became too great to stay up there a moment longer.

His eyes moved towards me as I climbed down. Amund took some fish off the fire which sat in the corner of the dwelling, a clay chimney rising above it. He put them down on the table and began slicing them apart. But Catesby did not notice anything but me.

"What time is it?" I asked, hoping it would provide a distraction.

"A little before sunset." He said solemnly, as if he was afraid, I had heard what they had been speaking about. "When did you wake?"

"A moment ago." I replied, more abruptly than I intended. "I have not slept like that since I was a child."

Amund handed me a slice of fish meat and some water and urged me to eat and drink. In the cold light of day, he seemed different. As if last night some higher power had taken over him, now he was nothing more than he had always been. I wanted to ask him how he got his scar, but the right moment had not presented itself. He seemed a little less content, as if at any moment he would be ready to face something untoward. There was no sign of a woman around here, it struck me as odd that I had only just noticed.

"I am grateful for your hospitality." I said, certain he would be grateful for our departure. "But we will not impose upon you another night."

The knife in his hand was deftly placed on the table. He clasped his hands together and then wiped them on the cloth about his loins.

"There is no need. You are welcome to stay here as long as you require."

Requirement wasn't something I had given much thought to. Where we were heading must not get lost within adventure.

Catesby did not say anything, I realised the response was entirely down to me.

"I have to make it to the House of Consorts." I sighed, "My grandfather was going to send me there to learn all I need to know. But my uncle gathered the elders and they tried to stop me."

Amund nodded. "If your uncle had any sort of real power, he would not have needed to gather anyone. We gather the elders for things such as the union between two people. For the solstices and the equinox. If we have bad crops or if the fish do not bite, we do not call the elders if we have a grievance. Unless there is a war at hand, but war does not involve such trivial matters."

Catesby offered his own opinion. "He hates you because he hates *her*."

Perhaps I had known that all along. Perhaps it was nothing more and nothing less than that.

"Myth and legend are all very good." Amund said, recalling our stories of night. "But they do not eradicate the truth. They can shroud it and protect it and serve its purpose well. But the truth will always have its place."

"The truth has never been something easily offered to me." I surmised, looking to Catesby for agreeance.

He looked down. I noticed that he would not look anywhere else. If I did not have his honesty, his and no others, I had nothing and then I knew. With the certainty of knowing something without having it spoken out loud. I knew, so he did, and it was more than he could bear.

There was a sadness in his eyes as he looked downward and I shared in it. I could not come and go without his blessing, nor could I come or go without him by my side. He was my safety. He was my truth. He was to me what I had been to Rohan. His protection, his love was all encompassing.

But it was not the same, not quite. I knew it. I think, perhaps, Elora had known it too.

I wondered if he had come to this conclusion before I had. Just one silent thought, fleeting as it may be and if Elora had heard it... did Astala know it too? He would not look at me now. I did not dare to ask him why. This was not as it had been with Caleb. But as I tried to remember the curve of his jaw, there was only Catesby's face. I had forgotten to think of him. How had I forgotten to think of him?

I remembered that old ache, that old need and it remained but it was changed. If I was meant to continue loving him with conviction during our time apart, had I failed? There was growing repulsion within me, a voice telling me this man was the brother I had shared the womb with. But I could not recall that, nor could I recall anything which tied me to him the way a brother ties to a sister. All there was instead was a void. All around it was the sense that this man had made sacrifices for me. He had come to me first.

"As I said." Amund's voice broke into the thickening air. "I am very rarely wrong."

Catesby finally looked up. But not at me. I did not dare to ask what he could possibly be wrong about.

"Finola..." He turned his attention to me, his scar bending as he smiled. "I have something which may be of interest to you."

From within the fold of his cloth, Amund retrieved something he had kept well hidden. He handed it to me with a closed fist and dropped it into my open hand.

"What is it?" I asked, inspecting the strange object.

"A memory." He replied. "You did not come here by chance, Finola. You were meant to come here. Your mother knew that this day would come."

Catesby drew breath. Finally, he looked at me, at the thing in my hand.

"You knew her?" I breathed; overcome with something I could not put into words.

Amund nodded, I knew now why my welcome had been so incredibly warm.

Memories were not things we recall in our minds eye. Memories were things we could remove and place outward of ourselves for others to see. Memories were small, round stones that were cool and smooth to the touch. Memories were black as a raven and yet reflected the sunlight perfectly.

"Place it in the water." Amund instructed. "And you will see."

He dropped another stone into Catesby's hand and pointed out towards the shoreline. "There are pools of water within the rocks at the edge of the bay. Go there."

I wanted to drag stories about my mother from Amund's mouth, but he smiled evenly and walked out. Regardless of us being there, he had things to do and our presence couldn't prevent it.

"Not today." I said, placing my stone aside. "Go if you will. But I will go another day."

Catesby raised an eyebrow. "For once the truth is placed right within your hand and you will not witness it?"

Strange as it may seem, I hoped by keeping it at bay it might serve a higher purpose. I liked it here and the fear that whatever lie within the memory stone may prompt us to leave sooner was very real. I wanted to wrap myself in the warmth of Seohl Bay a while longer. While he was clearly frustrated, Catesby did not argue with me.

Perhaps this was one of the reasons why I had come to love him so. His persistence in keeping an even temper was not lost upon me. One of my brothers had been quick to anger and the other was as cool as a morning breeze in spring.

I watched him carve outside Amund's house, his knife gliding down the wood as if it were spun silk. All around me it seemed that the day was winding down, but I had slept and was not tired at all. Boats appeared down at the shoreline, and fin men brought in baskets of fish that the young ones brought into the village. Others were gathering by the village fire to eat, while little ones ran wild laughing and playing with no interest in the onslaught of night. There came the sound of muffled drum once more and I wondered if towns and cities were ever this alive.

We stayed, perhaps, far longer than I intended to. But it was not without its lessons. Seohl Bay had captured my attention, I was inclined to stay indefinitely. I had lost count of the days when I encountered a seal lying on the rocks, basking in the warmth of the day. Its sleek and black body majestic and round, somehow it did not seem to sense me as I stood, enchanted, and watched.

I wondered where it had come from and if it had ever seen Eynhallow. It was becoming a morbid theme, wondering if any of the more ancient Finfolk had ever set foot upon the other 'Aheem.

The lazy seal rolled on the hard surface, back and forth as if it could not satisfy a scratch. I wondered if it would come to its senses as I moved closer. There was a brief moment of unease as I stumbled, my foot catching within the rocks as I tried to remain unseen. The seal stopped and flipped back over, big deep eyes searching for me. I was never certain if it saw me, only that when I thought perhaps it did, it slipped effortlessly off the rocks and disappeared into the water as if it had never been there at all.

I was bitterly disappointed. I wanted to transform myself into one of these beautiful creatures, but I had only ever known wings. The faithful birds seemed to follow us, or perhaps they only followed Catesby, but in recent days the skies had seemed empty.

Without trees, the birds fled to the cliff faces that sat at each end of the bay. The bay itself was so large and vast, I dared not imagine how far they had to fly before they reached us.

He waited for me in silent frustration. Although he never spoke the words out loud, I knew what he wanted. He wanted to know the contents of his memory stone and let them take us onward on our journey. A journey that would ultimately take me away from him, but one that he was willing to take regardless.

Sometimes he would go out on the fishing boats with Amund and be gone until the light began to fade. Sometimes he would sit and carve little images of men and women from driftwood and rock and give them to little Amund and the other children to play with. He filled his days, one way or another, while I seemed to be standing on a shoreline once more waiting for something to happen.

"Why don't you go in?" Amund asked, one evening, as he came to bring me food from the village fire.

I sighed and took the bowl of freshly cut fish, it had been cooked in a strange green herb I had no name for, and it smelled oddly like grass on a cool spring morning.

"And then would I be able to shift into the form I wanted just by getting into the water?" I asked, knowing the answer would not be easily given.

Amund shrugged, his scarred face turning downward. "Who is to say what comes easy to one person may not be quite so easy for another."

"I have no right to think I even could."

"You are still young with much to learn. But that does not mean you have not learned already. I have seen it. You are quick to doubt yourself and this prevents you from doing the things which you desire."

Amund was looking at me, expecting me to react somehow. But all I could do was watch the water and it felt so much like home I almost let my heart be consumed by it. I was still her; I was still that girl. In some small measure.

"Forgive me." I said, turning away. "Perhaps one day I will be able to thank you for your wisdom."

"Do not thank me." He said, abruptly, "Thank only yourself."

With a careful hand, that moved with the speed and grace of a swooping bird, he pushed me off the rocks and into the water. His voice, fading fast, telling me to give in to desire.

I wasn't certain of myself, that was true. But as my body hit the water, I did not feel the cold and breathlessness of it. Instead I allowed it to engulf me. Death would be something, perhaps the greatest truth of all. But I did not die.

Instead, I watched as the water began to clear. Rocks and seaweed began to coil around me. I was still in my usual form, the material of my dress clinging to my skin like another layer I did not need. I struggled to free myself from it. But when I did, I let it go, not bothering to care how naked I might appear when I resurfaced.

Down here was eerily quiet. Not like being underneath water on Eynhallow. There were no murky depths here, only clear blue that gave way to dancing shadows from the strange light above. The seabed was even and yet in complete disarray with those beautifully coloured weeds. Every now and then, tiny speckled fish would dart in and out of the dancing water vines. My hair was floating around me, I could see it above and beside my field of vision. Not only was it quiet, but it was also very still. The water held me perfectly below the surface, but above the seabed. I could not breathe, but I found that I had no need for air in my lungs. Without the gills behind my ears, surely, I would drown?

I could see the creature approach through the weeds and climbing vines. I knew what it was, but what struck me most was that I was not afraid. It would be impossible to know fear down here. The feel of the seal against me was almost more than I could take. With a body so soft and streamlined, it ran a careful flipper up my spine as it moved swiftly beyond me. I twisted in the water to see where it had gone, but it had already turned and was fast approaching me again.

This time I took hold of it and allowed it to take me wherever it may go. My hands firmly holding the swishing flippers, I was able to see the deep and cursive scar underneath the pitch-black eye. I released my hand and watched him, wondering how Amund could have been standing on the rocks with me only a moment ago and had now taken on this elusive form. It was beyond my capabilities; I knew that now. Perhaps smaller creatures were much easier to shift into? If indeed I possessed the ability at all. I had wondered often if it had been a fluke that I had taken flight.

With great disappointment, I began to resurface. When I broke, the air above filled my lungs and I praised the feel of it against my wet cheeks.

Amund leaped onto the rocks nearby, his sleek body rising from the water like it had somehow been part of the wave. Without hesitating he began to shift back into his natural form, and I found that I could not take my eyes off him.

It was not the unashamed way that he did it, nor the fact that I knew he would be naked thereafter. Something inside me told me this was sacred, and I should look away. It was her. That dear old woman who had raised me on the land. The one I had called Mammy once. It was her voice ringing in my ears as the colour of Amund's skin began to shimmer from black to silver and then back again to whatever it had once been before. His bones did not crack like mine had, everything seemed to move more fluidly, and I was envious of it. There again was that voice that spoke of sin.

Once he was done, he picked up his loin cloth and hastily wrapped it about him. Then he looked at me, still treading water and offered me a hand. But I was acutely aware of my dress which languished somewhere in the depths below.

"Your naked body does not give me desire." He said, almost as if he were about to laugh. "If that is what you are worried about."

These human things were dragging me under. These human thoughts and human dispositions. These human voices inside my head. He had already seen it, with those deep black eyes. The same eyes which looked at me now. They had already seen my body. Touched it even. Would I be bashful now?

"It's not that..." I managed, noticing the fabric floating near a rock nearby.

Amund followed my gaze and went to fish my dress out of the water. With a careful hand he scooped it up and wrung it out. As I pulled myself out and clasped the dress back onto my body it felt as though I was wearing a false skin. Perhaps this was why the Finfolk dressed so simply and minutely? Flesh was clothing, almost as if it were a pair of shoes or a Sunday hat.

"I'm sorry, I failed you." I said, bowing my head.

But Amund lifted my chin with a curved finger and he felt so much dearer to me then.

"Did you learn something?" He asked.

My heart lifted as I felt the dress, which was still dripping wet, on me like a second skin. I knew that he had not pushed me into the water so that I could take another form but so that I could know what I needed to do in order to take whatever form I chose when I chose it.

"There is much to learn in peaceful times. It will come to you in time, you cannot wish for all knowledge and all power to come to you because that is what you think must happen. I did not wake up one morning with this scar. It was my greatest lesson of all."

Lucie Howorth

Chapter Six

BLOOD BROTHERS

atesby was different at night. He turned into a person I barely recognised in daylight. By the fire he was thoughtful and often quiet, unless I burdened him with questions which required long winded answers. I wondered why he seemed so troubled, but it was the one thing I would not ask.

This night he seemed particularly distant. In his hand he turned his memory stone and watched its smooth edges glow in the flames. Little Amund came and sat by his side, his face immediately changed from one of deep thought to a smile I knew was only put there for the sake of a small child.

We ate fish and bread and drank the juice of a fruit I had no name for, it was sweet and left tiny seeds on my tongue. But it was moreish, it wasn't until I had drunk too much of it that I realised it was potent.

I came to realise these cups in my hands were filled with something close to wine, I drank them down like water. But it did not seem to matter. All around me was merriment and laughter and dancing and drums. I could hear the sound of a pipe being played somewhere in the distance but could not see where it came from. Always I could hear it but never see it.

Tonight, was different. It wasn't the usual evening gathering to eat and talk about the day's events. It felt as if the atmosphere was building to something. The fruit wine had gone to my head so much so that I did not seem to care that Catesby was in no mood to talk. I thought I saw his face almost drop as I approached him.

"Do you despise me, brother?" I asked, in a playful tone that was entirely unlike me.

He winced. It was the first time I had ever referred to him as such. I cocked my head to the side and decided it was best to put my cup down.

"Of course, I don't." He replied, indignant and void of all humour. "But you are drunk and Little Amund has asked me to take him back home."

It wasn't far, I didn't venture a response as Little Amund placed a sleepy hand into Catesby's.

Yes, I was drunk. I had never been drunk before; I wasn't certain it was something I found any pleasure in.

The fire danced before me, flames licking outward and upward as if releasing tiny spirits into the air. I wasn't certain of how long Catesby had been gone when he somehow returned, I realised I had been hypnotised.

"Is Little Amund asleep?" I asked, not taking my eyes from the fire.

"Yes, by some miracle." He replied, referring to great sounds of the celebration.

I finally found the strength to break away and look at Catesby's melancholy face. "What is all this for?"

"Today is what they call a Solstice. When the light above us is most strong and powerful."

I looked up to where he pointed and noted the way the darkness seemed to linger in purple hues that did not quite reach pitch black. How had I not noticed? How had I not known?

"There will be a gathering at the ring of stones in White Mount. A celebration in my village. Much like this one."

I was sad for him; I noted a tone of reproach as he spoke but then he smiled, and it was the first time I had seen him smile in what felt like a very long time.

"You miss your village." I sighed, "Perhaps it is time you went back to it."

"I will, in time." He sounded optimistic about that. "I am content to be here, for now. Wherever you are, that is where I will be."

Maybe it was the drink that clouded my mind, but I couldn't help but disagree. "I don't think you are content."

He wasn't smiling anymore; I was sorry for what I had said.

"Perhaps content is not the right word, but you seem to linger here and so must I."

I could feel the way he needed to be near me. He had taken on this journey and never once asked anything of me, and I suddenly felt selfish and ashamed that I had only noticed his sullen face.

I had not stopped to think of his thoughts and where they might lie. I wasn't a good person, not really. I was fixated entirely on my own agenda. I was failing entirely at every test which had come to pass. I was locked in my own skin, despite shifting into a bird, there was something preventing me from taking on any other forms. I had often thought of Caleb and if I was honest with myself, my journey had begun with him in mind.

But somehow that had gotten lost along the way. My mind had wandered from thoughts of him, to other things which occupied my mind.

"You are faithful." I said, still drunk and now no longer caring whether I was or not. "I am an unworthy sister."

He placed an arm around my shoulder, to prevent me from falling. I hadn't known that I was about to until he stopped me.

"Please, do not say that..." He almost sounded as if he were begging. The way his voice seemed to tremble as he spoke.

He had mocked me once. When he would smile at me, knowing that he knew all the things which I did not. I had almost forgotten the last time he had done that. How long had we been here? How long had I been here at all? How much I had changed. Yet, I still did not know what he meant.

"Do not say what?" I asked plainly, placing a careful hand to my forehead.

"Sometimes I wish that you were not my sister at all, then I would not be bound to you. But I am bound to you, I do not know yet if it is a blessing, or a curse."

I was hot, I could feel my skin burn. The fire was close, and the air is already full of warmth. The Solstice marked the beginning of summer. If, indeed, there were seasons to be marked here. I was certain I was too hot to touch and shifted my body away from his.

"I have been a curse." I confessed. "You need only speak with the one I called mother."

He did not move to console me once more.

"Would that I could."

I was once again sorry that he hadn't been there with me on that lonely isle. I could not wish that for him, yet I somehow wanted him to know the solitude from which I came. For a moment I was drawn to his eyes, it seemed that he wished for me to say something more. But my mind was swimming in drunk thoughts which made little sense and I could feel my body begin to sway again.

All around us, I could see them moving, dancing and singing and raising their arms to the sky above. It was glorious and daunting, soon they came to us to bring us forth into the celebrations. I didn't feel much like celebrating then, Catesby had let it be known when he declined to dance saying that he needed to go and check on the sleeping Little Amund.

I was sad that he didn't dance with me and I was afraid of the reasons why. Where was Amund? Why had he left his son in Catesby's care? I had not seen him all night.

So, he didn't go anywhere, he remained and watched as I was pulled around the fire and a garland of white flowers was placed upon my brow. One of the women from the village anointed my face with a sweet-smelling oil and blessed me with a single kiss to my lips. When they were done with me, Catesby was smiling again and I realised that no matter how warm it was by the fire, it could not measure the heat within me whenever he smiled.

Perhaps chaos gives us courage. There seemed to be no restraint tonight. I couldn't really say what had changed, if anything. It was as though I had within me all the love and hate and regret I had ever felt all at once. He wasn't with me and hadn't been with me for so long it struck me as odd when suddenly I thought of him.

But it wasn't really him. It was a version of him that he had once been, with a version of myself that I had once been. The only truth I had was the one surrounding me in that moment, and it was not Caleb.

"I think I'll go and lay down with Little Amund." I whispered.

I was drained of meaning. I could no longer try to figure out what anything meant. I pulled the flowers from my hair. Catesby's smile went with it. He stood to my height, our eyes level and I couldn't hear the drums anymore.

"I'll go back with you." He offered, but he knew I would decline.

I shook my head. "I'm afraid, Catesby." But I did not cry. "I don't know who I am."

The concept of not knowing who oneself seemed strange to him, I knew in the way he furrowed his brow in response to me.

"You are Finola."

Whatever that meant, it was lost to me. I was done with the celebrations. The night had lost all of its shine. With a pounding head I tried to make my way back to Amund's place, but each step seemed to feel heavier than the last. I almost laughed at the absurdity of it. Despite my protest, Catesby took my arm and guided me away from the village fire.

It was then that I saw him. As inconspicuous as a tree, except where there are no other trees to be found. He had known where to look, it seemed, amongst the crowd.

He did not smile; he did not share in the merriment. He was not here to break bread. I pulled away from Catesby, the sudden chill that ran down my spine a sobering bolt.

He was not alone. I recognised faces from White Mount, from the castle and the village below. They did not smile either, I was suddenly aware of a hostile silence that began to resonate over music that no longer played. I reached for the sickle knife that hung at Catesby's side always, but he had already unsheathed it and poised it in a curled fist. It was a small blade, but its sharp edge cut into the darkness and I was afraid no longer for myself.

"You are certain Little Amund is safe?" I asked, in a low voice almost in a whisper.

Catesby nodded as their presence became known. The death of the music brought a halt to the dancing and in turn, all eyes searched for the source of their cull. From the firelight I saw the strongest step forward, while others stepped back.

"Astala banished you." Catesby said, through gritted teeth, brandishing his knife as Esson stepped forward.

Their cloaks were black as tar, Esson pulled the hood down slowly to reveal the raven black hair that had once flowed long and free had been shaven to reveal a head of dark tattoos. I had only sinister memories of men with tattoos, my resolve almost broke.

"And banished I am." He said, cold and without a hint of emotion. "Tell me, where do the banished go?"

Then, there was a hint of a smile. I noted four men stood behind him, each of them carrying tall spears with curved blades that glinted in red firelight. It was as if all had ceased to move. I almost felt as if breathing would break the silent repose.

From beyond the fire people began to move aside. But Catesby did not relent. I had not seen Amund that night, it struck me as odd that I had only begun to notice. When he suddenly appeared at the front, his face was grieved and lost in a memory that had been buried far too long. He did not carry a weapon. His hands were open, I almost feared we had trusted in the wrong man.

"We do not want a fight, Esson." Amund said, his voice low and authoritative.

I knew then that I barely knew him. Where had he been? His touch was unwelcoming now as he placed a hand on Catesby's shoulder and urged him to fall back.

"What makes you think that I have come here to fight?" It seemed he was surrounded by blades, his words made folly.

Amund placed himself between Esson and the rest of us. If one swift movement came without warning, he could be felled at any moment.

Catesby still clutched his knife, still alert to the posed threat. But still, I doubted he could thwart any attack with the tiny thing. Even if he could, they would have killed Amund before he had chance to strike back.

"We do not have weapons here. We are fishermen and do not wish to fight you in these times of peace."

Esson's lip curled in distaste. I had not missed that face, nor had I any tolerance for it now.

"Fishermen." He scoffed. "Is this what the leader of a great army has been reduced to?"

Amund closed his eyes, as if he had been struck down, but no blood had been spilled.

"Another time, another life. Please, I have a young son now. Will you not greet us in peace?"

For a moment I thought Amund was begging.

"Tell me, Amund, what sort of life did you envision for yourself after your own banishment?" Esson asked and although there seemed to be whispers exchanged, nobody moved to display their shock at this revelation.

Save for me.

"Banished?" He looked at me with sorrow in his eyes. "Why did you not tell me this?"

"Perhaps." Esson offered, without a hint of remorse, "For the same reason he did not tell his own brother the whereabouts of his lost daughter."

I felt the bitter stab of intended betrayal. I could not process it though; my heart began to pulsate with love and hate and mistrust and rage simultaneously.

I could see that Esson's revelation was meant to impose a wall between those who would stand against him, but I did not feel any rage towards

Amund. He was a man I had come to know as great and kind, when I thought about it soberly, *of course* he was Astala's brother.

There was a shared sense of power in that bloodline, and perhaps this was why I had felt at ease in his house. Whatever grievance had befallen between the two, it did not extend to me. Now I fully understood why Amund had been in possession of my mother's memory stones. Why he had waited all these years to give them to us. He had betrayed his brother, perhaps, in some way, but he had not betrayed me.

"We must choose our loyalties." I said, almost as if in a dream. "Sometimes we cannot remain true to everyone we love."

It wasn't until I spoke the words that I knew them to be true. It suddenly hit me that I did not refer to Amund and Astala, but myself. I was no better than anyone that had ever lied or cheated. I was not pure; I had known this for many years. But had I truly accepted who I was until this very moment?

"Why are you here Esson?" Asked Amund, with renewed purpose. "You have not set foot outside the borders of White Mount since the wars ended."

"And since I am banished, I am required to do precisely that, Uncle." Esson used a broad and mocking smile as he spoke.

It was as if all the bad within him had been boiling away and somehow overflown.

"And you think there is anything for you here in Seohl Bay?" Amund asked, "We have nothing to offer you."

"He is here for me." I interjected, but Amund placed an imposing arm before me so that I could not advance.

"Of course." Amund agreed, "But that does not mean we have anything to offer, still."

Esson thought about this for a moment. His eyes moved from Amund to the knife in Catesby's hand and then to me as I stood trembling behind them.

"Perhaps *I* do."

There was an exchange of confusion. But Esson seemed to relish the whispers and disbelief that he had anything to offer which could be of any value. But he knew he had piqued some interest. Including my own.

"And if I agree to hear you? Will you take your weapons and leave us?" Amund said diplomatically, offering Esson a seat.

Esson did not rescind. I was in no doubt as to who the stronger of the two men were, but appearances seemed important to Esson. Now more than ever.

He ran a hand down his shaved scalp, the black ink moving with the swift stroke. I wondered if they had been there before, underneath his hair, or if he had put them there after his banishment?

There was something about fin skin that made tattoos somehow more beautiful. There was a depth to them, ink that had penetrated the tiny scales seem to shine in the right light. When Esson's hand moved down, he took the ink with it, the symbols seemed to shimmer.

"It has come to my attention that we are all in need of a new awakening." He addressed us all, to my horror, all seemed to be listening. "My father may have brought about a peaceful age, but at what cost? Our gratitude has made us his slaves."

"Speak with a careful tongue." Amund warned.

Esson did not heed his words.

"There was once a time when Finfolk and Mankind alike walked the earth together, moving between the realms as if they were one and the same. Finmen fought in the wars of mankind on their battlefields, utilising our weapons and skills to defeat their enemies. In turn, men came to 'Aheem and fought *our* wars on *our* battlefields. Before the legends, before the gateway was built." His eyes turned to me. "The isle of Eynhallow was *ours*. They told us our blood was starting to die. That there could only be a chosen few allowed to dwell amongst us. *That* was a war that will stay with us, always."

Amund was growing weary. "History, Esson. It is all history. What place has it here and now?"

"Don't you miss the sun, Uncle?" His voice was almost a whisper.

Amund bowed his head, I feared that he agreed with this madness until he began to approach Esson with a careful hand which he laid upon his shoulder.

"Esson. With each age of peace there must come sacrifice. I have lived here for many years and found joy again. I found me a woman who bore me a son. She was a great healer, knew the art of magic. When the time came for her to leave us, she agreed to leave our son here so that he might grow to be a skilled fisherman. There is no shame in that. I do not wish to fight another war just to have the sun shine on my face once more."

I wondered what kind of woman Little Amund's mother must have been. It gave me comfort to know she was not dead. I had heard much of these great wars of the past, but they seemed to be locked in a shared consciousness that wished to be forgotten. I knew that I bore witness to something here, perhaps a moment that would become part of a history I belonged to.

"I believed in you, back then." Esson offered, but not humbly. "You stood at the front and demanded that each of us fight to the death and give our lives for the cause. Now you stand here not even a shadow of that man."

Amund was weary. "I do not wish to be that man again. You must take your people and find somewhere to live out your life with your beautiful wife and child. There is no great victory in disturbing the peace and you will not succeed."

Had I known what was in his mind that night at the ring of stones, I would have run back to Eynhallow. I should have gone back. I was certain now that I was a pawn to ignite a greater plan.

"She is not going to the House of Consorts." His finger raised to point at me, "I will feel the sun upon my face again."

Silence. Consuming silence and only the crackling fire to break it. Catesby took my hand and I could feel his pulse rage wildly, perhaps he knew something which I did not?

"Is that your greatest fear?" Amund asked. "You have always known, haven't you? It was never in your destiny to be High Priest. The time of Priests is over. When Astala dies, you know what will come to pass."

Esson curled his lip more fervently, it trembled with rage and I could see those blades begin to shake in angered hands.

But Amund did not stop. "Yes, my nephew... You cannot bring about this while ever she lives, can you?"

Catesby stood back, took me with him whilst Amund stepped forward along with those who would defend him. None of them were armed save for the tiny knife in Catesby's hand.

"There are those who will follow me." Esson preached, "I do not stand alone. There are those who will walk the shores of Eynhallow once more."

I could not stifle a mocking laugh that came from the very pit of my soul. I broke free of Catesby's hand, moved to approach where Esson stood. Again, Amund moved to stop me.

"There is no Eynhallow to walk upon." I said, feeling the rocks beneath my feet as ingrained as the soft ground I stood upon now. "Only death and solitude and a land which does not want to be walked upon."

He did not want to believe me; I could see it in his eyes as I moved beyond Amund's restraint. If he wanted to kill me, he would have taken my life sooner.

"Let me tell you about Eynhallow." I could feel the words as tears welled in my eyes. I had not spoken words such as these before. Only thoughts that remained within me like dreams.

"It is not part of the world. Or any world. It killed everyone, banished those who did not succumb. Until there was only us left and then, it killed my father. For each person who tried to walk those shores after, it all but killed them too. What makes you think you won't be next?"

Esson smiled, as if death did not favour him. "So, the land is ready for this war too."

Perhaps he did not anticipate my own smile. For when my face moved, his diminished.

"Eynhallow will kill you." I whispered. "For *I am* Eynhallow..."

I could feel it then. The spark which ignited the fire within me. He did not wait for it to burn, instead he raged forward and shook the foundations of the Solstice night.

It was only a moment, so brief and fleeting, but it was all it took for those blades to come down. I fell backwards, pulled by unseen hands. They passed me back, back and back again until I was lost behind a sea of clashing spears and voices reaching pitch as they screamed and sent the village into disarray.

Through the chaos and fear I saw Amund and in his hand was one of the spears Esson's men had brought. Without hesitation he drove it into one of the cloaked figures who had tried to fight back. He moved quickly and fiercely, taking out one of the men who had tried to kill him from behind. Had I done this? Was this my doing?

Amund swung the spear high above his head and shouted for all of us to run, the blood dripping down from the blade onto his scarred face. He was not a fisherman. Had he ever been a fisherman? If he drove fear into my heart, I wondered what he had been like on the battlefield and yet, I could not run. I would not.

I moved against the crowd that ran against me. Their direction in stark contrast to my own. Someone grabbed my hand, when I looked it was one of the human consorts who had come here to be with her Finman. She was terrified.

"Tell me true. I must know. Is there no world to go back to?" She asked, as if the thought of going back had crossed her mind more than once.

"How long have you been here?!" I asked, but she shook her head as if there was no answer to that.

If she had come from Eynhallow, hers was a face before my time. Yet she did not look much older than Mammy had been when I was a child.

She was pulled from me before she could speak another word. I could smell death; it was in the air now. I could see Amund and Esson with bloodied spears in their hands and it seemed that amidst all the chaos they had somehow come to this moment and when I saw the blood on the ground I was glad that I had not witnessed it.

"Stand down Esson!" Amund commanded. "Let us not spill each other's blood."

The four men who had come with Esson lie on the ground. Two of them were dead, the other two writhed in agony as blood spurted from mortal wounds.

It occurred to me that immortality was not granted to them, yet unwounded their lives stretched out further and wider than any human could endure. I wondered if their death was the same as ours and if it wasn't, which one awaited me?

"I will not." Esson seethed, "I will kill you if I must."

Catesby emerged from Amund's side, the knife in his hand saturated in fresh blood that snaked up his arm. He brandished the knife still, even though he fought to control his fear. I didn't want to know if he had killed anyone, perhaps neither did he. Amund and Esson faced each other, spears poised. I knew neither of them would yield.

I wished that Astala were here. I wished that he would appear as he would so often in White Mount and bear witness to this madness.

It seemed to me that he had the power to stop this, him alone.

They circled, as if waiting for the other to strike. I wondered if Astala would appear from the dissipating crowds and bring forth an end to it. But I knew it was nothing but a futile wish. Nobody was coming. Everyone had fled, save for a few who would fight beside Amund. Esson was gloriously outnumbered.

"You can try to kill me." Amund wagered, "But it will not change the fact that she is here, and she will sit in Astala's place."

I did not want to sit in Astala's place. Of course, I didn't. What a ridiculous presumption. They need not fight over it.

"Have I not a say in this?" I asked, hoping they would lower their weapons. "I have no desire to that end."

"Desire or no." Said Amund, "It is why your mother sent you to the other 'Aheem. It is why you have returned."

This fact seemed to enrage Esson. His spear flew high above his head, he let out an almighty battle cry. Amund met him in direct combat, pulling his spear back and around himself causing Esson to jump back as he advanced. Catesby ran to my side, the blood on his hands covering me as he tried to shield me. But I did not see it, nor did I feel the warmth of it until much later.

Amund was the stronger of the two, Esson knew it. But he had youth and speed on his side, he moved to tire his opponent. If Amund had already killed the other men I was in no doubt that he could kill Esson with one blow, but it seemed that he did not want that. Whilst Esson was dancing with his spear, Amund was looking for a moment to strike and when he took it, I could not watch any longer. The blade sliced across Esson's bare chest, opening it like a gutted fish. Amund brought his spear around as Esson fell to his knees and with one swift movement he sliced the arm from Esson's body.

I could only stare at the dismembered arm on the ground, the fingers still curled in a cursory fist. Amund was breathless and remorseful as he threw his spear away from him. He moved to wrap one of the cloaks which lay on the blood-soaked ground around Esson's torso. If he did not bleed to death it would be a miracle.

Esson, with empty eyes, looked at me and it seemed that he accepted his defeat in the face of his loss. He allowed Amund to wrap his wound, after a moment's composure he stood. He did not cry out in pain. He did not look at his arm on the ground. He did not take his eyes from me.

"The Greenfolk will heal you." Amund said flatly, still catching his breath. "If you can make it to the trees, you will live."

He didn't want that. He didn't want to be touched. There was a strange silence in the air now, deep breaths hanging in the balance. I had never seen blood like this, not even on frostbitten grass in the dead of winter when those foxes took their chances.

Finblood. Everywhere. Death. Everywhere.

"You think me evil, Uncle?" Esson asked, his voice thin and barely there. "I love my people. Enough to lead them back into the sunlight."

Amund was not convinced. "I do not think you evil, nephew. But no good can come of your intentions."

He inched away, silent as if his tongue had been cut in place of his arm. His defeat would taste bitter. But he had his life. As he staggered away, I could feel the breath return to my lungs as I realised I had been holding it. Amund dropped to the ground, exhausted, I noted he was wounded.

"Leave it." He demanded, regarding the chunk of flesh missing from his calf muscle. "I've had worse."

He walked away without a limp or a hint that he had just fought for his life. People began to come out from their hiding places as Amund walked through the village. They thanked him and graced him with kisses to his hands, he accepted their gratitude with humility, and I wondered if he had always been their protector. Much like Astala, Amund was a good man. I would not doubt that again. But his was a more brutish way. If Amund headed the White Mount army, surely Astala had tended the wounded? It grieved me that they had quarrelled.

My attention was soon drawn to the carnage left behind. Catesby poked the severed arm with his knife distastefully, wrinkling his nose at it almost as if a moment ago he hadn't been ready for a fight.

Together we bound the bodies and the severed arm in bloodied cloaks and placed them side by side. I was struck by the weight of them, how I felt nothing as we moved them. The Finfolk were built bigger than half bloods. Somehow, we retained much of our humanity on the outside. But as Catesby moved their tall and sinuous bodies with ease, I knew it was a strength beyond what humanity could lend.

He was weary as we made our way back to Amund's home. The light had begun to change, signalling the birth of day. Amund was sitting at the table, his mind lost in thought as we came inside. He nodded a halfhearted acknowledgement of us and then returned to his own mind.

I went to lie with Little Amund. Who I knew now to be a distant cousin. He was warm and undisturbed; I felt my body tire as I laid my head down. Catesby followed, taking the space beside us. At first, I had missed the feel of a bed around my bones but in time I had become accustomed to sleeping on the floor on nests of grass. I was resolved to remain here.

"You must wash the blood from yourself." I whispered, noting the dark red stains on Catesby's pale skin.

He looked at himself as if for the first time. "It's not my blood."

He turned around and fell into a deep sleep. But I could not rest. When Little Amund began to stir I felt his body leave, but I did not move. I was afraid to go back out there to face the whispers and condemnation.

Eventually I fell into a half sleep, where I seemed to hear all the sounds of the village outside, but I was rested enough. Perhaps I slipped further than I thought, for when I opened my eyes it was darkness which greeted me, and Catesby had cleaned the blood from his arm.

Amund seemed withdrawn in the days after Solstice. He took his son out on the boats with him each day and seemed to want to keep him close.

Catesby told me, in secret, that he had been with a woman on the night Esson came and he felt tremendous guilt that he had left us unprotected. I tried to tell him, in those days afterwards, that he had not failed to do what was right. But he would reconcile it within himself in time, that much I knew.

The people of Seohl Bay seemed to slip back into normality, showing a great resilience. Although I had wanted to stay, it seemed that with each passing moment my time here was coming to an end.

The events on Solstice night had unnerved me, and even without his arm I feared Esson would return. I spent my time in the water, swimming with seals and learning from them. But their form still evaded me, I had to accept that perhaps I would never know the water through their eyes.

Chapter Seven

THE CONSORTS

I t was six days after Solstice when she found me. Standing on the rocks waiting for me to emerge. I knew her face, I had seen it before. Troubled somehow and melancholy.

I pulled myself out of the water, unashamedly naked now and able to dress in front of this stranger without hiding my human form from her. She was human too. The woman who had taken my hand and asked me if there was no world to go back to.

She humbly bowed her head as I approached, an action reserved for greeting those in a place of power.

"No, do not greet me as such." I said, bowing in return. "You and I are the same."

I knew what she had come for. I did not need to ask. Yet her demeanour gave me cause for concern. We were utterly alone, yet she was afraid of being seen. She beckoned me away from the rocks and I followed her to where the cove ended, and the sharp curve of the cliff face jutted out into the open water.

Here there was a small cave that had been cut into the rock of the cliff face. The water was knee deep and accessible if you stepped carefully. As we approached the mouth of the cave, I was surprised to see items of clothing hanging from ropes that stretched across the opening. Fishing nets were strewn across the rocks, inside there was a crude fire pit with fish smoking above it. There were animal skins on the ground, they resembled bear skins but much larger. I had no name for this creature, but I was immediately intimidated by its size. She bade me sit upon it, offered me a drink of water.

Her hospitality was entirely human.

"What is this place?" I asked, sipping on the coolest and clearest water I had ever tasted.

She was not young, as she sat beside me her bones ached as she reached the ground and yet, she was entirely beautiful and had chosen to wear her hair long as the Finwomen did, pinned back with fish bone clasps. She wore a simple cloth dress that was soaked from wading through the shallows, but she did not seem to care.

"It is only a cave." She shrugged, "But it is where I live."

"Why do you not live in the village?" I asked, inspecting the moss that grew up the cracks in the cave walls.

Finally, she smiled. "When you have lived in solitude, it is all you ever really know."

She spoke of Eynhallow. I could not hide my joy.

"Strange." I noted. "How once I hated to be there and now it seems that my misery is remembered fondly."

She nodded in agreement and for a moment we shared a collective of memories. But I had never seen her face upon Eynhallow. She was not a Munro or a Guthrie or a McAvoy, or even a McDonnal.

"You want to know how I came to be here." She said, it was not a question. "Perhaps you would like something stronger to drink?"

I had been drunk before and I was not ready to revisit that sensation. If I could hear her words on water alone, I would be strong indeed. She poured herself a drink of something else and took a long swig, swallowing hard.

"I have not even thought about this in such a long time. I have had no need to. But it seems to me that you coming here has turned this world upside down." She said, in an accent that was strange and muddled.

If indeed you could turn worlds upside down. All I'd ever wanted was to know where I belonged, whether it was upright or no. It would be a world turned on its head that would be mine, after all.

Perhaps I had always known the strangest of places I would always call home. I had been odd on Eynhallow. Odd and sad and a mystery. Would I always be so?

"It was not my intention." I told her, "I only came here to find out who I was. Apparently, that too is not something so easily come by, no matter which world I am in."

She seemed to sympathise with me, it was a great comfort. I began to see how dwelling in a cave by the sea might be more appealing to one such as us. Who had known a winter of solitude.

"Are the winters still long?" She asked, almost stepping into my thoughts.

I nodded gravely. "And getting longer still."

"I remember my last winter on Eynhallow. I was young then, and full of longing to be away from the island. I thought I might go to the mainland and travel south, but as you can see, I was not bound for that fate."

There was a wistful look in her eyes. As if remembering those old dreams was almost laughable. She took another long swig; I was compelled to ask her for her name.

"Margaret." She said, "But I have not been called that for so long... He used to call me Nettie. Because I would gather the fishing nets for my father and sometimes tangle myself within them. That was when he came to me. To cut me from the nets and call me Nettie."

I didn't remember any fishing nets on Eynhallow. Only the doleful thrum of cattle and birds.

Whatever her name was, she took a deep breath and looked me in the eye. "That was a hundred years ago."

Before I ever walked those shores, she had been born, lived and should have died. But here she sat before me, on the cusp of middle age, only a hint of a wrinkle as she spoke the words.

"These are the things they teach in the House of Consorts. Things I cannot say, but if one day you reach their door you will know yourself better for it. There is no hidden truth there. It is what they might call a grave sin in the other 'Aheem, to keep these truths from you."

And yet I had lingered here in search of them.

"He was not there. I did not see him for many years, but when finally, the day came for me to leave he waited for me in the long grass meadow outside the closed door. Here we have dwelled ever since."

Whoever he was, I presumed he was one of the fishermen I had seen pulling their boats onto the shore, he had obviously leant her some of his longevity.

"Are you happy here?" I asked, afraid that she had indeed been dragged here against her will.

Her lips drew a thin line, her eyes wrinkled. "Who among us is happy all their days? Certainly not I. But I have not wished to return. Not until..."

She drew breath and leaned in carefully. "I do not know if I have been here for a hundred years. I tried to keep track of the passing of days, but I lost it. Perhaps it is more than a hundred, perhaps it is less. But it seems to me the land I left behind is forever altered. Sometimes my mind would wander back, I would be reminded of it. Tell me, is there none left?"

I couldn't imagine the Eynhallow of her youth.

"There is my brother Rohan, his wife, our cousin Bethan. There is his mother too." I found my throat choking on the words as I spoke. "There is also another house, being built from the rubble of those that were burnt when sickness killed almost everyone. If ever it was finished, I do not know. If it was not, then I dare say those three are the only ones left. If they did not find the wit to leave."

She nodded; a nod filled with sadness. "And Esson will be free to take it back."

With one arm? I tried to imagine him coming up against Rohan. Finfolk were slight in stature, but their strength far exceeded any humans that I had witnessed. As graceful in their movements as they were, I wondered if Rohan's strength could match their fluidity. I didn't want to imagine it.

"There is a world beyond Eynhallow where none of us exist. It is only a small patch in the ocean, unwanted and unkept. Even there the stories have all but died. If Esson wants to exist in a world where they do not believe, then his fight is greater than he thinks it to be." I said, almost laughing at the absurdity of the people in Evie looking upon a Fin man for the first time.

"I remember the mainland." She said sweetly, this woman lost in a world she had not been born into, "Is there still a Church in the village?"

Evie had not changed. I imagined that church standing there when all else had fallen. But still, I smiled at the memory of standing in the church yard on Rohan's wedding day. However bittersweet it was.

"I have seen more of this world than I ever saw of the other. I spent my life on Eynhallow, only sometimes in Evie. The rest of it is unknown to me. But it is familiar, still, even now. I cannot recall how long I have been gone from it."

She began to throw sticks in the fire pit, ready to conjure flames. "I remember the day you came. The word spread like wildfire and reached us here in the bay. From that day to the Solstice there has been 300 days in between."

My eyes met hers in horror, obvious that I had thought it to be much less. She set a layer of dry moss above the sticks and waited for the smoke to rise.

"I suspect time moves differently here." Conscious that I had already felt the passing of time much more slowly. "Has it been a hundred years here or a hundred years there?"

She drew a long breath as a fire sparked to life in the pit at the centre of the cave. "For me, it no longer matters. I was young when I came here, my life has been here. My children have grown here and all I have are memories. A hundred years here is perhaps two hundred on Eynhallow, perhaps more. I knew that my mother and father would have died by the time I left the House of Consorts. But you cannot give yourself over to such thoughts."

How could I not? How could I live knowing Rohan could be an old man, never knowing what became of me?

"I can see you are troubled." She noticed, and it was the first time anyone had ever addressed the fact. "You have had to fight to know yourself, I see that."

Tears pricked at the corners of my eyes. This woman, who was a stranger to me, she knew me best of all.

"We are on the verge of unrest." She foretold, staring into the growing flames. "The peace of the land is coming to an end."

"What does this have to do with me?" I asked incredulously, closing my eyes for the briefest of moments to wonder.

But she was lost in the flames. They reflected in her eyes, and for a moment it was as if she was not with me at all. When finally, she looked up, she seemed grieved. The time for small talk was done.

"You are the key to everything, Finola." She said in a whisper, "The one who will keep the peace and sit in the Castle at White Mount when Astala's day is done."

I began to shake my head. The tears began to spill down my cheeks. "You cannot know this."

And yet, she had known me.

"Nim took the child to the gateway, wrapped in her arms, she climbed to the foot of the waterfall and plunged into the waters below. Her child was screaming silently in the water, but she could not soothe her. She mourned the child she had left behind, for there had been two of them. One of them in the 'Aheem below and one in the 'Aheem above. Theirs was the last blood of Eynhallow. For she would not bring her consort back, she feared for his life and those of her children.

There was a quarrel between the children of the High Priest. Their father promised to keep the peace as he always had, kept his son close to his side, hoping that one day he would give up all his thoughts of taking back the land which they no longer dwelled upon. But Esson's heart was black, there was no hope.

Only Nim had known this to be true and when she quarrelled with her father she did not listen to his pleas for her to remain. He would protect her; he would make everything right. But she did not believe him, she had seen her brother's intentions and so had Astala. The child that she took was given to her human father upon the land of Eynhallow, the child that she left behind was kept by his grandfather. Both of them grew never knowing of the other, only their names a testament to their parallel lives. Finola, named so for her Finblood.

Catesby, a human name from the land he would never know. Nim could not bear to see the end she knew would come, so she asked her Uncle for help. He took her far away, gave her food and tools to survive and promised never to tell a soul where she was. For many years she walked alone, in a land where the trees grew taller than the mind's eye can conceive.

The wind whistled low through the long vines and branches and the sound was as if someone was crying in pain, eventually it drove her mad. Awaking without her senses, she somehow found herself being lifted above the canopy where the wind could not reach. There the Greenfolk gave her the strength to carry on. For she never forgot her cause. The Finfolk must never return to the other 'Aheem. The world of men has changed. They have forgotten us. She never let go of her sacrifice..."

She drew back from the flames and clutched at her chest. My hand instinctively flew to the little pocket on my dress, it was empty.

"Where is it?!" I demanded, "How dare you..."

Taking a long wooden stick, she stoked the fire and pushed the smooth black stone from the building ashes. It was strangely cold to the touch as I placed it back within the folds of my skirt, the violation still stinging. I hadn't been ready to know what was within the stone. She did not have the right to take it from me.

"Would you have looked within for yourself?" She asked, nonchalantly placing a pot above the fire. "Time is running out, Finola Gray."

"I would have." And it was true. "In my own time."

She was not sorry for what she had done. Her eyes were serious as she looked within mine.

"I tell you, Finola, there is a time to lament and a time to fight. If you do not go to The House of Consorts, it will be too late. There will be none to keep the peace when Astala is gone. Only you can truly understand. Eynhallow's day is done. Only you can prevent this."

I could not bear it. I ran from the cave, stumbling over rocks, my shins bleeding as I hit the shallows below.

I was afraid. But more than that, I was angry.

I could hear her calling after me as I ran, telling me to turn for The House of Consorts. Who was she to presume what was best for me? I could feel the memory stone weighing me down as I ran, wondering how she had managed to take it without being caught.

Of course, I had not known how long she had been standing by the rocks while I was in the water. I cursed myself for not noticing sooner.

Amund and Little Amund were gutting fish when I returned, with Catesby sat peeling something that looked like potatoes into a basket. All of their eyes shot up as I came inside, breathless and bleeding.

Of course, they fussed over me and tended to my minor wounds. Little Amund asked me if they hurt, but I came to realise they didn't. I told Amund who had come to seek me out, and his reaction told me he was not surprised.

"The Consorts, they are meddlesome at times." He said, waving his fish knife around, "It is rare to have a human consort in these times. Easy to forget some humans have been here for an age. Still, they consider themselves equal and, in some ways, perhaps they are. But they have their own concerns, ones which we cannot share. This woman which you speak of, I know her husband well. He is a hard worker; I don't think she meant you any harm."

Harm or no, she had intruded upon me and I had no desire to speak with her again.

Catesby was quiet and thoughtful as ever, enquiring if I was feeling myself throughout the rest of the day. I felt as if I had not spent enough time by his side of late and had neglected his loyalty. I had spent too much time in the water, where I was vulnerable. But as I spent more and more time away from the ocean, I felt stronger and comforted with him near me.

I did not ask Amund about the powers of the memory stone, or how the memories were ignited by fire as well as water. I found that I did not want to see the contents of it for myself, afraid that Nettie had somehow been wrong or what if she wasn't?

I saw her lingering in the village, as if she sought out my face amongst the others. I kept Catesby close by, I think he knew who it was I'd begun to fear in the end. He silently kept her away from us and I was silently grateful.

"Catesby..." I hushed, in the middle of the night. "Catesby..."

He turned in his sleep and opened his eyes slowly. Somewhere I could hear the sound of Amund gently snoring and Little Amund sniffling within the curve of his arm. But they slept deeply, all was well under this roof.

"What is it?" He murmured, rubbing his tired brown eyes.

I could not sleep. "I must speak with you..."

He sighed heavily. "Can it not wait until morning?"

No, it could not. I pulled my hair up and away from my face and raised my body from the floor.

"If I am to go to The House of Consorts, there will I be reunited with Caleb?" I asked, knowing full well that he did not have the answer.

I had given it more thought than I had cared to since my encounter with a human consort. If I was half human, then how could Caleb be my consort? If I was half anything, was I half in love with him?

Catesby sat upright, stretching his arms and I watched him closely. I knew his body as I knew my own, my eyes fully accustomed to the bare chests of all the Finmen and half-bloods and human consorts that had been chosen by Finwomen.

Catesby had always worn his loincloth, and that was the only part of him that I did not know. These thoughts came to me unbound, although I did not want to speak with Nettie again, I found that human part of me had been suffering, she had brought that suffering to the surface.

"I cannot say what will happen once you get there. I thought you were happy here?"

It wasn't a question of happiness anymore. Had it ever been? Laid back on his arms, I could see the lines of the cloth on his skin where he had been laid.

I wondered what would happen if I laid my head down in his lap, but there had never been such affection between us. I had known his hand within mine, but there had been no lingering embraces. Not like it had been with Caleb.

Why should I compare him to Caleb? If there were any comparisons to be drawn it should have been with Rohan. But when I thought about my brother, I could not place Catesby into that box. He did not belong there. If not there, then where?

I had known that I should think of Caleb more, although I had been distracted, I had wondered from time to time how he fared. I ached for him in those days in White Mount, when the memory of him was still raw. But time had drawn me closer to Catesby, I was certain this was not the way of it. I should love the man I chose. I should await him with loyalty and fierce passion.

Yet, I was slowly forgetting who he was. I was consumed with Astala and Esson, Elora and her strange powers. I was consumed with Amund and his son, the places I had been. I was consumed with all the things I could not do, all the things I wished I could do. But most of all, I was consumed with knowing that how I felt about Catesby could not be uttered out loud.

"It's time for us to go." I whispered, tears forming in the corners of my eyes.

I was afraid if I remained here any longer I would lose myself to him. If I was not where he was he would be forgotten to me, as Caleb was becoming now.

He did not agree verbally, only nodding as if he had been awaiting this day. We did not say our goodbyes to our Great Uncle. I could not bear it, to see Little Amund beg us not to go. We slipped out as silently as we could, before the light began to change above. The village still slept.

"Wait..." Catesby paused, "Let's go to the rock pools first."

I knew what he wanted. I could not deny it him. I had grown to love him.

Lucie Howorth

Chapter Eight

MEMORIES

The water was clear and still and while waves lashed against the rocks beside us, here we could see our reflections untainted by tide. Catesby had remained silent, his face stoic and unreadable.

But he had not been unable to hide the way his eyes searched for something within me. Something that mirrored whatever he felt inside. Here, I did not need to say the words. They remained unspoken and yet I knew that he heard them.

I love you, dear brother. I love you in ways I cannot begin to fathom. I do not love you like the brother I left behind, nor the lover I brought with me. I love you in entirely new ways and, I do not know what any of it means. I have never felt within me this way.

"I only ever saw these once before." Catesby said softly, "When I was younger. Astala used them to communicate with the elders. He would pluck his memories and place them within these stones. That way his thoughts were always safe."

I found that quite astonishing. "And yet he wanted his son to marry one who can read minds."

"He keeps the things he desires closest to him." Catesby shrugged, "It probably drove him near insane that you were so far away."

I wasn't there to lament that. Astala had been kind to me. He had watched over me; I did not need to know more than that.

I already knew the contents of my stone. Even if I had not seen them for myself, I had little desire to replay those second-hand moments. I urged Catesby to put his stone into the water.

"I don't remember her." He said, placing his stone by the water's edge. "Why should I pay any mind to what she remembers?"

He was angry, still. After all this time. I could taste his bitterness like the salt in the sea. He didn't need me to say anything in response. What could I offer? I did not remember her either.

He flicked his stone into the water diligently. The ripples remained clear at first, as if the disturbance was nothing more and nothing less than a stone breaking the surface. Then the ripples began to darken, the rocks beneath vanished into a cloud of black. I leaned over, blocking out the light. But all I could see was black water and nothing more. Catesby glared intently; his face fixed on something I could not to see.

I wondered how these strange stones worked. I had not seen anything in the flames when Nettie had used mine. Nor could I see the contents of Catesby's now.

I watched his face closely; he did not seem to cast any emotion as he watched. Whatever it was that he saw, it can't have been troubling to him. I began to wish that I had the courage to look first. I couldn't bear that I did not see it. The water remained black and taunted me, Catesby still did not offer me a moments glimpse upon his face.

When the water began to clear again, the blackness seemed to return from where it came. Catesby scooped the stone up and I was surprised to note that he had been holding his breath the entire time. He fell back, panting for breath. His throat flexed hard, the hair upon his neck flecked with perspiration.

He wasn't with me for a moment, his eyes looked through me as I tried to bring him back to me.

I was desperate to know what he had seen. But his eyes were vacant, even as I screamed into his face. My hands scrambled to shake him into the present moment. My fear and frustration growing with each passing breath, I curled my hand into a fist and urged him to look at me before I did something I might regret.

He closed his eyes as I uncurled my hand. When he opened them, he saw me. I realised I had drawn myself close, my body arched over him as he lay upon the rocks. He had scared me.

"I do not ever want you to do that to me again." I told him, inching away so that he could rise.

It had been in moments such as these that I had revealed to myself those parts I had tried to hide. I was not who I once was. I was a shadow of that girl. I missed her sometimes when I craved the familiarity of shorelines and stone fireplaces. I wished that I could talk to her and tell her that there was no need to fear the water. I wished that I could tell her it was ok to be in love. The things I feared now did not reflect the life I once had.

Once I had been afraid of touch, but I did not stop it now. Catesby took my hand into his, his entire body slumping into mine with the sheer exhaustion of carrying the memories he had seen. I pulled him into me, as close as I could. A tempered heartbeat pulsing in my chest, his head lay softly against it and I felt him rhythmically breathe in unison with it. I wondered if Astala had always known and sent him to me first so that I would love him best.

"I was on Eynhallow…" He whispered, his lips against my collarbone as he spoke. "I saw my father."

I could not stop the tears from falling. Of all the memories she could share, she gave him that one. I let him bury his face within my hold upon him and I was reminded bittersweetly that he was my brother.

"Tell me." I said through gritted teeth. "Tell me what you saw."

"Nothing at first." He gripped me tighter. "And then it seemed to me that I stood not apart, but behind and everything she could see is what was given to me. She was angry at her father and ran further than she meant to. She jumped into the water at the foot of the mountain falls. That is the way back."

He pulled away so that his eyes might meet mine. Suddenly he was animated and excited, he smiled so broadly that I could not stop myself from mirroring him.

"There was a great tide and it pulled her in, I could feel her body as it came to the surface on the other side. It was... almost as if... she had not known what would happen to her. She went to the rocks and climbed onto the land. She sat there for a very long time just watching the waves. He found her there and she was too afraid to speak to him."

I knew that. The only word she had ever given him was my name.

"But she let him speak to her. She listened. He was young and handsome to her; she was beautiful and strange to him."

He fell silent as his smile faded. I could feel him shed his previous excitement.

"He told her stories about the people on the island, told her where she could find him if she ever needed him and she went back to him once more to make love to him." He shook his head, spirals of black hair falling down about his face. "He knew what she was. Even when he begged her to speak, she would not. He knew what she was. He loved her and she loved him."

I wished that I could have seen it. I wished that I could have seen him one last time. Even through the eyes of another, it occurred to me that I had forgotten to remember my father.

"Did you know that he had a brother called Catesby?"

My heart sprung to life, I stared in complete desolation that I had never known that.

"He died when they were children, but she loved listening to him talk about the people he had loved. He talked about Catesby a lot; she loved the name so much she gave it to me."

I knew why she had given this to him and not to me. I'd been given sixteen years of him. Catesby had need of this, the need was much greater than mine. What she had given me was something else entirely. She needed us both to know *why*.

"What else did you see?" I asked, content now to hear it from him and nothing more. "Did you see The Hylands?"

He shook his head. "He never took her there. They always remained where they could never be seen."

Perhaps he had glimpsed at their moments together. He seemed to be satisfied with all this was. I felt some warmth for the mother I had never known for giving him a precious gift.

"I'm glad." I sighed, feeling the weight of my own stone heavy in my hand. "I'm glad you got to see him."

"Humans are afraid of loss." He noted. "He was so afraid to lose her, but she wasn't afraid to lose him."

"Perhaps she knew he would wait for her for the rest of his life." I felt a prick of something like resentment break that warmth. He had waited and had died still waiting. Until he could no longer look at me because of her.

"No. I think it is just humanity." He surmised. "Love is different... up there."

He was staring straight at me. Not through me anymore, he saw me now and I could not hide.

"Your consort. Why do you love him?" He asked, "Why did you bring him with you?"

I had not dared to think of Caleb this morning. Each time I had it had burned within my chest and threatened to end me.

I had accepted our time apart as a rite of passage and only allowed myself to dare dream that we would be reunited when I was given the hope of going to The House of Consorts. I did not want to tell him any of that. I did not want to tell him why I loved Caleb or why I had brought him with me, and it wasn't because those thoughts were mine to keep. It was because I didn't want *him* to hear them. Or perhaps it was because I had begun to doubt that I did love him, after all.

"You only talk of such things because of what you have seen. Their love is not my love."

His hand curled around my wrist, all his fingers wrapped perfectly around it and swallowed it. He pulled my fingers apart and took my stone.

"I'll give it back." He promised. "But I do not talk of such things because of what I have seen. I had hoped that by now I'd have a wife and children. I've seen it before. I've seen *love* and it never came to me."

I could feel my throat begin to tighten, the air in my lungs disperse. "It will."

He didn't let go of my wrist. "Do you know how time passes here? Not like there. Do you know how many years old we are on your world? How our immortality remains intact because each moment that passes is so much more fleeting?"

I could feel the thrum of my heartbeat louder. "No, tell me." I breathed, almost in a whisper.

He inched so close that I could feel his breath on my skin. "I have not loved for a hundred years."

I tried to remember how old I was, how old I had been on Eynhallow. How long had I been here? Was Rohan dead? I had been twenty, maybe twenty-one…

"I cannot hear this." I said, finally allowing my voice to sound out beyond emerging sobs. "If I do then I shall be the ruin of all I have wrought."

He backed away, as if my bidding was his desire. But he looked saddened and placed my stone back in my hand.

"I know that you are my sister." He said, rising from my embrace. "Do not think that I forget that."

I did not want him to go. "But you are not my brother!"

Catesby turned, his face yielding to physical pain. "Do not say such things."

But I could only speak the truth. "I'll ruin myself anyway, as I always have."

He shook his head as I stood to meet his height. "I did not think that I would love you. Now I am bound to you."

He had been alone. He did not say it, but I knew that he had been so completely alone. I shared in that. I had been alone, and I did not know how much until I looked into his eyes and saw myself reflected.

"And I, you." I told him and I meant it.

It did not matter that I had loved Caleb. That him and I had found each other at the edge of the world and jumped off the precipice together. It did not matter that he had carried me in his arms when I could not carry myself. Catesby did not carry me; he walked at my side and shared this strength that had never been there before.

"You sent the birds." I said, memories of flocking wings and broken feathers. "It was you, wasn't it?"

I could feel myself become dizzy with adrenaline. "When they came to rebuild... His name was Simon."

Caleb had caught me in his arms. But Catesby had sent the birds.

"It was always you wasn't it?" My breath was low and quick now, threatening to strangle me. "Tell me true."

He never said it. He didn't speak. There was a tremble on his lip when I thought he might say the words but instead he pulled me into him and kissed me.

I should have protested; I should have pushed him away and told him it was wrong. But there was not a single drop of me that wanted to. This kiss was not of desperation, but of necessity. Should I spend my life wondering what a kiss such as this consists of or yield to its power?

There was no fear in this kiss. His mouth was soft and certain and moved in perfect synchronicity with mine. I did not feel the rocks below nor the breeze. My eyes were closed, and I did not care. His body trembled against mine, I felt his fear in his fingertips that slipped down the curve of my back. I was aware of myself, in this same dress he had given me the night we left his village, that he had seen what it was underneath. Still, I did not care.

When his mouth moved away, the taste of him still there, I was reluctant to open my eyes and see if there was regret in his. His hand remained upon my cheek and I heard him whisper my name.

"Open your eyes." He said, when I did, he smiled. "Sweet Finola."

There was a note of trepidation in his voice which betrayed him. I had not ventured further than a kiss, I did not dare to ask if he intended to lay me down. It struck me that I found myself wanting him to. Regardless of the rocks beneath. He was breathing hard and heavy, a low deliberate sound I had never heard from him before. He would only look at me, forehead to forehead, breath warm and sweet.

"Forgive me." He said, his voice breaking on hysteria.

Forgiveness was not something I knew. I wasn't certain if it even existed. So, I did not murmur as he pulled me closer and I could feel his intentions. I submitted myself willingly.

He was unsure of his touch. But it was not unpleasant. There was a breeze hanging in the air above us and it ran across my skin as he removed my clothing. The rock was hard and smooth beneath, his body coveted me. I was no more certain of my touch, my fingertips trembling as they ran down the curve of his back. His eyes were dark and intense, as if they could not take all of me in. In them a madness and frenzy of a desire he had buried and did not dare resurrect. Perhaps neither of us could control it.

His breath was heavy and quick, hot on my cool skin as he ran his lips down the length of my neck. My mind did not run back to all that it had once known. Not how I had thought it might. A moment imagined a thousand times can only be lived once. It was not with the person I had envisioned. But it would have been unfair of me to wish for it now. I did not want him. I did not wish that it was he in Catesby's place. Even as hot pain lashed at my thighs, I could not muffle the sound which escaped my lips as I realised he was inside me.

There was no sky or rocks beneath. Only him and I, the pain that came with each thrust that I welcomed. I could not take my eyes off a tiny scar that sat above his eyebrow. I had not noticed it before, and it came as quite a revelation to me. He was trying to be gentle, as much as anyone could be whilst fighting against their nature.

There was not one single moment that I could say was defining. There was a rhythm between us, and it all became as one. My body responded to his, to the heat which was rising. Heat was such a shock to my already awoken system. I did not know heat, only cold and dark nights.

Warmth was not within me, yet it churned a cauldron of fire in my belly as I saw in my mind's eye the first flush of winter snow. I knew somewhere… somewhere in a world I could not touch it was cold and desolate and I had taken the spring and summer from them.

It was here within me and about to expire in great turmoil. Catesby began to convulse, his body stiffening with an almighty groan that was both relief and apology. I did not seem to conclude what we had done, only that it had occurred, and I was no longer a virgin and y et, I rejoiced in that. I had not been turned away by his touch.

It was a silent reproach which greeted us both. He lifted himself from my naked body and tried to look away. I pulled my dress about me, unsure if I should feel shame or contentment.

There was a reserve about him now, his fists were curled into balls that went white at the knuckles. Perhaps this was the usual response and I was uninitiated? He appeared to want to speak, but no words came out.

I could only lie there and hope that I had not disgusted him. I began dressing in silence, my eyes to the ground. He did not look at me until I had clasped the final whale bone at my shoulders.

"It would be an insult to ask for forgiveness." He said, his voice a shadow of sound. "But I will ask for it someday once again."

I would have spoken, but his body began to shiver. His eyes burned into me, as if they knew I would catch him if I got too close. His skin trembled, the shape of him began to move. I did not see his bones give way, nor the exact moment he shifted. It seemed that at one moment he was whole and in the next he was something else entirely.

Perhaps I had blinked? My hands reached for him but all they found was the air he left behind as he took flight. A black feather lay at my feet, the sky filled with all the birds which followed him. Forgiveness was not something I knew how to give. I could not say it to him. I could only watch as he flew away, taking all my hope and strength with him.

I did not throw a stone into the water. I gathered it into my dress with the single black feather and resolved that if I screamed, I would not stop until my throat gave way to silence. I could not scream; I could not cry. I could not allow myself to feel.

I had known the desolation of loss before, I was not that same girl who had stood at the window waiting for snow to thaw. I did not forgive him. I vowed that when he asked for it, I would not grant it to him. He did not hold the right to fly away before the fight.

I looked into the sky, unsure what hung above it. I held my body together, shaking bones which threatened to spread wings and seek answers. I did not go back to the Village. I did not say the goodbye that Amund deserved, or little Amund. There was nothing for me there now, there was nothing for me anywhere. I could only go where I had been heading regardless.

I was filled with a sense of fear as I took my first step alone. But as I made my way across rock and sand a bird flew overhead, I resolved never to look upon it. If he could lay with me and love me and still fly away, there was humanity in him like the day Caleb left the shores of Eynhallow.

Men were weak and indecisive. Even those who were only half the blood of man.

A part of me died. Maybe it was the human, maybe it was something else. Maybe it had to die, because I could not go it alone with fear in my heart.

There was an ache between my legs, blood that I did not notice until I found myself too far away from the water to wash it. But I refused to care. I could not drown in abandonment. I was not an island at the edge of a forgotten world. I'd forsaken that place, that girl. Betrayal somehow made the world that little bit uglier.

It did not matter which world, all of them were perhaps one and the same and that same grief would transcend. I was not a vessel anymore; I was not carrying that burden of guilt and shame. I had done what I had done, and I had not run from it.

Perhaps, in one way or another, I had killed Nathan Munro all those years ago when I was young and foolish. Perhaps I had driven my own father to the insanity which killed him. Perhaps I had placed the hate my Mammy had come to have towards me in her heart myself. I had done all this and still, I was here.

Catesby had not taken anything from me, for there was nothing I was willing to give. I reserved the right to my virginity, despite the blood and the sensation of him still between my legs I would not allow the desolation of his loss to consume me. I wondered if I would go against my better judgement if he returned to me, but as I made my way further and further away from the shore, I was certain he had gone from the sky.

Lucie Howorth

Chapter Nine

ALONE

I had lost most of what I had carried. The dress which had covered me previously had been torn to make wraps for my bloodied feet that had carried me across land and water. My hair was ragged and swept by relentless wind. When they found me, I had not the strength to protest. I knew they meant me no harm, even as they carried me up into the canopy of trees that wound around each other in branches that seemed to belong to not just one tree, but all. They placed a leaf at my lips and sweet nectar dripped into my parched mouth. It was like a dream, one that I had lived before.

Faraway voices and deep oval eyes peered down at me in blurred visions. This is what they had done for my mother.

I was awake for a moment, perhaps on the verge of sleep the next. I looked down and they had put me in a dress made of deep green cloth. No whale bones to clasp it together, just thread made of something I had no name for.

When I was strong again, they brought me a broth to drink and allowed me to sit amongst them, their curiosity piqued in hushed tones and pensive glances.

They were not like their water dwelling kin. They were more in tune with the magic here, even their skin echoed the trees. Theirs was a hue of autumn leaves and their scales seemed not to dance in the light but move like wind not water.

Nor did they share the same language. Their words were alien to me but so beautifully spoken that I did not care. I could feel whatever it was they tried to convey. Almost as if it were implanted within me.

They allowed me to wander their land above the trees. Bridges of vines and woods connected them one tree to another, some had grand platforms where fires could be built safely, and others had places where small wooden cabins had been carved from bark and branch.

When the light changed to night, all illuminated, I wondered how anyone could not be enamoured by it. But then, there was none down below who knew of it and I was saddened by it. I wished that Catesby had been with me to witness it. But how could he have been?

I knew that by being alone I had brought myself here. I knew that being alone was not the demon which had sat upon my shoulder, but the angel who had promised me that all would right itself.

"Solitude is a gift."

I spun at the sound of words I could understand. Of course, Astala would know this place. I ran into his arms and buried my head into his bare chest.

"Grandfather..." I called him so, affectionately and allowed him to run a hand through my hair. "Have you come to bring me back?"

"When you have already come this far? Never, child." He pulled my face up for him to inspect. "You are weary. But you are not done."

So much to say, so much to confess. He would know all of it, I did not doubt, I wondered why he had not come to me sooner.

He bade me walk with him, through the treetops and beyond. The Greenfolk bowed their heads in revered respect as they passed us as he in return bowed to them. We walked until we reached a small clearing. At the end of the forest where all could be seen.

There, beyond the trees, lie The House of Consorts.

"Where have you been?" I dared to ask, "You are always this place or that. Is that the way of it for you?"

He drew in a deep breath. It seemed that all this world was a turning cog in a number of many, Astala had been turning it for longer than I dared to imagine.

"I grew up in White Mount and it will always be my home. Where I am most… settled. But I cannot be a High Priest if I am only where my heart desires. I know every inch of this land, its people and when I am gone, I hope that I have served and taught them well. Whatever way it is for me, so it has been for all before me and so shall be for all after me."

I was in awe of him. I could not hide it.

He appeared too young to carry such burdens, yet I knew he was weary in a way that only a man such as he could be. His eyes focused intently on the building between the hills and felt a sadness that drew me in.

"What grieves you so?" I asked, with genuine concern for his mounting melancholy.

He looked down at me. "You are the first of your kind to dwell in The House of Consorts. A decision which has brought a bloody end. I know my son to be impulsive and quick tempered. But he is not always wrong. They may treat you with great indifference, if you do not show them what you are made of."

I tried to fathom the way he spoke of a man he had banished, with almost affection and tolerance. Perhaps this was something I had yet to learn.

"I am yet to know what I am made of." I confessed.

Astala shook his head gravely. "You are not the same girl who arrived here. You have made it here alone, without knowing quite exactly which direction to take. Could Finola of Eynhallow have done that?"

Finola of Eynhallow was afraid. I found there was fear in my heart still, but it had shifted. The things which scared me now were not the same. Things such as water and going into it were fears that were long quenched. Now I was kept anxious by wondering if Caleb still loved me. Wondering where Catesby had gone. Wondering if Esson had survived his wounds. Wondering where my mother was.

"You look for meaning, always." Astala pointed out, a rare smile forming. "What if there is no meaning? What if this is simply the life which is yours to live? What if that is all there is and all else is what you make of it? You can learn all there is to know, understand all there is to be understood. But will it change our destiny?"

I had a feeling that he was trying to comfort me. That all the things which had been denied me meant nothing anyway, what I would learn would serve only a general purpose. Perhaps he was right. Did all the wisdom in all the world's truly change who we are meant to be?

"You are who you are, Finola Gray, be it that scared little girl or the woman who brought herself forth without a light to guide her. You will know yourself when you enter the house. That much I promise you."

I realised I would not see him again for a very long time. He was not going to remain here and await my emergence. This was his goodbye.

"Thank you, Grandfather."

Catesby had not been wrong when he said that Astala had been more kind to me than anyone else. He had watched over me my entire life, even when I had never known. He allowed me the freedom to walk whichever path I chose, even if it meant disturbing the peace. He had secrets, that much I knew. But what I knew was enough to know that I trusted him, and I loved him.

"Ah, my little one..." He breathed, in a solitary moment of weakness, allowing himself to embrace me not as High Priest but as my mother's father. "You must go now... when we see each other again, I will know you better."

But would I know him better?

It seemed to me that the enigmatic Greenfolk knew Astala well, bowing their heads in acknowledgement as they passed by. His comings and goings were like threads which wove this world together. If only he could weave the threads of his own family back as one.

"Where is Esson?" I asked, afraid that I would not like the answer. But I asked regardless.

Astala hid his pain well, but not completely. There was a stab of something intangible in his face as he tried to stabilise his expressions. He wished that I would go and fulfill this burgeoning destiny. But first, I would ask this.

"I received word that he had passed into the border of a land far to the north. Of this, I cannot say more. The north is mostly barren, you will be taught well in things such as history and geography enough to know why soon enough. Place not your worries in where Esson lies. He is weakened from his wounds inflicted in Seohl Bay. That is all that I know."

His children scattered to the wind, his grandchildren parted on strange and tumultuous terms. Perhaps this was his sacrifice for the peace of a world which had been quietened for too long. I would go to The House of Consorts and I would learn all I could, and swiftly. I could feel it in my bones, the edge of hysteria once more.

But I was no longer afraid, I knew the chaos of war would reunite the family I had never known. The chaos of anything other than solitude on a lonely isle would bring me to myself.

Astala kissed my forehead softly, when I closed my eyes, I knew that when I opened them, he would be gone.

The Greenfolk whispered on the breeze as I left the forest, my name on the wind. I looked back only once before turning towards the mountains ahead and the castle which lay between them.

It was the last time I ever doubted myself about going back. That moment when I knew I had finally reached where I had been going.

The path which lead towards the mountainous twins was clear and uncompromising. The trees gave way to a clearing that looked out towards the House of Consorts. It was a revelation to me. It did not rise the way Astala's had, it did not seem to be a part of the mountain itself.

Someone had put it there, to be sheltered and hidden from whatever lay beyond. It reminded me of the gateway at the bottom of Eynhallow sound. That strange colour, that grand opulence.

It became clearer to me as I approached. Turrets lined with windows, the breeze picking up silks which hung in the frames that reflected the luminous sky. The stone was not white, but grey, like the stone of my home. The meadow around me seemed to sing of the colours, greens and browns and yellow grasses moving this way and that.

I was still weakened, still weary and bloodied from my journey alone. Never truly knowing if the direction I was going was the right one.

But the grass felt soft on my bare feet, and it carried me on my way. It was truly a thing of beauty. Even as the door came into view, its beautifully ornate arch decorated in gold with knockers made in the image of dancing fish hanging from the dark wood.

I felt calm and sighed deeply, an audible sound that carried on the wind.

"That is your first mistake." Came a voice from where I could not see. "You will not feel calm again for a long time."

Naturally I halted. There was the sound of grass on the wind, but nothing more. But I remained calm, nonetheless.

"I have made many mistakes." I confessed to the bodiless voice. "I can barely remember the first."

"That is an old life." They continued, still refusing to show themselves. "There are many more to come."

I saw a flutter within the grass to my side, the colours gave way to a figure which moved too swiftly for me to see. Perhaps they did not want me to see. I was too exhausted to play games.

"I do not doubt that." I agreed, almost in a whisper, as I carried on my way.

Whoever it was remained with me for a little, I felt their presence close by until it was there no longer. It felt as if the house was perpetually on the horizon, each time I looked up it felt further away the closer I became. Then it was there, and I did not have to walk anymore.

There was an ancient set of steps which lead to a door within a door. At either side of the arch stood two stone pillars with vines that snaked around each curve. Tiny pink buds threatened to bloom around the winding green stems, I could smell their sweetness already. I wondered why a door of such grand size was needed, if perhaps giants had once been here.

The ornate knockers were still shining in the dimming light and I was struck by their perfectly carved beauty. But it was the smaller door that opened, and I felt ridiculous for thinking that it would be otherwise.

Lucie Howorth

Epilogue

There was and is a house which stands alone within the waters of Orkney. Upon Eynhallow. The winters were always long and bleak, with no sunshine or hope. The summers seemed to laugh at us in those dark months, mocking us with memories of stolen days in the warmth. If there was such a thing as summer. The Hylands seemed to exist in a world forgotten and us, in turn, forgotten too.

But I had not forgotten. Nor would I ever exist in any world without recalling the bitter cold of my youth. There was no land without sea, perhaps I was both of them. As I stepped into the House of Consorts, I knew that I was a wild fox trying to survive where it did not belong. They saw me and they fed me. Perhaps there would be some of them who would fetch their guns against me.

"Finola Grey." Said a voice which I recalled, from within a hooded cloak in the darkness.

A torch ignited, flames licking away at the black as the door closed behind me. I saw their eyes beneath the hood, and they were entirely human.

"You were in the grass." I said, uncertain how or why I knew that.

I wasn't brave or courageous. But I knew she was. She was everything I was not. Even as we stood in the torchlight, I could feel her powers. Her knowledge.

"I was." She confessed. "As I was in all the other places I have been."

Her eyes were not old. But they had seen things I could not fathom.

"Where?" I asked, afraid that I already knew the answer.

"The winter of 1852 was unrelenting." The words echoed around walls I could not see. "It drove us to the edge of tolerance."

A solitary tear slid down my warm cheek. Whatever she was doing, whatever she had hoped to achieve it was cutting at the core of me.

"And now?" I asked, hoping my voice did not betray me. "If I stay here, I will not be allowed to go back, will I?"

She did not say one way or the other, but I knew. There had been a purpose for me once, I had not remained to see it through.

"Your winters are waiting for you, if you so wish."

There was no way back, no truth if I took what she was offering me. What horrors lie ahead for me that she would allow me to return to my human life before all else?

"No. I will not know another winter." I said, the breath of my voice moving the flickering torch flame.

I don't know what made me say it. Whether it was because I knew my fate no longer belonged there, or if perhaps I'd always known.

"You wish to know if your brother perished." Her face moved to the side; a pair of flushed red lips came into the light. It was not a question, nor a presumption. She had known what I had thought.

"I shall not know peace. Until I know of that." I was afraid regardless, to know if Eynhallow still stood.

She was not perturbed. "You will know a great many things, Finola Grey. None of them can be taught if your heart is not here."

She was human. But she came to me as one who had never known humanity. I wondered if her heart had ever been anywhere else and somehow, she seemed to know the way things once were.

I could not see the room in which we stood. Only faint outlines of things which were shrouded in the dark. Whoever she was, she knew the layout perfectly and when she reached out to place the flaming torch in a cast iron holder, it seemed to appear upon a pillar I hadn't known we were standing next to.

From within the folds of her cloak, she revealed an old and worn book bound in whale skin. As she opened it I noted the pages had writing in a language I could not read.

"Rohan Grey of Eynhallow." She said flatly. "Son of William and Mary Grey. Born in the Winter of 1840. Died in the spring of 1910. Outlived his wife, who perished in childbirth with the fourth of her sons in her twenty fifth year. They buried him on the Island with his father and mother and there it is said, they still remain. But no other."

The tears came more heavily, of sadness and regret. Sadness that I had not the knowledge to know the passing of time and the regret that I had not remained to greet his sons. But there were tears of contentment too. That he had known love and so his ghost was where it wanted to be. I had to accept that I had chosen this.

"What happened to her... the one I called Mammy?" I dared to ask, afraid that if I didn't, I would be a prisoner to wondering.

I knew she wondered why it was that I should wish to know. Her eyes narrowed, as if she knew that there was a God which had come between us.

"Mary Grey did not survive the Winter following the marriage of her son. Hers was a quick death, void of any thought. Is that what you wished to hear?"

It occurred to me that I had not cared what I heard. She was gone and with her God. All of them were gone. But not only that, they had been gone far longer than I could have anticipated. If time slipped away much quicker in the other 'Aheem I wondered if my body would turn to ashes if I ever graced the shoreline again.

"What of the house? The one they came to build after the others were burned to the ground. Is it still there?" I was almost growing hysterical, and she knew it.

She flicked to another page of her book.

"There are none that stand upon Eynhallow now. Only the bones of an old ruin, which has always stood. That alone will remain."

She spoke of the kirk, which had been a ruin always. I was surprised to find comfort in that. But a sickness tugged away at me that The Hylands was lost to a memory that existed now within none save for me.

"Are you satisfied, Finola Grey?" She asked then, her voice still flat and emotionless.

I remembered when I was a child. I would run the length of the island with a ribbon in my hand. Whichever way the wind blew, so did my ribbon. Whichever course it took, the wind would sway it so and I was satisfied. But I had not been for a very long time, I had not come here for satisfaction.

"No." I responded, with disdain. "It does not satisfy me at all. Time is my enemy."

She moved to retrieve the torch, placing the book of strange words back within her cloak. It seemed that we stood in an empty room, the sound of my voice becoming more of an echo against the stone I knew was there. But it did not feel real. We could have been standing anywhere, at any time. My mind began to run into the darkness.

Would I turn to dust if I stepped foot on Eynhallow soil? Did the death I had not courted still await my human flesh? Is that why she hinted at my return? There on her lips was a wry smile so fleeting, but I had seen it, nonetheless. Some things the darkness could not hide.

"Time is a veil, Finola Grey. Yours and mine have run in accordance with one another before this."

She reminded me of a whale I once knew, who spoke in riddles and truths that would not reveal themselves. Even now I wondered if this darkness was for her benefit and not mine.

"Is that so?" I asked, half caring for an answer. "You speak as if you have known me."

There was a hint of that smile once more, I tried to place it within smiles I had seen before. I wondered if my memory was failing me. I had been afraid of it.

"There was a child in me once, as there was within you. When neither of us knew this path. Do you not remember Finola?"

There was a flash of firelight in my eyes, for a moment it blinded me. But when I blinked into the black, her face came into view. At once I knew her. The vast years that had slipped by began to move backwards, however many of them there had been for me, and her. She had aged, but no more than the age we had always shared. She had seen things, all of them had shaped her.

"No... it cannot be."

She had died. I had seen them take her body. I had grieved for her. There was sorcery here, I did not believe that it was potent enough to raise the dead. Yet... here she was and here was I. Perhaps it was me who had died?

"No, you are not dead. Not yet." She said, "And neither am I."

"But the others... they died."

It was like coming up for air. The realisation that what I thought I had once known was a dark lie. What was any of it for? The Finhag stories and Nathan Munro washing up on the shore? Who made it to the mainland, and who didn't?

There was a knowing look in her eye, if I gave myself over to the darkness then somehow, she would reveal the light, but even though I recognised her face I no longer knew her.

"Jenny..." I whispered.

Her eyes flashed unacceptance. "They call me Jen."

Not Jenny McAvoy. Who shared a boat with me to church on Sundays? Who ran with me in grass and sand until our shoes filled with it?

"They took you?"

She lifted the torch above us so that the fire illuminated her eyes. They bore into me with such intensity I felt my blood run just that little bit quicker.

"A finely orchestrated thing." She said, "I had thought that I would come to know you here sooner. But everything has a moment all its own. I was not taken. But I did not come willingly either. They did not bury me. They let my body into the water, and I did not wake up in heaven."

There was a prick of sorrow in my heart for her. Something inside her had died, if not all of her, even though she stood before me becoming more real as my eyes beheld her. I wanted to embrace her, but I feared she would recoil from my touch.

"Are you a consort?" I asked, "Is that the way of it for you?"

She allowed a smile to reveal itself. "I am. He found me; he knew that I was not dead."

I tried to remember the years which had gone by, both here and there. She had been here a very long time and was still here.

"When will you be ready to be gone from this place?" I asked, afraid of the answer.

She was looking at me almost with pity. I wanted to end this conversation, but I felt as if it was part of my initiation.

"Our time here is measured by what we learn. Some have been here longer than others, of those who are left. There are not many of us, the time of Consorts coming and going are long gone. I feel like my time here is almost done, as is perhaps the House itself."

If there were no more consorts, there would be no need for a House. This fact made me feel sorrow and in a sickening way, I wondered if it was this which Esson was trying to prevent. If the two worlds collided once more, the House could be full again.

Jen flinched. "We must begin immediately."

The flame began to move down a narrow corridor. I followed it diligently. Where it went, I did not know. But I knew, even in the darkness, that I must follow. There was a breeze that came from somewhere, the scent on it sweet and reminiscent of a garden in spring. It was all I had as I walked on, caged by darkness behind me and a blinding flame before me. I did not dare to ask where it was, she was taking me.

As I walked, I felt the prick of sadness reach me as I came to thoughts of the life I had left behind. But only for a moment. When we reached the end of the corridor, the torch went out.

And so did I.

Acknowledgements

I have always been a writer since a pen was put in my hand as a child at school. Other children would choose to play games after they completed their work, I chose to get a sheet of A4 paper and write short stories about Topsy and Tim who were popular children's book characters in the 1960s.

As it was the early 90s, nobody really knew who Topsy and Tim were, and I reveled in this. As the years went on my stories moved from sheets of A4 to Microsoft Word. I dipped my toe into the world of "fan fiction" before it was ever really a popular literary choice.

But fantasy was always where my heart lay. I started writing Finblood under the working title of "Winter" when I was a stressed-out stay-at-home Mum. Writing had always been my escape, but I had struggled to finish projects since having children of my own.

This was going to be my life's work. I had no idea how long it was going to take me to complete or how immersed in the world I'd created. I kept my writing secret and never let a soul read my words. It wasn't until the invention of the Kindle that I started to entertain the idea that one day I might allow another to read my work.

I simply enjoyed drifting away, listening to Bon Ivor and Mumford and Sons to set the mood for each chapter. I had to abandon the story altogether when I hit a terrible case of writer's block during a transcending time in my personal life.

I always knew I would return to it though and two years later I picked up where I had left off with a new idea and a new personal life. Meeting my second husband Pete proved to be the catalyst for getting my work published.

He took the story and became, in essence, my editor. He believed in me and the quality of my writing enough to let another person in to something that had been just for me since I was five years old.

I finished the book, but I had not finished the story. I had created something which had more to give. I would like to thank Pete for giving me the opportunity to bring my stories to others. To my two beautiful children who have grown up watching Mummy write, but never really knowing what it was I wrote and, to the rest of my friends and family who I hope will enjoy reading it.

About the Author

Lucie Howorth's debut novel is the result of many years of hard work, determination and overcoming many personal struggles, both mentally and physically. A huge Game of Thrones fan, both the TV and book versions and Wuthering Heights by Emily Bronte are just some of the inspirations she has used to complete this book.

Whilst she follows her ultimate dream of becoming a best-selling author and to follow in the footsteps of her heroes, Lucie works full time caring for people with learning disabilities and as a full-time mother to her amazing children, Jamie and Evie.

Everything Lucie has done in her life has always been for the benefit of those around her; her children, her (very lucky) husband, her whole family. This is the one thing that is truly for herself.

You can follow Lucie for future updates on her work and novels by following:

www.instagram.com/thiscreativeoutlet

Lucie Howorth

Finblood

Printed in Poland
by Amazon Fulfillment
Poland Sp. z o.o., Wrocław